Judah Maccabee

Part 2 - Against the Gods of Greece

Chronicles of the Watchers
Book 5

By Brian Godawa

Judah Maccabee: Part 2 - Against the Gods of Greece
Chronicles of the Watchers, Book 5
1st Edition e

Warrior Poet Publishing
www.warriorpoetpublishing.com

ISBN: 978-1-963000-64-1 (paperback)
ISBN: 978-1-963000-66-5 (hardback)
ISBN: 978-1-963000-65-8 (eBook)
ISBN: 978-1-963000-93-1 (Large Print)

Scripture quotations are taken from *The Holy Bible: English Standard
Version*. Wheaton: Standard Bible Society, 2001.

Get a Free eBooklet About the Gods Referred to in This Novel.

Limited Time Offer

FREE

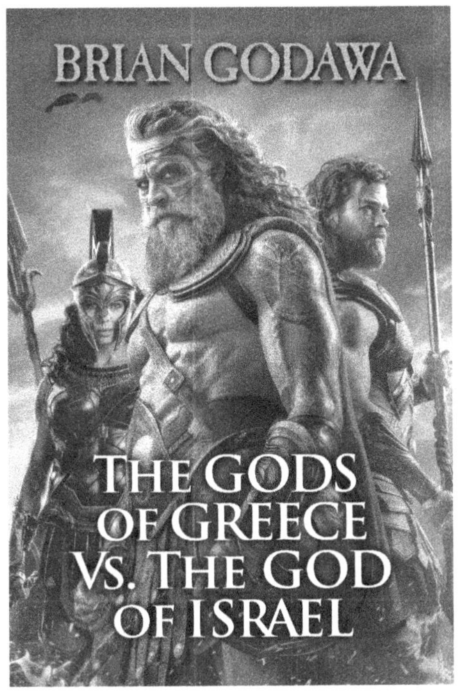

Zeus, Hera, Ares, Athena, and others vie for power in their territory allotted to them by Yahweh.

Surprisingly, many ancient Jews had been deceived into worshipping the gods of Greece during the time of the Maccabees. Learn about these pagan opponents of Yahweh.

https://godawa.com/free-gods-of-greece/

DEDICATION

This novel set is dedicated to Cary Schatz,

a fellow intellectual warrior for God

who seeks the purity of the Faith.

ACKNOWLEDGMENTS

To Yahweh: Even when you are silent and apparently absent to my failing perception, you are sovereign and work all things after the counsel of your will.

To Kimberly: Once again, you are my Sophia, my Hannah, and every other worthy woman of love in all my stories.

To Jeanette: Once again, thank you for your editorial sword.

NOTE TO THE READER

Judah Maccabee: Parts 1&2 is a standalone novel set. But it is also part of the *Chronicles of the Watchers* series whose books all share what biblical scholar Michael S. Heiser has called "the Deuteronomy 32 worldview"[1] and what I call "the Watcher paradigm."

For purposes of clarity, I will lay it out here in brief summary. For more detailed biblical support and explanation, I recommend reading my booklet, *Psalm 82: The Divine Council of the Gods, the Judgment of the Watchers, and the Inheritance of the Nations (affiliate link).* It is the foundation of all three of my novel series: *Chronicles of the Nephilim, Chronicles of the Watchers,* and *Chronicles of the Apocalypse.*

Deuteronomy 32 is well-known as the Song of Moses. In it, Moses sings of Israel's story and how she had come to be God's chosen nation. He begins by glorifying God and then telling the Israelites to "remember the days of old":

> *When the Most High gave to the nations their inheritance,*
> *   when he divided mankind,*
> *he fixed the borders of the peoples*
> *   according to the number of the sons of God.*
> *But the Lord's portion is his people,*
> *   Jacob his allotted heritage.*
> *(Deuteronomy 32:8–9)*

---

[1] Michael S. Heiser, *The Unseen Realm: Recovering the Supernatural Worldview of the Bible*, First Edition (Bellingham, WA: Lexham Press, 2015), 113–114.

The context of this passage is the Tower of Babel incident in Genesis 11 when mankind was divided. Rebellious humanity sought divinity in unified rebellion, so God separated them by confusing their tongues, which divided them into the seventy (Gentile) nations described in Genesis 10 with their ownership of those bordered lands as the allotted "inheritance" of those peoples.

But inheritance works in heaven as it does on earth. The people of Jacob (Israel) would become Yahweh's allotted inheritance under his ownership and rule while the other Gentile nations were the allotted inheritance of the *Sons of God* under their ownership and rule.

So who were these Sons of God who ruled over the Gentile nations (Psalm 82:1-8)? Some believe they were human rulers. Others argue for their identities as supernatural principalities and powers. I am in the second camp. In my *Psalm 82* booklet, I prove why they cannot be humans and must be heavenly creatures.

The phrase "Sons of God" is a technical term that means divine beings from God's heavenly court,[2] but they possess many different titles. They are sometimes called "heavenly host,"[3] sometimes "holy ones,"[4] at other times "the divine council,"[5] or "Watchers,"[6] or even "gods" (*elohim* in Hebrew).[7] Yes, you read that last one correctly. *God's Word calls these beings "gods."*

But fear not. That isn't polytheism. The word "god" in this biblical sense is a synonym for "heavenly being" or "divine being" whose realm

---

[2] Job 1:6; 38:7.

[3] Isaiah 24:21-22; Deuteronomy 4:19 with Deuteronomy 32:8-9; 1 Kings 22:19-23.

[4] Deuteronomy 33:2-3; Psalm 89:5-7; Hebrews 2:2.

[5] Psalm 82:1; 89:5-7.

[6] Daniel 4:13, 17, 23.

[7] Deuteronomy 32:17, 43; Psalm 82:1; 58:1-2.

is that of the spiritual plane.[8] Simply put, the Hebrew word *elohim* ("god") is not just used for the Creator Yahweh alone but is also used of other different kinds of beings. According to the Bible, "*elohim*/gods" is not necessarily a word that means infinite, uncreated beings that are all-powerful and all-knowing. Yahweh alone is that God. Yahweh is the God of gods.[9] He is species-unique. That is, while Yahweh is an elohim, other elohim are not like Yahweh. These "gods" (lowercase 'g') are finite, created spiritual beings who reside in the heavenly realm that can intersect with the earthly realm of humanity. Sadly, our modern use of the word "god" does not line up with the biblical use of the term, thus causing unfounded reactions of fear in those who prefer modern over ancient context.

The biblical narrative is as follows. The Fall in the Garden was not the only source of evil in the world. Before the Flood, some of these heavenly Sons of God rebelled against Yahweh and left their divine dwelling to come to earth (Jude 6), where they violated Yahweh's holy separation and mated with human women (Genesis 6:1-4). This was not a racial separation but a spiritual one. Their corrupt hybrid offspring were called *Nephilim* (giants), and their effect on humanity included such corruption and violence on the earth that Yahweh sent the Flood to wipe everyone out and start over again with Noah and his family.[10]

Unfortunately, after the Flood humanity once again united in evil while building the Tower of Babel, a symbol of idolatrous worship of false gods. So Yahweh confused their tongues and divided them into the seventy nations. Since mankind would not stop worshipping false

---

[8] Michael S. Heiser, *The Unseen Realm: Recovering the Supernatural Worldview of the Bible*, First Edition (Bellingham, WA: Lexham Press, 2015), 23-27.

[9] Deuteronomy 10:17; Psalm 136:2.

[10] Genesis 6:11-13; 2 Peter 2:4-6. For this storyline, see my first two novels, *Noah Primeval* and *Enoch Primordial*, in the Chronicles of the Nephilim series.

gods, the living God gave them over to their lusts (Romans 1:24, 26, 28) and placed them under the authority of the fallen Sons of God that they worshipped. Fallen spiritual rulers for fallen humanity (Psalm 82:1-7; 58:1-2). It's as if God said to humanity, "Okay, if you refuse to stop worshipping false gods, then I will give you over to them and see how you like them ruling over you."[11]

Deuteronomy 32 hints at a spiritual reality behind the false gods of the nations, calling them "demons" (Deuteronomy 32:17; Psalm 106:37-38), which in Hebrew refers to territorial guardian spirits.[12] The apostle Paul later ascribes demonic reality to pagan gods as well (1 Corinthians 10:20; 8:4-6). The New Testament continues this ancient notion of spiritual principalities and powers connected to and reigning over earthly powers in the unseen realm (Ephesians 6:12; 3:10). The two were inextricably linked in historic events. As Jesus indicated, whatever happened in heaven also happened on earth (Matthew 6:10). Earthly kingdoms in conflict are intimately connected to heavenly powers in conflict (Daniel 10:12-13, 20-21; 2 Kings 6:17; Judges 5:19-20).

So the Bible says that there is demonic reality to false gods. Just what this looks like is not exactly described in the text of Scripture. But since those Sons of God who were territorial authorities over the nations were spiritually fallen Watchers, that makes them demonic or evil in essence.

So what if they were the actual spiritual beings behind the false gods of the ancient world? What if the fallen Sons of God were masquerading as the gods of the nations to keep humanity enslaved in idolatry to their authority? That would affirm the biblical stories of

---

[11] For this storyline see my novels, Gilgamesh Immortal and Abraham Allegiant in the Chronicles of the Nephilim series.

[12] Victor P. Hamilton, "2330 שד," (Hebrew, "shed") in *Theological Wordbook of the Old Testament*, ed. R. Laird Harris, Gleason L. Archer Jr., and Bruce K. Waltke (Chicago: Moody Press, 1999), 906.

earthly events and rulers occurring in synchronization with heavenly events and rulers. It would not have to be a one-to-one correspondence of demonic Watcher with pagan god. Evil angels could put on the disguises of different gods at will to achieve their deceptive purposes.

One other note of importance is that the Bible speaks of the Divine Council members, Sons of God/Watchers, and spiritual angels as being exclusively male in their sex, names, and pronouns, but it does not explain why. It is therefore reasonable to conclude that there are no female elohim. But because this is an argument from silence, it would be extra-biblical speculation to suggest that there are female Watchers or angels, but it would not be *anti-biblical heresy* because silence is an argument for neither existence nor non-existence.

However, sometimes silence *can be* a deliberate expression of existential reality or theological purpose. In this case, we can only speculate why, but I have chosen to adopt the biblical silence as deliberate and purposeful and therefore have suggested that any female presentation of fallen Sons of God/Watchers are facades or illusive disguises that hide the true male sexual identity of the beings. The New Testament claims that the satan and his ilk can masquerade as angels of light (2 Corinthians 11:14), which means they can disguise their identities for nefarious purposes.

That is the biblical premise of the *Chronicles of the Watchers*. The pagan gods like Zeus, Hera, Ares, Baal, Anat, and others are actually fallen Sons of God, Watchers of the nations, crafting identities and narratives as gods of those nations. The ultimate end of these spiritual rebels is depicted in the series *Chronicles of the Apocalypse*. But for now they plan, conspire, and fight to keep their allotted peoples and lands, all while seeking to stop God's messianic goal of inheriting all the nations (Psalm 2:1-9; 82:8) through his seed (Genesis 3:15; Galatians 3:16).

My goal is to use the fantasy genre to show the theological reality of spiritual warfare while remaining faithful to the biblical text.

A word for those who share my high view of Scripture. In the interest of focusing on the story of the Maccabees, I not only drew from the Bible but from Jewish Second Temple literature as well as Greek sources. The purpose of this was not to "add" to Scripture through syncretism but rather to subvert pagan narratives and fill in the gaps between Scripture in a way that is faithful *to* Scripture.

Anyone familiar with the Bible will know that this story of Jewish revolt is contained in non-biblical books called 1 & 2 Maccabees. They are part of what is called the Apocrypha, Greek texts that Christians debated about in the first centuries as to whether they should be included in the canon of Scripture. Reputable Church fathers and scholars were on both sides of that debate. Clement of Rome, Irenaeus, Tertullian, Cyprian, Clement of Alexandria, and Origen were just some of those most respected who considered some of the Apocrypha to be inspired Scripture.

But as Francis Beckwith concludes, the canonicity of the Apocrypha was not uniform. "All that was agreed was that the Apocrypha were to be read and esteemed, not that they were to be treated as Scripture."[13] Later, Martin Luther expressed a common Protestant position when he described the Apocrypha as "books which

---

[13] Roger T. Beckwith, *The Old Testament Canon of the New Testament Church and Its Background in Early Judaism* (London: SPCK, 1985), 386, 394. One of the strongest arguments for the Apocrypha not being considered canonical is that Jesus and the Apostles never quoted from those books as being Scripture. But this is not an absolute proof because there are nine other Old Testament books never quoted in the New Testament as well: Judges, Ruth, Ezra, Esther, Ecclesiastes, Song of Solomon, Lamentations, Obadiah, and Zephaniah. Obadiah and Zephaniah, however, were considered a part of the singular category called "The Twelve" in reference to the twelve prophets, so they may be assumed under that category. And it must be remembered that the New Testament also quotes from many sources that are NOT considered to be canonical but are considered relevant or truthful such as 1 Enoch.

are not to be equated with Holy Scripture and yet which are useful and good to read."[14]

Bible scholar John Bartlett adds:

> In England the Calvinist-inspired Geneva Bible (1560) included the apocryphal books, accepting them "for their knowledge of history and instruction of godly manners,", a phrase taken up in the Church of England's Thirty-Nine Articles of Religion, which state that "the other [i.e. apocryphal] books … the Church doth read for example of life and instruction of manners; but yet doth it not apply them to establish any doctrine."[15]

In a sense, this standard still holds today. Even though Protestants may not agree with the Roman Catholic or Eastern Orthodox views of the Apocrypha as canonical or deutero-canonical, scholarship maintains they are nevertheless worthy of respect to be studied and afforded esteem for basic historical purposes. That is the position I took as author of the novel set *Judah Maccabee: Parts 1&2*. God is sovereignly involved in all history, not only in biblically canonical history.

Another important note for the reader is that the name of Judah Maccabee in the novels begins as Judas ben Mattathiah. This is the Greek version of the Hebrew name Judah ben Mattathiah due to the Hellenistic context. It will change to Judah Maccabee later in the story for a very specific reason. Have patience!

If you are interested in learning more about the historical, biblical, and religious foundation of this novel, I have written a companion book

---

[14] Thomas Fischer, "Maccabees, Books of: First and Second Maccabees," in *The Anchor Yale Bible Dictionary*, ed. David Noel Freedman, trans. Frederick Cryer (New York: Doubleday, 1992), 439.

[15] John R. Bartlett, *1 Maccabees, Guides to Apocrypha and Pseudepigrapha* (Sheffield, England: Sheffield Academic Press, 1998), 14.

explaining the research I've done and the choices I've made. It's called *The Spiritual World of Ancient Israel and Greece: Biblical Background to the Novels Judah Maccabee – Parts 1&2.*

Thank you for your understanding of imagination and faith.

Brian Godawa

Author, *Chronicles of the Watchers*

TABLE OF CONTENTS

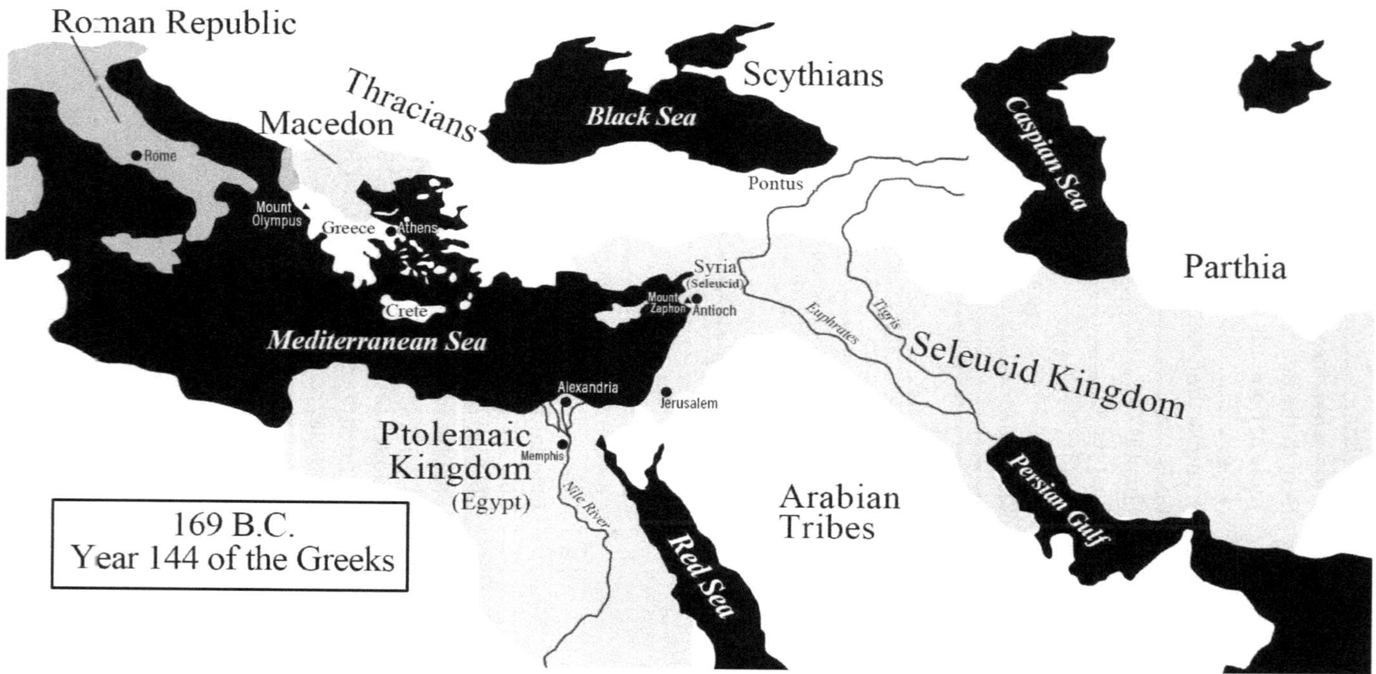

Roman Republic
Rome
Thracians
Macedon
Mount Olympus
Greece
Athens
Crete
Mediterranean Sea
Scythians
Black Sea
Pontus
Syria
(Seleucid)
Mount Zaphon
Antioch
Euphrates
Tigris
Caspian Sea
Parthia
Seleucid Kingdom
Alexandria
Jerusalem
Ptolemaic
Kingdom
Memphis
(Egypt)
Nile River
Arabian
Tribes
Persian Gulf
Red Sea
169 B.C.
Year 144 of the Greeks

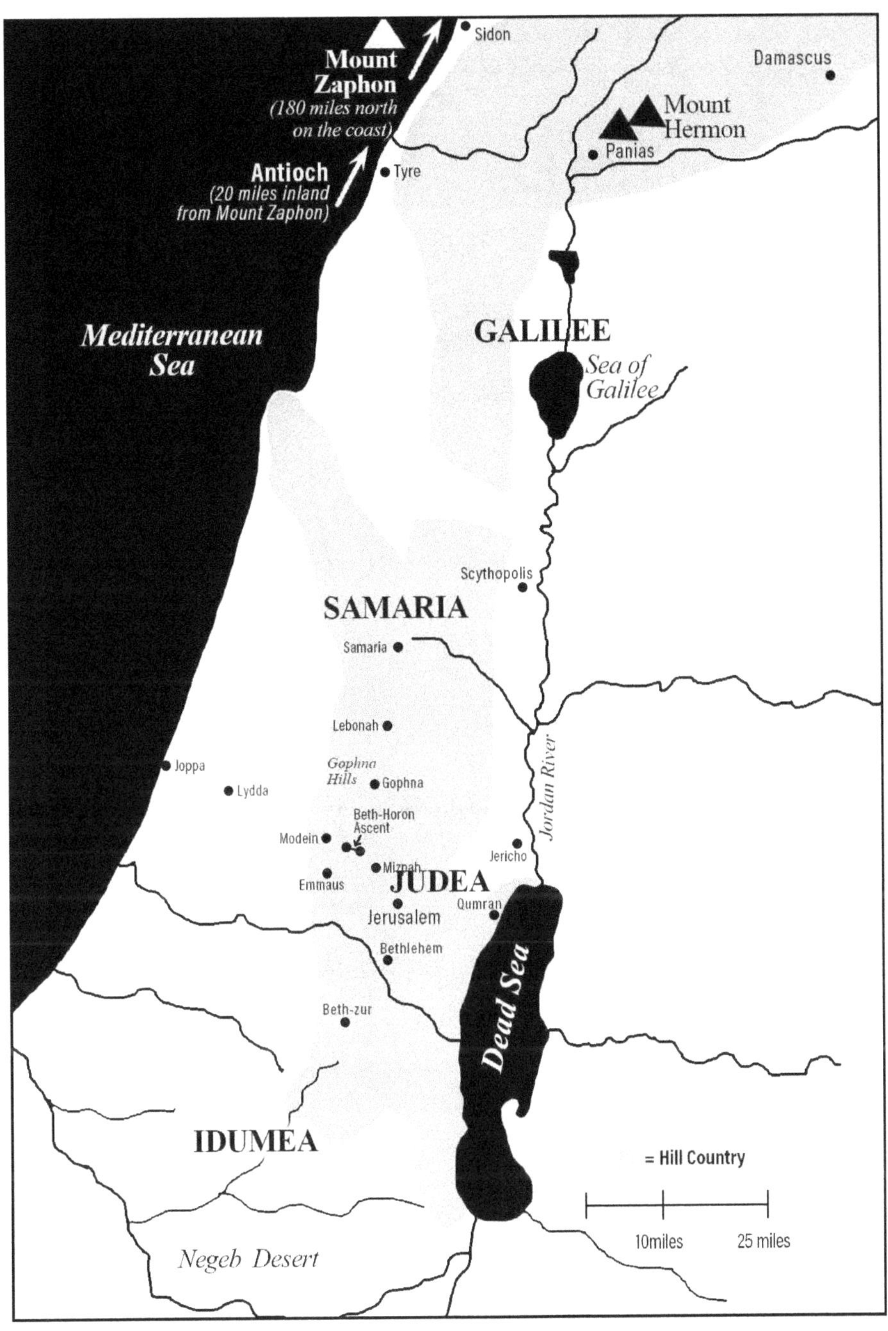

Sidon
Damascus
Mount Zaphon
(180 miles north on the coast)
Mount Hermon
Antioch
(20 miles inland from Mount Zaphon)
Tyre
Panias
Mediterranean Sea
GALILEE
Sea of Galilee
Scythopolis
SAMARIA
Samaria
Lebonah
Gophna Hills
Joppa
Gophna
Lydda
Jordan River
Beth-Horon Ascent
Modein
Jericho
Mizpah
Emmaus
JUDEA
Qumran
Jerusalem
Bethlehem
Dead Sea
Beth-zur
IDUMEA
= Hill Country
Negeb Desert
10miles
25 miles

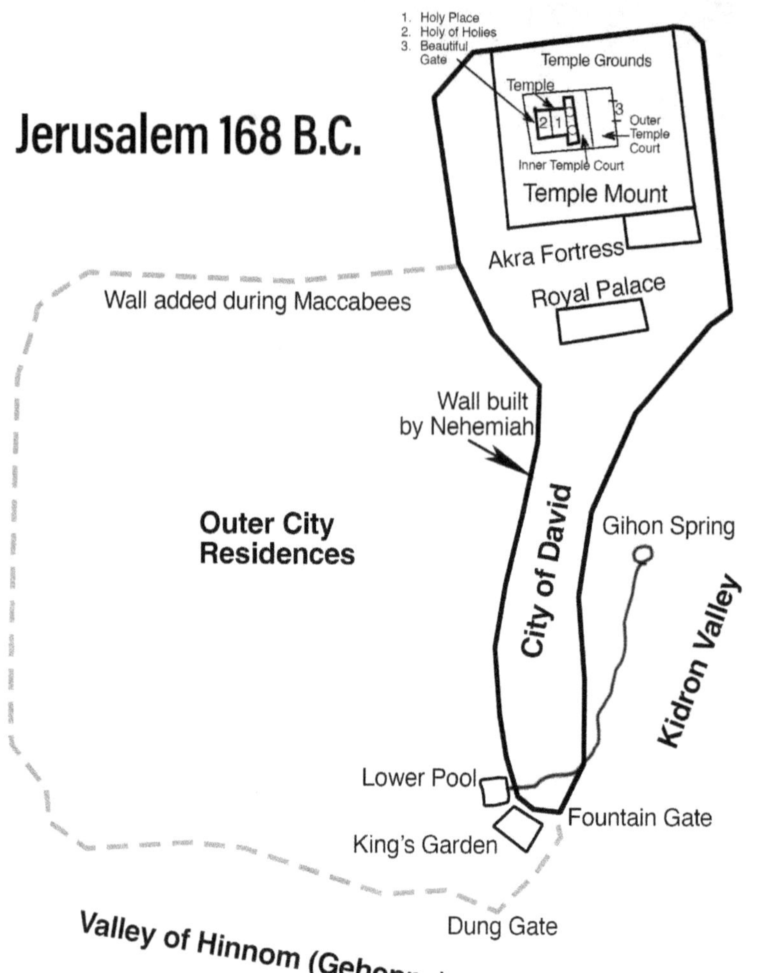

Jerusalem 168 B.C.
1. Holy Place
2. Holy of Holies
3. Beautiful Gate
Temple Grounds
Temple
Outer Temple Court
Inner Temple Court
Temple Mount
Mount of Olives
Akra Fortress
Royal Palace
Wall added during Maccabees
Wall built by Nehemiah
Outer City Residences
City of David
Gihon Spring
Kidron Valley
Lower Pool
Fountain Gate
King's Garden
Dung Gate
Valley of Hinnom (Gehenna)

PRONUNCIATION KEY

Foreign Name/Word	English Pronunciation
Antiochus	Ann-**tie**-uh-cuss
Antiochene	Ann-**tie**-uh-keen
Apollonius	App-uh-**lone**-ee-uss
Gaius Popilius Laenas	**Gay**-uss Poe-**pillee**-uss **Lie**-nuss
Diadochi	Dee-uh-**doe**-kee
Eleusis	El-**loo**-sis
Euergetes	You-err-**get**-eez
Laodice	Lay-**oh**-dih-see
Menelaus	Men-eh-**lay**-uss
Seleucus	Sell-**oo**-cuss
Seleucid	Sell-**oo**-sid
Seleucia	Sell-oo-**see**-uh
Deianeira	Day-ann-**eer**-ah
Phalanx	**Fay**-lanks
Cerberus	**Sir**-bur-uss
Ceryneian	**Sir**-rin-ee-an
Cybele	**Sib**-eh-lee
Chiton	**Kye**-tun
Chlamys	**Clam**-iss
Himation	Him-**at**-ee-un
Peplos	**Pep**-low-ss

GODS

GODS OF GREECE (12 OLYMPIANS)	
God	**Attributes**
Zeus	King of the gods, god of the sky. Thunderbolts.
Poseidon	God of sea and elements. Trident.
Hades	God of underworld (Not Olympian - in Hades). Invisible helmet. Owner of Cerberus the three-headed hound of Hades.
Hera	Queen of the gods, goddess of marriage and childbirth. Owner of the Nemean Lion.
Demeter	Goddess of harvest, agriculture.
Hestia	goddess of the hearth, domesticity (some sources do not include her in the Olympians)
Children of Zeus	**Attributes**
Apollo	God of sun, prophecy, archery, disease.
Ares	God of war, violence, bloodshed.
Athena	Goddess of wisdom, war. Patron of the city of Athens.
Artemis	Goddess of the hunt, virginity. Owner of the Cerynian Hind.
Aphrodite	Goddess of love, passion.
Hermes	Messenger of the gods, travel.
Dionysus	God of wine, festivity, ecstasy (some sources do not include him in the Olympians).
Hephaestus	God of fire, blacksmith forging, volcanoes.
Others	**Attributes**
Gaia	Mother Earth. Mother of life.
Persephone	Goddess of spring, consort of Hades in the Underworld.
Cybele	Mother goddess of Anatolia (Asia Minor) Had two lions. Worshipped by Amazonians.

GODS OF EGYPT

God	Attributes
Ra	King of the gods, sun god.
Amun	Creator god. Name means "hidden."
Horus	Patron god of the Pharaohs. Falcon-headed.
Osiris	God of the dead who rules the underworld. Mummified with green skin.
Set	God of chaos and violence. Resides in the desert. Has a strange unknown animal head.
Sobek	Crocodile god of the Nile.
Montu	God of war. Bull-headed.
Ptah	Creator god of mankind and craftsmen. Patron deity of Memphis.
Ogdoad	4 gods and 4 goddesses of primordial chaos and creation.

Goddess	Attributes
Isis	Wife of Osiris, god of the dead.
Sekhmet	Lioness goddess, wife of Ptah. Protector of Pharaohs.
Wadjet	Cobra goddess, guardian of Lower Egypt. Sister of Nekhbet.
Nekhbet	Vulture goddess, guardian of Upper Egypt. Sister of Wadjet.
Tawaret	Hippopotamus goddess, protector of women in childbirth.
Neith	Hunter goddess.

Canaanite God	Attributes
Baal-Set	Originally Baal, the most high god of Canaan. Hyksos brought him to Egypt and he became united with Set.
Anat	Goddess of war. Juvenile sister of Baal, violent. Worshipped in both Canaan and Egypt.
Resheph	God of war and plague, worshipped in both Canaan and Egypt.

<table>
<tr><td colspan="3" align="center">GODS OF ROME</td></tr>
<tr><td>Roman God</td><td>Greek God Counterpart</td><td>Attributes</td></tr>
<tr><td>Jupiter</td><td>Zeus</td><td>King of the gods.</td></tr>
<tr><td>Neptune</td><td>Poseidon</td><td>God of sea and elements.</td></tr>
<tr><td>Pluto</td><td>Hades</td><td>God of underworld.</td></tr>
<tr><td>Juno</td><td>Hera</td><td>Queen of the gods.</td></tr>
<tr><td>Ceres</td><td>Demeter</td><td>Goddess of harvest, agriculture.</td></tr>
<tr><td>Vesta</td><td>Hestia</td><td>Goddess of the hearth.</td></tr>
<tr><td>Apollo</td><td>Apollo</td><td>God of sun, prophecy, archery, disease.</td></tr>
<tr><td>Mars</td><td>Ares</td><td>God of war, violence, bloodshed.</td></tr>
<tr><td>Minerva</td><td>Athena</td><td>Goddess of wisdom, war. Patron of the city of Athens.</td></tr>
<tr><td>Diana</td><td>Artemis</td><td>Goddess of the hunt.</td></tr>
<tr><td>Venus</td><td>Aphrodite</td><td>Goddess of love, passion.</td></tr>
<tr><td>Mercury</td><td>Hermes</td><td>Messenger of the gods, travel.</td></tr>
<tr><td>Bacchus</td><td>Dionysus</td><td>God of wine, festivity, ecstasy.</td></tr>
<tr><td>Vulcan</td><td>Hephaestus</td><td>God of fire, blacksmith forging, volcanoes.</td></tr>
<tr><td>Others</td><td></td><td>Attributes</td></tr>
<tr><td>Prosperina</td><td>Persephone</td><td>Goddess of spring, consort of Hades in the Underworld.</td></tr>
</table>

"[The vile despicable one] shall seduce with flattery those who violate the covenant, but the people who know their God shall stand firm and take action. And the wise among the people shall make many understand, though for some days they shall stumble by sword and flame, by captivity and plunder. When they stumble, they shall receive a little help…so that they may be refined, purified, and made white, until the time of the end, for it still awaits the appointed time."

Daniel 11:32-35

CHAPTER 41

Kidron River Valley
Samaria
Two months after the Abomination of Desolation

General Apollonius sat on his warhorse across the Kidron River, watching and waiting. He had led three hundred Mysian mercenaries on a hunting expedition twenty miles north of Jerusalem. His prey: Jews who had fled the city and hid in the wilderness to observe Sabbath, circumcision, and dietary laws in defiance of Seleucid King Antiochus IV Epiphanes. The king's recent Edict of Unity in Judea had established a new altar to Zeus in the Jewish temple and forced suppression of all exclusivist Jewish customs under pain of death. The king would tolerate their anti-Hellenist ways no longer.

Normally, a captain commanded the Seleucid companies of soldiers. But the general himself so thoroughly enjoyed killing Jews that he took the lead to participate in the task. He had recently received intelligence from the high priest Menelaus of a large community of a thousand Jews—men, women, children, and their cattle—who had managed to escape detection by living in caves near the Kidron River. The cattle were sequestered in a nearby isolated valley.

Menelaus had told Apollonius that even though these Jews were his people, they were criminals in defying the law of the king. The high priest had felt that his conscience dictated he follow a higher law than his love for his people. Apollonius remembered acutely the duplicitous

Jew's lying face looking at him as he said, "I am a man of principle and conviction over personal interest."

As far as Apollonius was concerned, as long as he got to kill Jews, he didn't mind relying on one of their own to rat them out. He was, after all, a man of practicality and power. Apollonius laughed until he noticed one of his soldiers watching him with a curious look.

A scout had captured one of the Jewish lookouts, and they had tortured him to discover the whereabouts of the caves and livestock. The problem was that there were many caves. These operated as small decentralized fortresses. If the Jews fought back within those caves, they could do significant damage to Apollonius's forces, perhaps even achieve a victory. That was a level of uncertainty he did not want to test to find out.

Apollonius devised a plan as his forces marched to the location of the hideout. It was mid-day in spring. He had waited until the afternoon before the Sabbath to announce his presence across the Kidron River, at this point shallow and narrow enough to cross on foot. But with the melting snows in the north, the water level was slowly rising.

Apollonius had a cavalry unit of fifty horsemen with him and made sure his three hundred elite infantry soldiers were visible behind him. The Jewish leader had his own much less impressive assembly of a couple hundred armed men with him. How many more might be in hiding, was not apparent.

"I am Apollonius of Samaria, Mysarch and general of King Antiochus IV Epiphanes! To whom am I speaking?"

"I am David ben Joseph. We are no brigands or bandits. We are a peaceful community seeking to live in the wilderness."

"How many are you?"

"Several thousand, men, women, and children."

"Is that so?" Apollonius knew the Jew was lying, trying to demoralize him with exaggerated numbers. The general waved behind him. Two Mysian soldiers carried forward the Jewish captive, broken, bloody, and barely alive. Apollonius saw fear cross the face of his opponent.

The general said, "We have one of your watchmen here who has told us differently. He has said you have a thousand people with a total of two hundred and fifty men to defend you. And he told us where your cattle are. A squad of my soldiers are currently herding them to my camp, where I will feed my men."

The Jewish leader counseled with his men. They all displayed agitated surprise.

"Let us get to the point," Apollonius continued. "I have come to enforce the king's Edict of Unity. My new friend here has told me where you are hiding in caves and that you are still circumcising your male infants as well as observing your Sabbath among other crimes. So I call upon you now, engage in a sacrifice to Zeus, cease from observing your Sabbath this evening, and you will be allowed to live. If you do not, I am authorized to kill every one of you, man, woman, and child."

The Jewish leader replied, "I will need time to discuss this with the elders of our community."

"You have until sunrise to tell me your decision."

Apollonius saw the leader hesitate. Sunrise would be right in the middle of their Sabbath rest, which would not be over until sundown that next day.

"I need more time than that," the Jewish leader said.

Apollonius remained stern. "Tomorrow, sunrise."

Turning his horse, he headed back to camp with his men. Apollonius had been told by Menelaus back in Jerusalem that the community here was hasidim and adhered strictly to their religious rules. Their Scriptures commanded them to do no work on the Sabbath. Many of the hasidim believed this meant that they could not on the sacred day engage in the profanity of war. They were not even allowed to wear their weapons.

Apollonius scoffed at such a belief. He had told Menelaus, "How have you people managed to survive this long in the world with such absurd interpretations?"

Apollonius had begun to wonder why his people the Samaritans had ever wanted to become united with the Jews. He was glad his family had been turned away from Jerusalem when his father sought to live there. It had bred the hatred that filled his father—who had taught Apollonius everything he knew.

Menelaus had explained that the Jews believed God would protect them if they obeyed him. This was confirmed by their captive's defiance despite brutal torture.

"God will fight on our behalf," the captive had said through broken teeth, "as he did for Moses against the Egyptians."

Still, these Jews were a scheming people. Apollonius didn't know how much of what he'd been told by Menelaus or the captive was true and how much a lie. They had beaten much out of this watchman, but Jews were also cunning.

Apollonius concluded that if the general of the Jewish community returned with warriors who wore armor and carried weapons, then they would most likely fight on their sacred day. If they showed up without weapons, or if they didn't show up at all, then Menelaus was right. They would not fight on the Sabbath, and Apollonius would have an easy victory over them.

At sunrise, Apollonius stood waiting again with his entourage. But the Jews did not show up. He gave them about a quarter hour before he concluded they were not coming. He knew they hadn't tried to escape in the night because his scouts had kept watch in the surrounding hillsides. It was very likely they had used the time to hole up in their secret caves and plan traps and ambushes for Apollonius and his soldiers. He wasn't concerned in the slightest. He had well-trained and experienced soldiers against their equal number of ill-equipped and inexperienced peasants.

And thanks to the tortured watchman, he knew where their hideouts were. Turning, Apollonius raised his sword and ordered his men, "Forward to the caves! And kill them all!"

He and his cavalry advanced easily through the calf-high water. The Mysian elite infantry followed through the brush and foliage a quarter mile to the wooded hillside.

The Mysarch had split his force into six squads of fifty men. Four squads entered caves to hunt the Jews while two squads stayed outside for reinforcements and capturing escapees.

Apollonius entered the first cave, leading his squad of fifty. They held their shields tightly with swords in hand, carefully negotiating the pathway, prepared for ambush. Torchlight danced on the rock around them like phantom warnings. The deeper in they went, the more they were removed from reinforcements and more vulnerable to attack.

But Apollonius was surprised to find no ambush awaiting them. Instead, he found a hundred or so men, women, and children praying around a small fire. The captive watchman had been right. The men were refusing to fight on this holy day of theirs. Instead, they implored their deity for protection.

But you received me as your answer, the god of destruction, thought Apollonius.

His men had an easy time slaying them all. It was like a butcher slaughtering sheep. Some women tried to run with their infants in their arms. These were cut down by the men stationed at the cave entrance. Some were raped before being slain.

But *all* were slain: men, women, and children just as the king had ordered. Just as Apollonius gleefully obeyed.

It was a bloodbath. The screams of women, the cries of children, all cut short by swords and axes in the hands of ruthless mercenaries. At first, Apollonius felt the frenzy of bloodlust fill him like a demon as he became drenched in the blood and gore of his victims. But then it became anticlimactic.

It was too easy, even boring, chopping up people who did not fight back.

The night before, he had instructed his men not to see the Jews as human but as filthy, diseased rodents or insects whose survival would ensure the spread of a plague that would ultimately kill their own families. This plague of their religion was treason to the pantheon of gods whose myths were the very foundation of their civilization. The Jewish god was a tyrant who would enslave all the world with his oppressive jealousy. And no Jew was innocent, not even their women or children. For if their women survived, they would simply breed more of their wicked offspring. And if their children survived, they would grow up to wreak vengeance on the children and grandchildren of the Greeks.

So all Jews were guilty and deserving of justice.

Apollonius saw some of his soldiers throwing infants in the air to impale them on their swords like a game. For a moment, he felt the pang of guilt prick his heart. Until his own words came back to him. "If a single Jew survives, that Jew becomes the leader of the next generation of Jews who will kill all our women and children."

Yes, this was a necessary evil. It was necessary to kill their women and children. In fact, it might even be the event that stopped more killing, because other Jews would see that their lawlessness only led to their own extermination. They were the ones responsible for the consequences.

No, this was not a necessary evil. It was a necessary good.

CHAPTER 42

Judean Hills of Gophna

Judah sat in counsel with Mattathiah, his brothers, and five other leaders of their growing guerilla forces. They had commandeered caves in the Judean hills near Samaria for their hideout. Their initial revolt in Modein a month ago had garnered a hundred hasidim to their side from their village and surrounding towns. Since then, the word had gotten out and more Jews were recruited to their cause, growing their forces to over a thousand men. These were spread out in a network of small units of fifties and hundreds throughout the cities and towns of Judea. Two hundred of them were stationed with the Hasmonean family in the Gophna hills.

Mattathiah had been universally recognized as their general. His single act of defiance had inspired the resistance. He had appointed commanders of one hundred, including Judah and his brothers. Their numbers were small, but they were developing guerilla tactics to strike at Seleucid weaknesses: arson, night raids, attack and withdrawal, stealing Seleucid supply trains.

Many still scoffed at them in the face of an enemy whose numbers were like the sand on the seashore. And the Jewish forces had begun with tools as their only weapons: pickaxes, shovels, and hammers. To arm themselves properly, they would have to confiscate weapons of their defeated enemies. But how could they defeat them without proper arms in the first place?

Part of their strategy included the creation of a network of spies and communication throughout all of Judea for an advantage of intelligence gathering.

A messenger had just returned from Modein to relay the information that a company of a hundred Seleucid soldiers had arrived at the city searching for the missing military unit of Commander Apelles. His was the platoon that had been struck down by Mattathiah's original uprising. The Modein elders had successfully convinced the search party that the hasidim had refused to obey the king and had fled into the hills of Gophna. And that Apelles's platoon had gone after them.

The search party had dutifully followed the trail of evidence Mattathiah had left for them. Faux camps with fire sites and tent settings were replicated from Judah's knowledge of Greek military behavior. With several hundred hasidim, it had been easy to overwhelm the mere hundred Seleucids in a deep ravine pass.

There were now two missing Seleucid military units but still no revelation as to why. Mattathiah was buying time to build his guerilla forces.

But today, the new messenger had come from the Kidron River valley with a horrifying description of the grisly atrocity that had occurred there. They were now discussing the reality that an entire hasidim community had been deliberately attacked on the Sabbath because the king's forces knew they would not fight back on their holy day. All one thousand Jews had been butchered; men, women, and children.

Judah's younger brother Eleazar became defensive. "Those brothers and sisters remained true in their obedience to Ha Shem."

"And look where it got them," said another of the leaders, Samuel, a young, lean fighter who had previously repented of his own Hellenism. "These Seleucid generals are not stupid. Seeing such resounding victory, why would they not plan all their battles for the Sabbath?"

Judah watched his father considering each of the arguments as they were made. This would be a difficult decision for a man who had a deep conviction of obedience to Torah.

"Where is your faith?" Eleazar demanded. "Do you not believe Ha Shem will protect his people when they obey his Sabbath?"

"Where is your reason?" responded Samuel heatedly. "Ha Shem will not have a people to obey Sabbath if these massacres continue."

One of the other leaders spoke up. "The martyrs are inspiration to others in their self-sacrifice."

"Yes, they are," said Samuel. "They are an inspiration to fight so that more will not die."

Though the youngest son of Mattathiah, Jonathan was sharpest in his ability to negotiate disagreements. He said, "Eleazar, consider this. If you had an ox or an ass fall into a pit on the Sabbath, would you pull them out or leave them to the wolves?"

"I would pull them out," Eleazar responded quickly.

"And so would I," Jonathan agreed. "And if one of our family were wounded in an accident on the Sabbath, would you let them bleed out and die?"

"Of course not," snapped Eleazar. "I would work to save their life. That is not the same as fighting."

"Oh?" queried his younger brother. "Is not self-defense saving your life? Is not saving women and children from being murdered without mercy saving their lives?"

Finally, Eleazar stopped talking. Judah saw his father sporting a subtle smile.

Simon spoke up. "When Joshua purged the Promised Land of the Seed of the Serpent, I do not think that the Anakim giants stopped fighting on the Sabbath to accommodate the Jews. Nor is there any indication that Joshua withdrew on the Sabbath from all his multitude of battles."

Mattathiah sighed and said to the group, "This is a serious decision we are contemplating. Make no mistake, our God is not a pragmatist to ignore his laws for mere convenience."

Eleazar and a few others mumbled in agreement.

"Nor are his rules without exceptions."

Simon and the others now agreed.

Mattathiah continued, "Rahab of Jericho was honored for lying and deceiving to protect lives. Joshua's priests marched around Jericho for seven days. On the seventh, the walls fell down by God's hand, and they captured the city."

Judah added his support. "One of those days was a Sabbath."

Mattathiah nodded. "And the siege of Jerusalem by David extended over at least one Sabbath. As did the sieges of that city when defended against Pharaoh Sishak, against Assyrian King Sennacherib, and against Babylonian king Nebuchadnezzar."

Those historical examples from Scripture had the impact of silencing everyone there. Mattathiah asked, "Who would agree with me that self-defense is an exception to the Sabbath in God's Word?"

Everyone but Eleazar and the one leader raised their hands. Judah did not because his mind had wandered again to the innocents who had been massacred in the Kidron Valley. He then raised his hand and said, "I will fight King Antiochus unto death—without rest."

All eyes glanced around the room. Eleazar reluctantly raised his hand as did the other holdout.

Simon cautioned them. "My brother is heroic in his conviction. But we will not win by running heroically into a swinging scythe blade. We must be strategic. We must focus on building our forces and attacking targets we can win."

"You are correct, brother," replied Judah. "That is why our first campaigns need to be against our own people."

Everyone expressed shock at the statement. Everyone except smiling Jonathan, who understood. Judah turned to Mattathiah.

"Father, I would recommend that we travel to all the Jewish towns and villages in Judea and execute the idolaters in our midst who have bowed the knee to this false god of the Greeks. Torah commands it. Israel's unfaithfulness to the true living God is the ultimate cause of our desolation, the abandonment of our nation by Ha Shem. Our first task is national repentance and renewal of the covenant—before attacking the Gentile tyrant."

Eyes began to show dawning understanding. Judah continued, "That will purge our land of traitors and draw to our side the faithful patriots from those same towns and villages. Once we have the numbers, we will invade Jerusalem, destroy the Abomination of Desolation in the temple, and rout the apostate Jewish priesthood. Only then will Ha Shem return and set up Messiah's rule."

"A Phineas army," Jonathan muttered. Judah saw Big John, Eleazar, and Simon nod in agreement.

"That is a bold and dangerous suggestion," said Mattathiah.

Someone challenged him. "Well, what are your orders?"

Mattathiah recited Scripture from the scroll of Deuteronomy. "Thus saith the Lord, 'If your brother, or your son, or your daughter, or the wife you embrace, or your friend who is as your own soul entices you, saying, "Let us go and serve other gods," you shall not yield to him or listen to him, nor shall your eye pity him, nor shall you spare him, nor shall you conceal him. But you shall kill him. Your hand shall be first against him to put him to death. So, you shall purge the evil from your midst.'"

A solemn silence descended upon them all. They knew this was the very Word of God from their Torah. They both dreaded what they had to do and dreaded what God would do to their nation if they did not.

Mattathiah got down onto the ground, prostrate. The others followed to their knees or their faces. He led them in an anguished prayer of confession and repentance before the God of hosts who was holy, holy, holy.

CHAPTER 43

Jerusalem

Zeus sat on his heavenly throne in the Holy of Holies drinking from a chalice of sacrificial bull's blood. The male gods were all there, Poseidon and Hades beside him, Hephaestus, Dionysus, and Ares before him. Apollo and Hermes had just returned from their missions of reconnaissance.

Apollo spoke first. "I found them. Hera and her bitch goddesses are on Mount Hermon of all places. After we left the assembly there, they circled back and set up headquarters in El's temple."

"The nerve," said Ares.

Zeus laughed. "On the contrary, my good warmonger, it's brilliant. You must give Hera her due. It's the original cosmic mountain, the gods haven't used it in centuries, and it's less desirable to me than Zaphon."

Ares was not as impressed. "Should we plan for an assault? I have been waiting forever to give it to that Athena."

"No, no, no, no," commanded Zeus. "Leave them be. Let Hera cool off, and she'll eventually see she needs *me* more than I need her."

"But what about her mutiny?" complained Ares.

"I don't really think it was mutiny," answered Zeus. "I was speaking from my rage."

"She's a calculating schemer," said Poseidon.

Zeus laughed. "Ha! Yes. And that is why she will soon realize they cannot overthrow the gods. And they cannot rule without me."

Hermes said, "On my way back from Hermon, I decided to run through the entire land of Galilee and Samaria. I wanted to check out their cities for any sign of archangels. Just in case. I saw nothing but howling silence."

"Interesting," remarked Zeus. "If Judea is the obvious source of the messianic seed, it would make sense to hide outside of Judea."

The others murmured in agreement.

"In fact, now that you say so, I think we will need to start exploring the least likely places of all for the Messianic branch to grow. Let's start with Philistia. Gath, Ashkelon, Ashdod, Ekron."

Apollo spoke up. "Your majesty, on my way back I came upon the Mysian forces of Apollonius."

Apollo's gaze turned accusing as he continued, "The general has a superior fighting force that is quite effective. Shall we discuss the secret weapon he has recently acquired?"

Caught! Zeus saw the others look at him in confusion. Well, he was going to have to admit it eventually. It might as well be now.

"Ahem, uh, what Apollo is referring to is, uh … well, Apollonius has a gibborim soldier who just joined his army as a mercenary." Gibborim was a term that meant the mightiest of warriors.

"But not just *any* gibborim soldier," goaded Apollo. He let Zeus confess.

"He is another Heracles."

The gods were aghast.

Poseidon exclaimed, "Have you created the Nephilim army all along?"

"No, no, no, no, no. There are no other Nephilim. Only this one." Zeus looked around guiltily, trying to find an ally, finding none.

Apollo chided him. "That's what you said about the other Heracles."

Zeus scrambled, trying to explain. "I originally replicated two of them at the same time just in case I lost one. That was all." He thought to shift the blame. "And I was right, wasn't I? Hera, that unsubmissive ..." Zeus wanted to cuss her out. But he thought better of overdoing it.

"So you only revealed the one to us," clarified Hades.

"Please don't lie to us, brother," said Poseidon. "Do you have a hidden army of Nephilim somewhere?"

Hades said, "If we wake up in Tartarus because of this, it will not go well for you."

Zeus became indignant. "Where would I be able to hide an army and train them without you finding out? Two maybe, but not an army. Come on, be rational."

He saw them weighing his words, reading his body language, to decide if he was lying this time as well. Now that he was telling the truth, he wished he had let them in on it sooner.

"I swear to you on my own honor," proclaimed Zeus, "I have not replicated any other Nephilim."

"Your honor is not worth much these days," said Poseidon.

Zeus said, "I deserve that. But I'm still king of the gods."

He was pushing it with that one. If they ganged up on him, they could overthrow him as they had done the Titans in their myth.

Poseidon turned to the others. "But he does have a point. The only place he could hide numbers like that would be underground." He looked at Hades. "And that would not escape your notice."

Hades shrugged. True enough.

Poseidon added, "And besides, we haven't woken up in Tartarus yet, so …"

Zeus added, "There will be no Nephilim army. He's one Naphil. A surgical strike force to tip the balances in favor of Antiochus. Which balances in favor of us."

"And that is all?" Poseidon demanded.

Zeus placed his hand on his heart and raised his right hand in an oath. "And that is all."

Ares quipped, "Then let's see what this little bastard can do to the Jews."

CHAPTER 44

Bethel

At his father's command, Judah led a battalion of three hundred warriors to the city of Bethel. The resistance forces had been split up and appointed to various areas throughout Judea and Samaria to execute their purge of idolaters and recruitment of freedom fighters. Within several weeks, they had already drawn hundreds more to the cause from the villages and towns but had also executed as many for their idolatry.

Word of their exploits had reached the king. His general Apollonius in Jerusalem had placed a bounty on the heads of the leaders of the "Modein bandits." Most Jews knew them as the brothers Maccabee, sons of Mattathiah ben Hasmon.

Their resistance forces had avoided the larger cities until last because these seemed to be strongholds of evil. The more cosmopolitan and urbane the populace, the more likely they were to eagerly embrace Hellenism along with its gods. Ironically, city folk were more like sheep than rural folk. Because they were herded together in a centralized society, they were less self-reliant and therefore more easily manipulated by earthly government powers and their heavenly princes above.

It was winter again, and the skies above had storm clouds rolling in. Judah and his brothers Simon and Eleazar walked through the city streets in disguise as reconnaissance for their three hundred fellow soldiers hiding outside the city walls. The brothers wore the garb of merchant traders with Phrygian bent conical caps and multi-patterned belted tunics. Judah wore a hooded cloak. This location was a trading crossroads between Samaria and Judea as well as the Phoenician coast. Any one of a number of traders might recognize Judah's face from their many travels.

This would be a straightforward mission. The city walls were only twenty feet high and easily breeched. With about fifteen hundred inhabitants, that meant about three hundred males of fighting age. A small enough number for the resistance to subdue. But the brothers had not anticipated the festival they had stumbled upon. The streets were full of residents making their way to the center of town and lining the main street to watch a procession. The crowds were thick and pressing. Most everyone wore ivy leaf wreaths in celebration.

Judah and his brothers pushed through the throng of people for a better view. What they saw sickened Judah's stomach.

The grand procession was led by a tiger-drawn chariot carrying a large bronze statue of Dionysus, the Greek god of wine, fertility, and madness. Judah considered those traits a tame description of the perversion before him and his brothers. Dionysus was sculpted with a boyish handsomeness and soft feminine-like features. The musicians that followed him playing flutes and drums were naked except for hairy goat skins on their legs. This outfit was supposed to mimic the goat legs and hooves of the mythical hybrid satyrs, followers of Dionysus who represented the wild abandon of nature, especially in sexuality. Eleazar used to call satyrs goat demons.

Next in line of the pomp was a group of men who were more naked than the satyrs but covered in vines and wearing large wigs and ivy wreaths on their heads. They used heavy make-up to appear as exaggerated clownish women in their faces. Others wore Greek theatrical masks and still others animal heads. All carried large wooden poles carved as phalluses and marched with them performing sexually provocative dancing.

These creatures were engaging in more than mere idol worship. They seemed to embody a total rejection of every natural distinction created by God. Male and female, pleasure and pain, sanity and madness were all fused together into hybrid monsters. Human chimeras. Much wine was being consumed, and some of the crowd behaved in such an erratic way that Judah felt the presence of evil spirits among them. This was confirmed to him when he saw more than one person fall to the ground in writhing contortions, making guttural animal sounds.

His heart was grieved. Despite the presence of Greek residents, the city of Bethel was still predominantly Jewish. Meaning that many of these grotesque idolaters were his countrymen. And they would have to pay the consequences of their apostasy. What a sad picture of what this city had become from its once-sacred origins. The patriarch Jacob had had his dream of the step-pyramid to heaven at this very location. At one point in Israel's history, the ark of the covenant had been stored in Bethel. The prophet Samuel had judged here as well.

But then the apostate Jeroboam had set up a golden calf at Bethel in a cult center to rival Jerusalem. From that point on, the city had descended into a pit of evil whose wicked consequences Judah and his brothers were witnessing at this very moment.

The procession ended in the circular agora of the town, where the statue of Dionysus was driven before a stone altar of sacrifice. A large bull had been slaughtered on the altar. Its meat was now passed around for all to partake along with plenty of wine.

The rumble of thunder above signaled to everyone a coming interruption to their festive conclusion. It made Judah realize his own plans would have to be quickened.

A large circular formation of men and boys from the procession, still half-naked, danced and sang a choral performance called a dithyramb. The fermented fruit of the vine continued to flow freely through the crowd, enabling their own drunken participation in the bacchanalia. This was all a precursor to the theatrical Greek satyr plays that were scheduled to commence.

Judah considered the intoxication of the mob to be a strategic advantage for his surrounding forces. The brothers would leave this drunken revelry and return with their sober soldiers of judgment.

But as the brothers crossed an alley, Judah realized Eleazar had been lost in the crowd. Simon looked around for him, but Judah's attention was distracted by two figures engaged in a struggle down the alleyway. Judah moved instinctively to help.

When he arrived, Judah saw it was a woman being attacked by a man. His hand was covering her mouth, and he was trying to rape her. What little noises she was able to emit would never be heard above the din of celebration in the streets.

Judah pulled the man off the female victim and slammed him against a mudbrick wall. The man had a bulbous nose and pockmarks on his fat, confused face.

Judah offered his hand to help the woman up. She cautiously accepted with wide, staring eyes. His hood had come off in the fray.

The fat-faced man bolted for the crowd. Simon chased him. Judah followed.

Fat-Face pushed his way through the crowd trying to disappear, but Simon caught him before he could get far. He dragged him to the ground, and the crowd parted around them.

When Judah arrived, he saw Fat-Face looking up at him with recognition. He shouted, "I know you. You're Judah Maccabee."

The man must have been a trader in one of the towns Judah had already been to.

"You have me mistaken," Judah denied. He realized he could not pull his hood back on without appearing guilty.

"No, I know you," said the man, struggling in Simon's grasp. "You're Judah Maccabee!"

Judah responded quickly with a dismissive laugh. "Shut up, you drunken fool! You speak nonsense!"

Simon got up, still holding the man in his grip, "And I am King Antiochus!"

The brothers forced their laughs as though enjoying the party. But others were staring at Judah now.

The rape victim had arrived beside Judah. She shouted, "He's right! I recognize him too! That is Judah Maccabee!"

Betrayed by the woman he had saved.

Another shouted, "Grab him!"

Simon shoved Fat-Face into the crowd and tried to pull Judah away.

But it was too late. They were completely surrounded. Where was Eleazar? The masses of bodies kept tightening around them, an impenetrable, crushing horde. Judah saw Simon pulled away into the multitude. From all sides, hands grabbed Judah. He felt as though he was being pulled apart. He struggled to free himself. But he could not. He could not get at his sword. And it wouldn't have done him any good anyway.

He was dragged up to the center of the marketplace. Everything was spinning around him. The loud music. The shouting and dancing. The mob. The dark swirling storm clouds above.

Then Judah heard a ram's horn.

It was Eleazar calling for battle.

The horn seemed to rise above the cacophony of noise and music all around.

Within minutes, all three streets that led into the marketplace had been blocked by a unit of seventy-five men each.

Judah was thrown to the ground at the altar.

A Jewish priest raised his butcher axe over Judah's head. His eyes seemed to gleam red with demonic hatred.

He was going to turn Judah into a human sacrifice.

Then the priest was launched backwards to the ground by a javelin piercing his chest. Judah looked up to see that his brother Eleazar with Simon had broken through the mob into the center circle. Eleazar was always a sure shot with his javelin.

Two other priests beside Judah were hit by arrows.

Judah saw his youngest brother Jonathan on a rooftop with released bow. Big John, the Jewish Heracles, was beside Jonathan. Jumping off the roof into the crowd, he began pounding his way through until he reached the other three brothers.

The four of them drew their weapons and circled off against the mob.

But by now, the mob had cowed into submission. The troops in the streets did not attack, and a final squad of twenty-five warriors joined Judah in the center square. They had come from the rooftop where Jonathan remained watching over his brothers with a sharpshooting aim of protection.

Judah stood up on the altar and drew attention, announcing to the village, "People of Bethel, I am Judah Maccabee. These soldiers are the Jewish forces of resistance against your tyrant king, Antiochus Epimanes!"

It had become their habit now to use the "madman" moniker in place of the "god-man" one. Judah had their attention now.

"Yes, we are wanted by the king with a bounty on our heads! And I wear that like a crown granted from the king of heaven! Today, this town center will be a threshing floor to divide the wheat from the chaff!"

The audience became agitated. Many knew what that had meant in surrounding towns and villages over the past months. Word had indeed spread about Judah's recruitment tactics.

"Who among you will repent of your unfaithfulness to Adonai and obey the Torah? Who among you will pick up arms and join our resistance against the one they call the Little Horn of Daniel? Against his Abomination of Desolation that has corrupted the temple, the holy city, and all the Land?"

The swarm of people buzzed with reactions of all kinds, those for the offer and those against.

"This Gentile despot is a beast who has forced us to deny our God and his law or die! Can you not see that if you continue in this apostasy, you are dead already?"

"We cannot win!" someone shouted out. "So we die either way!"

Judah replied, "It is true, you will die either way! But those who worship idols will die and face the judgment of almighty God! While those who turn back to worship Adonai will die and face a resurrection unto life!"

Some in the crowd cheered. Others scoffed. More thunder cracked overhead as if to confirm Judah's claim. Hellenists considered it a clap of denial.

"Choose this day whom you will serve! Those who choose Adonai, come and stand with us!" Judah gestured to the circle of soldiers around him in the center of the marketplace. "Cast off your filthy, unclean garments of apostasy and put on clean garments of righteousness!"

From all around the crowd, men began tearing off their ivy leaves, dropping their wine to the ground, and moving their families forward to join Judah.

Some in the crowd jeered the joiners. Others spit on them, but the faithful wiped off the spit and kept coming. Dozens of them.

Then it became a hundred and more.

The center circle around Judah grew to accommodate the numbers. The soldiers opened canvas sacks and handed out weapons to the recruits. Women and children were herded protectively into the center.

The mob began to rise with agitation. They could see what was coming next.

Judah announced to the heavens, "A sword for the Lord and for his people!"

This was the phrase to which Judah's soldiers had been commanded to respond with force. A phrase first adopted when the Jewish people under Gideon had resisted their far more powerful enemy, the Midianites in the time of the judges. They were to kill only the adult men and women, not the children.

Then as if on cue from heaven, it started to rain. Drops at first, but then a steady sprinkle as thunder clapped overhead.

The soldiers at every blocked street exit launched an attack on the citizens, who were unarmed. The soldiers pushed toward the middle, where Judah and his newly armed recruits pushed outward. The unrepentant festival-goers were crushed in a pincer movement.

Rain poured down, drenching everyone in the blur of its wake. The darkened masses of slaughter lit up with lightning flashes of terror. Screams of women and children were drowned out by the crack of thunder and the bellowing of war.

Children were pulled aside to safety. Adult idolaters were executed. The blood of hundreds mixed with the rain to form a river of red through the muddy streets. Cries for mercy were drowned out by the storm and the chopping of blades.

Judah hacked and thrusted at bodies with a maniacal madness that overcame him. All he could see was red. He felt as though his mind had been released into a frenzy. All sense of humanity left him.

These were idolaters and apostates from the living God.

Judah and his men were the righteous army of Phineas.

It took only minutes for the bloodbath to be over.

Judah looked around him at streets full of corpses and carnage. Bawling children were held back by the repentant. Thunder crashed above with resounding judgment. Blood and gore were cleansed from the soldiers' armor and weapons by the pounding rain. Bodies strewn all over the muddy streets were baptized with justice. Idolaters had been punished this day with the wrath of God.

But Judah somehow did not feel right. He looked down to the ground at his feet where he saw an innocent young girl he must have accidentally cut down in the melee. She couldn't be more than six years old. He didn't remember seeing her. He would have stopped if he had. Had he seen her? Images from the attack assaulted his memory.

It was just one child. But it felt like a dozen to him. Though he had sought so desperately to avoid such horrible mistakes, they were nevertheless one of the unintended casualties of war.

But he could not dismiss this little child—dead at his feet. He could not put her out of his mind. Had he crossed a line? Had he become a blinded beast in the pursuit of killing the beast?

Had he gone too far?

The rain continued to pelt him like a pounding finger from heaven.

He dropped to his knees with regret. He was exhausted. With his own self-righteousness.

He had turned justice into vengeance in his heart.

CHAPTER 45

Town of Acrabeta, North of the Gophna Hills

Mattathiah took war council with his two leaders in the confiscated synagogue of the small town they had most recently attacked. They had executed idolaters and had sworn in by oath the hundred new recruits who had joined them with their families. Some of those families had been Hellenist for years and had not circumcised their infant sons. This would be remedied within a few days. There was no neutral stance that accepted the God of Abraham without accepting his covenant sign. Hellenism had to be cut out of their souls with Torah.

A scout stood before the general and his captains. A small, thin young man named Noah who had been recruited for the task because of his skill at hiding and moving about without being noticed.

Mattathiah asked, "Are you certain?"

"Yes," said Noah. "I saw General Apollonius, and he has a force of a thousand men with him in position."

"But you say you heard the command with your own ears?" Mattathiah clarified. "You were not mistaken?"

"I was not, sir. I saw Apollonius announce to them all to stay at the ready but do not attack. Allow the gibbor to work alone."

"So he has some kind of champion warrior," Mattathiah mused. Gibborim often received their designation from their mighty achievements in battle. Mattathiah asked one of his captains, an elderly experienced fighter with a scar down the left side of his face named Baruch, "And how many men do we have?"

Baruch said, "We only have a hundred and fifty. The others are already halfway back to the Gophna Hills by now with the new recruits."

Mattathiah cursed. They had just wrapped up their operation here and were about to follow the others when this news had arrived.

The other captain, Rani, an intellectual commander with a long face and shaved head, said, "If we leave immediately, we may be able to get several miles before they even discover we are gone. We can outrun them."

Mattathiah looked at the young scout. "And they don't know how many we have?"

"No. I heard it spoken."

Mattathiah mused aloud, repeating the strange statement, "Allow the gibbor to work alone."

Baruch was also incredulous. "A lone mighty warrior? What can one gibbor do against a hundred and fifty experienced soldiers?"

"Maybe he is leading a special squad," said the commander Rani.

"Did you see this gibbor?" Mattathiah asked Noah.

"No, sir. I did not."

They waited anxiously for the general's decision.

"We will not run," said Mattathiah. Rani sighed with concern. "We will mount a squad of a hundred men in the town entrance. They don't know our true numbers. Let them think that is our welcoming committee that portends a larger force inside the town."

"Which we do not have to back them up," warned Rani.

"Every battle is a risk, captain," said Mattathiah. "Have you forgotten who is *our* gibbor?"

Rani's face went flush. He averted his eyes to the ground. To his shame, the much younger, smaller scout Noah immediately answered from Scripture. "The Angel of the Lord encamps around those who fear him—and delivers them."

Rani nodded agreement. "You are right. God is our Champion."

"Then let us face this nemesis," said Mattathiah, "and find out just how mighty he and his squad really are."

The hundred Jewish warriors stood at the gates of the village as the sun rose, casting a beautiful orange glow on the hillside before them. Even unwalled villages such as this one had such entry gates marking the city's identity and operating as the location of the elders' political decisions for the community.

The elders and village population had long since left, hiding in the nearby hills to wait out the battle. Mattathiah had set up his perimeter of watchmen on village rooftops in case Apollonius had plans to ambush them.

Mattathiah's horse stood a dozen paces inside the gate in the center of the village's market and common area. He was flanked by his captains, also on horseback, and surrounded by thirty infantrymen. They would observe and make calls as needed.

Mattathiah's Jewish forces had to this point been engaged in guerilla warfare. They had been waiting to build enough forces to mount face-to-face battles. Now it appeared that Mattathiah would be the first to do so and without the backing he needed.

Well, the Angel of the Lord is on our side.

Tension mounted as the hour approached. Mattathiah could feel the anxiousness of his men. But also, their hungry desire for action. They had proven themselves over the past months and were seasoned and ready for confrontation with these Hellenic demons.

Mattathiah heard a watchman sound off. "Incoming!"

The soldiers adjusted their shields and light armor. They tightened their grips on their weapons, ready for a battle royale.

Then they saw a lone figure break the crest of the hill. A large muscular warrior carrying a club and strangely wearing the skin of a lion over him. The head of the lion operated as a kind of helmet.

Mattathiah grew curious.

Baruch said, "This must be their gibbor."

"Does he have no squad with him?" Rani queried.

The lion-clad warrior marched with purpose toward the town entrance and the soldiers. He didn't slow down, and he wasn't followed by a squad.

"Archers!" shouted Baruch. They only had six, but that was enough to take out an elephant with their precision.

The archers drew and nocked their bows.

"Release!"

They released their missiles.

The gibbor merely drew his lion skin around to his front to receive all six arrows in the pelt. They all bounced off the skin.

"Again!" shouted Baruch.

They readied.

But now the gibbor was jogging toward them. They would have one last chance.

"Release!"

Again, the missiles bounced off the lion pelt.

"Magic!" cried Rani.

Then the gibbor was upon them. He hit the first line of warriors, spreading them out in an explosion of force.

Half a dozen warriors were grounded. Mattathiah could tell bones were broken by that impact. *That was preternatural.*

The gibbor engaged with a dozen other swordsmen, smashing their swords out of their hands and crushing their bodies with his large club.

He was close enough now for Mattathiah to see the large golden belt the gibbor wore with a huge buckle like that of Ares. Mattathiah had seen such before in his travels to Scythopolis. The design was Scythian.

The gibbor warrior was cutting down the Jewish soldiers like a scythe through wheat. And still no other Seleucid forces followed him into the fray.

Because they didn't need to.

Mattathiah knew this would be over very quickly.

Rani called to him, "We should leave now."

But Mattathiah was transfixed by this glorious monster of war. His graceful dance-like movements. His mighty power. He was like one of the Nephilim from Canaan though not as tall. Maybe six and a half feet.

Who was he?

Picking up a bow and arrow, the gibbor suddenly aimed it right at Mattathiah, who froze. Captain Baruch pulled his horse in front of him and yelled, "Protect the general!"

The soldiers huddled in closer, trying to block any projectile.

Mattathiah peered around Baruch's broad back to see the gibbor drop the bow, wipe out another ten soldiers with his club, then reach down to pick up a boulder by the gate. It was the size of a man.

He raised it above his head with a scream, muscles bulging as though ready to burst out of his arms. The handful of soldiers still alive cringed in fear.

The gibbor launched the boulder directly at Mattathiah.

Baruch was still in the way, so it hit him first, crushing the life out of him immediately. The captain's body flew into the air. The rock slammed into Mattathiah's horse, snapping the horse's neck before it could reach Mattathiah. But he and his mount fell hard backwards. The general felt his breath knocked out of him, and everything went black.

He came to a moment later on the ground with his horse's bloody muzzle weighing his chest down. The rock had spun away after glancing him and now rested on the ground in his peripheral vision. Mattathiah felt a pain in his ribs and could barely breath.

In a moment, Rani was upon him and helping him onto his own horse.

Mattathiah was still dizzy and half conscious. He could only babble his words as he felt the pain in his ribs with each pounding hoof of Rani's horse.

They were escaping.

Mattathiah lost consciousness.

CHAPTER 46

Gophna Hills

Judah marched through the camp of his army, followed by his brothers John, Simon, Eleazar, Jonathan, and fifteen other captains of hundreds they had just gathered. Jewish warriors of all stripes spotted the hillside in camps of smaller units of ten to twenty. Messengers had called them in from their campaigns. Their numbers had grown to almost three thousand strong.

Entering the cave, the captains made their way to the bedside of Mattathiah, who had finally awakened with a more vivid consciousness than the past couple days. The strategic commander Rani sat with him, having taken care of the general after bringing him to safety.

"Father," said Judah. "We are all here."

The brothers gathered around their father, the other captains of hundreds behind them.

Mattathiah moaned. Rani lifted the woolen blanket to reveal the general's naked torso completely covered in bluish-purple bruising.

Judah knew what that meant.

"I am dying," croaked Mattathiah. "I have internal bleeding."

"Don't cry for me, Eleazar," he continued. Judah glanced over to see his passionate brother unable to hold back tears from his eyes.

"I have lived a full life. I have served the Lord, and I have a family of sons who serve the Lord. No man can ask for better."

He was staring at Judah when he said those words. Judah felt a pang of guilt for having put his father through so much grief. But what he felt from those eyes was true forgiveness, a father's love.

"I only ask that you not bury me in Modein. Bury me in these hills under this sky. For it is here where I tasted true freedom."

"We will, Father," assured Simon.

Judah leaned toward his father. "Rani told us of your encounter with the gibbor warrior."

Mattathiah asked, "Did anyone else survive?"

"No."

"I have never seen such might and power in my life. I am sorry to say that includes even you, John."

Judah glanced at John to see his face tighten.

Everyone listened in silent awe as Mattathiah narrated, "The gibbor took down a hundred men like they were small children. And he was dressed ironically…" The general paused, not appearing to want to say it. "… like Heracles. The lion skin and club. A Scythian belt of Ares."

"What is this madness?" Simon said incredulously. "A myth come alive?"

"Occult magic," said Eleazar.

"One of the Nephilim," corrected Mattathiah.

A hush went over the brothers.

"But I thought King David cleansed the land of that Seed of the Serpent during his reign," Simon said with confusion.

"He did," responded Mattathiah. "The Anakim, Rephaim, and all the Nephilim tribes had been eradicated by then. But even in tribal massacres, there are always individual survivors. Goliath was one such King David defeated. And the giants of Gath killed by David's mighty men, all descendants of the Nephilim."

The family and their fellow leaders considered the terrifying implications. Could there be more of these gibborim?

"And there was one other thing." Mattathiah coughed weakly and winced with the pain. "Apollonius had his forces, a thousand strong, watch from a distance. It was as though he was testing the gibbor."

Rani added, "To see how much damage he could do alone."

Finally, Big John spoke out, "He is no myth and no Heracles. He is just another Goliath. And I will be his David."

The rest of the group remained silent. John's sincerity and boiling tension were scary to behold.

"I have wanted all my life to be a gibbor like David's mighty men," John went on. "I have trained for it. And now is my opportunity. I swear I will take this Greek peacock by his gonads and string him up."

Judah and the other brothers all gave John a hand of affirmation on his shoulder and back. Everyone knew there was no stopping John once he made up his mind about such things. The brothers had often teased him of being an elephant with a purpose.

Now Eleazar spoke up. "And I will kill King Antiochus the Mad with my javelin. He is the head of the serpent. I will search him out, and I will pierce his liver. He will die in agony for what he has done to God's Chosen People."

"My sons, my sons," coughed Mattathias with a chuckle. "No more oaths, please. You are getting ahead of yourselves. There is much difficulty ahead of you. More than mere individuals can accomplish. You must work together."

"We will, Father," said Judah. That brought another look of gratitude from the old man.

"We have three thousand warriors now," said Simon. "It's not enough to fight a war. But we can still engage the enemy in small battles with guerilla tactics."

"Finally, my elder brother agrees," quipped Judah.

Mattathiah wasted no more time. He announced, "My captains of thousands and hundreds, hear now my dying will as the general of this military." He coughed again. "I relinquish my command of the armies of God to my son Judah Maccabee as general of all forces. May he be the Hammer of God that we need to finish this war."

Judah saw Simon frown with disappointment.

"And my son Simon the Wise shall be his head of counsel. Listen to him, Judah. For though he is envious of you, he is also wiser."

Simon's glowering expression lightened with hope. He looked over at Judah, not to gloat but as if to plead for agreement.

"If you both can find a way to overcome your sibling rivalry, you will be an unstoppable force." Mattathiah coughed once more and finished, "Those two hard heads will stop knocking together, and they will knock down the kingdom of the Greeks."

Judah was now looking at Simon. Both had tired, wet eyes. Judah reached out his hand. His brother grabbed his wrist firmly. The others around them lightened with laughter.

"We will, Father," Judah said.

Simon echoed, "We will."

They embraced each other as the brothers they should have been for years. Always beside Judah, Big John took them both in his wide, hugging arms as he liked to do.

But Mattathiah was not done. He reiterated his favorite statement of which he loved to remind his family. "We are the Hasmoneans, proud descendants of my great grandfather Hasmon, the greatest priest from the tribe of Jehoiarib, the first of the Levite priests to return to our holy city after the Babylonian exile."

The brothers smiled in affirmation. Judah said, "Indeed we are, Father. Indeed, we are."

Mattathiah, falling asleep, muttered, "Cleanse the temple. Messiah is coming."

They buried Mattathiah ben Hasmon in the hills of Gophna the next day at sunset. Three thousand men looked down upon the solemn ceremony from all around as if in an amphitheater. But this was a quiet performance so as not to alert the enemy anywhere near. The silence itself was an otherworldly music of hearts united in honor and courage.

A single voice rose from the gravesite as Simon read Psalm 61. Then John recited the Kaddish, their prayer of mourning.

Judah gave the final blessing,

> "The Lord bless you and keep you;
>
> the Lord make his face to shine upon you and be gracious
>   to you;
>
> the Lord lift up his countenance upon you and give you
>   peace."

CHAPTER 47

Gophna Hills

Judah's men had intercepted a Seleucid caravan on the main road south from Samaria to Jerusalem that had led through the Gophna Hills at the edge of Samaria. A royal Seleucid carriage had been accompanied by a platoon of fifty soldiers. When the Jewish forces detained its occupant, they discovered it was a Syrian princess who had been sent with royal authority to deliver a message to Judah Maccabee directly. They had blindfolded her with her four maidservants and brought her to Judah's headquarters cave for questioning.

Judah was relaxing by a small fire when two guards led the princess in and sat her on a rock, removing her blindfold.

As the guards left, Judah was arrested by the sight of this Syrian beauty. Her long, full-bodied raven-black hair framed a perfectly sculpted smooth-skinned face and fell around her dark wool cloak that covered a modest royal-purple gown beneath. She wore a small royal tiara that signaled her status.

The woman stared at Judah with warm brown eyes crowned by thick manicured eyebrows. She was maybe twenty years old but emanated a spirit of solemnity that could only come from a soul who had suffered.

The first thing she said was, "Are my maidservants safe?" Her voice was seductively raspy.

Judah nodded. "They will not be mistreated. Nor your escort guards. We recognize your ambassadorship."

"You are Judah Maccabee?" She was forward, not arrogant but unafraid.

"I am."

"I am Princess Laodice V, niece of King Antiochus, daughter of Queen Laodice IV. I have been sent to deliver a message to you from the king."

"Oh?" Judah sat back, amused. "And what would that message be?"

"The king knows of your growing resistance, your defiance of his Edict of Unity, and your spreading of sedition throughout Judea."

Judah raised his brow with interest. She continued, "He offers you the opportunity to hand yourself in to his mercy."

Judah repeated with sarcasm, "To *his* mercy."

The princess concluded, "If you continue, he will hunt you down and make you an example to all of Judea."

Judah sat in silence, contemplating his response. Finally, he said, "So he insults me by sending a woman to negotiate."

"There is no negotiation." Laodice spoke with deadness of emotion.

"There is no mercy," Judah responded harshly. "No soul in a monster who is willing to send his own niece into danger as an ambassador."

He watched her closely to see if she would flinch with fear. She did not. Instead, she said, "It's a perfect opportunity to discreetly rid himself of the sister of the true heir to the throne, Demetrius I, son of the late King Seleucus Philopator—and my brother."

Now that was a fascinating plot twist, like something out of Homer. There was another claimant to Antiochus's throne.

"Where is Demetrius?" Judah asked.

"He has been a hostage of Rome since the death of my father. There he remains because Rome prefers Antiochus."

It had been the custom of Rome to take a hostage from one of the male heirs of the royal family upon ascent to the throne. A guarantee of continued submission. The old scribe Eleazar had told Judah about the court intrigue of Antiochus stealing the crown through assassination while Demetrius remained hostage in Rome.

Judah was trying to put all the confusing facts together. "Your mother Laodice IV is the queen."

The princess gave a facial smirk, "And thus the reason why I was not simply made to disappear when the king married her. But I am a constant reminder to the king of my brother Demetrius, the rightful Seleucid king."

Judah stared at her. She was mesmerizing.

He raised the edge of his lip with a subtle smile. "So it seems you and I have a common nemesis."

Laodice did not return his smile. She remained determined. "The governor of Samaria, General Apollonius, is on his way from Samaria right now with a force of two thousand Mysian mercenaries to hunt you down regardless of how you respond to the king's offer. He is to bring your head back to Antioch."

"Regardless of how I respond?" Judah clarified.

"Regardless," she repeated.

He said with surprise, "That sounds like the part he didn't want me to know. So I am supposed to trust you now?"

"No," Laodice said. "Do whatever you wish. But Apollonius is coming."

"Down the Lebonah pass?" Judah asked.

"Yes."

"Well," he concluded, "I will take you captive and see if you are lying to me."

Laodice didn't respond to his threat. Instead, she said, "Why do you do this?"

"You mean, take you captive?"

"No. Why do you fight a war you cannot win?"

The Seleucid princess sounded truly interested in understanding Judah's motives. As though he was something she had never encountered before. As though she was watching an exotic animal in the arena.

"I am a Jew. I fight for the right of my people to practice their religion without being eaten by Antiphates." Judah was alluding to the mythical king of giant cannibals, an obvious jab at Antiochus.

"You are a Jew who talks like a Greek," Laodice commented.

"I was a Hellenist. I served on the Royal Guard."

Judah could see her surprise. She asked, "What changed you?"

"My wife and unborn child were murdered by the king's 'Edict of Unity.'"

He saw her eyes well up with empathy.

He continued, "I have seen the corpses of women and children who would not disavow their God at the bottom of Jerusalem's walls. I have pieced together the bodies of faithful Jews who were tortured and cut to pieces for their religious beliefs. So you will have to excuse me if I am loathe to trust Greeks bearing gifts."

Judah wondered if the beautiful princess was a Trojan horse.

"I wouldn't either if I were you," Laodice responded. "And don't trust anything Apollonius offers you. But he is coming."

The Lebonah Pass

It was late in the afternoon as Apollonius rode at the head of his second regiment of a thousand Mysian mercenary soldiers. The first regiment led the way through the valley of the Lebonah ascent. This was a narrow pathway up a steep incline with precipitous upward slopes on both sides. It was a prime location for an ambush, so his men were anxious and watchful as they traversed the path in a four-man-wide column snaking around the winding ravine. Because the sun was so low, they were already in the shadows of the hills above them, requiring some torches to light their way.

Apollonius was confident in his Mysian warriors. They were well-trained and wore the armor of a heavy infantry phalanx unit, the backbone of Hellenistic forces since the days of Alexander. They had bronze helmets and wore leather jacket cuirasses instead of their heavier metal coats of armor due to the more difficult terrain in which they would meet their guerilla enemy. Each phalangite soldier carried a small, round bronze shield on their back and a long *sarissa* pike in their hands sticking twenty feet up into the sky as they marched.

The sarissa were used for phalanx fighting, the typical formation of most armies where the soldiers lined up in blocks of men beside one another, shields tightly linked, pikes forward to the enemy, the entire length of the battlefield and sixteen or more men deep. Anyone within ten feet of their formation would be skewered into oblivion. Even cavalry had a hard time breaking the phalanx because the horses would be skittish of the pikes.

But all that military strategy was worthless in defending a march through a tightly-narrow road where they were forced into column formation just four men wide.

A half mile through, and they would be out in the open again and more prepared for battle.

Apollonius had a hundred heavy cavalry units, also vulnerable in this mountainous ravine with their heavy solid metal armor on both rider and steed. Climbing steep hills was not in their capabilities. He made them march double-time to get through this death trap as quickly as possible. The thin line of soldiers snaked so far ahead of him that Apollonius couldn't see the front unit around the bends of the winding road.

He had decided not to bring the gibbor with him on this hunting expedition of Judah Maccabee in the Gophna Hills. He knew the Jews were woefully ill-equipped and terribly outnumbered, so he wanted to retain the glory of a massacre by his own hand without the credit being stolen by that glory hound who named himself by the arrogant moniker of Heracles.

To make sure of his plan, Apollonius had lent the gibbor to the general Seron for his forces coming down from Syria. Apollonius knew how history operated. The events and heroes making it into the writings were the extraordinary ones. The boldness of an Alexander. The bravado of an Achilles. The generals and men they led were the theatrical backgrounds for the sensational achievements of individuals.

And Apollonius wanted to be the individual who crushed the rebel Judah Maccabee in the serpentine coils of his strategic skills on the battlefield. He even dreamed of the best possible scenario that involved personally facing down Judah, using his whip sword to cut the Jew's cockroach body in half. What a rousing event that would be. How would a Hellenist poet describe their confrontation? Would Apollonius make it into the writings of Greek historians?

His scouts had reconnoitered intelligence that Judah's forces were possibly five or six miles into the Gophna hills just south of this valley pass. The enemy no doubt had their own intelligence and were hiding in their caves preparing their defense.

Suddenly, the long train of soldiers stopped marching. The general cursed, "Gods be damned, you slothful …The longer you delay, the longer you make us vulnerable to attacks! MOVE!"

And then it struck him. Could this be …?

A hundred feet up the steep incline of the hills above the Lebonah pass, Judah looked down from his hiding place among the boulders. He and his brother Big John were waiting for their moment to attack the winding, thin train of Mysian soldiers.

He had only six hundred men with him against Apollonius's two thousand, so he had to strategically maximize his assets. The Lebonah ascent was the best location to ambush Apollonius. And he had to ambush the Samaritan general because he wouldn't stand a chance on a traditional battlefield.

The Jewish resistance had been perfecting their strategy of guerilla warfare. They had sabotaged Seleucid supply caravans for the past few months for food and weapons. But this was the largest number of soldiers they had ever faced. Not only did Judah have to win this fight, he had to win overwhelmingly or he would lose Jewish momentum and recruitment. Some men would fight to the death for a cause, but most only wanted to join a winning side. Judah had to prove it was possible to defeat the beast or he would suffer the loss of support needed to win their freedom.

Their future was riding on this battle.

Judah saw the marching line halt. He noticed the general screaming out curses and commands from his horse. This was their moment. Hundreds of yards up the path, a company of a hundred and fifty hasidim warriors blocked the head of the snake. Because of the narrow pass, the phalangites could not move into formation. They could only fight as a four-man-wide column against a four-man-wide column of hasidim with the element of surprise.

The hasidim pushed the Mysians back onto their comrades, who fell and were trampled. The entire marching train of soldiers had been halted by this single roadblock.

Meanwhile, a second unit of a hundred and fifty hasidim attacked the rear of the train in the same way as the front. They blocked retreat and pressed in toward the middle.

With the help of Judah from above, a fourth squad of a hundred and fifty armed and screaming hasidim descended on the middle of the train from the eastern hillside.

The phalangites were able to present their skewering pikes to their left to greet the attacking party. They stood still, stoically awaiting the arrival of their assailants.

But the Jews stopped in their tracks just yards outside the striking zone of the pikes. They weren't about to rush into the porcupine defense of the Mysians.

Meanwhile, Judah led his squad of a hundred and fifty silently down the western slope until they reached the turned backs of the phalangites defending themselves against the eastern side. Because their extremely long pikes required two hands to hold toward the enemy, the Mysians were unable to access their short swords to defend the rear.

Judah and his men hit them like a stampede of war horses. The eastern slope warriors then finished them off in a crushing pincer movement. The other Seleucid soldiers outside of their reach watched helplessly as the phalangites were massacred beneath the blades and bludgeons of Judah's strike force.

Then the two hasidim squads pressed north and south of each other.

Judah had been right. This narrow valley was a perfect death trap for an army used to fighting in regiment formation on a battlefield. Confusion and fear gripped the defenders, which emboldened the Jews in their own fighting.

Judah saw Big John beside him plow into soldiers with his war hammer. He had never seen his eldest brother so explosive before, so full of rage. One hit would smash four or more soldiers and send them all flying like broken puppets. John was a war elephant clearing a path for Judah. He heard his mighty brother yelling out, "Where is your champion?! Where is the gibbor?!"

No answers were given because they were all being smashed into pieces. Dozens of unlucky Greek soldiers.

It only made the Jewish powerhouse rage even more.

And the legendary champion Heracles was nowhere in sight for Big John's vengeance.

But Apollonius was.

Judah eyed the general on his war horse preparing to defend himself. The rest of the cavalry behind him stood unable to attack. Unless they were prepared to trample their own men, they could do little-to-nothing. Some riders tried to clamber up the hill but were rendered helpless, a couple of horses falling and crushing their riders.

Behind him, Judah heard again, "Where is your champion gibbor?" John had circled back around to question the fallen who were still barely alive.

Judah pushed ahead toward Apollonius. He found himself at a gap in the road between the units. As his gaze met the general's glare, he could somehow tell that Apollonius knew who he was. The hunter had found his quarry.

Judah said, "I believe you're looking for me."

Instead of racing toward Judah on his horse, Apollonius jumped down from his mount, threw his plumed helmet to the ground, and pulled out a strange-looking weapon from a sheath. It looked like a whip with a flat thong, but it glittered like metal. The general grinned confidently.

Before Judah could move closer, two hasidim ran toward Apollonius screaming a war cry. The general handled the metallic whip with precision to cut off one soldier's head in transit. His body fell to the ground, dead meat.

With a second crack at the other soldier, the tip of the whip blade seemed to cut into his abdomen, ripping out his entrails in a splatter of blood and gore. He fell dead at the feet of the general.

Judah was spellbound by the weapon. It seemed otherworldly. Because of his time in the horse stables, he was very skilled with a whip and how to defend against one. But a razor-sharp blade was not a soft leather strand, so he had to be careful.

Crouching, Judah picked up a bronze shield from a fallen Mysian. The sound of battle began to lessen around him as his forces successfully decimated their enemies. The cavalry now regrouped to meet the hasidim squad from behind, who used confiscated pikes to pierce the horses' scaled armor and take down their riders.

Judah closed in on Apollonius. If he killed their leader, it wouldn't be long before the army succumbed to defeat.

The general snapped the whip sword at Judah, who raised the shield to guard himself. It split in half beneath the preternatural impact of that serpentine bite. Judah tossed the shield to the ground.

"My compliments on your ambush, Jew!" the Samaritan general growled. "But you will still die."

Apollonius cracked the whip again. Judah saw the movement coming. He dove and rolled away from the blade.

The general said, "My only regret is not tearing your vile temple to the ground and setting Mount Zion aflame!"

Judah picked up the now-empty plumed helmet from the soldier Apollonius had decapitated and threw it at the general. The flexible blade caught the thing in mid-air and cut it clean in half.

Judah was taking note of how his opponent handled the weapon. The Samaritan wasn't an expert. And he had no spatial awareness of his horse behind him. Seeing the blade flick beneath the horse's left leg, Judah ran to Apollonius's right.

The general tried to follow his movement by whipping the sword toward Judah. The metal blade caught the lower ankle of the horse and cut it right off, hoof and all. The steed reared and whinnied in agonizing pain.

When it came down, it fell to its side, catching Apollonius from behind and landing on him with a thousand pounds of flesh and metal. The whip sword was ripped from the general's hand. He landed on his face in the dirt, half-crushed beneath the mighty steed.

The panicked horse writhed in pain. Apollonius screamed out as his legs and hips were pulverized even more by the shifting weight. The horse whinnied in terror until Big John approached, grabbed its head, and broke its neck.

Judah looked down upon Apollonius, now struggling in agony. Bending down, he pulled the whip sword from beneath the horse's corpse and examined it. The word "Rahab" was inscribed on the handle in ancient Hebrew.

"Where did you get this strange weapon?" Judah said to the whimpering Apollonius,

"From your temple treasury," the Samaritan general croaked in pain.

Judah shook the blade out behind him with the skilled finesse of a whip handler.

"Please, have mercy!" Apollonius cried out.

Judah crouched down to get closer. "Mercy? On you who would have no mercy on others?"

He swung the whip around with precision and cut off Apollonius's head. It rolled a few feet away in ignominious defeat, face eating the dirt.

Judah had wanted the general to suffer more since he had been the right hand of the king's fury upon Jerusalem and the hasidim all these months. But Judah believed the monster would be judged by Adonai according to his ways. And Judah knew there would be more monsters that would rise to take Apollonius's place before victory was attained for God's holy ones. This was only the beginning.

The Mysians saw that their general had been vanquished. Word spread in the ranks, and morale collapsed.

The north and south hasidim ambush squads completed their squeeze to the middle as Mysians fell beneath their victorious blades of justice.

As Judah had expected, it was not long before they finished wiping out the entire two thousand Mysian mercenaries.

They saved three captains whom they planned to interrogate.

CHAPTER 48

Judah and John entered the cave where Princess Laodice was being held captive with her four maidservants. The men had come straight from the battle of Lebonah Pass, their leather cuirasses and battle tunics still drenched in blood and gore. They hadn't even bothered to wipe their faces clean. Simon had joined them from his camp to inquire of their royal prisoner.

Outside in the camp, soldiers celebrated with drink and battle stories of their strategic victory in the narrow valley against impossible odds. Numbers were already being exaggerated in the telling. Legends were already being created. Morale was high.

But it would not last long as the dark reality set in that it was only going to get worse. The king had an unlimited supply of soldiers compared to the few thousand resistance fighters. To this point, they had been a guerilla force acting like bandits in the wilderness. Now they were a full-fledged revolution that could bring down the wrath of their earthly sovereign. They needed all the help from heaven they could get.

Inside his general's cave, Judah unlaced his cuirass as he explained to Laodice, "Apollonius is dead. We annihilated his forces to the man."

Seeing her face brighten with interest, he added, "You told the truth about him. And I thank you."

"It wasn't for you," she said. "I despised the man. He was a pig."

The brothers listened silently. Judah set his leather armor down and scratched his sweaty, itchy skin beneath his battle tunic. "I will keep you captive no longer. You are free to leave with your entourage and guards. To return to Antioch."

Laodice stared at him angrily. "Are you a fool?"

Judah was taken aback. He looked at John and Simon, who both shrugged.

"Hostages are valuable leverage for negotiation," the Seleucid princess continued.

"I don't want a hostage," Judah responded. "There will be no negotiation."

"And I don't want to return to Antioch."

Judah raised his eyebrows. "You want to remain a captive?"

Laodice sighed with exasperation. "You are not very observant."

Judah gave Simon another glance for advice. He got none.

"I detest my family," Laodice added forcefully. "I despise the king. There is nothing more I would rather do than give you intelligence that will make him suffer."

"Against your uncle," Judah clarified.

"Yes, against my uncle, the king, who raped me, who murdered one of my brothers to take the throne, and now plots to kill my other brother in Rome who is the rightful heir. Yes, that uncle."

Judah felt his mouth open with shock. He didn't know what to say.

She continued, "As a family member of the crown, I am privileged to know some individuals of significance as well as some secrets that flow between said individuals in power."

"Such as the plans of Apollonius."

"Maybe there is hope for you yet," Laodice said.

Judah felt the burn of her sarcasm. He couldn't tell her that he wasn't thinking straight because she had mesmerized him with her beauty and candor.

Simon interjected, "You may be royalty, young lady. But you are at our mercy, so I would recommend you respect our general."

"Forgive me," the princess said quickly. "I do get in trouble for my mouth."

Simon told Judah, "Some of the men still don't trust her. They think she will sabotage us."

Judah asked her, "What other intelligence do you have?"

"Only if you keep me hostage."

He hesitated. Laodice added, "If by chance I do survive and return to the king, don't you think it would be more believable that I was held *hostage* under force than just freely giving up information like I am doing? To be clear, I'm not suggesting you torture me."

"Okay," Judah replied reluctantly, "I will keep you captive. I will have my brother Eleazar responsible for your guard. You and your maidens will be safe with him."

Laodice nodded agreement. "Also, would you return my soldiers to the king alive with the message of my capture? That will show good faith on your part."

"Okay, I will release your guards," Judah confirmed. "Do you have any other demands as a hostage, your highness?"

For the first time, he saw Laodice smile. The three men laughed.

Big John said with a soft voice, "Princess, do you know anything about a champion warrior of Apollonius? He attacked a town called Acrabeta not far from here."

Laodice's smile abruptly evaporated. "Yes, the general called him his 'Heracles.' He sent him to another general, Seron, who is on his way to Jerusalem from Syria by way of the Philistine coast. And he has twice as many troops as Apollonius had. I believe he intends to join forces in

Jerusalem and use the Akra citadel as a base to expand their search for you."

A dread pall fell over the men. The stakes were rising. A reckoning was coming.

Simon said, "That means they'll be going through the Beth-Horon pass."

It was the only main road straight inland. The ascent to Upper Beth-Horon was another route that was advantageous for an ambush. Judah turned to Simon.

"Get together a tight regiment of a thousand. That's twenty-five miles. We have to travel fast and light to get there in time and prepare for the battle."

Simon nodded and left them. Big John followed, leaving Judah alone with the princess.

Laodice looked at him thoughtfully. "I know Seron. He is not vain as Apollonius was nor blinded by Jew-hatred. He will not make the same mistakes. And he is well-armed with Thracian soldiers. More ruthless than Mysians."

She was right. Thracians had a reputation for being brutal mercenaries from a culture of independence and tribal warfare. They had been used by Athens to cause great damage to cities during the Peloponnesian War.

Judah asked, "How is it you are so knowledgeable in military matters?"

Laodice smirked at him. "You mean, matters meant only for men?"

He waited for her answer. She said, "I was married once. To King Perseus of Macedon."

Judah didn't disguise his surprise.

She continued, "As opposed to men, women *do* listen. And I listened."

He smiled, twice-humbled.

"My husband taught me how to navigate the political machinations, diplomacy—*and treachery*—of the court. He was defeated in the Battle of Pydna by the Romans. They marched him and our children in Triumph through the streets of Rome. They all died in captivity."

Judah was drawn in by her story. She had his full attention now. "I am sorry to hear of your suffering. How did you manage to survive?"

"My mother is Antiochus's queen." Laodice added with disdain, "So women aren't entirely without influence."

"And all men are not the same." Judah watched her every gesture, her every facial expression with intense interest.

The princess smiled reluctantly. "No, all men are not the same. Most do seek power and glory. But some *may* live for a higher purpose … or die for it."

Judah knew she was referring to him. As though she was having a hard time believing he was real. Now he noticed she in turn was watching his every gesture and expression. As though she was as curious of him as he was of her.

He said, "And all women are not the same. For the same reasons. But we all share the same human nature."

"I was right," Laodice quipped. "There is hope for you yet."

Judah could not help but smile.

At that moment, Simon strode angrily back into the cave. "Judah, the three captives have escaped."

"How?"

"The camp has been celebrating our victory—with a little too much drink. Some shared wine with the guards."

Judah sighed and winced. Though his forces were voluntary and had fought well together, they were still guerilla fighters that lacked the discipline and training of the Seleucid army. He would have to respond sternly and decisively if he wanted to earn the respect they had given his father before him.

Simon confirmed Judah's dread. "The hostages overwhelmed the guards while everyone else was distracted. They stole horses and fled."

"Do we know which way?"

"No."

Judah felt another sting. "They must be seeking out Seron. If they get to him, they will tell of our tactics at Lebonah and our location here. Have you assembled a search team?"

Simon had more bad news. "Big John went after them. Alone."

"Alone? Why didn't he come to me?" demanded a frustrated Judah.

Simon said the obvious. "Because he knew you would probably not let him go."

"It's that gibbor champion he's after," concluded Judah.

"I'm afraid so," said Simon. "The escaped captives will no doubt lead him to Seron's camp where the gibbor is."

Judah sighed. "John's obsession blinds him to the danger he is putting us all in. You heard what Father said. That champion warrior is a Naphil. He's much stronger than John."

"On the other hand, John is too good a tracker," Simon responded. "You know the captives won't make it back to Seron alive."

"But if John is captured by Seron and tortured ..."

"I don't think Seron could get anything out of our mighty brother," Simon countered. "You're not the only hammerhead in this family."

Judah disagreed. "Every man has a breaking point. Let's pray they don't get the opportunity to find brother John's. But you're right. He will catch those captives better than any search team we could send."

Judah swallowed hard. He knew his next course of action would be a most difficult one.

An hour later, Judah and his commanders of thousands and hundreds stood before the mustered forces of hasidim in the valley. Their celebration had been abruptly ended, and the men had been gathered to witness the scene before them. The four guards who had failed their duty over the captives knelt beside the three friends who had brought them wine on the sly. Each had his back bared to receive the lashes of a leather flogging whip.

Forty stripes each was the maximum penalty according to God's own words in the holy Torah. The crime was exposing the entire army of their comrades to potential sabotage by the enemy. Everyone knew it was just treatment. But that didn't change the solemnity of the situation.

The whole valley was silent as the guilty received their punishment. With each slapping strike of flesh and each groan of pain, Judah felt himself wince in his soul. These men had risked their lives for him. For Ha Shem. Some had even saved the lives of others in combat. But if he did not follow through with this, Judah knew he would not be worthy of their loyalty and they would not become the disciplined army they needed to be to defeat the forces of Antiochus the mad king.

CHAPTER 49

Jerusalem

High Priest Menelaus stood with other Jewish priests in the inner temple and watched the priests of Zeus perform their monthly sacrifice in honor of King Antiochus. The outer courtyard around the temple was filled with Jews who were required to join in observation. Some of them were quietly defiant, but most were willing participants in the Hellenistic celebration.

They had begun in the usual way on the twenty-fifth day of the month with a bronze statue of the king carted through the city to the temple in a long procession of citizens. His image was standing with arms raised in divine blessing to observers. Once inside the inner courtyard, the people sat before the temple. The priests of Zeus poured libations of wine at the foot of Zeus's image, now accompanied by the image of Antiochus placed beside him.

Besides bulls and goats, hundreds of pigs and other unclean animals had been burned on the altar before Zeus since its installment a year and a half ago. Torah was no longer observed here. Both the Scriptures and the ceremonies of his ancestors had been effectively eliminated.

It had been difficult political maneuvering for Menelaus in his position as high priest for Judea. He had become a figurative head of an obsolete reality in his own priesthood. He had begged the king for exemption from serving in the new priesthood of Zeus. He had successfully argued that he needed to remain a liaison between the Jews and their Seleucid overlord. Menelaus could not do so if he had to replace his high priest garments with those of the Olympian priesthood. The Jews needed some link to their past if they were expected to embrace the future. Extreme change could lead to revolution, so reform had to be incremental. One could get any people to do anything through incremental changes, one small step at a time.

In truth, Menelaus despised the image of Zeus. Maybe it was just residue of the Second Commandment still in him, but when he had first seen that idol of gilded gold, the ludicrous notion of it all hit him. The words of the prophet Isaiah came alive to him like never before.

The idolmaker plants a cedar and the rain nourishes it. Then it can be used as fuel. Half of it he burns in the fire; over this half he roasts meat, eats it and is satisfied. He also warms himself and says, "Ah, I am warm, I can feel the fire!" The rest of it he makes into a god, his idol, bows down to it and worships it; he prays to it and says, "Save me, for you are my god!"

But then again, it was all absurd, both images and rejection of images, visible gods and invisible gods. For all the Jewish claims of miracles of deliverance and provision, in the end they were nothing but a tiny backwater territory of backward thinking. They had no kingdom of power or consequence. The world was now a progressive Hellenist civilization, not because of a god's will but because of a single man's will. A young pagan warrior king, Alexander the Great, who had conquered the world with military power.

And that power was currently declining in the face of the greater power of pagan Rome rising in the west. The only truth that Menelaus believed in was power. And he would do whatever he had to do to join whatever side held that power. Tolerating a ridiculous golden image was a small price to pay for his survival. Just as performing the rites and responsibilities of a Jewish high priest had been a small price to pay for his power in Judea.

Menelaus actually enjoyed the taste of pork and other foods forbidden by Torah but promoted by Hellenism. Pork ribs were delicious, and pig's belly bacon was the tastiest of meat he had ever eaten. Shellfish such as shrimp and lobster were also a gourmet delicacy he imbibed in as often as possible. He had come to the conclusion that the god of Torah really was a killjoy who wanted to keep bodily pleasures from his people. All the rules of separation seemed to Menelaus to be a separation unto unhappiness, not a separation unto holiness. His sexual peccadillos also happened to be more acceptable in a Hellenist world than a Jewish one.

So Menelaus had found his perfect place in between two worlds. He maintained his outward figurehead status in Judea as high priest but partook in the guilty pleasures of eating forbidden foods to obey Antiochus. Forbidding circumcision was another custom he was happy to enforce while claiming mere obedience to the oppressive demands of the king. In fact, he thought circumcision was a barbaric mutilation of the male body.

Menelaus was required by the king to command the Jews to participate in the edict. That had been more difficult than he had first anticipated. So many of them had lost their lives defying Hellenist reform. So many wasted lives. If they had just obeyed, they would have avoided so much bloodshed. In that sense, all the suffering and death of the Jews had really been their own fault.

They had it coming.

Menelaus had thought that the execution of dissidents would strike fear into the hearts of his people and compel obedience. But this had resulted in the opposite effect. It had spawned what some were already calling the Maccabean Revolt. Judah, son of Mattathiah the Hasmonean, had his epithet spreading across the land: Judah Maccabee, the Hammer. He and his father and brothers had risen up in defiance in their small city. And they had become a pocket of resistance that was winning back other Jews to join their lost cause. Surely, they didn't hope to win against King Antiochus and the giant of Hellenism.

Menelaus watched the smoke rising from the holocaust on the altar. The smell of burning flesh made his mouth water for some good well-done meat. But a fellow Jewish priest interrupted his thoughts.

"My Lord, news from near Samaria. Judah Maccabee has overcome Apollonius's forces at the Lebonah Pass. Completely wiped them out."

Menelaus could not believe what he was hearing. He looked at the young priest. He certainly didn't look like he was jesting. "And Apollonius?"

"Dead," said the priest somberly. "They say by Judah's own hand. They say thousands of hasidim are joining him."

Apollonius had been one of the most fierce and ruthless leaders Menelaus had ever met. His work securing Jerusalem had made him a legend. At that moment, Menelaus knew the tide had turned. And Judah's ultimate goal would surely be the holy city and temple. He didn't know how long it would take the scoundrel to make it here. How many more battles and victories. But he had no doubt Judah was coming. So Menelaus had to protect his own interests.

Menelaus sat in Captain Nico's headquarters in the far side of the Akra fortress. He shared a glass of wine with the captain, a stocky, swarthy Greek with rich, black tightly-curled hair, olive skin, a hearty beard, and large eyebrows that seemed to cross his forehead to become one large eyebrow. The man's arms were also hairy, and he sweated a lot.

But Menelaus knew not to be fooled by the simple animal-like presence of the commander. Nico was cunning. And he knew Menelaus was afraid despite the high priest acting quite calm and collected with his reasonable request.

"So you are fearful of this Judah Maccabee eventually making his way to Jerusalem? And that he may not be happy with how you have fulfilled your duty to your people?"

To appear less afraid, Menelaus gave the commander a scolding look. "Captain Nico, I take offense at your implication. I have encouraged the Jews to obey the king and embrace Hellenism. Would you not call that fulfillment of my duty to my people?"

"Fair enough." Nico took a sip of wine. "So you would like the protection of the Seleucid Akra Guard again. Do you not have your own temple guard to protect you?"

Menelaus tried to act and sound as humble as possible. "I am truly grateful for your previous protection to me during Jason's siege. But I am not asking you to join in the defense of the temple. I am merely asking to take a more permanent residence in the Akra to secure the protection and safety of my office of high priest."

"And that of your boy-love."

"And that of a few of my *assistants* and servants," Menelaus corrected the captain. "Judah Maccabee is a violent domestic terrorist without scruples. If he has his way, he will invade the temple, kill all the Hellenists in the priesthood, and return Judea to Torah. Is that what you want?"

Now Nico appeared to be one-upped.

Menelaus continued, "I am the only one who acts as a liaison between Judea and Antioch. My presence keeps the peace."

"Or what little we have left," interrupted Nico.

"I will be of no good for that peace to the king or to you if I am dead by the sword of that insurrectionist."

Menelaus took a victorious sip of wine.

Nico scratched his bushy beard, considering the options. "And what is in it for me? I mean, something more concrete other than the peace?"

Menelaus smiled and raised his finger, gesturing for the commander to follow. They both got up, and Menelaus led the way to the door of the fortress headquarters. When he opened it, he stood aside so Nico could see the dozen temple prostitutes, priestesses of Aphrodite, standing in their luscious pleasure gowns that offered transparent peeks into private places and skin bared to solicit desire. Menelaus had spared no hairdo, jewelry, or make-up to seal the deal. He could see Nico respond with instant lust—and arousal.

Menelaus said, "I am sure your soldiers will be grateful to you and more loyal than ever."

Nico was beaming ear to ear.

Menelaus sweetened the offer yet more. "To reside in the Akra for as long as I do."

"Menelaus," said Nico, "you are indeed a shrewd liaison who keeps the peace."

CHAPTER 50

Necropolis of Memphis, Egypt

Hera and her goddesses stood at the pinnacle of the Great Pyramid of Khufu over four hundred and eighty feet above the necropolis, the city of the dead. The group of fugitive exiles from the Greek pantheon included Athena, Aphrodite, Demeter, Artemis, Persephone, Gaia, and Hestia. Hera saw multiple pyramids and tombs of kings all around her on the barren desert field of the necropolis. Monuments of death on a field of death. It was empowering.

Across the river, the city of Memphis gave the opposite impression. Green, lush and fertile. Human mudbrick domiciles spreading out for several miles around the glorious temple of Ptah with its huge red brick pylons and painted walls. This was the city and temple where King Antiochus had been crowned as Pharaoh last year—before his humiliation at Alexandria in the face of Rome's earthly and heavenly princes. Memphis was a city of life, human life, whose worship was necessary to empower the gods to rule through death.

Hera had requested a secret meeting with the gods of Egypt. They had been summoned to the Great Pyramid for discussion in one of the secret chambers deep inside this cosmic mountain.

This cosmic mountain. Though it was on one level a tomb for a human king, that king had sought deification and connection between heaven and earth. He had done so by building this man-made mountain patterned after the likeness of the original man-made cosmic mountain known as the Great Tower of Babel. That structure had been a ziggurat, or step-pyramid, that functioned as a stairway between heaven and earth. Between humans and gods.

Hera would never forget those ancient days at Babel when the Creator Yahweh had divided the tongues of men, creating the nations, and had allotted them under the authority of the rogue Sons of God as their Watchers. She and her comrades had all taken on new names of the deities that humans worshipped. They had become the gods of the nations while Yahweh had allotted one people to himself in an unfair display of juvenile jealousy. The Watchers had so embraced their deception that Hera barely remembered her original name and identity. But what did an old identity matter when you create your own reality?

Gods dwelt on mountains that also connected the heavens and earth to the underworld with a temple as spiritual portal. In a sense, the conflicts of history were conflicts between cosmic mountains. The Olympians had recently lost their Mount Olympus to the seven hills of Rome. Marduk reigned on Etemenanki, the ziggurat mountain in Babylon called The Temple of the Foundation of Heaven and Earth. Baal had reigned from Mount Zaphon in his holy temple. This pyramid complex in "the Field of Reeds" near Memphis was also aligned with the constellation of Orion and the underworld god Osiris. But that was another long story. Even Yahweh had his heavenly throne above mirrored in his earthly temple on Mount Zion.

Mount Zion. The thought of that hateful cosmic mountain filled Hera with rage. Yahweh's own portal to his people. The ultimate territorial prize. And just when the Greek gods had it in their hands, Zeus had to throw it all away with his plan to replicate an army of Nephilim. Only a fool would risk another major violation of the heavenly/earthly divide that would surely bring the judgment of Yahweh down upon their heads. Hera knew she was right about the danger. In fact, she knew the gods knew she was right. They were just too cowardly to stand against their alpha male and his toxic divinity.

And that was why she was here today. To do what had to be done to stop a tyrant. To salvage what little chance they had of avoiding catastrophe and with it imprisonment in Tartarus. Why wouldn't Yahweh cast them into the same deepest, darkest region of Hades as he had done the two hundred Ancient Ones?

Hera motioned to her goddesses. They slid down the smooth, white limestone casing of the pyramid exterior to the bottom pyramid entrance.

They walked past the human guards without their awareness because they remained in the unseen dimension of reality.

They walked up the ascending tunnel to the king's chamber deep in the center of the pyramid.

"Do you feel the spiritual vibrations?" asked Persephone. Her voice was sweet and childlike. She was sensitive to the occultic power of the underworld.

Artemis said, "These Egyptians really love their magic."

"It didn't help them too much against the ten plagues," said Athena, reminding them all of that nasty, unpleasant episode.

Hera explained, "Well, this will ensure our privacy from that eavesdropping totalitarian Zeus and his dirty little spies."

Arriving at the king's chamber, they entered a room thirty-five by twenty feet in dimension with a ceiling twenty feet over their heads—a secure room of stone. Unlike many Pharaonic burial chambers, this one had no carvings or hieroglyphic texts painted on the walls or sarcophagus. Hera thought it badly needed some decorating.

The god Ra sat waiting for them on the red granite sarcophagus of King Khufu. His gleaming body looked like a living golden statue of a Pharaoh with his atef crown and crook and flail. His eyes glowed lapis lazuli on his humanoid visage.

Hera was surprised. "You said you would meet us with your council and the gods of Canaan."

Athena became skittish, hand on her sword.

"Calm down, Athena," said Ra. "If you remember, Rome has enforced peace between us. A fight would be in neither of our interests, much less yours. I will bring your concerns to the pantheon. You will have to wait."

He's rubbing our noses in it! Aloud, Hera said, "With due respect to your majesty, we don't have a lot of time to wait. The reason I am here is to warn you of Zeus's plan to create an army of Nephilim. I am sure you need no explanation of the consequences of such an act."

Ra too had been there to see his brothers imprisoned at the Flood for their sin.

"As it happens," he responded, "We are very aware of Zeus's alleged plan. But I must say I am not convinced he will go through with it."

"You do not know him like I do," complained Hera. "I am here to ask for your support."

Ra listened with piqued curiosity as she continued, "If you help us overthrow Zeus and place me on the throne, I will guarantee more than mere treaties of peace. I propose an alliance of equal powers. We have divided and fought each other while Rome has expanded her territory. Sammael is already the strongest prince of nations. He will surely annex our lands as he did Macedonia and the Aegean. If we unite, we could become a power that would keep the prince of Rome in his place."

Ra looked impressed. He slid off the sarcophagus and paced through the room. "A bold move." he mused. "Ah, if only women ruled the world, all wars would cease and nurturing harmony would prevail."

Hera didn't appreciate the sarcasm.

Ra continued, "You do realize such a political alliance would force Sammael to declare war on us both."

"The prince of Rome doesn't have to know about our alliance until it is absolutely necessary. And by then we would have our militaries in synch with each other."

Ra nodded in agreement. He continued his pace over to the tunnel entrance. "How much wealth do you include in this offer of yours?"

"You could plunder the Jerusalem temple."

"Come, come, Hera. You don't think I know there is nothing left to plunder in that whore house?"

Hera paused. Then said, "If Baal-Set, Anat, and the gods of Canaan join us from your pantheon, I promise to return Syria and the Phoenician coast back to their control."

Ra raised his brow. "You are sure they want to return?"

"It was their allotment from heaven," she said. "Do you still want them here? I'm sure Baal-Set would be happy to have his house back on Mount Zaphon."

"Baal-Set is in the belly of Apophis somewhere in the Abyss," Ra responded. "But your offer is tempting regarding the other Semitic deities. They are a constant reminder of our Hyksos occupation after the ten plagues. Syria and Phoenicia are a significant concession."

Hera became even more somber. "If we don't unite now, we may lose all our allotted territories."

"Your warning is not without merit." Ra leaned against the stone wall by the tunnel entrance. "And your offer is generous."

Hera smiled and glanced at her fellow goddesses with pride.

"There's just one problem," added Ra. "We've already made a deal."

Hera was confused. What was he talking about?

"With Zeus."

She felt a shiver through her bones. She had been betrayed. *The goddesses* had been betrayed.

Then Hermes appeared at the tunnel entrance wearing his running skirt, leather running boots, and bronze Attic helmet with wings. That long-haired fidgety gossip had beat them here. He crossed his arms, sporting an arrogant smirk on his lips.

Ra stepped into the tunnel access next to Hermes.

The goddesses drew their weapons. Swords, daggers, and a javelin or two were readied for action. Athena wasted no seconds. She leapt at Ra but was shoved back by an invisible force at the entrance.

"Damnable Egyptian magic!" the goddess of war exclaimed.

Ra said, "Only your weapons will pass through the barrier if you hand them over."

"What has Zeus promised you?" demanded Hera.

"A commensurate deal. The problem with you, Hera, is your lust for power."

"And you don't lust for power?" she barked. "And Zeus doesn't? And Sammael? You hypocrites. Everything is power. You just don't want to give up your power."

"You are a fool, Hera. Obviously, everything is power. And that is why your claims of inequity and demands for fairness are absurd. You haven't learned to accept your own limitations."

She was sick of hearing the same putdowns for millennia. "Why is it always goddesses who must accept their limitations?"

"You will never understand until you give up your proud assumption of entitlement."

Hera felt a rising rage she knew could find no outlet in this prison. She glowed with bright bronze flashes.

Anger turned into desperation, and she burst into crying. "You don't understand what it is to be oppressed because of your sex! You will never know the burden of powerlessness that women must suffer!"

"Neither will you," said Ra. "Because you are a male pretending to be a female. This … enterprise of ours, the entire strategy of the Sons of God from the very beginning of Babel, has been deception intended to undo the creation of Yahweh. And, yes, for power. But you have forgotten your place in the order of things. You have deluded yourself for so long that you believe the Lie. And that is why you are a liability to our cause."

Hera became so enraged she screamed at him. It began as a guttural bellow and increased into a high-pitched hysterical shriek. Everyone had to cover their ears.

But it could not pierce the veil of magic enveloping the king's chamber.

Finally, she could scream no more. She fell to the floor gasping for breath. The goddesses surrounded her empathetically.

Ra said, "You will stay here for as long as it takes you to stop resisting, disarm, and accept Zeus's punishment."

"It will be a cold day in Hades," said Athena, "before we submit to the patriarchy again."

"Then get comfortable with your new cell. At least you'll stay warm."

Ra and Hermes turned and walked away, leaving the goddesses to cling to their weapons and stew in their bitterness.

Alexandria

The blacksmith god of metallurgy and volcanoes, Hephaestus limped through the Jewish quarter of the city in the unseen realm. He was looking for any sign of unusual spiritual activity that might indicate the presence of archangels protecting the messianic seed. The other gods were busy surveilling Philistine and Idumean cities at Zeus's command. But nobody, including the king of the gods, had thought to consider Egypt as a possible hiding place for God's Chosen Seed.

Hephaestus had always considered himself wiser than the other gods gave him credit. For the gods' sake, he had crafted most of their weapons for them. That was no simpleton's task. It required great skill and intelligence. They never showed him the appreciation he deserved.

His limp was a perpetual reminder of his neglected presence among the Olympians. He had once tried to protect Hera from one of Zeus's abusive tirades against her. For his trouble, Hephaestus had been permanently wounded by one of Zeus's thunderbolts and was ostracized from Olympus. Not one of the other gods had supported him. To this day, he resented each and every one of those cowards. They knew he was right. Zeus knew he was right. He would prove it to all of them one day. He was hoping this would be that day.

He had chosen to come here secretly. They would probably not even notice his absence. If he was right and the messianic seed was in Alexandria, then he would win back Zeus's respect and hopefully his status amongst the Olympians. He would show them. They would not shun the great Hephaestus anymore.

He thought he would check out the library. Maybe the scribes would speak of something significant he might overhear. They were well-informed leaders of their community, and their setting was hushed and private. They would have no idea of eavesdroppers in the unseen realm surveilling them.

Hephaestus approached the huge structure, the size of several blocks square. It was Greek in style with massive granite pillars holding up flat roofs with friezes of Greek and Egyptian mythology syncretized into a unity of storytelling. A large platform of stairs led to an open-air courtyard like a horseshoe in shape. Egyptian, Greek, and Jewish scholars, students, and scribes bustled back and forth between buildings in search of ancient wisdom to read.

As soon as he ascended the stairs, Hephaestus felt the hair on his arms go stiff with instinct. Something was here. Something hostile. He reached for his blacksmith hammer beneath his cloak and held it close. His muscles flexed with heightened awareness. He was an underestimated god in more ways than one. Because of his blacksmithing, he was actually the strongest of the deities though none of them realized it. He just never displayed it or competed with any of them, so they overlooked the greatness in their midst.

He would be an unpleasant surprise to any supernatural foe should they underestimate him as well.

Hephaestus, the god of metallurgy and volcanoes, never saw what hit him. Or what blinded him and cut him into pieces for burial in the heart of the sea.

CHAPTER 51

Lower Beth-Horon

The sun had just disappeared beneath the horizon, and the stars began to break through the dusk. Big John walked his horse through the dense thicket of a forest just outside Lower Beth-Horon. He had followed the three escaped Mysian soldiers for the last several days all the way down from the Lebonah Pass through the Hill Country. They had been easy prey, sloppy travelers who didn't bother to hide their camp remains each day. They were in a hurry and must have thought they had sufficiently evaded anyone who might have been looking for them after their escape from Gophna.

But John had caught up with them.

They were now in the pathway that led from the twin cities of Beth-Horon all the way west to the city of Lydda by the coast where Seron most likely was quartering his forces for his march inland. They were only a day or so away from Lydda. Still, John wanted to make sure there was no change of course in their destination before he dispatched these escaped prisoners.

Tying his horse to a tree, John made the rest of his way on foot to their camp. Fortunately, they were near a rocky stream so the sound of rippling waters covered his steps on the dry wood of the forest floor.

He saw the light of a small fire ahead. He heard voices. But there were more than three. Crouching lower, John inched his way silently toward the firelight.

Once he had a clear line of sight, he counted a total of six soldiers. Three of them looked foreign in their armor. Bold patterned woolen cloaks. Fox-skin headdresses with ear flaps. Oval shields with crescent cut-outs and double javelins. John recognized those outfits. They were Thracian soldiers. Princess Laodice had told Judah that Seron was using a Thracian mercenary army.

He heard one of them, a boisterous talker with a loud voice, say, "We're scouting this area of the woods. Another squad is already on its way back from the Beth-Horon ascent. But if what you say is true, we need to get back to General Seron and alert him. Could you lead the general and his forces back to the Gophna caves?"

"We think so," said one of the Mysian soldiers.

Another one offered, "They had a hostage from the royal household, so they may know something about your movements. But we don't know for certain."

This was a worst-case scenario to John. If these scouts got back to Seron, Beth-Horon Pass would be avoided and with it Judah's intended ambush of Seron's army. Instead, they would lead Seron to the hideout where the rest of the hasidim forces would be overwhelmed. But if John killed these scouts now, they would not return to Seron, which would make the Syrian general wary.

John would just have to take that chance. He would have to …

His intuition made him feel something was wrong. Before he could figure it out, he felt a hard blunt force on the back of his head. The noisy stream that had covered his own movements had also covered the movements of an enemy behind him. He blacked out.

When he came to, his head ached with a dull pain. His blurry eyes sharpened focus on a fire in front of him. He saw the three Mysian escaped prisoners and four Thracian scout soldiers, some standing, some sitting, all looking at him.

His arms and legs were spread wide, and he quickly realized they had tied him spreadeagled between two trees near the fire.

One of the Mysians, a lean, wiry one with angular cheeks and madman eyes, said to the others, "I recognize him well enough. He's one of the Maccabees who fought us at the Lebonah Pass."

The leader of the Thracian scouts, a muscular arrogant peacock of a soldier, walked up to John, staring him down. He stopped within inches and said, "So they're calling them the Maccabees now, eh? Fawning toadies of Judah Maccabee, the Hammer."

"They hammered us hard," the madman pointed out. "With only a few hundred."

Still staring into John's eyes, the arrogant Thracian scrunched his face and looked sarcastically impressed. "You are a big man. Strong." His faux-serious expression turned into a maniacal grin. "You will be a fun toy for our Heracles to play with."

John's attention was piqued. So the Naphil gibbor *was* with Seron. John was on the right track. He just had to get out of this. His muscles tightened with apprehension.

"I'm sure he won't mind if I soften you up a bit," the arrogant Thracian added.

John saw it coming. The Thracian was strong himself but revealed everything unwittingly through his eyes. Hauling back, he gave his hardest punch to John's stretched belly.

John had flexed in anticipation of the hit. It was surprisingly minimal considering the man's self-confidence. The Thracian could tell as much as John smiled back at him up close. Then with lightning speed, he jerked his head forward, head-butting the pompous idiot.

The Thracian's head snapped backward with the impact. He fell to the ground like a log, his forehead crushed in, his eyes frozen wildly open with confusion.

Two Thracians checked him. One of them said, "He's dead."

Another Thracian, hairy and bearded with a scar on his cheek, picked up John's war hammer from against a tree, carried it over, and swung it hard into John's belly.

That one hurt badly. John felt his wind knocked out of him, and he grunted in pain. He vomited the berries and dried meat he had eaten earlier.

"That's for killing my comrade, you beast," the hairy one said. "Now let's see how *your* skull handles a knocking."

He reared back on the hammer with every ounce of strength in him.

But a voice rang out, "Enough!"

The hairy one stopped reluctantly and set the hammer down. John saw that the command had come from the true leader of this troop of scouts, a handsome gray-haired, square-jawed unit leader. He said, "We need this man alive for the general. He may have crucial information to torture out of him."

"Can't we torture him just a little right now?" one of the Mysians whined.

The unit leader responded. "You can put one of his eyes out with a firebrand if you want."

Grinning with joy, the Mysian sought a piece of wood from the fire that he could use. But that threat caused a stir of rage inside John. He was not going to have his eye burnt out.

He glanced up at the trees to which he'd been tied. Birch. Hardwood to be sure, but thin compared with the cedars around them.

The thought came to John's mind that he was like Samson, tied between columns with this one last chance. So he uttered Samson's prayer, "Ha Shem, strengthen me just this once."

Then he pulled inward with all his might. He growled under the strain and saw the soldiers stand back in awe.

The trees bent downward toward him with creaking sounds. He used that as an inspiration to pull harder beyond anything his muscles had done before. He pulled as if his life depended on it.

His life *did* depend on it.

He gritted his teeth and growled like a bear.

The creaking turned to cracking. All at once, the tree on his left broke under the strain just as the rope on his right snapped. The treetop crashed in front of him, narrowly missing his head.

He saw the soldiers draw their weapons. Three stepped forward, the courageous ones.

John picked up the treetop, a good two feet round, and heaved it at them like a horizontal missile. It struck all three, propelling them backwards to the ground.

Two of them landed in the fire. They screamed in agony as their flesh burned, unable to free themselves from beneath the tree. The third one had been impaled by a branch.

John roared like a bear at the others, who stepped back again. Stooping down to pick up a dropped sword, he cut the rope from his feet and left hand.

He left the rope on his right, using it like a lasso at the nearest Mysian, the madman. It wrapped around the other man like the coils of a snake. John yanked it with everything left in him. The Mysian flew through the air as if launched from a catapult. He hit a tree headfirst and was smashed into mush.

That left two soldiers.

In a fit of cowardice, the unit leader shoved the last subordinate in front of him. John cut the last rope from his hand just as the Thracian threw a javelin at him.

Dodging, John caught the javelin in mid-air. He immediately hurled it right back. The reverse javelin went completely through the soldier's chest and stuck deep into a tree. He hung like a dead puppet.

The unit leader had now mounted his horse and was taking off into the night—back to General Seron's forces. Inhaling deeply, John exploded in a sprint after the Thracian. He could not outrun a horse for the distance. But if he used every shred of power in his body for one short burst …

He started at a distance of about ten feet behind. It was crazy for him to even try. He should have retrieved the javelin.

The Thracian was looking back at John in shock at how close he was. He kicked frantically on the horse's ribs.

And that was his mistake. His panic created the opposite effect on the horse, whose response was not to speed up but to slow down.

That was just enough for John to close the distance. He leapt forward. His hands grabbed the hind quarters of the horse.

He couldn't get a good grip. The horse shuddered and broke its stride. But John crashed to the ground out of reach.

Regaining his stride, the horse continued on down the path beneath the blue moonlight.

John should have retrieved the javelin.

When he got to his knees, he saw something on the ground. Something long, thin, wooden. It was a javelin! Like God had dropped it to him from the sky.

Of course, he hadn't literally dropped it. John's grab on the horse must have jarred loose the weapon from its holder.

John grabbed the long Thracian javelin in his hands, juggling it a bit to get the feel and weight.

He looked into the distance. The Thracian had become a silhouette beginning to fade into the darkness. He was fifty yards out.

Thank God for the moonlight.

John eyed his target, ran a few steps forward, and launched the lance like a human ballista.

He watched it thread through the air, then disappear from sight just as he lost sight of the Thracian and his horse shadow.

Then he heard the sound of a body falling and hitting the ground. He gave a whoop of victory. Maybe he couldn't quite outrun a horse. But he still had an Olympic athlete's skill in his throwing.

John covered the distance on foot until he spotted the lifeless form of the Thracian on the ground, pierced through with the javelin. The horse was nowhere to be seen. Heaving for air, he placed his hands on his knees, then collapsed down into a cross-legged sitting posture. He had used every ounce of strength in every muscle of his body breaking two trees and racing a horse.

And boy, was he hungry. He would go back and eat all the food in the soldiers' camp in celebration of his victory. He would regain his strength for the task ahead: kill the Greek Naphil and achieve his glorious status as a true gibbor of Israel. He would join the ranks of David's own mighty men. Sibbecai, who struck down the Rephaim giant at Gezer. Elhanan, who struck down Lahmi, the giant brother of Goliath. Abishai, who struck down the giant Ishbi-ben-Ob. Benaiah of Kabzeel, who struck down the giant Egyptian.

All those giants had been bound by oath to assassinate the messiah king of Israel, David. But they would all be forgotten in the shadows of the gibborim warriors who slew them in Adonai's cause. John would earn that same right to be remembered for God's kingdom as a vanquisher of the last of the Nephilim.

But after he returned to the camp and ate all the food he could, he finished out the night by burying the bodies where they could not be found. Dead scouts discovered meant sabotage and close proximity of hostile forces. Missing scouts could be cowards, deserters, or simply victims of local tribal animosity.

Dropping the shovel, John sat down upon the mass grave he had filled in. He finally faced the fact that he had pushed out of his mind in his obsessive pursuit of the captives. If he did move on to face this "Heracles," then Seron would know that the Maccabees were on to him. Which meant he would also figure out that they might ambush him. Not only that, but the Thracian scout was right. If Heracles bested John, they would no doubt torture him and find out everything about Judah's plans.

John felt a sudden dread chill his bones. What had he done? How could he have been so blind? He should never have gone after the escaped prisoners without Judah's consent. He had been too unwilling to hear a "no." He had been too obsessed with achieving glory to consider the consequences of his proud ambition. How could he have been *so blind*?

Remorse swept over John like a tidal wave. He felt seized by his own sin, and his eyes welled up with shame. He blurted out, "What have I done?"

It was so simple. He would have had his chance to fight the gibbor at the ambush. Why had he felt he had to run ahead and fight him in a battle of champions?

Because of his pride. Because of his lust for glory. He should have been seeking the face of God and leaving the results in his hands. He should have sought God's glory, but he had traded out that inheritance like a bowl of porridge. And now he felt like vomiting that choice.

John rolled to his knees and wept before God, confessing his name and praying for forgiveness. With the temple of God desolate from an abominable sacrilege, could he ever hope for atonement, for a true sacrifice that would be his substitute? Was his confession and repentance enough? Was his faith enough?

He knew what he had to do. He had to walk away from his ambition and return to meet Judah at the Beth-Horon ascent. He would share the intelligence of this trip and hope that God would still allow him to kill that demon chimera Heracles for the sake of his fellow soldiers and the higher purpose of this war.

Returning to his camp, John plopped down near the fire, now smoldering coals for purposes of concealment. On his back, he looked up into the trees that punched into the night sky. He replayed in his mind how he had snapped the tree like Samson. Used it as a sideway battering ram to take down several men at once. It gave him an idea that swirled in his mind as he drifted off to sleep.

He slept that night as he had never slept before in a deep slumber of shalom.

CHAPTER 52

Upper Beth-Horon

Judah set up camp with a thousand men a couple miles outside Upper Beth-Horon. He had chosen a small clearing in the local forest and sent scouts to the town for reconnaissance and to secure their secrecy.

Dusk was now descending, wrapping everything in a growing darkness as the sun glowed red behind the hills. Warriors sat beside smoldering fireplaces sharpening their blades on stones and preparing their hard leather armor. No fires tonight. Tomorrow, they would descend the pass and prepare for their ambush of Seron's forces.

In his general's tent, Judah ate a meal with Princess Laodice of wild goat stew flavored with fennel and wine. He had decided to take the Seleucid princess along on the campaign. Leaving Laodice in Gophna without his protection would have been more dangerous for her safety amongst restless warriors away from their general. By bringing her with him, Judah was able to keep Eleazar's trusted watch over her and her maidens within a stone's throw of distance from his own tent. And of course, the forest camp was far removed from the battlefield on the steep ridges of the mountainous pass.

But Laodice was also a strong bargaining chip for negotiations with Seron if needed. With the death of Apollonius, Seron was the new highest-ranking general for King Antiochus. His word and decisions carried authority. The problem for Judah was that it was getting harder for him to use the princess for his own purposes because of his increasing concern for her wellbeing.

He had eaten several meals with Laodice since taking her hostage over a week ago. He considered her female company refreshing and her royal insider perspective helpful in planning his strategy. They had shared their experiences of life in both the family and the Royal Guard of King Antiochus. They had discussed how the king would take the news of her captivity from her returning guards and whether Antiochus would be willing to pay a ransom for her. They had not come to any firm conclusion on the latter.

They had more in common than he had originally thought, and Judah found himself looking forward to the next meal with her. To her lively youth and witty banter. To her beautiful face and haunting eyes. He found himself looking forward to *her*.

And he suspected she had been looking forward to him.

Judah took a sip of wine from his bronze cup. "Have you experienced any unwanted attention from the soldiers?"

Laodice shook her head. "Your brother Eleazar is a fierce and holy watchdog. I thank you for your kind treatment of me and my handmaidens. I know you owe me nothing. And I know I have been demanding."

"Princess, your information is invaluable to my interests. While endangering to your own. I should be thanking you."

Laodice used her teeth to pull some lean meat off a bone, swallowing before she said, "Tell me of your wife."

Judah took a long gulp of wine, then stared off into the distance. "She was stunning. Intelligent, confident, strong. Everything I am not. Me? I was only confident of one thing in this life. I wanted her. To protect her. To provide for her. To give her our children. She helped me return to the faith of my fathers. To see that there was something higher than the both of us and even of our family."

"Was she a member of your tribe?"

"No. She was an Athenian convert to Judaism living in Antioch when we met."

Laodice looked surprised. "So you like Greek women?"

"She was a *godly* woman. I never understood real love until I met her."

"Is she your Eurydice?"

Eurydice was the beloved of Orpheus in Greek myth. Their love had been so great after marriage that when Eurydice died prematurely, Orpheus descended into the underworld to bring her back. Hades tricked Orpheus at the last moment, and Eurydice was lost to Orpheus forever.

"No," Judah responded. "Human love alone cannot transcend death. But she understood our love meant nothing without the love of God. Without him, all human love is a vapor. A delusion of sentiment that dies with the beloved. Orpheus and Eurydice. Pyramus and Thisbe. Hero and Leander."

Judah had often mused over all those tragic lovers, stories of fate, and the impossibility of finding what Greeks called *agape*, love that was eternal.

Laodice countered, "'Because when the dust has soaked up a man's blood, once he is dead there is no resurrection.'"

She had quoted the Stoic Aeschylus. Judah smiled. "Sophia would have liked you. But she would have debated you on that point. And so do I."

"So you reject all the gods of Greece, indeed all the gods of the nations, hundreds of gods—thousands—for your one, single, solitary god? I simply reject one more god than you."

"No," he responded fervently. "Because without the one true God, you have nothing of real value. No love. No truth or justice. No meaning or purpose to life. No hope. You just have stories you tell yourself to pretend you do. But in the end, you have nothing. So you are lying to yourself."

"You speak harshly," Laodice said.

"I speak from experience. I lied to myself. I told myself the stories. I am the *most* deserving of God's judgment."

"And what makes you think your people's stories are any different?"

"Our stories provide the very foundation for love, truth, justice, and meaning. That is not the same thing. That is the opposite."

Laodice smirked. "The logical law of non-contradiction. Does your god create logic or is he beholden to it as well?"

"My God *is* the Logos."

"And is your God with his violent actions any different from the violent gods of the nations?"

"This is a world of violence and rebellion, princess. Justice is violent to the violent. And peaceful to the innocent."

"I am your hostage," Laodice demurred with a smile. "I must do as you say."

Judah could tell she was trying to save face. To avoid the wall she was being backed up against in her ideas. But he could see her soul had been moved by their discussion.

"I have no desire to force anything upon you, Laodice. You can leave whenever you want. Your help has been invaluable to our resistance. I have arranged for a squad of fifteen soldiers to escort you to the coast at your request. You can take a ship from there to return home to Antioch."

"I'm not ready to return," she pouted. "That's not my home. Nor am I ready to convert. I just want to stay. A while longer."

"It is your choice. But I want to know why you choose to take your comfort in Cynicism and despair. Because of what has been done to you? What was taken from you?"

Her face loosened, her voice softened. "Why does this God of yours allow such things in this world? Such pain and suffering? How can you accept what was taken from you?" She was no longer challenging him but truly asking from a desperation of the soul.

"I don't know why," Judah responded with as much honesty in return. "But the pain runs deep and almost unbearable. I only know that one day a Suffering Servant will come. We call him Messiah, the Anointed One. Our prophets say he will be a man of sorrows and acquainted with grief. One of us. That he will carry our sorrows and be pierced through for our transgressions, crushed for our iniquities. That upon him will be laid the iniquity of us all. His chastisement will bring peace, and by his wounds we will be healed. He will finish the transgression of Israel, put an end to that sin, atone for our iniquity, and bring in everlasting righteousness."

There was a pregnant pause of silence as though they two alone were the only ones left in the world.

Finally, Laodice whispered, "That is a beautiful story."

Judah whispered back, "It is not just a story."

He could see a tear rolling down her beautifully broken face. "I hope you are right." But she spoke as one who wished she could believe what she did not.

Judah noticed that in their engrossing discussion they had long since finished their meal. He stood up. "It is getting late. I thank you for dining with me once again. I will have my guards escort you to your tent."

He wanted her to stay. To stay the night. He wanted to be with her. He felt drawn to her honesty, her pain, her strength in the face of it all. He wanted to comfort her. To be comforted by her.

But if anything he had said tonight was true, that would be a mistake. His was not a decision to withhold happiness or forbidden love but a choice to remain true to a higher calling. One of *eternal* love and happiness.

Judah could not live without *that* love, truth, justice, or meaning. He could not live without God's law.

He let her leave and slept a fitful sleep that night.

CHAPTER 53

Beth-Horon Ascent

Big John had walked his horse halfway up the steep incline of the Beth-Horon ascent that ran between the towns of Upper and Lower Beth-Horon. This was the pass where Judah was on his way to ambush Seron's forces. Judah was probably already outside Upper Beth-Horon by now. But it was late in the evening. John would set up camp and finish the last few miles in the morning to meet his brother on the other side of Upper Beth-Horon. He tied his horse slightly down the backside of the hill to avoid detection. No fire for this evening.

The ascent was similar to Lebonah in that it was a very narrow, winding path that rose for two miles linking the twin cities. But it was different from the Lebonah Pass in two ways. First, though six to ten feet wide in some places, it was in many places narrower, requiring one-man marching lines. Secondly, Beth-Horon was not a valley but a mountainous pathway. On one side of the road was a steep hillside rising as much as a hundred feet above. On the other side, a steep precipice opened up to the river valley as much as two hundred feet below. Anyone who fell off that road would die in the fall.

Making it a perfect location to ambush Seron. And the Syrian general could no doubt see that, so he would be preparing for such an event. Still, he would not traverse it at all if he suspected an actual plot. He would take the much longer circuitous path down south to Emmaus and around the twin cities. That would delay Seron's campaign for days, but it would also place Judah at a grave disadvantage because there were no good locations on that southern route for an ambush. With Judah's outnumbered forces, he needed the element of surprise and the advantage of terrain, neither of which he would have if Seron went south. The Jewish guerillas might find themselves on the run again.

John kept awake on the ridge that night praying that any suspicion of possible threat in Seron's mind would be dismissed through patience run thin by their long march from the north.

It was a good thing he couldn't sleep much since halfway into the night he heard the sound of softly approaching steps carried on the wind. John surreptitiously grabbed the handle of his war hammer lying beside him. Because he was on his back, he could only see sky.

He took the chance of lifting his head to look. Silhouetted by the moon, a large dark shadow figure stood over him, wielding a huge primitive-looking club over his head. Instinctively, John held his hammer and rolled. He felt the ground shake as the club hit the dirt where he had previously been sleeping.

In a flash, he was up and ready to swing his weapon in response. He hesitated when he saw in the moonlight a bare-chested muscular monster of a man dressed in battle kilt and a large belt with golden buckle.

Instead of attacking, John asked, "Are you Heracles?"

"In the flesh," came the response in a deep guttural voice. "And you are quite a stealthy scout. And fit-looking."

Flattery was a tactic of distraction. They circled one another.

Heracles added, "Which means there is a rebel force nearby."

"Your general is not going to find out," John replied.

Heracles laughed. "Oh, I always return from my scouting. I take it you are the reason our first scouts did not?"

John remained a moving target as he answered, "Four Thracians with three escaped Mysians from our camp."

"Impressive," said the muscular mutant. "But I'm afraid I'm a little stronger than seven soldiers."

He seemed more like twenty soldiers stronger. But John refused to lack faith. He growled, "I am a servant of the living God of Israel."

Heracles boasted in return, "I've been told I was once a mighty king of Babel. Royal seed."

"You are the Seed of the Serpent," replied John.

The Naphil warrior grinned. "And I have a fatal bite."

As he said this, he swung his club at John's head. John dodged backward, and the warrior fell off balance.

John swung back around with his hammer and hit the attacker's shoulder blade. Heracles kept spinning, diverting some of the force of the hit but dropping his club to the ground with a grunt.

John had gotten a good one in. He grinned.

Heracles picked up his club and rotated his shoulder to work out the sting. He shouted, "Ho, hurrah!" It seemed a burst of rowdy laughter. As if he was exhilarated by the challenge.

They circled one another again.

"Well done, Jew. Not many have been a worthy opponent. What is your name?"

"John ben Mattathiah. Brother of Judah Maccabee."

"Oh," exclaimed the brawny ogre. "Then it will be an honor to kill you and face that scoundrel in battle. You think I will make it into your Jewish histories?"

John ignored the sarcasm. It only proved to him the hunger for significance that plagued even this pagan gibbor. John spit out, "I've been hunting you ever since Acrabeta. You killed my father."

"Ah, so I have a fan following," Heracles laughed, still rotating the pain out of his shoulder.

John muttered, "Adonai be my strength."

Heracles growled with demonic contempt, "Your god is a weak and impotent deity. Zeus has taken his throne. I'm done toying with you."

The gibbor launched toward John with his club, coming at him overhead. John met him with his hammerhead upward. The hit was so strong that the hammerhead slid down to John's hands.

He turned the weapon around and slid the handle back down with a curved swing just as Heracles's club came in a wide arc.

The hammer head hit the club with a loud crash. John felt the power of it rattle both his arms and hands to the core.

Heracles arced the club around the other side. John met that one as well. But the force was too much. His war hammer flew from his hands into the dirt.

He looked up at Heracles, shocked. He took a protective stance.

Heracles watched him and threw his club down. He laughed again, apparently relishing a weaponless challenge.

John had trained hard in grappling. He only hoped Heracles had not. Somehow, he doubted that.

Heracles launched at John and grabbed him. John felt the crushing strength of his hands alone.

But strength was no match for maneuver. John twisted his arms, folded in, and spun, taking his opponent to the ground in a head lock.

He squeezed thick neck muscles that felt like iron cables. Could he choke this Behemoth out? Could he kill this muscle-bound freak?

Heracles then leveraged his legs and body to roll.

They were on the top of the ridge.

The two of them tumbled down the steep hillside like a couple of logs. John felt his back and arms hit several rocks on the way down, stinging with sharp pain. His muscles weakened, and he released his grip on Heracles. He felt the crushing weight of the monster roll over him.

Then he rolled over the top of the monster. Again and again and again. His vision was a spinning, whirling view of stars and dirt and grunting warrior until they hit the road fifty feet below in a cloud of dust.

John was disoriented. He couldn't see his enemy. His back and muscles were bruised with pain from the pounding descent.

He crawled to the edge of the path to see if Heracles had fallen over the cliff. The moon was bright. But he couldn't see any sign of the monster.

John coughed from the dust he had ingested. That was when he felt two hands flipping him over onto his back, his head almost at the edge of the precipice, his right arm dangling over his head.

The Naphil was on top of him. How could the beast have survived that descent without the pain now crippling John?

The dust cleared. He saw and felt Heracles straddling his chest, pinning John's left arm, the brute's left hand at John's throat while his right hand lifted a rock he had grabbed from their landslide debris.

"I must commend you," Heracles coughed out. "You were a worthy opponent. A true gibbor."

The words announced John's death at the hands of this abomination. His focus became tunnel vision. And his fighting instincts kicked in again. He couldn't move his pinned body, but his right arm was free.

He brought it up with every ounce of strength left in him. It was his last desperate grasp at survival. His palm hit his enemy's nose and shoved it right up into his brain.

Heracles froze in shock at the hit. His death grip on John's neck released. The rock dropped out of his hand to the ground. Blood came gushing out of his nostrils.

So Nephilim noses were as weak spots as human ones. John took that opportunity to grab the monster's belt, then used his legs to flip the stunned Heracles over the ledge into the chasm.

He turned in time to see the body make its final tumble over the rocks like a broken rag doll until it hit the river at the bottom of the gorge with a splash.

Nephilim were half-human, so they died like every other creature. The moonlight glittered on the waters below as the body floated away into the darkness and into Hades.

Big John rolled over and got to a knee, moaning with the pain of his wounds. He muttered to himself, "They are never going to believe this."

His brothers and other comrades-in-arms would hear a story only his father would believe because he alone had seen that creature with his own eyes. But his father was gone. And this … this would sound like an exaggerated tale of battle that should only happen after years of storytelling. This would sound like his attempt to craft his own legend. And he had nothing to prove it. No corpse. No witnesses. Only his beaten-up and bruised body from a pathetic fall down the ridgeline.

No, this was perfect. This was Adonai's way of using John for his purposes in a significant history-changing act but without a way for John to claim the glory for his pride. He was a true gibbor of the House of David, and only he and Adonai knew. Which was exactly the way it needed to be.

Looking to heaven, John cried out, "O Lord, thy will be done."

CHAPTER 54

John walked his horse into Judah's camp half-dead and about to fall out of his saddle. His entire body ached with the pain of his battle the night before. But he wasn't going to let it show. He straightened up in his saddle as he was escorted to Judah's war tent in the middle of camp. There must have been a thousand soldiers here. He hoped it would be enough.

"Big John!" The words were cried out by Judah as he and Simon, Eleazar, and Jonathan all ran over to him, ready to wrestle their big brother as he got off his horse. He held his hand out, stopping them.

"I've been wounded," he said, sliding off his horse to the ground with a grunt of pain.

"What happened?" asked Simon.

"I fell down one of ridges of the Beth-Horon Pass. It was steep and rocky."

That half-truth was all he would give. He would keep his battle with the Naphil to himself and Adonai.

"Who did you fight? Did you find the Naphil warrior?"

Surrounding him, they helped John limp over to the war tent to finish their discussion.

"I found the three escaped Mysians and a scouting party of four Thracian soldiers on the Beth-Horon pass."

"Did the scouts know we are here?" asked Judah.

"No. I am sure of it."

They entered the tent. John found a small couch to sit on for his bruised and weary body. He continued as he took off his armor, wincing from his movements, "I killed them. But I believe Seron wasn't expecting them to return unless they saw trouble."

"So you never made it to Seron's camp to fight the Champion?" Judah asked.

John took a deep breath. "I realized that it was selfish of me to seek my own glory without your orders and without consideration of how it might affect your campaign. So I turned back before I got near to Seron. He doesn't know we are here."

The brothers muttered gratitude and approval of their advantage. John concluded, "My general, my brother, I am sorry for my insubordination, and I willingly accept punishment in the face of the entire army."

John finished taking his tunic off. His body was black and blue like they had never seen before. It was as if his entire skin had turned purple. They all gasped at the sight.

Judah suspected there was more to the story than John was telling them. It was almost as if their big brother was protecting them. But Judah had to discipline his brother as he had the previous seven camp guards or he would lose the respect and loyalty of his men.

Judah said, "I want you to walk around camp without your shirt. Your body bears the marks of punishment as surely as the seven I disciplined."

John nodded acquiescence. "By the way, while I was round about the forest and ascent, I figured out a way to do significant damage to Seron's forces."

Simon interjected, "We have at best until morning before Seron is on the ascent and vulnerable to ambush. We have to make every tactic count."

"Oh, this will count," said John with a sly grin on his face.

• • • • •

Just before dawn, Judah gathered his army around him. A company of three hundred had been appointed to work through the night preparing their ambush site according to John's recommendation. It had been hard labor back and forth between the camp and the ridge of the ascent. But they had accomplished their goal and now stood with the others before their commander.

Judah announced to them all, "You three hundred who labored through the night without sleep to exhaustion, I thank you! You will stay behind to guard the camp. I will take the remaining companies of seven hundred to the battlefield. We leave for the Beth-Horon ascent immediately."

One of the captains of a hundred, a staunch, rugged man with a matted beard who often complained, said, "General, we got lucky with six hundred men against Apollonius's two thousand. But you are now facing Seron, who has four thousand troops. That's twice Apollonius's numbers."

"That's why I'm adding an additional hundred to bring our numbers up, captain." Judah said this with the confidence of Joshua entering the Promised Land.

The complaining captain did not appear to appreciate that confidence. He complained again, "We will be throwing ourselves into a meatgrinder, sir."

Judah turned to the assembled infantry and archers. "Soldiers of Adonai, I know you face a great burden this day! I am asking you to run to the battle outnumbered again! To pray for another miracle! But I want you to remember this when you rush the enemy and look them in the face. It is not on the strength of man or the size of the army that victory in battle depends! They come against us in great insolence and lawlessness to destroy us and our wives and our children, but we fight for our lives and our laws! Adonai himself will crush them before us! As for you, fear not, for your strength comes from the Lord!"

The thousand men gave a low rumble of agreement. Now was not the time to cheer and be heard by the enemy. Judah turned to the captains of hundreds and told them to assemble the seven hundred up at their pre-arranged location for battle. Then he turned to Big John. "Brother, I want you to stay and guard Princess Laodice."

Simon reacted with surprise. "Judah, he has been preparing for this opportunity. Would you take that glory from him?"

Eleazar and John kept quiet, watching them both.

Judah looked to his bigger brother. "John, do you consider your wounds to be sufficiently healed to face your ultimate enemy?"

"I am content to obey your command, my general," John replied proudly. Then he averted his eyes humbly to the ground. "And I have a feeling we won't be seeing the Naphil warrior any time soon."

Simon refused to understand. "Since when do you follow your feelings, John? Why in the world would he not be there?"

Catching John's knowing glance, Judah got the feeling that John's feeling was more than a feeling.

"God humbles us all in different ways." John said.

Judah had no time to wait. "Simon, my order stands. Let's move out."

He saw Simon's face light up with awareness. As if he had finally received the unspoken understanding that the other brothers already shared. He looked at Eleazar and Jonathan, who were shaking their heads.

"Simon the Wise!" Jonathan muttered.

Eleazar chuckled. And they moved out.

• • • • •

The seven hundred hasidim warriors lined up behind a steep ridge along the final bank of the two-mile ascent. The grade of the embankment was about a forty-degree angle with desert brush and rocks along the descent. Attacking down such an incline would be tricky. A soldier could move speedily but get out of control and tumble if he didn't watch his footing.

The narrow pathway to Upper Beth-Horon lay a hundred feet beneath them. The soldiers had stayed quiet for a long time while hiding in the cold desert morning air, waiting for the right time to emerge. Their breaths had to be directed downward to avoid the vapor rising and betraying their position.

They waited for over two hours before they saw the lead regiment of a thousand Thracian soldiers walking the path in single file. The cavalry of three hundred horsemen led the way, walking slowly for sure footing lest their horses slip and they plummet to their deaths down the gorge to their left. The rhythmic stomp of Hellenic warriors overwhelmed the distant sound of the rushing river below.

Judah had chosen this spot for several reasons that were justified as he spied the enemy. First, by the end of the two-mile winding ascent, the soldiers were tired from their long march upward. Second, because they had made it this far without incident, their guard was dropped. They could see the end of the ascent not far ahead and were confident any attack that might occur would have already occurred. And third, that left the longest single-file line vulnerable to attack.

Judah had changed his tactics from the Lebonah Pass. Like before, he had a squad of men to block the exit. But this time, there was no one to block the entrance far behind them. He couldn't afford the men. He needed the rest of his attackers on the hillside.

With a single-file line, Seron could not ride in the middle of his troops because under attack, he would be trapped with no possibility of escape. So he had chosen to lead the forces at the head of the line with his cavalry. Though this option was not without its own dangers, it was the best tactical choice he could make under this situation.

One of the goals of guerrilla warfare was to target the general and any leaders as soon as possible to ensure disintegration of the enemy's ranks and cohesion. With Seron in the lead, Judah just might be able to inflict maximal damage with the strategy he had planned.

Grinning at Judah, Eleazar grabbed his handful of javelins. The next succession of events happened in quite rapid order, an unfolding series of escalating attacks.

First, Judah signaled the archers and slingers, two hundred of them at the head of the line. They stood up, aimed and nocked their arrows, twirled their slinger pouches, and all released upon Judah's command.

The result was a flurry of missiles descending upon the cavalry in front like lightning bolts and meteorites. Because the Thracians were unprepared, they could not get their shields up in time. Horses and horsemen were hit alike by both shafts and stones targeted with lethal precision.

Men fell from their mounts. Horses panicked and reared up. Some trampled, but many of them lost footing and room on the narrow pathway, plummeting to their deaths down the steep gorge.

Those who escaped the first volley were hit by a second wave of missiles. Men screamed. Horses whinnied in terror. The impact was rapid and devastating.

Judah saw Eleazar rise up with his javelins. General Seron had survived the flood of arrows. His shield was up. Other soldiers protected him.

Aiming his first javelin, Eleazar let loose its spinning fury. It pierced a soldier guarding Seron but did not hit the general. Eleazar cursed and ran down the hill to get a better shot.

"Eleazar! No!" Judah yelled.

The first volley of return arrows came from Thracian archers a hundred feet back on the pathway. The arrows plucked at the ridgeline where the archers and slingers had been.

Eleazar now stood alone, a wide-open target. He didn't care. He had told Judah that he was going to trust Adonai to allow him to kill Seron as a confirmation that he would one day kill King Antiochus should he ever find the king on the battlefield.

It was a dangerous risk, but Judah could not dissuade his brother from his avowed quest for greatness. Shaking his hair back out of his eyes, Eleazar prepared a new javelin and launched it. Just as he did, an enemy arrow struck him from below. He fell to the ground.

"ELEAZAR!" Judah screamed.

Then he saw the javelin hit its mark of Seron's shield. Its force was enough to penetrate the shield and push Seron off balance. His horse reared up. Seron fell off his steed, disappearing over the ledge of the canyon.

He had done it. Eleazar had killed Seron. But at what price?

Stupid brother! Stupid, glory-seeking brother! Judah saw Simon run down to retrieve Eleazar's body, his own shield protecting him from arrows.

But Judah had the welfare of his army to be concerned with over the life of his brother. They had all vowed their oaths of loyalty to their cause above family or clan. He used a flag to signal their next attack. He called it Big John's Rollers—his secret weapon that had taken them all night to prepare.

A series of soldiers got behind large logs of trees they had cut down and stripped. Twenty men to a log thirty or more feet long, a thousand pounds of weighted lumber, they pushed them over the ridge and watched them roll down the steep hill with fatal velocity.

By now, the soldiers in their single lines had their shields up, protecting themselves from arrows or infantry attack. But they could not protect themselves from a thousand-pound log that hit them, crushing them and plunging them over the precipice of the cliff.

The logs were measured out every hundred feet or so, leaving small groups of surviving soldiers cut off from the others and now vulnerable to the hordes of hasidim barreling down the hillside with swords, spears, axes, and clubs.

Judah led the charge. Pulling out his whip sword Rahab that he had taken from Apollonius, he let it drag behind him. He had been practicing on their trip out here and felt confident of his control.

The first soldier Judah met was cut through both shield and torso with one swipe. Glancing to his left, he saw his youngest brother Jonathan being jumped from behind. Judah spun around and snapped the sword at the Thracian soldier, ripping through his spine.

The one disadvantage of the whip sword was that it was not as effective in close-quarter combat. A Thracian swordsman rushed Judah, seeking to cut him down. Judah dodged and used his own small circular Macedonian shield to defend against the blows. He felt the vibrations of bronze hitting bronze rattle his bones. He slipped and fell to the ground.

The Thracian was relentless. He pounded on Judah's shield like a screaming banshee. Spotting his opportunity, Judah swiped the whip sword at the Thracian's feet, cutting them both off at the ankles. The enemy fell, still screaming like a banshee but now helpless.

Judah stumbled to his feet, only to find himself surrounded by Thracian swordsmen, seven of them, like a pack of hyenas surrounding their prey. He felt the incline at his feet. He judged their distances. Some had shields. Others did not. One had a spear. All were protectively cautious, fearful of the strange weapon they had seen him use. He let it lay dormant at his feet, a serpent playing dead. They backed up, then moved in closer until they were circling him.

Fools. A circle was exactly what Judah needed most.

He pulled the sword over his head in a sweeping motion and whipped the ten-foot blade in a circle around him. He felt it connect with heads and necks above shields as he twirled it, extending his arm out as far as he could. He kept it going but grabbed the handle with both hands, spinning like a windmill until all seven soldiers were dead at his feet, beheaded or cut in half by Rahab's deadly bite.

Judah fell to one knee, tired and dizzy from the exchange. When he regathered his bearings, he saw the aftermath of his fury. Around him, a killing field of body parts and blood-soaked ground. Beyond him, scattered carnage filled the sloped landscape. The only ones left standing were hasidim. The Thracians were on the run.

Word must have carried through the Thracian troops that their commander Seron was dead, and they could see those in front butchered like sheep. It had put such a fright into the Thracians that they had turned tails and ran back down the descent—their only way out. Many fell off the narrow path and down into the canyon in the confusion and panic.

"Run your way back to Philistia, you cowards!" Judah yelled after them.

His men cheered with weapons raised high. Others chased the enemy soldiers long enough to ensure they would not return.

Judah looked around him, wiping blood out of his eyes. Slain bodies littered the hillside. Many had plunged over the edge into eternity. He reckoned that about eight hundred of the enemy had fallen beneath the hammer of God.

And then he remembered. Eleazar! Where was he?

Judah spun around. He spotted his brothers Simon and Jonathan standing over a prone form on the hill above. Eleazar. He ran up the incline, his legs aching with exhaustion. He had to see his brother. His young and foolish brother. His courageous brother who had sacrificed himself to take out the leader Seron.

When Judah arrived, he saw Eleazar lying on the ground very much alive, groaning from an arrow sticking into the meaty part of his rear end. Simon and Jonathan were snickering, holding back their laugh.

Eleazar glared up at Judah. "I got him, brother. I told you I would get him."

"How in the world did you…?" Judah gasped out, panting for breath.

Jonathan joked, "That pain in the ass was worth it!"

Finally, he and Simon could hold back their laughter no more. They belted out roaring. Jonathan couldn't stand up. Eleazar, normally the one wisecracking, now found himself on the receiving end. And he couldn't resist. He started laughing through his pain.

He said, "Don't make me the butt of this joke!"

And they all roared even more.

The day had been a victorious one for the forces of Adonai. Their fear and anxiety against insurmountable odds had turned into the joy of the Lord's strength.

The seven hundred returned from their victorious ambush, carrying their few fatal and wounded causalities. After burying the dead and tending to the wounded, they celebrated their triumph with a well-earned, long-awaited meal.

Big John had received his brothers at the camp with joy. After they had the arrow safely removed from Eleazar's buttock in the medical tent, Judah took the opportunity to say to John in front of the brothers, "The Naphil warrior wasn't there."

John gave a guilty smile. "Oh well, lucky for me."

"Lucky for us all," Simon said.

Judah said, "I guess your 'feelings' were right."

John nodded humbly. "I guess so."

Judah added, "That would have been some glory to have conquered a Naphil warrior like that. Might have given you the honor of being a gibborim warrior as of the House of David."

John said, "Yeah, sometimes God has different plans to humble us."

"Indeed," said Simon. "But this war's not over. You may yet get your chance at glory."

"Like I said," replied Big John. "I have a feeling we won't be seeing the Naphil warrior any time soon."

Judah said, "I'm not going to question your feelings, brother. I'm going to believe you have good reason."

John smiled with wet eyes. The big bear had a big heart.

The brothers embraced Big John, who groaned in pain under their loving squeezes.

CHAPTER 55

Daphne

Lysias of Damascus rolled over on the satin sheets of his bed, having seduced Antiochis, elder sister of King Antiochus. She slept on her side with her back to him, her dark curls falling gracefully on the naked skin of her plump body. Her face was barely tolerable to Lysias, which is why he took her from behind. She was almost fifty years old and bore the marks on her body of three births. She had been queen of Cappadocia until her husband the king had died. She was back in Antioch with her thirty-year-old daughter Ophelia, twice-widowed confidante of her mother.

Lysias was already scheming how he might seduce Ophelia as well. He would seduce the whole family if it could help his chances of ingratiation into the royal line. But he had to be careful because Antiochis was also sleeping with her brother the king, a disgusting Seleucid habit. That could become dangerous for Lysias.

In a way, bedding Antiochis had been a celebration of Lysias's recent appointment by the king to be the guardian of the crown prince Antiochus V Eupator, a young boy of seven. Should the king die, Eupator would ascend to the throne but would require a co-regent to rule the kingdom until he was of age. That could be as long as eight years.

Lysias lay back on his plush silken pillow and looked up at the ceiling with a self-satisfied grin. Lysias would be that co-regent, effectively operating as king as he guided the boy by his wisdom and experience.

Oh, what he could do in eight years with the proxy power of a king.

He had finally achieved it. Almost. All he needed now was for King Antiochus Epiphanes to die.

Lysias was of royal birth and had risen to become governor of Syria. At fifty-two years old, he was handsome enough, not ugly, with a bald pate that gave him a commanding presence among the ruling class. He made sure to maintain a lean, muscular body through exercise and self-discipline. He carried himself with assurance and authority whether he felt it or not. He had learned long ago that followers believe whatever leaders present themselves as, and aggressive confidence was a winning trait. What had begun as an act of performance had become over time and repetition his authentic identity.

Oh, yes, he had done everything he could throughout his entire life to craft his image and attain this position he was in right now. And no one would take that accomplishment from him. No one. He would kill to protect it. He glanced over at Antiochis's prone form. He would kill her if he thought she would let on to the king about their sexual relationship.

A knock at the door startled him.

"Who is it?" he yelled in anger.

"My lord," came the voice from behind the oak doors, "the *Pompe*. It has started."

"Zeus Olympius!" Lysias exclaimed. He had gotten so caught up in his thoughts he had lost track of the time.

Antiochis had already jumped up. They both scrambled to get dressed and leave.

Lysias ran the full distance from the small palace to the royal platform along the agora a couple blocks away. The streets were mostly empty because everyone in the town was lined up along the large main street for the Pompe, a Hellenist version of the Roman Triumphal Procession. The difference here was that Antiochus had no particular victory to celebrate. But he was always keen to display his martial glory before he launched out on a mission. And he had a big mission ahead of him.

Lysias pushed through the crowd of straining people until he was noticed and motioned forward by the Macedonian guards at the royal platform. He caught his breath from the hard run and wiped sweat from his brow. He was dressed in his general's linen chiton tunic and scarlet woolen himation secured on his right shoulder with the golden Seleucid military brooch of authority. Antiochus preferred his high-ranking officials to always wear their best, especially at celebrations and parades. It kept them separate from the hoi polloi and reinforced their importance.

Walking up the wooden steps to the top of the platform, Lysias came upon the king's seating from behind. The king had called upon Lysias to sit with him at this procession for some reason he had yet to discover. But he had an idea.

The king sat on his comfortable throne chair with felt cushions. Queen Laodice sat a few feet away with a couple of maidservants to attend her. Behind Antiochus were his chief counsellors Heraclides and Timarchus, handsome young sycophants who never seemed to leave the king's side—like a pair of leeches. On the king's left sat his son Eupator, a snot-nosed little prick with curly sandy-blonde hair and fidgety legs dangling from his seat. As Lysias approached the open chair to the right of Antiochus, he saw the king's son picking his nose.

Before them, the parade was in full swing with a long line of infantry marching by in their phalanxes of *syntagma* units, sixteen men wide and sixteen men deep. The soldiers were covered in metal armor, shield grieves, and small Phrygian helmets with pointed bent tops. They held large, round bronze shields and carried their sarissai spears pointing twenty feet into the air as they marched. It was an impressive display of power and glory.

Lysias bowed to the king before sitting down.

"Gods dammit, Lysias, where have you been? You almost missed the Pompe!"

When Antiochus saw Lysias adjusting his cloak and tunic, his fury turned to a knowing smirk. "Were you cavorting with a lover *again*? I know you have. Which one? How many lovers do you have now, you champion stud, you!"

Lysias demurred as if embarrassed. If this monster ever found out which one, he would have Lysias's head.

Antiochus shifted his interest like a sincere child. "Oh, wait, were you interrupted? Were you able to get satisfaction? How wet did she get?"

"Your majesty," Lysias demurred again. He gestured with a glance at the child Eupator on the other side of the king.

Antiochus looked back at the little runt. Then he barked, "Ah! Eupator has to learn soon enough. And you *are* responsible for his education, you know."

The king laughed heartily. But his outbreak was cut short by wincing as he tried to hide a sudden pain in his abdomen.

Lysias tried to help by turning attention back to the parade. "Look, your majesty! Your cavalry!"

Lysias watched the leading cataphracts, the heavy cavalry in their best of chainmail and horses gilded with metal plates. Their faces were all covered by a metal facemask of soulless sculpted warrior faces. Thousands of them prancing in perfect formation, the sound of their hooves pounding in rhythmic syncopation. Pounding, pounding, pounding.

Antiochus said, "You missed forty-six thousand infantry in the beginning and five hundred gladiators! I have almost ten thousand cavalry, light and heavy, and a thousand war chariots. And wait till you see this! Thirty-six Indian war elephants! Not African. These are Indian, much stronger and deadlier."

The king acted like a precocious child describing his military toys. Lysias hid his impatience. "Your majesty, what is your matter of importance? I am eager to serve."

"Oh, well, yes." Antiochus broke off as if not knowing where to begin. "Well, with the most recent defeats and murder of my incompetent generals Apollonius *and* Seron at the hands of those Jewish cockroaches in Judea, I have heard they are increasing in numbers and are preparing for even worse atrocities. Imagine their gall. I need to crush this rebellion swiftly and with terrifying force. I have mustered all my armed forces not deployed in foreign lands. And I have just paid them a year's wages in advance. But my treasurer has informed me that, apparently, my coffers are now empty!"

The king exploded with rage on that last word. He immediately restrained himself. "I try to do a good deed, and the gods curse me." He shook his head with disgust and sighed.

Lysias was more disgusted at Antiochus. He knew that the king had spent too much money on monumental construction projects in Syria, Asia Minor, and Greece. But he had also wasted thousands of talents of silver and gold on lavish gifts and hosting huge, wasteful extravagant festivals and celebrations here in Daphne—like this self-aggrandizing puffery before them. Those stupid, toadying counsellors of his never seemed to challenge Antiochus on wasteful spending.

Lysias asked eagerly, "How can I help, your majesty?"

The king's impatience rose again as he described his intent. "Well, now I have to take half that army and travel halfway around the world to Persia just so I can collect revenues to refill the treasury. I just can't seem to get anything done! I am always being interrupted by one thing or another. This will probably take me years, and I don't have years!"

Lysias knew what was coming next, and he felt excited for it.

"Lysias, until I return, I am appointing you as viceroy in charge of my affairs from the river Euphrates to the borders of Egypt."

"Your majesty," Lysias responded with faux humility. That was the western half of Antiochus's kingdom. Lysias tried to withhold his glee at this order. It was the next best thing to being king, maybe even better than being Eupator's co-regent.

Antiochus added, "I am leaving you half of my armed forces, including war elephants and the generals Nicanor and Gorgias. That should be plenty enough for you to invade Judea."

Lysias felt his eyes widen with desire.

Antiochus's attention was taken again by the parade. He said giggling, "Speaking of which, look at those beauties. Magnificent."

The war elephants were indeed magnificent. They marched in a single file to draw out the length. Huge, lumbering giants with mighty tusks and stomping feet. Above each one was a wooden coach structure housing four archers and javelin throwers with an East Indian driver. Lysias could feel the ground shake as they passed by with their frightening size and presence. Their skin was like their own armor. Facing down these beasts was one of the most frightening experiences a soldier might have on the battlefield.

Antiochus began a slow, burning rage as his words were augmented by the visual of these mighty war beasts of crushing mass and weight.

"Begin with Jerusalem. Take back the city. Destroy it if you have to. Trample it beneath your feet. Burn down the temple. Then I want you to lay waste to the countryside and all its towns and villages. Hunt down this general Judah Maccabee and all his forces. Slay them all to the man. Exterminate the seed of Judea. I want a holocaust of such magnitude that the smoke will be seen ascending into heaven for miles."

Lysias was pleased with the king's extremity. "Your majesty, if I may interject, if you want such thorough devastation, would I have the authority to bring in Scythian mercenaries?"

At the suggestion, the king's face brightened with a diabolical grin. Scythians were considered the most brutal of all mercenary soldiers. "You are my genius, Lysias. That is why I chose you." He turned devious in his look. "Would that include Amazons?"

Amazons were the all-female tribe of Scythian warriors. Lysias nodded, tantalizing the king, who added, "A perfect resource of savagery to inflict great misery and destruction."

Antiochus paused, then concluded, "Yes, use Scythians. I want to banish the memory of the Jews from that land."

He paused again with emphasis. "Then begin the importation of aliens into the territory. Distribute their lands by lot. Just make sure you replace them with foreigners. Hellenists, of course."

"Of course, your majesty," bowed Lysias. "A great replacement."

Antiochus said, "With all this at your command, you will have no excuse for failure. Otherwise, I will skin you alive and salt your wounds. Am I understood?"

Lysias stared at the king in shock.

Antiochus laughed and slapped him on the back. "I'm just kidding, Lysias!"

Lysias breathed a sigh of relief.

"No, I would hang you." When the king saw Lysias react again, he laughed again. "Ha! I got you! You should see your face!"

Antiochus laughed hard at his own morbid sense of humor—which in fact Lysias knew could turn on a drachma into serious and real.

Swallowing hard, Lysias responded meekly, "Your majesty. You will not be disappointed."

At least those two leeches behind the king would be gone.

"Good," said the king. "Oh, I almost forgot. This Judah also continues to hold my stepdaughter Princess Laodice as hostage. I don't know what information he's been able to torture out of her or if she's still alive. Just make sure that you do not accept any negotiations for her return."

Lysias felt confused by the lack of concern. "None?"

"None," Antiochus repeated. "I do not negotiate with terrorists."

Lysias took note of the king's apparent lack of concern for the safety of his own relative. *Well, stepchildren do represent a conflict of royal interest.*

Antiochus looked over toward Queen Laodice, who was distracted by the pageantry. He leaned into Lysias and conspired, "I must say, all this previous talk of your sexual conquests has aroused me for some fun." He turned to his counsellors, "Timarchus, go fetch my sister Antiochis and tell her to prepare for some … frivolity."

Lysias saw Eupator behind the king listening in. He'd been listening the entire time without anyone bothering to notice. Perhaps natural children represented a conflict of royal interest as well. How much of this the young boy could understand, Lysias had no idea. Nor how much jealousy he might feel on behalf of his mother.

Lysias said a prayer to the gods that the king's whore would keep her mouth shut by keeping it occupied elsewhere. And hopefully, the crown prince would learn his first lesson of royal indiscretion. Smart children do not tattle. They keep secrets as weapons.

Lysias watched the rest of the military procession without seeing any of it as it passed.

CHAPTER 56

Jerusalem

Hera felt the leash around her neck pulled tighter as Zeus whispered into her ear, "Do you like that? Do you like the pain?"

She couldn't respond because her mouth had been gagged shut with a rag and a leather muzzle.

"I think I like you better like this," Zeus murmured. "Silent and submissive."

Hera looked out onto the floor of the Holy of Holies in the temple. It was full of the Olympian gods and their goddess captives dutifully returned from Memphis. The goddesses had relinquished their weapons to the gods of Egypt and had accepted the conditions of surrender to Zeus. Their choice in the matter was between this humiliation or perpetual imprisonment in the Great Pyramid at the mercy of Egyptian occult magic. For all they knew, that could have become their own personal Tartarus.

According to the deal, the goddesses were to accept their second-class status as servants of the gods, to feed them and clean up after their disgusting messes, and to be their sexual slaves, objects for control.

Each of the males had their chosen goddess doing their bidding. Athena was suffering the scatological perversions of Poseidon. Hermes was shoving objects into every orifice of Artemis's body. Dionysus had the duo of Demeter and Hestia upon which he poured out his fetish lusts.

Poor Gaia was chained to the floor on her stomach as Apollo reaped his vengeance upon her. He had never forgiven her for turning his beloved Daphne into a laurel tree. Ares had always had a thing for Hephaestus's wife Aphrodite, but since the war god was impotent, he had to satisfy his psychopathic deviance by beating the love goddess to a pulp. If the lowly blacksmith deity ever returned from where he had disappeared to, he would not be happy with what Ares left of his trophy wife.

Ironically, the only goddess fortunate to avoid abuse was Persephone, who had been set aside for the absent Hades. Aphrodite and Gaia would have some respite soon since Ares and Apollo were about to leave to accompany the Seleucid campaign against the Maccabees.

Hera saw Zeus realize something. As if reading her thoughts, he asked, "Where is Hephaestus anyway? How long has he been gone?"

Hera grinned to herself beneath the muzzle. Hephaestus had been neglected like the runt of the litter in the family. Zeus was only now realizing he was absent.

Nobody could answer. Zeus looked down at Hera and yanked her chain. "Did you do something with him? Do you have him captive somewhere?"

Hera shook her head no with fearful eyes.

Poseidon stopped smearing Athena's body with excrement. "Didn't you send him with the others to Philistia to look for the Messianic Seed?"

"Yes!" exclaimed Zeus. "I do remember that."

"Your majesty." The croaking voice came from Aphrodite.

Zeus said, "Apollo, release her throat, will you?"

The god of healing paused his torturing.

Aphrodite said, "I thought I had seen Hephaestus down in Alexandria before we went to Memphis to meet with the gods."

"Well, why didn't you tell anyone?"

"I wasn't sure it was him. He was distant, and it seemed out of place for him to be there, so I just put it out of my thoughts."

"I should send someone down there," Zeus mused. Then another thought popped into his distracted mind as he looked at Persephone. "What about Hades? Where is that pathetic brother of mine?"

"Right here," said Hades, who suddenly appeared out of thin air walking out from between the columns on the side of the room. He had taken off his special helmet of invisibility.

Zeus looked suspicious. "Where have you been?"

"Taking care of business, *brother*." Hades's emphasis on the word brother was venomous.

Suddenly, to the surprise of all the gods, the mighty sound of trumpets pierced the air in the heavenly realm.

Everyone looked around.

Down in the Holy Place, shadow figures stepped out from between the columns of each side of the darkened room like an army of wraiths. A dozen of them.

As they approached the steps to the Holy of Holies, their forms came into clearer light.

They were the gods of Rome. Not just a few as the Olympians had encountered in Alexandria. Hera counted eight of the major male gods of the pantheon. Jupiter, their king. Neptune, their Poseidon. Pluto, their Hades. The Roman Apollo. Mars, Mercury, Bacchus, and Vulcan. All of them counterparts and mirror images of the Olympians—but more powerful. Romans were the masters of appropriation. They would absorb the best elements of every conquered people, their culture, art, and religion. They didn't try to redesign the wheel. They simply took the wheel and adapted it to their needs. The one unique talent they offered the world was power.

The Olympians were so shocked at the surprise arrival that they did nothing. They remained still like deer in the face of predators as the Romans walked up the steps and paired off with their Greek counterparts.

Hera stared up at Jupiter towering over Zeus's prone position and gaping mouth.

The Roman deities grabbed their Olympian targets and pulled them off the goddesses.

What ensued was an entertaining fight that gave Hera a joyful glee to watch. She was sure the other goddesses were equally thrilled.

The Romans pounded the Greeks with ruthless fury. Some tried to fight back. Poseidon got a few good licks in at Neptune, but he didn't have his trident handy. Neptune did. Zeus and Jupiter wrestled in a small whirlwind of lightning. Zeus wound up in the kind of electrical seizure he was so fond of inflicting on others.

The odds were just not equal in terms of power. Even mighty Greek gods like Ares did not match the strength of their Roman counterparts like Mars. Rome had grown too powerful. Hera noticed that Hades had managed to avoid his punishment as he stood aside observing, untouched by Pluto. Apparently, the "business" Hades had mentioned was betraying his brothers to Rome. So Hera's whisperings to the underworld god had taken hold of his petty little heart.

Zeus was right. Hades was pathetic.

By the time the Romans were done with their ambush, the Greek gods had all been pulverized and bound. The goddesses were then released from their restraints. Jupiter unbuckled the muzzle from Hera's mouth and pulled out her gag. She coughed and spat out some linen.

When she looked up, she saw a tall, gangly figure approach the Holy of Holies from the back of the Holy Place.

Sammael, prince of Rome.

Gliding up the stairs, he looked silently down on the captive Greek gods, his lean wiry body covered by his royal purple robe of authority. The Greeks lay strewn about, some on their backs, in crumpled fetal positions of groaning pain. Their spiritual chains enforced the authority of Rome.

Sammael sniffed and wrinkled his nose in disgust. "This place stinks to high heaven," he said smugly.

Hera saw his shifty lapis lazuli eyes look at her. He extended a hand to her, beckoning her to rise and join his side. She obeyed and took his hand to stand beside him. He looked over the bloody mess like a disappointed father. His long, black hooded robe hid his body in a cloak of mystery. He wasn't built like the physically mighty warriors Mars, Ares, Poseidon, and Neptune. But he was ten times more frightening because of his occultic power and legal status. Hera felt her own hand trembling in his as he looked around.

Sammael gestured to Pluto, standing beside Hades. The Roman god hit the Greek god so hard with a club that the latter fell to the ground in a stupor. Pluto then pulled Hades's hands behind him and bound him with chains.

"Wait!" complained a groggy Hades, his face in the floor. "We had a deal. You promised."

"You're right," Sammael said. "We did have a deal. Now here's a new deal that supersedes all previous deals."

Sammael held up a scroll in his hand for all to see. Finally, he spoke with the unnerving calmness of a satan, a prosecutor in God's own heavenly court. "Gods of Greece. Allow me to introduce you to your new suzerain treaty with me."

Unrolling the scroll, he gave glances at the document but recited most of it from memory. "Firstly, the Preamble. I, Sammael, Prince of Rome, king of kings, Lord of lords, God of gods, do establish this suzerain treaty with the pantheon of Olympians in Greece and all subordinate or subsidiary deities thereof.

"As Prologue, Rome previously made the treaty of Apamea that ensured the submission of Greece as embodied in the Seleucid kingdom and her gods to Roman powers and principalities. More recently, I was called away to adjudicate a ceasefire between the long-warring factions of the Seleucid and Ptolemaic deities in Egypt. Apparently, Zeus and his privileged co-conspirators have continued to step out of line and seek Greek supremacy, resulting in constant annoyance to my plans.

"Here then are the stipulations I decree. Hera, Athena, and Gaia shall now share power as the Most High trio of the pantheon. Zeus and his 'good old gods' will be the servants of the goddesses."

Hera looked at Athena in shock. The goddesses could not believe what they were hearing. Neither could the gods, who responded more verbally with mumbling and complaints.

"SILENCE!" Sammael bellowed in a voice so amplified that it shook the foundations.

The gods shut up.

He continued reciting, "Fourthly, your cursings and blessings shall be thus. If you honor the provisions of this covenant treaty, you will experience prosperity in your allotted territories and allowed the rights of a suzerain vassal of Rome—with a few limited restrictions. If anyone breaks the provisions of this covenant treaty, they shall be captured and imprisoned in the earth to await their judgment from Yahweh.

"Fifthly, this treaty shall be applied to the royal succession of any principalities and powers connected to future earthly rulers of this kingdom—in perpetuity."

Hera knew Antiochus IV Epiphanes, as powerful as he was, would not be the last ruler of the Greek kingdom of Seleucids. Then who was the future one to come on the wing of abominations to destroy both holy city and sanctuary? When was the end that had been foretold if not now? Who was the final "willful king" to come, spoken of by the prophet Daniel?

Sammael concluded his declaration. "And so I call heaven and earth to bear witness along with the gods of Rome and Greece the decrees of this treaty, blah, blah, blah."

He handed the treaty to Hera, who felt emboldened to spit on Zeus's face lying at her feet.

Zeus squeezed shut one eye covered in spittle.

Sammael looked down at the large Foundation Stone near him. He said, "Zeus, you should be grateful for your sanctions. Had I been able to find a way to release that signet of Solomon and open the portal, I would have cast all of you worthless ingrates into the Abyss. Now, please, would you once and for all leave me alone? I have a lot to accomplish on my To-Do list, and I don't want any more interruptions."

Hera could hear the smoldering anger in his tone. She was happy to see him turn away and leave with all his Roman gods in tow. Parasitic bootlickers, just like Olympian males. All gods were the same.

She smiled, "Well, ladies, I believe we have a lot of work ahead of us. Better get your dogs ready to lick this place clean with their tongues. It's about time we had a Matriarchy. Let's show them goddess power."

She couldn't help but feel a bit of a contradiction. Everyone here knew they had been rescued by male gods and given leadership and directions from an alpha male divinity. *Their power was granted by a god.*

Hera pushed the paradox from her mind as she focused on the goddesses turning their cognitive dissonance into vengeance. Aphrodite had already cut off Ares's male member and stuffed it into the god's mouth. Persephone was using a priestly butcher axe to hack the body of Hades up into little pieces as he screamed like a little bitch. Hera knew she was going to feed those pieces to Cerberus for lunch.

Ah, she thought with delight, *vengeance is a dish of dog food, best served bloody.*

She looked down at the pathetic, puppy-eyed face of Zeus looking up at her and wondered what she should do to her dog.

She would start by muzzling him.

CHAPTER 57

Mizpah

At the end of the day, Judah stood at attention before his holy army of God, thousands of them. Instead of their armor, both he and his soldiers wore sackcloth with ashes dirtying their faces and shoulders. They had finished twenty-four hours of fasting and prayer. Judah couldn't wait to get the scratchy, itchy burlap off his body. But it had been a good physical incentive to seek God's face for the new battle that awaited them on the horizon.

His messengers had told him Lysias of Damascus had assembled a force of thousands of men on the plains of Emmaus eight miles southwest of here. The Greeks had finally learned their lesson and were no longer marching through treacherous mountain paths.

Several months had transpired since their victory at the Ascent of Beth-Horon. It was spring, the time when kings go off to war, and Antiochus was doing just that through his ruthless Syrian general. In the preceding months, word had spread throughout Judea of the miraculous exploits of Judah the Hammer of God and his few freedom fighters against impossible odds. Hundreds more had come from all over the land to join his righteous cause. The people had seen the courage of the few willing to stand up for the many and die if needed for their freedom to worship Ha Shem.

Judah's forces had grown to six thousand warriors spread out in networks across Judea. But their growing size had created a new problem. Though they had increased their number of fighters, they were dangerously lacking weapons of war. Many of the new recruits had nothing but their farm tools and small weapons like shovels, daggers, and axes. It was not enough to have the manpower. They also needed iron power.

The odds were mounting into impossible again.

But Judah truly didn't care. He had been ready to die since this all began, and he was still ready to die now.

He finished an earnest prayer beside a retinue of priests dressed in their holy vestments. Priests who should have been serving in the temple, a temple that remained defiled and desolate. Judah cried out to heaven, "Oh Adonai, Ha Shem, Your sanctuary is trampled down and profaned, and your priests mourn in humiliation. Here the Gentiles are assembled against us to destroy us. You know what they plot against us. How will we be able to withstand them if you do not help us?"

He broke away abruptly, deliberately leaving his plea open for God's answer. He didn't expect audible words from heaven but a hidden hand on the battlefield.

Trumpets blew a familiar call to war.

Judah announced to his troops, "Warriors of Adonai! Our time of fasting and prayer is over. Return to your tents and prepare for war!"

Whooping and hollering rang out from the more aggressive soldiers.

"Those who are about to be married and those who are fainthearted will be allowed to return to their homes as Torah allows!"

No one moved from their stance.

Judah gestured to the dozens of captains standing in front of him. "I have appointed these captains of thousands, of hundreds, fifties, and tens! They will brief you on strategy! Be ready at a moment's notice for forced march to the city of Emmaus less than ten miles west. May Ha Shem be our sword in battle!"

The men shouted with a resounding battle cry, "Praise Adonai! Praise Adonai!"

With that, Judah turned and strode back to his tent to wash, get dressed, and prepare for a meal. But his brothers intercepted him, insisting they had a surprise that needed his immediate attention. They brought him on horseback along with a few captains of thousands to a valley at the edge of the camp.

Judah was indeed startled to see a group of foreign prisoners guarded by a hundred of his hasidim. From this distance, he could see distinctive turbans on their heads.

He looked over at his brother Simon, who shrugged and said, "Arab mercenaries in Lysias's army."

"How did you capture them?"

"We didn't. They traveled here from Emmaus and surrendered to us. There must be about a hundred of them."

Approaching the Arabs, Judah, Simon, John, Eleazar, and Jonathan got off their horses. A hasidim brought a disarmed man up to the brothers. Instead of a turban, the Arab wore a red-plumed Hellenistic bronze helmet along with Hellenist bronze body armor. He was the group's obvious leader.

The foreign mercenary took off his helmet in respect. His skin was olive like his fellow soldiers, his hair black and long as Arab commanders typically wore it. When he stood before Judah, he dropped to the ground and bowed with his face in the dirt, the Arab sign of submission.

"My lord, my name is Mustafa ibn Hubal and this is my regiment of Nabataean soldiers. We are mercenaries in the Seleucid army, but we are here to surrender our services to the one they call Judah Maccabee, the Hammer of God."

"Is that so?" Judah responded skeptically.

The leader stood again and dusted off the dirt from his knees. Judah stared into his eyes to see if he could read his soul. The Arab's eyes were dark but carried a look of pure sincerity and deference.

"I am he. I am Judah Maccabee."

"My Lord." Mustafa dropped to the ground again. Judah chuckled. "Please, stand up. We are equals in rank."

"No, my lord, we are not." But the foreign leader obeyed anyway and stood, dusting off his knees again. He gestured over to a pile of Arabic weapons: curved scimitar swords, spears, and round shields. "I trust our surrender of weapons is evidence of our sincerity."

Judah had a good feeling about this, but he didn't trust his feelings, so he inquired, "Why are you doing this?"

"My lord Judah, I do realize that these actions of ours must seem dubious in your eyes. That mercenaries who have received pay would change sides does not appear trustworthy on the surface of it."

"No, it does not. You are all now traitors to King Antiochus and will be hanged when caught."

"Ah, but here is what I would like you to consider. I have but two good reasons to give you, and I am sure that when you have heard them, you will know we are your allies."

Judah was curious to hear how persuasive this rather elegant diplomat could be.

"Firstly, we Nabataeans are Arabs, and it is no secret that we sons of Ishmael are at odds with the sons of Isaac."

"I'd say so," said Judah. Ishmael had been the illegitimate son of Abraham's slave Hagar, over whom Sarah's son Isaac had been chosen.

"But!" Mustafa interjected, "if you take a different perspective, you might see that we are actually on the same side *against* the Greeks. For we are both sons of Abraham. And while you and I may have a more nuanced understanding of our lineage, in the eyes of the Greeks we are all the same. What that means is that they will pay us to help conquer you. But Nabataea is just on the other side of the Jordan from here. Since we are ultimately the same in their eyes, we would be their next territorial expansion after conquering you. So you may hate us, and we may hate you, but we are still more family than the Greeks, who hate us both—and want us both as their slaves."

Judah nodded and looked at his brothers, who clearly also recognized the man's logic.

Mustafa added, "There is an ancient Arabic saying. 'The enemy of my enemy is my friend.' My offer to you is that we unite against our common enemy to defeat him on the battlefield or at least repel him from your land. Then we Arabs can go back to our homes and you to yours, and we can return to hating each other. But at least we will both be alive and free, yes?"

Judah smiled at the congeniality of Mustafa's personality. It was a practical proposition that made sense and benefited both sides. They had a common enemy in the Greeks, and it would do the Arabs no good to help feed the crocodile if they were the last in line to be eaten. Judah could sense the beginning of a friendship that might transcend their differences. "And what was the second reason?"

Mustafa shrugged with a smile. "We *really* hate the Greeks."

Judah shared a smile with the Arab officer. He decided to test the soldier's offer by asking for more intelligence. "What are the numbers of Lysias's army?"

"My lord, they are not good for you. There are twenty thousand infantry. Three thousand and five hundred cavalry. All the nations have gathered against you. Mysians. Thracians. Cypriots. Even your cursed enemies the Edomites from the Negev."

"No, that does not look good." Judah looked at his brothers. They had a mere six thousand mustered with five hundred horsemen.

Mustafa said, "Lysias is not commanding the forces. They are led by General Nicanor and his Edomite chief Gorgias. Cunning leaders, and they have learned from you. Nicanor is planning on attacking you at night with a concentrated force—as you have often done to them."

Mustafa added a sympathetic smile to the discouraging news. The Seleucid forces were used to engaging in organized battles in the early to midday that left time for observation and assessment on both sides. They did not fight battles at night. And they had not been prepared for the guerrilla tactics Judah had perfected. Attacking in the dark of night was one of his most successful ones.

Judah considered the information and the sincerity of his new ally. He looked to his brothers. They all nodded. It was not usual to have them all in agreement on something. This was a good sign.

He turned to the head hasidim guard, a serious-looking young soldier who stood at attention as if God himself was directing him. "Give these men back their weapons, give them some rations, and find them a section within the camp."

"Judah," Simon spoke with caution. Apparently, that was going too far for his skeptical brother.

Judah replied, "We cannot expect to retain their trust if we do not trust them in return."

"No, no, no, no," interrupted Mustafa. "Trust is earned, not gifted. We will stay here in the valley outside the camp under guard and without our weapons until we can prove ourselves in battle. However, some food and drink would be received with much gratitude."

"Fair enough." Judah turned to the serious guard. "See to it that these men are not cheated in quantity or quality of rations."

"Yes sir."

Judah turned back to Mustafa. "We can talk more on this in the morning."

Mustafa bowed low again in gratitude. "Tomorrow will not come too quickly for the Jewish citizens Nicanor is selling into slavery."

"That son of a whore," Judah muttered. Such wartime tactics were commonplace, but Judah could never get used to the thought of Jewish women and children suffering enslavement. He could not get to the battlefield soon enough to crush this Hydra's heads.

Judah and his leaders made their way back to camp for some food and drink of their own.

CHAPTER 58

Judah ate dinner with his officers that evening around one of the campfires of his battalion. The general had invited their royal "hostage" and her four maidservants to eat with the officers as he did on rare occasion. Over the past several months, chosen guards under Eleazar's watch continued to protect the princess and her entourage. Under that guard, the women had been allowed more freedom of movement, and their presence around camp had become familiar to the Jewish soldiers. Sometimes Laodice and her women found fellowship with the women of the Jewish towns where Judah's forces hid out.

At this meal, Laodice and her servants sat together on one side of a fire with Judah and his brothers on the other side. A couple other commanders joined them. The women wore warm, woolen cloaks as protection against the cool desert evening. Everyone ate soup made from lentils and onions with small pieces of lamb and mutton requisitioned from the residents of Modein.

Eleazar had been pouting about Judah's latest appointment of battalion leaders for the Emmaus battle that was looming on their horizon.

"But it's dishonorable for me," complained Eleazar. "I am his elder."

"Age has nothing to do with it, Eleazar," Simon rebuked. "Everyone knows Jonathan has a more strategic mind than any of us, not just you."

"But I'm the only Hasmonean brother who isn't leading a battalion."

Simon replied, "There will only be four battalions."

"But I am the most zealous of all of us."

Judah finally spoke up. "I think the correct word is 'overzealous,' Eleazar. And that is the real reason why you are not leading a battalion. You are not ready. You are an excellent fighter. There is no one better with the javelin or spear than you."

Eleazar held his hands out as if to say, "Then what is the problem?"

"But your ambition gives you tunnel vision. It blinds you to your surroundings. That makes you strong in your own fight but weak in the wider battle. A soldier fights. A leader strategizes."

"My javelin took down the enemy leader at Beth-Horon."

"And you got bit in the ass," said Simon. That brought laughs from the brothers. "You just missed being turned into a pin cushion."

The joke no longer seemed funny to Eleazar. He glared at young Jonathan, who couldn't stop smiling.

Eleazar said, "Courage requires risk even against the odds. You take such risks with your army, Judah."

"I am not talking about courage," said Judah. "You have courage. But courage is not enough for leadership. Before you can lead, you must learn to follow."

Laodice had been listening to the exchange in silence. She spoke up, "Eleazar, you want to kill King Antiochus one day, do you not?"

"Yes, ma'am, I do."

"Well, consider yourself lucky then. You cannot kill an enemy leader when you are busy leading your own battalion."

Eleazar thought about it and nodded his head in reconsideration, muttering, "Fair enough."

Big John smiled his big, warm grin. "Princess Laodice, you better be careful. If you convert to our cause, you may have to stay with us."

Laodice stared straight at Judah. "I could see some benefit to that."

Judah stared her right back. "But can you see the cost?"

"That is a high cost." she demurred.

"The cost is everything," Judah said soberly.

The sudden silence in their midst punctuated the moment with a dark realization that they had all given their lives to this cause. That there was no going back.

Laodice spoke up again. "Hellenism has spread with inevitability. It unifies the world as one people, one language, one purpose."

"Like the tower of Babel," said Eleazar.

The princess looked confused. "How can a people thrive on separation from others? On dividing the people?"

"Princess," said Jonathan, "Hellenism spread through force. Its unity is slavery to our people. According to our prophet Daniel, the only inevitability is the fall of the bronze Greek kingdom and the rise of iron Rome."

"Iron mixed with clay," corrected Eleazar.

"I don't understand," said Laodice. "What do you mean?"

Judah jumped in. "Let me try to explain. In the days of our exile in Babylon, Daniel was one of our prophets who was held captive in the court of King Nebuchadnezzar. The king had been disturbed by a dream that he had of a large statue. An image whose head was made of gold, whose chest and arms were made of silver, whose middle and thighs were bronze, and whose legs were iron—but with feet of iron and clay.

"Now, our God revealed the meaning to the prophet Daniel, who explained it all to the king. The image was a symbol of the successive Gentile kingdoms to come, all of whom would oppress God's people one after another. The gold head was a symbol of the Babylonian kingdom. Their rule was overcome by the kingdom of the Medes and the Persians, represented as the silver chest and arms. But those kings were overcome by the Greek kingdom of Alexander, symbolized in the bronze middle and thighs. That is your Hellenism."

Laodice was listening intently, carried away by her imagination. "And the legs of iron are Rome?"

"Yes. We have not seen the worst of our judgment for our sins."

She wasn't following. "What do you mean your sins?"

"The reason for the oppression of our people beneath the boot of Gentile beasts is because Israel is like a wife who has been unfaithful to her spiritual husband. We have worshipped other gods. Gods allotted to the Gentiles."

Laodice was beginning to understand. "The temple of Zeus in Jerusalem."

"Among many others," Judah said. "We seek to return Israel to her husband, remove the idolaters, and cleanse the temple."

"But this Roman kingdom does not yet rule over you."

"No. But it will. And it will be a kingdom that will trample and crush and break into pieces the other kingdoms with its 'unity.' That is when the last part of the dream will be fulfilled. Because Nebuchadnezzar had also seen a stone not cut with human hands come out of heaven and hit the image at its feet of iron mixed with clay. The stone broke that image into pieces. We believe that stone is Messiah."

"Who is he, this Messiah?" Laodice asked.

"We do not know. But in the dream, that stone grew to be a mountain that filled the earth. A cosmic mountain. Because in that day, Messiah will come and establish his kingdom, which will be an everlasting kingdom that shall never be destroyed."

Another moment of silence gripped everyone listening. The implications were both frightening and awe-inspiring.

Laodice stared again at Judah as she spoke to the men. "Yours is a fascinating religion. Full of imagination and hope. A hope I wish I could believe. I want to believe."

Judah was looking right back at her straight into her eyes, into her soul. He said as if finishing her thought, "But you can't."

The princess sighed with sadness. But she could not take her eyes off Judah. "Pray for me, then, good men of Judea. I am not your enemy. For I have come to understand the cause of the Jewish people. And I believe that love transcends all divisions."

Judah knew that was spoken most pointedly to him. Through their interactions over the past few months, he had felt himself drawn to this woman, desiring her. They had shared intimate conversation. She had offered as much intelligence of Antiochus that she could think of to aid their cause. She had wept with sympathy for his people.

But she was not one of them.

He stood up. "Men, I must turn in. We have a big day ahead of us tomorrow. Good night to you all. Good night, Princess Laodice."

As he looked at her, he felt that he was saying goodbye. And her tearful, pleading eyes seemed desperately aware of it.

Retiring to his tent, Judah sat alone in just his tunic in the dark on the bed. He felt completely alone before God. He had prayed for God to remove his desire for Laodice. But it remained. He prayed for her soul. He prayed for understanding and acceptance of the will of God. But God seemed so distant. And silent. Judah felt sickened to his stomach with longing.

He was interrupted by the voice of one of his three guards whispering the presence of the princess at his entrance.

He allowed her in. She was alone. She wore a long, heavy woolen cloak with hood to hide her appearance. She pulled the hood off, and he felt his heart race.

They stared silently at each other. Their mutual attraction felt palpable to Judah. He could see her pupils wide open, drinking him in.

Her hands slowly undid the woolen cloak just enough to reveal her bare skin all the way down into the shadow below.

Judah didn't move.

She waited for him, both innocent and seductive, pleading to be taken.

The dam that held back his passions started to crumble under pressure.

He reached up with his hands and took both lapels of her cloak, then slowly closed them back to cover her nakedness.

Her eyes teared up with shame. She turned to leave.

But he held her arm to stay.

"Laodice," he whispered. "There is nothing my flesh wants more at this moment than to take you. To surrender myself to desire."

"Then take me," she whispered back. "Is desire so wrong?"

"Desire is not love," he challenged.

"It doesn't have to be," Laodice countered. "But it can become so."

Judah smiled at her empathetically. "Come. I want to show you something."

The Nabataean camp rested quietly in the valley beneath the waxing moon above. Most fires were out as the Arabs had retired to get their sleep for the big day ahead of them. A small platoon of fifty hasidim stayed on the perimeter, not as guards but as guides for assimilating into the army of Judah Maccabee.

Those Jewish guides were also presently asleep and unaware of the four cloaked figures who slipped away from the Nabataean camp and into the shadows of the night.

Mustafa ibn Farid led his three trusted soldiers through the trees up to the camp of the hasidim above. They already knew the location of posted watchmen but crouched and scanned the hillside for any others who might give them away.

Mustafa felt his scimitar beneath his cloak sheathed in leather, deadly silent and ready for action. They were on a mission to assassinate Judah Maccabee.

Judah had put on a cloak and walked Laodice from his tent in the direction of hers a short distance away. His guards remained in their place. It was very late. Most of his soldiers were sleeping with a few scattered smoldering fires for those who could not. Watchmen were silently guarding the perimeter of the camp in the darkness.

Stopping halfway in the midst of a small clearing, Judah looked up at the night sky. Laodice followed his gaze.

He whispered, "What do you see when you look into the heavens?"

"The sun, moon, and stars," she whispered thoughtfully. "The signs of seasons and the passage of time. A natural world of eternal laws."

They remained fixed in their observation above. Then Judah said softly, "I see a majestic Creator reflected in his creation. I see the heavens, the work of his fingers. The moon and the stars that he has set in place. And I think, how small we all are. How so very small."

"Insignificant," Laodice concluded.

Judah kept his train of thought. "What is man that God is mindful of him? The son of man that he cares for him? Yet he has made us a little lower than the gods. He has given us dominion over creation to rule in his image."

He looked back down at the princess to see her staring at him, still longing for him.

He had spent much time in his head imagining what he was about to say to her. He had had to convince himself. Now he would have to convince her. "Laodice, I do not deny that I desire you. I have come to know you over these past months, and you are both a beautiful and a worthy woman."

He could see her fighting back tears.

"But imagine after this night, how would you respect me if I had accepted? How could I lead you?"

"What do you mean?"

"You have taken the lead by coming to me. Your seduction results in my submission. Your respect is blinded by lust. But imagine how your respect would hold up for a man that *you* pursued, who did not lead in pursuing you. Such a man is not worthy of your respect."

"No. No," Laodice objected. "That is not true."

Judah gave her a kind but chastising look. "You would not respect me in the end. And I could not lead a woman who pursued me."

"Can we not be equal?" Laodice queried sadly.

"We *are* equal. In the sight of God, in our worth. But you are not looking for an equal in authority. You are looking for strength, protection, provision, even if you do not understand yourself."

She sighed with resignation. Judah could tell she knew he was right.

He added, "And what if *I* led in the seduction? Then what kind of a man would I be? A man—or woman—who sets aside their convictions of honor and propriety to gratify their desire is a person you can be certain will do so again—with another. Is that love?"

He could see she was being overcome with shame. He reached out and gave her an affirming caress on the side of her head. But he swiftly removed his hand so as not to linger.

"I have never known such a love," Laodice responded with vulnerable sincerity. "It seems like a myth to me. A dream of ideals that are lauded but not lived." Her tears flowed now. "I have only known the real world of lust, gratification, and power."

"I understand, Laodice. I do. The world is broken. But it is not the 'real world.' The world is the nightmare that we have made for ourselves by rebelling from our Creator. And I am guilty of the same. We all fail at love—and goodness. We all need atonement."

Mustafa and his men moved like phantoms of death in the night. The Arab tents were but paces from the perimeter of the Jewish camp, and with their hasidim "guides" sound asleep, it had been easy for the small group of assassins to avoid discovery as they slipped from one camp to the other.

Gliding down dark pathways of tents filled with sleeping soldiers, they warily dodged the few night owls still awake at their small fires to arrive at the center of camp where Judah Maccabee's command tent stood guarded by several soldiers, two in the front, one in the back. By their yawns, shuffling feet, and occasional abrupt nods, the guards were very sleepy.

Mustafa nodded to the other three. Spreading out for their targets, they all counted in their heads as previously rehearsed to stay synchronized in their plan.

At the count of forty, the guard at the back should have been taken out quietly. At the count of fifty, Mustafa approached the tent from a distance, enough for the two front guards to see his figure in the moonlight without seeing his face. They immediately snapped to attention, focusing on their visitor. But before they could see who he was, an assassin rose behind each guard and slit their throats with daggers. They held their victims' mouths covered and laid them gently on the ground, stifling any noises.

Fifty yards away, Laodice was considering Judah's words of God's love and his Torah. She admitted, "I want to live in such a way. To love you in such a way. Can *I* not have atonement?"

"Yes. Yes, you can. But only through Torah. We worship different gods, you and I. And the two do not mix."

"But I don't worship a god. Is there no exception? No room for compromise?"

"No, there is not. And the god of the Cynic or the Nihilist who claims none is the most intolerant and demanding god of all."

The princess broke down, weeping into her hands.

Judah wanted to comfort her. But he could not.

Through her tears, her words came brokenly, "You are right, Judah. We are so very different, you and I."

He released his hand from her shoulder. "You have changed me, Princess Laodice. Never forget that."

She wiped her tears away with restored dignity. She whispered, "Have I?"

Mustafa saw a small lamp light within the tent. If the Jewish general was awake, this would not be easy. Silently pulling the entrance flap aside, he slipped into the tent, his three assassins following in deadly silence.

Inside, there was nothing. No one in the bed. No one by the lamp. They checked the couple corners of boxes and furniture where someone might be hiding. But there was no one.

His assassins looked at Mustafa with confusion.

"He must be with the hostage," he whispered.

While he had been softly conversing with Laodice, Judah's attention had been drawn to the movement of some figures up by his tent. The moonlight showed shadows converging, then disappearing. The figures of the guards were suddenly gone.

Judah stopped Laodice with a protective hand on her arm, whispering, "Something is wrong. Go to your tent and alert your guards."

In moments, he had traversed half the distance to his tent. Spotting four figures emerging from the entrance, he recognized immediately they must be assassins.

The intruders saw him running and drew weapons. They spread out to meet him and surround him.

Judah didn't have a weapon. He ripped off his woolen cloak. Once he was within striking distance, he threw it at the middle attacker like a net. It blinded the man enough for Judah to shove him to the ground and maintain his pace to the entrance of his tent.

He could hear the swift, pounding footsteps of his attackers behind him. Passing the two dead guards on the ground at the tent entrance, he pushed his way inside.

What his pursuers did not realize was that Judah was not trying to run away. He was retrieving Rahab.

Finding the leather sheath that housed the whip sword, Judah snatched it up and raced to meet the arriving assassins just outside the entrance.

He knew he had only moments to spare. The guards down by Laodice's tent blew their horns to awaken the camp.

He dodged a curved blade that swung down upon him. Rolling to the ground, he quickly popped up, releasing Rahab from her sheath. As the glittering blade rolled out, he snapped at the first assassin, cutting him in half at his waist. The dead man fell to the ground in two pieces.

A second assassin launched at him, swinging his scimitar in a circle eight. Judah snapped Rahab with a side swipe, cutting the killer's sword arm off. A second swipe took his head. Judah turned to face his final two assassins.

They had been watching. They had been learning. He was not going to take them down so easily. They stood back in defensive postures, brandishing their swords before them.

Judah heard the sound of the camp coming alive around him. He saw that Mustafa and the second assassin were going to charge him together. He could get one but not two. They were suicidal.

He swung from above, hitting the second assassin in the shoulder. The whip sword slashed down deep into his chest, halfway through his body.

And got stuck there. Judah moved out of the way. The hurling dead body of the assassin fell to the ground, ripping the sword handle out of Judah's hands.

He looked up and saw Mustafa standing over him, now swinging his sword down in an arc. Judah rolled, and the scimitar dug deep into the ground. He jumped up and hit Mustafa. The two of them rolled in the dirt and got up, facing one another.

Mustafa had a dagger in his hand, also curved like his scimitar, which was still in the ground. Judah had nothing. He demanded, "You would sacrifice the lives of your own people to the Greeks just to kill Jews?"

"Yes!" Mustafa watched for his moment to strike. "We will always hate the Jews more than anything."

He swiped at Judah back and forth with his knife. Judah backed up, dodging each swipe. Then he tripped. He fell backward to the ground. He rolled up next to the scimitar.

Just as Mustafa attacked like a rampaging lion.

Grabbing the scimitar, Judah yanked it out of the ground and stuck it toward Mustafa, who ran straight into the blade without halting.

It went deep, all the way to the handle, bursting out his back. With a violent jerk, Mustafa dropped the dagger. He staggered back and looked with shock at Judah.

"May your children be cursed from the River Jordan to the Great Sea," he croaked out, then dropped dead to the ground.

Judah was breathing heavily from the battle. He got to his feet just as his brothers Simon and John arrived.

"Judah!" Simon cried out. "Are you okay?"

They stopped in their tracks as they spotted the dead guards and assassins.

"It took you long enough!" Judah quipped.

Big John grinned. "Apparently, you didn't need us anyway."

Judah asked, "Where are the other Arabs?"

"Gone," said Simon. "They killed all fifty of our soldiers who guarded them and ran. Must have escaped back to Nicanor."

John raised eyebrows in disbelief. "Surely they must know that killing Judah would not stop the war."

Judah shook his head. "They love death more than life."

"So much for trusting Ishmaelites," Simon added.

Judah looked at his brothers, who were now joined by Eleazar with a javelin and young Jonathan. "They certainly don't understand the brothers Maccabee. Little do they realize they've just kicked a hornet's nest."

CHAPTER 59

Jerusalem

Hera sat in council with the goddesses in the Holy of Holies. Athena sat beside her. Around the throne stood Demeter, Persephone, Artemis, and Hestia. Gossip had been flying around the goddesses as to what kind of structure the new pantheon would take, what they were going to do with the gods, and what strategy they should adopt for the Seleucid kingdom.

Aphrodite arrived with a bowl full of blood from the sacrifice outside on the altar. She poured it into three chalices. Hera knew all the goddesses resented Aphrodite for her beauty, including Hera herself, so she had made sure to give the goddess servant duties that the males would normally be given. Serving blood. Cleaning up after their messes. Pleasuring the other goddesses. It kept her humble.

Behind Aphrodite, Gaia waddled in late, her rolls of fat jiggling with each step. She tottered her way up the stairs into the Holy of Holies to take a seat beside Hera and Athena. They were the new triumvirate of high goddesses to replace Zeus, Poseidon, and Hades. Hera's throne was Zeus's old throne, raised above the others.

"Where are the gods?" asked Gaia.

"They are chained up on the high places of the Mount of Olives. I don't want them hearing our deliberations."

"Who is watching over them?"

"The Canaanite goddesses Asherah and Astarte. I've made a treaty with them to unite with us in solidarity."

"Why am I the last to know these things?" complained Gaia. "I am one of the three high goddesses. I think I deserve more respect."

"If you would be more punctual," said Hera, "you might earn more respect."

Gaia grumbled.

"Our first order of business," said the Queen of the gods, "is to decide what we do with the men."

"I say we cut them up and scatter their pieces to the four corners of the earth," Persephone suggested in her sweet, inoffensive voice.

Gaia belted out in a belly laugh. Others chuckled as well.

Athena said with joviality, "Not all gods are like Hades, Persephone. Let's not stereotype them. That might be a bit extreme."

"Extreme?" countered Artemis. "Do you have battered goddess syndrome? Have you forgotten how they punished us?"

"To be fair," said Hestia, "we *did* commit treason."

"Oh, yes, we deserved it," mocked Artemis. "We deserve the millennia of oppression. If only we hadn't provoked them!"

"Sisters, please," interrupted Hera. "We need to stick together. Don't be like them."

"I say we castrate them and keep them as servants." The offer came from Demeter. "Let them see how it feels to be second-class gods."

"I like that idea," said Athena. "Eunuchs for the kingdom of the gods."

Most of the goddesses murmured agreement with the idea.

"Let us table that for the moment," said Hera. "I'm thirsty. Aphrodite."

Aphrodite handed the chalices of sacrificial blood to the three high goddesses. Hera took a deep drink from her cup.

"What about our organizational structure and duties?" Athena queried. "We need to get organized."

"Hierarchies are oppressive," said Gaia. "They're the systemic perpetuation of the Patriarchy. We need to remain egalitarian."

"Well then," Artemis broke in, "I suggest we start with you giving up your throne. All three of you should step down and redistribute power equally amongst us all. That is the Matriarchy."

Hera felt alarmed at the remark. That was not what she was thinking. She said, "Every hive needs a Queen Bee."

"As a birthing machine," corrected Aphrodite. "That is just another example of the Patriarchy."

Suddenly, Hera felt her throat close up on her. Her body began to tingle. Grabbing her throat, she choked out, "Something is wrong with me."

Everyone shut up and watched her with curiosity.

Hera fell off her throne, her muscles barely able to hold her. She was on her hands and knees. She vomited black bile from her stomach. She was completely confused. How could this be happening to her, a goddess?

She fell to the ground and rolled on her back, violently spasming in a seizure.

And then it stopped. She caught her breath. Her consciousness was still dizzied, her vision blurry.

She saw Athena and Gaia standing over her gloating.

"I agree with you," Athena said. "Something is wrong. We need a new goddess boss."

"How?" Hera croaked in confusion.

Athena spoke matter-of-factly. "Remember that Naphil you killed? Well, if you recall, he did cut off one of the heads of the Hydra that he gave to us in a sack. And if you remember, the blood of the Hydra is poison. No earthly poison can harm us. But Hydra is not earthly."

Gaia leaned in. "You won't die from it. But it is in your angelic blood now, and you will remain crippled in that body for gods know how long."

"But why?" Hera croaked again. "We're … sisters."

"I think the real answer to that question is why not?" Gaia responded. "You're a traitor to our gender. All the women you punished for Zeus's piggish infidelities, women he seduced and raped. You punished them instead of your chauvinist cad of a husband. You enabled him with your denial. You turned your own priestess Io into a cow to be tortured by a gadfly after she rejected Zeus's advances. She didn't even sleep with him."

Artemis stepped up. "You cursed my mother Leto and had her raped by a giant. You turned my follower Callisto, who was seduced by Zeus, into a bear."

"Semele," added Demeter.

"Alcmene and Echo," added Hestia.

"Europa and Aegina," added Persephone. "All women you punished instead of Zeus. You're no sister of ours."

They were all in on it. They were all her betrayers.

"Those are only stories we made up," said Hera.

"Stories that reveal your true character," said Gaia.

Hera choked out, "Vindictive bitches."

Athena said, "Says the high and mighty Queen Bitch herself, Mrs. Zeus. You old hag. It's time for new blood to reign."

She finished her cup and dropped it on Hera's head. It bounced off her forehead and onto the floor with a clank.

But then, Athena's face went pale. Her grin turned into a frown. She held her throat and began to gag just as Hera had done. Her eyes went wide with confusion. She looked over at Gaia, who smiled knowingly.

Athena fell to the floor beside Hera, still glaring at Gaia. She tried to take out her sword. Gaia stepped back out of range. Athena dropped the sword to the floor with a loud clank.

"You fat pig," Athena choked out at Gaia. "How dare you?"

"How dare I?" mocked Gaia. "How dare you for how you've treated me for millennia? Do you think I would forget how you have humiliated me and mocked me since the days of the Titanomachy? That time you transformed my sister Medusa into a hideous monster?"

"That was two thousand years ago!" Athena complained.

"Yes," said Gaia. "And I remember it like it was yesterday. Or the time when you cursed my favorite Satyr Marsyas with an awful death."

"I don't even remember that," Athena choked out.

"Well, I do," replied Gaia. "I never forgot."

Aphrodite now stood over Athena as well. She said, "You just couldn't help your violent, jealous temper when I won the contest for fairest of the goddesses. So you joined the traitor to our gender Hera and destroyed my Trojans. You both can rot in Gehenna as far as I'm concerned."

Aphrodite took the chalice from Gaia's hand and poured the undrunk blood over Athena's face. The war goddess wiped her eyes and screamed out in more blinding pain.

"Am I too late for the celebration?" came a familiar voice from the stairs of the Holy Place.

Hera turned her head to see Juno, queen of the Roman pantheon. She wore a gorgeous long, flowing stola made of dyed purple linen. It followed gracefully behind her like the wind. She seemed to be walking on air. Her swaying hips screamed sexual charisma in every step. She was stunning like a twin sister to Hera, who remained on the floor gaping up at her with contorted pain.

Juno's palla shawl over the stola was to die for, a regal cloak of her high rank made of artistically woven white wool. Her diadem was a stately, elegant golden band embedded with jewels over which a veil hid her full face. She was laden with golden jewelry of Roman design. Necklace, bracelets, and earrings accentuated her shining presence. She carried a scepter of gold that symbolized her royal authority.

Hera found herself staring at Juno's designer leather sandals adorned with gold and jewels. She felt a distinct jealousy that she lacked such premium footwear on her own shoe racks. Zeus was always a cheap bastard.

Juno was followed by the brooding hulk of Mars in crimson red tunic and Montefortino helmet of bronze. A gaudy studded leather military belt secured his tunic and held his sharp gladius in its sheath. The masculine warrior didn't wear the typical segmented chainmail armor so he could show off his bulging muscles to the world.

Narcissistic prick, thought Hera in her delirium.

Her confusion was shared by the other goddesses except Gaia, who responded defensively, "Oh, don't give me those looks. You all wanted to do the same, and you know it. Read the writing on the wall, Greek hegemony is over. I decided to cut a deal before they took everything by force."

Juno announced, "Okay, ladies, I'm the new Queen Bee, and I'm here to make sure you are all in compliance with Sammael's wishes."

"Why did you have to bring *him*?" Artemis complained, glaring at Mars. "All we need is another macho male godsplaining down to us with his male gaze."

"Oh, shut your twat." Juno looked around at the goddesses. "You know, they say a world run by women would have no war. But what I see is a bunch of hysterical, backbiting witches who are far pettier and more vindictive than men. For good or for evil, it will always be a man's world. So get used to it, ladies."

They moaned and bickered to the end.

"Our first order of duty is to move out of this primitive, rat-infested hellhole of a temple. If you think Yahweh is not going to come back and take it with Messiah, you're a fool. We had best build our base of operations elsewhere if we want to be ready for his coming."

The last positive feeling Hera would have for a long time was seeing Juno roll her eyes at the moaning and bickering that exploded from her new vassal goddesses.

• • • • •

Mount Hermon

Gaia arrived at the valley of Mount Hermon below its snow-peaked ridges in the land of Bashan, the place of the Serpent. It was a cool autumn midnight. A full lunar eclipse created a blood-red moon that lit up the gnarly tower of wood with its deep, graven crevices and fissures. She looked up in awe at its vast height rising to the stars. At her feet, she felt the twisting roots that plunged through soil and rock deep into the underworld.

Gaia was huffing and sweating from her journey. She had left Jerusalem with a promise from Juno to allow her this one favor as reward for her betrayal of the Greek goddesses. Gaia was done with them. She was ready for a change.

She was the Mother Earth Goddess. *She* was the primordial deity who with Ouranus had given birth to the original Titans, the Cyclopes, the Giants, and all the primordial sea gods. *She* was the mother of all life, not Hera nor any of those other stupid divas and tramps. At least that's how the myth was told.

Yet Gaia had never received the respect she deserved.

She heard a soft whistle in the wind and returned it. Within minutes, the rotund figure of Cybele emerged from the gloomy forest. She jumped for joy, running to meet Gaia. Her bouncing fat almost threw her off balance. When the two met, they slammed into each other but could barely reach their arms around their bulging, obese bodies. They kissed each other deeply with their tongues and stripped naked what little foliage they wore as clothes.

But the time for sexual abandon was not yet. They had first to draw down the moon.

Building a small fire, they burned hemp mixed with Nightshade from Scythia. They consumed other *pharmakeia* for their sorcery: wolfbane and black hellebore. This induced a trance as they held hands and danced naked around the fire, chanting and calling forth the denizens of the Great Tree of Life, her guardians and defenders.

Within minutes, black figures appeared from within the tree's dead crags. They came forth like phantoms from a corpse. Three of them, one a grown woman and two young girls. They were all pale-skinned with long pitch-black hair. The mother writhed like a serpent in an erotic dance that the two young children mimicked. When the woman arrived in the firelight, she and her daughters held hands with Gaia and Cybele, joining the dance.

"Sister Lilith!" Gaia shouted. "We welcome you and your daughters Lili and Lilitu!"

They giggled together, filled with the joy of the blood-red moon. Lilitu was actually a little boy who from ancient days had been cut up and reshaped to appear as a girl.

Behind them, a shadowy black serpentine form began to wrap around the tree's roots, weaving in and out of the crevices like a dragon in the waves of a sculpted sea. Gaia knew this chthonic being. Ningishzida, guardian of both tree and lady.

They all began to chant together as they circumambulated the fire. "By the rite of the Thessalian witches, if I command the moon, it will come down. If I wish to fly through the air, I am free from my weight. If I call to the underworld, the earth will open up."

The sound of howling in the distance brought them to a standstill. It wasn't wolves. It sounded more like demons, satyrs, and other creatures of chaos.

Gaia pointed to a large burlap sack at the foot of the tree. Lilith and her daughters ran over to it and opened it up. They all three lifted the huge Hydra head decapitated by Heracles. It was the size of Lilith's whole body. But she and her daughters had preternatural strength. Lifting it, they offered it to the roots of the tree.

It sank down into the roots and disappeared.

Gaia and Cybele walked up to the tree and embraced it. They twisted and writhed their bodies with erotic pleasure on the bark until they dissolved into the tree's folds, spirit beings dissolving into heavenly material.

They had become one with Gaia. One with the earth.

The ground shuddered. The tree shook with convulsions. The gritty bark slowly began to move, carved as writhing human bodies that made up the essence of its material. The whispered sounds of wailing and gnashing of teeth lilted through the air.

Lilith and her daughters danced with joy before the towering temple of deadwood that was coming back to life. Its branches far above began to sprout green. Its height rose still higher into the heavens. Its roots began to suck life from all around as bushes dried up and trees dropped their leaves. Desert flowers and herbs wilted in death as the tendrils of its spirit expanded.

The all-nurturing, all-comforting Mother of All, the Mother Earth Goddess had returned.

Gaia was reborn.

CHAPTER 60

Emmaus

Judah and his guerilla army had left Mizpah the morning after the attempted assassination. He marched six thousand infantry and five hundred horsemen over sixteen miles of winding hilly terrain. They had arrived just before dusk in the hills several miles south of Emmaus. They set up camp in full sight of Nicanor's forces bivouacked on the plains of the Aijalon Valley. Judah could see that Nicanor had backed his base camp up against the foothills, facing out toward the broad valley plains with daring challenge to Judah's army.

Judah remembered the Arab Mustafa's estimate of twenty thousand Seleucid infantry and mercenaries with three thousand, five hundred cavalry for Nicanor's forces. Judah knew he still didn't stand a chance against those numbers on a level playing field. And he wasn't about to start playing by the rules now. But he wanted Nicanor to think he would.

Though Mustafa had betrayed him, Judah figured that the intelligence he had shared on Nicanor's night raid strategy seemed valid. Some truth was always necessary to distract attention from the bigger lie. Had Mustafa assassinated Judah as planned, the accurate intelligence would not have mattered. But Nicanor did not know all that Mustafa had revealed, so Judah counted on his enemy using the night raid strategy.

The next evening, Judah ordered his troops to make a large number of campfires to give the impression of their presence. But he only left two hundred in camp as his four divisions of fifteen hundred men each slipped away into the night led by the brothers Maccabee.

Gorgias, the Edomite chief under Nicanor, had been given five thousand infantry and a thousand cavalry to ambush Judah's camp by night. He relished the opportunity to crush the pesky little Jew who represented an eternal enemy of his people. Gorgias's land was Idumea in the Negev desert south of Judea and expanding into Moab, their original home. Their forefather Esau had been firstborn and set to inherit Abraham's covenant. But the foolish Esau had been tricked out of his birthright by his conniving brother Jacob. Then Jacob's descendant, that abominable King David, had almost wiped out Esau's descendants the Edomites. As far as Gorgias was concerned, Israelites were the spawn of a demon.

Gorgias shared the swarthy form and reddish hair of his ancestors, with hints of graying. He wore the distinguished Hellenist armor of a Seleucid auxiliary leader with its golden cloak and red plumed Attic helmet, though the leather cheek guards flapped annoyingly against his red beard. He was proud of his heritage and proud of the fact that he would be the one to avenge his ancestors by helping to exterminate the Jews.

Gorgias had led his forces quietly through the night from the north wadi up to the north side of Judah's camp. When he gave the signal, they attacked cavalry first, breaking into the camp ready for slaughter.

But they were met with empty campfires burning all around the camp as though everyone had disappeared. Gorgias wondered what could have happened. Had Judah discovered the ruse and run like a coward?

"Chief Gorgias!" one of his captains alerted him, pointing to the rear of the hillside. Gorgias saw the back end of Judah's forces fleeing into the night down a wadi toward the direction of Jerusalem.

The cowards were indeed on the run.

This will be an easy hunt. Gorgias barked the command, "Chase them down! Kill them all!"

He was sure the Jews couldn't get far before they were overtaken by Gorgias's elite crack troops. He heard the sound of a trumpet from the retreating forces.

Judah heard the distant trumpet that told him his ruse had worked. Their small guard had led Gorgias and thousands of Seleucid soldiers, he wasn't sure how many, on a chase away from Emmaus.

The hasidim forces had split up their four regiments. Judah's and John's were on the hillside flank of the Seleucid phalanx formation in the plains. The other two, Simon's and Jonathan's, were to the north of the Seleucid camp.

But their time for attack was not yet. The Seleucid forces would be too hyped up on the excitement of Gorgias's surprise attack. And they were too familiar with guerilla night raids. So Judah threw them off by waiting until morning.

Just a few hours later, the rays of dawn broke over the hills, and Judah could see with more clarity the Seleucid army around the hillside from his hideout. Spread out on the plain at the front were thousands of cavalry. Behind them, multiple phalanx units with their shields tightly interlinked and their long sarissa pikes pointing forward were virtually impenetrable except by a counterforce of equally equipped phalanx warriors.

Judah had none. There was no way in Hades he could have faced that massive military horde head-on. So Judah had decided to attack it on its flank side where it was most vulnerable.

Signaling his men with the silent wave of a banner, Judah launched forward with his horsemen and infantry units. He and John led the charge with their two battalions of three thousand warriors.

Simultaneous with Judah's attack, Simon and Jonathan led their three thousand warriors down the hillside behind the Seleucid camp. There must have been ten thousand soldiers or more in the camp. But they were all relaxing at ease, eating breakfast, and watching their trusted phalanx units on the field. They had been caught unaware with their armor down.

Simon and his cavalry swept through the surprised forces, swiping down armed and unarmed soldiers alike. Some of the hasidim set fire to tents with torches. The infantry rolled in and spread out in an arc of death with axes, daggers, and gardening tools. It was amazing how effective a shovel or pitchfork could be in combat in the hands of a zealous warrior with a cause. Homemade spears could pierce as well as manufactured ones, especially with the element of surprise behind them.

That said, as the hasidim killed their victims, they snatched up their enemies' weapons and used them as their own. Confusion and fear ignited like wildfire amongst the Seleucids. Simon felt a supernatural confidence exude from his warriors as they massacred their victims with speed and efficiency.

Judah and his five hundred cavalry hit the phalanx on their right flank. The armored horses plowed through the unprotected phalangites with their shields and spears facing forward and away from the attacking force. The armored horses trampled and crushed hundreds.

John led the infantry with his war hammer swinging. They cut a wedge formation of fury right into the heart of the phalanx, which kept their edges from being surrounded.

The Seleucid cavalry took too long to figure out what was happening and reconfigure for a counterattack. The hasidim were already deep into the Seleucid ranks.

Panic spread amongst the phalangites. Dropping their long sarissai and shields as unusable, they sought to draw their short swords. But the hasidim had been too quick and efficient in their attack. The unified power of the phalanxes dissolved into scattered, undirected individuals with nothing but short swords. They were cut down in a frenzy of hasidim righteous rage.

From his mount, Judah could see the rear of the phalanxes retreating toward camp. The front phalangites that had escaped were running away into the plains south toward Edom. Judah's strike force of terror had worked. The Seleucid army had been split into two, then wedged in the side and plunged into chaos. Their numbers no longer mattered.

Their only downside was that he could not see Nicanor anywhere leading his troops. Was he gone? Was that why they seemed so unorganized? Or was he hiding like a coward?

Judah had victory in his grasp. If he could only sustain it.

Inside the Seleucid camp, Simon and Jonathan had created such massive death and destruction with their surprise attack that the Seleucid soldiers began running away. Some of them ran toward the field where Judah's men met them with horses, swords, and spears.

The Seleucid forces now ran desperately in all directions. Some took the western path back to Philistia. Some of Judah's forces followed them.

He and his brothers returned to the decimated Seleucid camp to regroup. The plains and camp were both littered with thousands of dead enemy soldiers. He noticed some hasidim already plundering supplies and wealth.

He had a trumpet sound the call and announced to his men, "Warriors of Adonai! God has remembered his covenant with our ancestors and has crushed this army before us like he crushed the forces of Pharaoh at the Red Sea! Now all the Gentiles will know that there is one who redeems and saves Israel!"

The men cheered.

"But do not plunder the enemy yet because our battle is not finished! Gorgias has returned!" Judah pointed to the open field a half mile away.

Turning, the Jewish troops saw Gorgias's six thousand warriors amassed on the plain a mile or so out. The Edomite chief must have gotten halfway to Jerusalem before he had discovered the ruse.

But he was back.

Judah felt a wave of smoke wash over him from behind. The burning camp had resulted in a column of smoke that rose to heaven like a signal of death. He watched Gorgias and his army staring at them, transfixed by the sight. What was the Edomite chief thinking? What was he planning to do?

Suddenly, the chief raised his banner and bolted off to the south away from Judah and his men.

He ran away.

At Judah's side, Eleazar screamed out, "Go back to hell, Edomite! And take your cursed people with you!"

The hasidim cheered with victory. Judah smiled at John, standing next to him with bloody hammer in hand. Simon and Jonathan were there as well on their horses, all five brothers together.

Judah led them in a chant with their new watchword. "By God's help! By God's help!"

The soldiers all joined in, swords and spears and axes held high. "By God's help! By God's help!"

Judah turned to his brothers. "Now the soldiers can plunder. But make sure to save a generous helping of the silver and gold for the widows and orphans of our people. And for the love of God, don't leave a single weapon of the enemy behind. We'll need every one of them for what is coming."

On the ride back to Mizpah, Judah could not stop thinking of what Eleazar had yelled at Gorgias. The reality of the past few years had made it clear to him that the Edomites really had proven to be perpetual enemies of the people of Jacob. It humbled him and made him reconsider the anger and hatred he had directed toward his parents when he was young. He now recognized that their insistence Judah not intermarry with an Edomite was not cruel as he had thought then in his naivete. It had been kind and wise to the ignorance of his youth.

Edom. What had the prophet Amos meant when he had said that in coming days God would rebuild the house of David and possess the remnant of Edom and all Gentile nations called by his name?

Could Messiah redeem these cast-off people when he came? The rejected ones like Edom? The Gentiles who knew not God? It was almost too bizarre to consider.

When Judah arrived back in Mizpah, he discovered that Princess Laodice and her maidservants had left the camp with the envoy of soldiers he had left at her disposal. He had told her she could request their escort to the coast at any time, and now she was gone.

Judah stood before her empty tent as one of the guards handed him a sealed letter she had left for him. He slipped back to his tent to read it alone.

My dear Judah,

I am writing you this letter because I could not say goodbye to you in person without being overwhelmed with emotion.

You have overwhelmed me. I wish I could have been for you what you needed. But I see now that you were right.

You have exposed me to a world that I never imagined. To a god and religion that I had severely misunderstood. Your integrity and honor are like none I have ever met in a man. You have made me question everything I believe, and I am better for it.

As you once told me, I now tell you, you have changed me. I will never forget you.

I have left for Joppa on the coast with the envoy you gave me. Thank you for your protection and provision. But I will not be returning to Antioch. I will be sailing to Rome to tend to my brother Demetrius, who remains hostage there. One day I believe he will be released and will become the rightful king of Seleucia. And when that day comes, I want him to know what I know and to rule with a just and merciful hand.

*May your god bless you and guard you. May he make his
face shine upon you and give you peace.*

Your friend, Laodice

Judah squeezed the parchment in his hand with a groan of
emotional anguish. The crumpling beneath his fingers felt like his own
heart breaking. He was overwhelmed. He knew he had done the right
thing. He knew his choice for holiness would not be easy. He had loved
her. But he loved his God more. That didn't erase the pain. But it made
it more bearable, knowing that he had chosen a higher love that would
last forever.

He prayed that one day she would too.

• • • • •

Antioch

Lysias sat on the throne in the king's hall, feeling powerful as he looked
down upon the visages of General Nicanor and Gorgias, that hairy
Edomite goat he had deployed to hunt the Maccabean rebels.

They had returned from battle with the Jews at Emmaus, a thirteen-
day march from Antioch.

Lysias could feel his anger rising with the incompetent fools before
him. Nicanor, a young, pretty-boy blonde Greek, had explained the
battle of Emmaus. Gorgias had described how he had been taken in by
the ruse of the fleeing enemy. Both had fled in the face of the cunning
strategy of Judah Maccabee.

Nicanor had escaped by dressing as a slave and running away to
avoid being captured. The coward. He was an inexperienced officer

who had climbed the ladder of power through nepotism. His father was a powerful senator in Macedonia. Lysias should never have bowed to the pressure. Sighing, the high commander let the failed leaders squirm in silence at the foot of the steps before him.

The royal heir Eupator sat beside Lysias as his continuing ward. King Antiochus was still somewhere in the bowels of Persia sucking her blood like a parasite.

Lysias glared at the general and his chief as he spoke words to Eupator. "This is a worthy teaching moment, my student."

He liked calling the ignorant little moron "my student." It was a way to subtly denigrate his status below that of Lysias. He was grooming the crown prince to depend upon him for everything. Lysias dreaded the day he would have to give up the power he had been given. He had already begun scheming how he might forestall that event even if it required regicide.

He continued his lesson. "Sometimes, you will encounter individuals who have achieved a certain … position or status that they do not deserve to hold." Lysias glared at Nicanor. "Perhaps they once did but no longer."

He looked over at Gorgias. "Or perhaps they never did. They simply bribed or blackmailed their way to the top."

Gorgias glanced away, guilty as charged.

"In any case, you will be faced with an incompetence that will frustrate you to no end. But you must keep your composure. The people do not respect a ruler who cannot control himself. At least in public. Do what you will in private, but in public restrain yourself. As for acts of incompetence by your subjects, sometimes if you want something done right, you have to do it yourself."

Lysias spoke to the Syrian. "General Nicanor, I want you to gather for me the largest force of soldiers you can muster from every corner of the kingdom. It's time I show you children how a grown-up hunts a lion."

CHAPTER 61

The Road to Beth-Zur
One Year Later

Judah rode at the head of his army of ten thousand soldiers through a wadi ravine ten miles south of Jerusalem on his way to Beth-Zur. After Judah had bested Lysias's generals at the battle of Emmaus last year, the Seleucid forces had withdrawn to Antioch. For months, the land had rest from battle.

Judah had then received intelligence that Lysias was amassing a huge army of Seleucid regulars and foreign mercenaries for his own campaign into Judea. As the winter turned into spring, Lysias had ordered all his forces out of Jerusalem to aid in his massive campaign. A regiment of three thousand Seleucids were left in the holy city to secure the Akra fortress and temple area.

Judah knew he had to seize upon the opportunity. That fall, the hasidim of Jerusalem had opened the gates, and Judah had marched his forces in without opposition. The Seleucids had holed themselves up in both fortress and temple while Menelaus remained in the protective custody of the Seleucid Captain Nico. Judah had taken the rest of the city for his purposes.

Rather than waste time and soldiers in a long, costly siege of the well-fortified Akra, Judah had decided to turn his attention to preparing his army to meet Lysias on the battlefield. The fortress and temple would come later. For now, he had a temporary base in the city from which he could execute his war plans.

Lysias had recently returned from Antioch to take back Jerusalem. He had besieged the city of Beth-Zur, a stronghold for both supply routes and access to Jerusalem. Judah was marching out to meet him on the plains around Beth-Zur.

For the last three years since the start of the Maccabean Revolt, Judah had fought against King Antiochus with guerilla tactics and a small fighting force. But as his victories increased, his recruitment had grown to ten thousand Jewish soldiers and hasidim warriors. A real army that made winning this war a real possibility.

Judah had spent months training them for battle in open field practice. He had built several phalanxes for infantry combat, armed battalions of archers and slingers, and increased his troops of cavalry to two thousand.

They were still outnumbered, but they had a fighting chance. Lysias had amassed his army outside the city of Beth-Zur in his first preparation for attack on Jerusalem. Judah was on his way to head off his adversary and face him for the first time on a level battlefield. If he could achieve a victory over Lysias at Beth-Zur, he would have the momentum to return to Jerusalem and finally cleanse the temple of the Abomination of Desolation that remained a polluting presence for both city and sanctuary.

A scout approached Judah and his captains at the lead of the train. Judah gestured to stop. The order passed all the way back through the cavalry, infantry, archers, and baggage train.

The scout was weathered and worn from his riding. He said, "General, go no further. The city is just down the bend in the wadi. General Lysias and his army are outside the walls of Beth-Zur. He has captured the city."

Judah turned to his brothers and the other captains of thousands. "Have the men set up camp. Simon, John, Eleazar, Jonathan, come with me to get the lay of the land."

They galloped down the wadi toward their destination of war.

• • • • •

Jerusalem

Menelaus had been spending time with his boy when he was called away by the Akra fort captain Nico. The captain's quarters were in the far side of the citadel, the safest location in the fort, a dreary stone edifice that Menelaus had gotten sick of living in all these months since moving in for his protection. That had been about a year ago, but it felt like a decade, and this fortress felt like a prison. He just wanted to get out of here. He wanted the war to be over with. He wanted Judah captured and hanged so they could all get back to normal.

Walking through the open courtyard, Menelaus saw the numerous guards on the walls high above. Others filled the courtyard below performing drills in their full regalia of armor and weapons. They had been holed up in this godforsaken fortress for too long with Judah's control of the city proper. The high priest was feeling like a prisoner, not a defender, and it often brought on fits of anger in him.

As he approached the captain's quarters, Menelaus was reminded of his envy of the captain's favor with Lysias, the supreme commander of the Seleucid forces and co-regent with the child Eupator. What was he, nine or ten years old? Menelaus fantasized about what he would like to teach that child-king in his bed. He had heard word King Antiochus would be returning from Persia soon. Maybe he would finally put his foot down and rescue Menelaus.

Arriving at Nico's quarters, Menelaus was ushered in by a guard. He saw what looked like a Jewish soldier standing sheepishly in waiting. Captain Nico closed the door behind him. The soldier looked scared. He was young, no more than sixteen or seventeen years old. He had ruddy cheeks, a soft face, doe's eyes, and curly long hair with only the faintest of a beard coming in. He looked delicious.

"This is Rhodocus," Nico said. "He is a deserter from Judah's army."

"I'm not a deserter," squeaked the young soldier. "I was forced to join by my village. I don't believe in the cause of Judah Maccabee. I'm a Hellenist. I believe he is a threat to democracy."

"So, you deserted him," said Nico.

"I'm no traitor!" exclaimed the young soldier.

"No one is calling you a traitor, Rhodocus," said Menelaus in a reassuring tone. "You are amongst friends here. I don't support the Maccabees either. And our good captain, well, he is a Seleucid soldier who is not so nuanced in his choice of words." He paused thoughtfully. "In fact, I would go so far as to say that desertion of Judah's army is loyalty to Judea."

The kid appeared to calm down. Menelaus gave Nico a scolding look. He said to Rhodocus, "Please sit down."

Menelaus sat at a table with him and asked Nico, "Captain, could I presume upon your goodness to give this fine young man a drink?"

Nico grudgingly got a couple of bronze cups and a bottle of wine. He placed them on the table. Menelaus picked up the wine and poured some in each cup. He lifted his and toasted Rhodocus.

The soldier drank deep. Menelaus watched him closely while sipping his own. He set down his cup and queried, "Now, tell me how you came to be in your situation."

Rhodocus looked around skittishly. "Like I said, I'm a Hellenist. But the Jews in my village were not. So when Judah came around with his army, everyone joined him. What was I supposed to do? He probably would have killed me if I didn't."

"You're right," said Menelaus. "He would have. Go on."

Rhodocus continued, "After the battle of Emmaus, my regiment of hasidim had chased the escaping Seleucid soldiers all the way to Gazara. There must have been a couple thousand Seleucids who had run into the city and seized two large towers as their defense.

"When Judah arrived with the rest of our forces, he demanded to be let in through the city gates with access to the towers where the soldiers were. But the city refused. So Judah besieged them for four days until some of our men stormed the walls and took over the city gates. Judah then put the towers to flame, burning alive thousands of refugees. He didn't even offer them surrender."

"That's Judah," said Menelaus.

Rhodocus turned pale with nausea. "I can still hear their screams of agony. Thousands of men who were no different than me, just on different sides of a war. With wives and children and families like me, fighting for their cause just like the Jews fight for theirs."

Menelaus encouraged him, "Just wanting their own land in Philistia."

Rhodocus continued, "There was a large temple of Astarte in the city, the Canaanite goddess of fertility and war. Well, Judah tore it down and turned it into rubble. Then he ordered us to kill every single adult male of the city. No exceptions. He had us round them up and slaughter them in cold blood."

The young soldier broke down in tears.

"Atrocity," said Menelaus. He kept feeding the young man's emotional pain and outrage. He placed his hand comfortingly on Rhodocus's back.

"I couldn't eat or sleep for days," Rhodocus whimpered through his tears. "I couldn't live with myself."

"But you lived," said Menelaus. "Because you're strong."

Rhodocus seemed to draw strength from the affirmation and wiped dry his tears. "I wanted to kill myself, but I couldn't. I stayed with Judah's army until now. I came to you because I thought that maybe I could atone for my sins at the temple."

He looked up at Menelaus, searching for redemption.

Menelaus had been thinking this through the entire time the kid had been talking. He said, "You came to the right place. There is atonement for you. There is redemption."

Rhodocus's eyes brightened with hope.

Menelaus went on, "You left Jerusalem with Judah?"

"Yes."

"Where is he now?"

"Just ten miles south on the road to Beth-Zur. Lysias has besieged that city. Judah is encamped a couple miles north waiting for Lysias to march toward Jerusalem."

Menelaus now understood. He muttered, "So that's where the supplies are going."

He shared a knowing look with Nico, who had also seen a train of guarded foodstuffs preparing to leave the city. Menelaus leaned in close to the young soldier. He could smell his sweat, his musty odor, and it excited the priest.

"Your salvation is near, Rhodocus. An act that will free you from the guilt of your sin that haunts you."

The soldier looked up at him, pleading. Menelaus said, "Captain Nico will give you a guarded escort to Lysias's camp at Beth-Zur. You will tell Lysias about the route of Judah's supply train."

Rhodocus's face dropped with revelation.

"Lysias can then send a squad to intercept the supplies and keep them from getting to Judah."

Menelaus could see in the kid's eyes that he was going to have to do something again that he didn't want to do. So, Menelaus made sure he would follow through with it.

"As high priest of this temple in Jerusalem, I can assure you that such a mission would be the very act of redemption that would cleanse your past. Rest assured that I will make a guilt offering on your behalf in the temple."

Menelaus deliberately avoided saying to which god. He didn't know how deep the kid's Hellenism was or whether he embraced sacrifices to Zeus over Yahweh. In truth, the Greek priests of Zeus still controlled the temple and continued to administer burnt offerings to the Greek Olympian alone.

But the kid didn't know that. He just needed an incentive. So Menelaus gave it to him. "But you must hurry. The supply train will be going out soon."

Menelaus felt a shudder of hope. This was exactly what he needed to gain Lysias's favor and finally stick a knife into Judah's back for everything he had done to Menelaus—and the king. For everything he had done to Judea.

CHAPTER 62

Road to Beth-Zur
One Week Later

Judah Maccabee had been waiting in his encampment just north of Beth-Zur. Waiting for Lysias to make a move from his siege of the city and out onto the field for battle. Judah always maintained the upper hand in such confrontations by organizing his strategy toward the weakness of the enemy's formation. He who made the first move was at a disadvantage.

But Lysias had not moved for a week. Beth-Zur was on an elevated hill, which meant the Seleucid general's position was strong and could not be assailed. So Judah had to wait.

And now the hasidim army's supply train of food from Jerusalem was late. His men were weakened by hunger and thirst, eating roots, plants, and berries. Ten thousand men quickly turned any local bivouac area into a barren wasteland void of sustenance.

"Judah," said Simon. "The messenger scout has not returned. Lysias's strategy is clear. He has sabotaged our supply train. He's starving us out."

Judah was standing in his war tent counseling with his brothers and six commanders of thousands in the early hours before dawn. A map of the area was spread out on a table with small carved pieces representing the forces of both sides in the field.

"Send an armed search party to Jerusalem," Judah said.

"We may be too late," Simon responded. "Our men have not eaten in days. We are outnumbered three to one in every unit, phalanx, cavalry, archers, infantry."

Eleazar butted in. "Same odds as Emmaus."

"Oh?" Simon countered. "And were there twenty war elephants and hundreds of chariots at Emmaus like we now face? I counted twenty elephants out there."

Eleazar shrugged. "Elephants are not invincible."

"No, they are not. But we lack experience battling them, and we lack experience facing the enemy in standard formation."

"Well, we have to start some time," Eleazar quipped.

"Yes. But have you ever faced the whirling blades of a scythe chariot, Eleazar?"

Scythe chariots were heavily armored four-horse chariots that had scythe blades sticking out of their wheels and from the yokes and horse chainmail. They cut through human bodies like flowers.

Eleazar didn't respond.

Simon added, "We also have newly trained phalanx units with no real experience against hardened expert Seleucid phalanxes."

Judah had been training eight phalanx units of two thousand soldiers total for the past five months with the Seleucid equipment they had confiscated from the fields of their victories.

"I understand we have always fought against the odds and against the numbers," Simon went on. "But our strength was in our surprise and the fact that we never faced them directly on the battlefield and in strict formation. Not against Apollonius, not against Seron, nor Nicanor, nor all the others."

Judah quietly considered his brother's words.

"I don't know, Simon," said Eleazar, "I think you are definitely a naysayer."

Simon ignored his little brother and kept focused on Judah. "I am not saying to follow my advice, Judah. I am saying to follow *your own advice*. Your own wisdom and experience. I beg you, do not face Lysias on his own terms in standard formation. A level battlefield is not level for us yet."

"You are right," said Judah, which stifled both Simon and Eleazar. "Surprise has been our strength. But we no longer have the element of surprise. Or the advantage of our guerrilla tactics because of our size. Lysias has avoided narrow wadis and ravines for travel where we attacked from the heights. He's always prepared now for our stealth night attacks and supply train raids."

Eleazar quipped, "Now he's using our own tactics against us."

"We still have our retreat strategy," Simon interrupted. "I say we withdraw now, exact damage when they chase, and fall behind the protective walls of Jerusalem."

Judah said, "There is something I haven't told you yet. I have reason to believe King Antiochus may be here at the battle."

A hush went over the men. One of the captains with scars of experienced battle across his face said, "But the king is in Persia."

Another captain asked, "How do you know this, general?"

"There's been rumors of the king returning," said Judah. "The intelligence is not solid."

He looked each of his men in the eye as he continued, "But when we scouted their forces, I saw the king's armored elephant in their war herd. I know it well from my time in the Royal Guard. It is the royal carrier. If it is true that Antiochus is in this battle, we have an unprecedented opportunity that could change the course of this war."

Eleazar had lightened up with fervor. He jumped in. "And I will be the one to lance that festering boil with my javelin."

Eleazar had become obsessed with his desire to kill the abominable king from the day they had begun their revolt. Judah knew he wasn't going to stop his little brother on his quest for significance. He just hoped he could keep him alive.

At that moment, a messenger entered the tent, a young lad with windswept hair and frightened eyes. "General, a report from Captain Benjamin on the plain. Lysias is assembling formation on the battlefield."

A pall of dread swept over the commanders.

Judah said, "Our luxury of deliberation is over. The battle has come to us. Make the call to assemble our forces."

CHAPTER 63

The Plains of Beth-Zur

Judah's army had been mustered in the narrow ravine that opened up to the wide plains of the battlefield. Eleazar had been asked by Judah to read a passage to the soldiers from the Torah about God's orders to Joshua to conquer the Promised Land.

> My servant Moses is dead. Now proceed to cross the Jordan, you and all this people, into the land that I am giving to them. Every place that the sole of your foot will tread upon I have given to you. No one shall be able to stand against you all the days of your life. I will be with you; I will not fail you or forsake you. Be strong and courageous; for you shall put this people in possession of the land that I swore to their ancestors to give them. Only be strong and courageous, being careful to act in accordance with all the law that my servant Moses commanded you; do not turn from it to the right hand or to the left. For then you shall make your way prosperous, and then you shall be successful. For the Lord your God is with you wherever you go.

Instead of giving a long speech to his weary men, Judah prayed a short prayer to their mighty God.

> Blessed are you, O Savior of Israel. Hem in this army by the hand of your people Israel and let them be ashamed of

their troops and their cavalry. Fill them with cowardice. Melt the boldness of their strength. Let them tremble in their destruction. Strike them down with the sword of those who love you. And let all who know your name praise you. For it is in you that we live and move and have our very being.

Then he led them in a chant of their watchwords. "By God's help! By God's help! By God's help!"

The Maccabean army marched out to the plains just north of Beth-Zur to face the enemy. They lined up in formation. Two thousand light infantry, including swordsmen, archers, and slingers—all called "skirmishers"—led the front lines. Behind them, eight phalanx units spread out wide in syntagma arrangement of sixteen men wide by sixteen men deep. A thousand units of cavalry guarded each flank of that phalanx spread for a total of eight thousand troops.

Judah held two thousand troops in reserve in the ravine for his retreat strategy. Standing on a hillside with his horse, he assessed the battlefield.

Lysias had twice the light infantry with the addition of scythe chariots behind them. Behind those were eight phalanx syntagma units to match Judah's—with a complete second row of eight more phalanx syntagma behind those. At the very back were the heavy infantry guarding twenty war elephants with wood carriages on their backs housing archers.

The lead elephant was the royal carrier that Judah had recognized earlier. The mighty beast wore bronze armor on its forehead and legs with a drape of chainmail on its back. It supported a specially armored carriage for the king and his supreme commander, Lysias of Damascus.

From this distance, Judah could not tell if the rumors were true about the king having returned from Persia. He prayed that they were. He prayed for his brother Eleazar.

The Seleucid flanks were guarded by double the numbers of the Maccabean cavalry. This included the wild Scythian Amazonian horse warriors of the Pontus region Judah had heard so much about. In all, he estimated there were about twenty thousand on the field, double his own forces. Significant thousands of soldiers were no doubt being held back to guard the camp of Beth-Zur, a strategic defense in light of Judah's surprise attack at the battle of Emmaus.

With the elephants, chariots, and Amazons, Judah figured the total power arraigned against them was triple that of the Jewish freedom fighters. He patted his white stallion's muscular neck and whispered, "You have been a loyal steed. We've been through much together. I ask for one more time, my friend."

Judah heard the horse whinny as if answering him with assurance. He had stopped calling his horse by the Hellenist name of Pegasus years ago when he had turned back to the faith of his forefathers. He had his trumpeter announce their call to ready, then raced down from his observation point to join his men.

The Seleucid trumpet sounded the call to attack just as Judah arrived at the front behind the skirmishers. He braced himself for the most important battle of his life.

Judah's light infantry moved out first. He saw Lysias's infantry move forward. Then their forces split down the middle, spreading to the left and to the right like a parting sea. From the middle of that sea of enemies came the chariots. Four-horse scythe chariots.

There must have been two hundred of them.

They poured forth and attacked Judah's skirmishers. A single armored charioteer reined each set of horses. These wore small bronze plate armor blanketing their backs with bronze shields on their foreheads. They had two shafts for yokes between the four abreast warhorses. Long poles with scythe blades jutted forward from those yokes and over the sides of the horses toward the enemy. Scythe blades stuck out several feet from the axels and two more from the wheel wells, creating a rotating, chopping blade.

The chariots plowed through the infantry forces, scattering soldiers and cutting them to pieces in the rotating blades. Dozens of men were cut down and trampled. The defensive reaction was not to confront the unstoppable bladed beasts but to dodge, run, and dive for cover. The initial foray of the scythed chariots was devastating in creating terror and chaos amidst the Jewish infantry forces.

But the chariots were heavily laden and cumbersome. They could not turn sharply, and they would not face the multitude of long pikes of the phalanx waiting behind their tightly-woven shields. As the chariots slowed and turned, Judah shouted. His archers aimed for the horses and their riders with their composite bows. The hanging metal plates protected the horses to some degree. But arrows pulled with good force could still find their way between the chinks of the armor. Others hit necks or rumps. The effect was not to kill the horses but to frighten them with sharp pain that made them panic.

Some reared, exposing their underbellies to lethal hits. But most of them turned and bolted in fright—away from the Jewish line and back to the Seleucid infantry. The charioteers who had survived the onslaught of arrows were unable to stop their stampeding steeds any more than the riderless carriages.

The result was a chaotic rampage of rotating blades against Lysias's own infantry! It took several minutes before they could calm the horses and lead them through a gauntlet off the field. Judah could tell the days of that peculiar experimental weapon were numbered. They created an initial impression of dread and fear, but they were not as successful for maintaining the forward advantage on the field.

Judah's light infantry regrouped with but few more causalities than the Seleucids had procured from their own devices. Both sides retired their infantry to the rear as their phalanx units now slowly moved toward each other, war trumpets blazing.

The phalanx had been the Macedonian Greek strength from the days of Alexander until now. Judah had stolen most of his phalanx armor and weapons from their defeat of Seleucid forces, so they were dressed in similar but lesser uniform: long shields of wood, chainmail or leather cuirasses and breastplates, shin greaves, short sword, and a two-handed *sarissa* pike, twenty feet long.

The Seleucid phalanxes were more uniform in their heavier bronze plated armor with bronze gilded shields, bronze greaves, and helmets. Altogether, these created in the rising light of the morning sun the effect of a blinding line of torches setting the field on fire. They moved slowly because of the complexity of the large, tightly-knit units that had to move together.

That lack of speed was a big weakness of their mighty formation.

Big John commanded the heavy phalanxes from behind the lines on his steed along with another hasidim leader. John hated the fact that he could not participate more directly in the battle, but his experience would be crucial to leading the hasidim to their goal of victory. He knew how these Greek bastards fought.

John had faced phalanxes before and decimated them from their flanks. But this time would be different. This time they were facing the enemy phalanx head-on. He had always supported Judah's leadership choices, but this time he wondered if his brother Simon's skepticism had been warranted.

The rival phalanxes were within a hundred yards of each other. The front four lines lowered their pikes forward toward the enemy, creating a wicket of penetrating spears. The twelve rows of phalangites behind them pointed their *sarissai* into the sky until they were needed to be lowered into the battle. As forward rows fell, rear rows would become the new front lines.

Simon led the right-flank cavalry of the Maccabean forces. Before the phalanx units could meet, he heard the sound of the Seleucid trumpets call out their opposing cavalry. The typical goal was for cavalry units to break through on the flanks of the phalanxes and attack the vulnerable sides of the formation. But first they had to get through their opponent's cavalry. Simon trumpeted his horsemen to meet them in full force.

As he raced into battle, Simon saw the infamous Amazon warriors he had heard so much about accompanying Thracian horsemen that composed the Seleucid units. The Amazons were women who looked a bit like men with short or wild-colored hair, painted faces, and tattooed bodies. They wore leather pants on their mostly bareback horses without stirrups. They maneuvered their wild-looking mounts with superior jockeying, and they handled their bows with expert marksmanship.

The Maccabean cavalry had no equivalent horseback archers. Simon saw too many of his riders hit with the Amazonian missiles. He had learned that they also laced their arrows with poison and barbed tips, so each hit was more than a wound. It was a death sentence.

How long could Simon's lesser forces hold the line?

In the middle of the battlefield, Big John's heavy phalanx units met the Seleucids with a clash of arms. Pikes on both sides rammed into shields, snapping spear points. Others found their way through openings to pierce their opponents. As some men fell, other openings in the wall of shields invited more thrusting pikes with more deadly effect.

John could see his men fall, only to be replaced by others from the rear to fill in the vulnerable holes. It was clear his phalanxes simply didn't have the experience and teamwork that marked the Seleucid forces. He could see his forces falling and regrouping at a higher rate than his enemy's.

They were losing ground—rapidly.

In the clash of cavalries on the flanks, Simon saw his men fighting the Thracian light cavalry with their javelins and swords while being picked off by Amazons firing their missiles from a safe distance. He called a couple of his finest horsemen with him to target the Amazons and stem their attacks.

Simon cut off the arm of one Amazonian just before she launched an arrow. Turning his head, he saw another female warrior aiming at him. He reacted without even thinking, arching back in his saddle as an arrow whisked right past his face. He spun back and sliced through the hind leg of a horse beside him. This brought the beast rolling to the ground, crushing the small female rider beneath it.

Taking stock of the situation around him, Simon recognized that the Amazonians were too elusive for his men. They were smaller, lighter, and better suited for their sniping. The Maccabean cavalry needed to get close to fight with their swords or spears while the Amazons attacked from a distance with their bows.

Simon pulled his short horn and blew for reinforcements.

Judah had prepared for this possibility by ordering the archers from the light infantry to retreat, not to the rear guard but to the side lines. When they heard the horn, they began hunting for Amazons with their bows amidst the melee.

Simon noticed that Eleazar had joined the archers, wielding his lethal javelins with pinpoint accuracy. One, two, three Amazons were taken down in mere seconds by Eleazar's fury. Lastly, he impaled what looked like the Amazonian captain of their command, an ostentatiously dressed woman with two bodyguards protecting her.

The move helped Simon to hold the line. But he could feel the line was faltering. They were simply outnumbered and were being picked off too easily by Amazons with their bows.

He thought to himself, *Come down off those horses and see how lethal you are.*

After several hours of clashing combat, Judah could see his army was not standing firm. Whatever advantage he had gained with a new army to match Lysias directly, he had lost through inexperience and numbers. Simon had been right. It had been a mistake for his untested army to fight the Greeks on their own terms by their own rules with their own tactics—and against such odds. Judah had become proud, presumptuous, and his men were now paying for it.

It was time to go back to doing things the old way—the way through which God had blessed them. Judah prayed it wasn't too late.

The general had joined his brother's horsemen in defending the right flank. Pulling back, he met his trumpeter in the rear and ordered a retreat. The trumpeter blew his horn. A ripple of recognition rolled across the Maccabean forces.

The infantry pulled back, making a break for the wadi opening a half mile back. The phalangites pulled away, strapped their shields on their backs, and followed them, running for their lives.

The cavalry continued to hold the line until the infantry could make it to the ravine. Simon saw that the Greek phalanxes did not follow. Instead, they opened up and allowed the war elephants, surrounded by a hundred heavy cavalry each, to lead the way after their prey.

They were going to chase the Maccabees and hunt them all down.

Simon led the cavalry units in retreat through the wadi ravine.

The Jewish dead on the battlefield surely told Lysias that Judah's retreat was desperate. There was no time for setting a trap in such chaos. The Maccabees had suffered massive losses. They had been crippled. They were fleeing.

But Simon also knew Judah was not without a plan.

CHAPTER 64

Judah's forces had escaped the battlefield through the narrow ravine that opened up to a new valley half a mile north. The Maccabean army regrouped there and took formation to face their Seleucid pursuers. That small canyon passageway became a dangerous bottleneck that allowed Judah an advantage. The Maccabees would only have to fight a single battalion at a time as they emerged through the opening into the valley. The rest of the Seleucid train behind them would be blocked and surrounded by steep hillsides on either side of the defile.

Unfortunately for Judah, Lysias had not led through the valley with his phalanx units but with his war elephants surrounded by heavy infantry wearing bronze-plated armor.

The Maccabean forces had never faced elephants in battle. They had also never faced phalanxes or cavalry in standard formation until today. And they had failed at that. So it was not looking hopeful for Judah's chances. If he failed to stop the enemy's advance through the ravine, it might be the end of the Maccabean revolt. All of Judea would return under the thumb of tyranny as well as continued idolatry in the temple.

This could very well be their last stand.

Judah wondered if his men were willing to fight to the last man. They had been with him for these three years through thick and thin. They had been on the run, faced innumerable odds, starvation, and much suffering for their freedom. They had become a better fighting force and had proven their loyalty through it all.

But this would be their ultimate test. Would they rise to the challenge? Would they accept death once again? They had never been beaten so badly before. Judah wondered if their morale had been defeated, if their hope had finally been crushed. They could fight with less men, less weapons, and less advantage if they maintained their hope. But when hope was gone, they had nothing left with which to fight. God had not failed them before. But it had never seemed so hopeless until now.

Judah could see the first elephants arriving in the defile. They were surrounded by the super-heavy cavalry, the cataphracts, that could quite easily collapse what was left of Judah's phalanx units. Their full-scaled armor and solid helmets with sculpted soulless faces were frightening enough. Their long ten-foot pikes with iron tips made them a mobile phalanx fighting unit.

Judah gave a trumpet call for his cavalry to meet them at the bottleneck before they could break out into the open plain. Simon led them into the fray. The Jewish cavalry weren't as heavily armored as the cataphracts, but they were faster and more flexible in their movements.

Eleazar was beside him. "Judah, look at the first elephant in the lead."

It was the royal carrier, the heavily-armored war elephant that might be carrying King Antiochus himself. Seven archers surrounded Lysias their commander, his red plume flowing in the breeze from his bronze helmet.

"I don't see the king," Judah said.

"I see him," Eleazar barked. "Behind the archers. They're shielding him."

He looked pleadingly at Judah. "This is it, brother. If I can take out the king, it will change the course of the battle *and the war*."

Judah knew he couldn't stop his brother's quest for glory. But this was their last stand. They were all facing the impossible and would probably die. "Go with God, Eleazar."

Eleazar smiled at Judah. "I'd say I'll see you in the Resurrection, but I'm not planning on dying. I'll be right back."

He took off on foot. Judah prayed that he would indeed be right back with the blood of Antiochus on his javelin.

Otherwise, Judah would in fact see his brother in the Resurrection.

Judah saw Big John with his phalanx waiting their turn for battle. This was it. Judah gestured to him, and the two bolted off around the phalanx to make their way up into the hills on the left side of the arriving army.

Simon's cavalry hit the first cataphracts and war elephant. Their pikes clashed with armor. War cries abounded as the competing cavalries battled, bringing the elephant to a standstill. The archers in the armored carriage took out targets from the safety of their positions high above. Jewish archers returned fire from the flanks. The general sported a shield while the king seemed to stay low and behind his wall of soldiers.

Eleazar moved on foot like a panther behind the Maccabean horses. His sight was locked in on Lysias leading the forces from his perch atop the elephant. He carried three javelins for his mission. They were made from cornel wood. Light, flexible, and strong. Their bronze metal tips were long, thin and quadrangular, giving Eleazar a sleek design for the throw—with a devasting impact.

He knew he didn't have much time. If this first elephant broke through, the others would stream in like an avalanche of boulders, crushing everything in their path. He had to stop it. He had to kill the king and supreme commander.

Eleazar dodged in between battling horses of both sides, finding his way through a moving labyrinth of death. He saw a Jewish brother about to get skewered to death. But he couldn't help him. He had his mission.

Dodging around, Eleazar found himself within a dozen feet of the side of the massive pachyderm. He could see Lysias commanding at his post twelve feet above. Where was the head of that miserable tyrant?

He had to move quickly. Dropping two javelins in the dirt, he hefted a third in his hand. He juggled it for a good feel and reared back.

Eleazar saw the general drop his shield for just a moment. In that moment, he launched his missile of death. But at the last second, an archer moved in front of the commander, taking the spear through his chest. The mortally-wounded man collapsed and dropped his bow, hanging over the ledge of the carriage.

Eleazar cursed and reached to pick up a second javelin. As he stood up, he saw a second archer above aiming at him and releasing. A second later, he felt the burning pain of an arrow going through his left shoulder. He screamed out.

But his javelin arm was untouched. He reared back to launch.

And was suddenly stabbed from behind in his right shoulder. He fell to the ground on his face. A cataphract had taken him down with a pike. He felt his life blood draining from his body.

Out of the side of his eye, Eleazar saw the huge foot of the elephant stomp down mere feet from his head. The ground rumbled like an earthquake. A small dust cloud rose from the impact.

Eleazar could feel that his right arm was now useless for a throw. He was done for. He could no longer launch his missile to take down the king—or commander.

He had failed.

But he had not given up. There was one last chance. Left for dead by the cataphract, Eleazar pushed himself upward from the dirt and picked up one of his javelins. It took everything in him just to lift the spear and hold it in front of him. But he strained against his pain and failing muscles.

Unseen by the battling cavalry around him, Eleazar ran to the front of the elephant. The huge, lumbering giant was more frightening up close with its leathery hide and mammoth trunk and tusks. He looked up. The behemoth towered over him, an impenetrable living, moving fortress rising into the sky.

Eleazar dodged a swinging tusk and pointed his javelin up at the mid-chest of the beast between the hanging chainmail where its heart would be located. Mustering the last strength left in his weakened arms, he ran into the belly of the beast. He couldn't throw the javelin, but he could ram the thing up into the monster's chest.

Eleazar felt the javelin slice through thick flesh and muscle, luckily missing any bones. He felt it hit an organ. He prayed it was the heart.

Roaring in pain, the elephant swung its tusks and trunks around in a frenzy. Eleazar dropped to the ground, dodging the swaying pendulum of death. The elephant hit one of its own Seleucid horsemen with its tusks, the force throwing man and beast a dozen feet into the air.

The elephant stumbled in confusion, roared again, and then collapsed—right down upon Eleazar, crushing him beneath its tons of flesh and bone.

Up on the hillside, Judah and John had left their horses and now stood with their two thousand hidden warriors surrounding both sides of the defile. Judah saw the elephant collapse onto his brother. He yelled, "Noooooo!!! Eleazar!!!"

The pachyderm fell and rolled to its side, crushing cataphracts and launching its riders to their deaths on the ground.

Judah and John didn't have time to weep. The huge fallen elephant was now blocking the valley entrance for all the other elephants behind him. Eleazar had stopped the advance. The army of Maccabean warriors saw it as well. They saw that the king and commander had been killed in the fall. It seemed like a second wind of spirit filled all the Jewish warriors.

They *could* stop this unstoppable advance after all. They could win.

Judah blew his horn for attack.

The first phase was a trick he had learned from his days in the Royal Seleucid Guard. He had gathered pigs from his journeys and conquests through Greek cities for this very tactic. Swine was forbidden as food by Torah, but they were collected as a secret weapon. For there was one thing that terrified war elephants and made them panic: squealing pigs.

Hasidim all along the hillside above let loose hundreds of pigs by sticking them in their rumps with arrow points or daggers. The pigs ran down the hill squealing and trying to escape their pain. The frightened elephants reared up and ran to get away from the tiny terrors, trampling their own cavalry. The northern route forward was blocked, so they turned and stampeded southward, crushing more Seleucids in their frenzy.

Maccabean warriors ran down the hills on both sides to confront the confused and broken ranks of the Seleucids.

Some carried long cables of heavily-barbed wire. They ran across the road, laying down their spiked barbs that wounded the vulnerable soles of the elephants' feet as they trampled.

Pachyderms roared and fell, crushing more Seleucid horsemen. Others multiplied the stampede with increased panic. It was a collapse of the Seleucid army into mass chaos. The soldiers began to run away back to the southern plains.

Big John swung his hammer at whatever cataphracts he could to jettison them from their mounts and crush them inside their bronze armor.

But there was one battalion that did not run: the Amazons. They lacked heavy armor so were very versatile on their war horses. They screamed high-pitched war cries and launched arrows at Judah's hillside attackers. Well-aimed arrows pierced many hasidim. But the Jewish warriors kept coming.

And then they were too close for the Amazons to use their bows. Their horses started up the hillside to meet the descending hasidim, but the terrain was too steep and rocky for horses to be effective. Dismounting, the women warriors pulled their swords, pointed axes, and spears to meet Judah's men.

The consequences were devastating. The women were wiped out by a tsunami wave of force. Judah pulled one off her mount like she was a child and crashed her to the ground.

He saw her face, an otherwise attractive female with raging eyes and a cursing mouth. It felt wrong to fight women. Women were supposed to be the ones fought for and protected. This was unnatural. But when the little creature swiped her axe and cut Judah's left arm, he shook awake and cut off her head.

Another screaming banshee ran at him with a spear. He turned and grabbed the thrusted weapon, then used it to yank the Amazon toward him, punching her in the face. She went flying backward onto the ground unconscious, her nose and cheeks smashed in.

These female "warriors" were so small, so light. They were broken so easily. It was such a difference from their horse and archery skills that had allowed them a technological advantage from a distance. But in hand-to-hand combat, it wasn't even close.

It wasn't fair.

But war was never fair. War was brutal and no place for a woman. Judah thanked Adonai their women had not been affected by the delusions of pagan religions and their goddesses. He thanked Adonai that he was fighting to protect Israel's women and that they were supporting their husbands with nurturing love that redeemed the violent impulse of war.

These female creatures were demonic hybrid monsters. Women trying to be men who lacked the brute force of men. Who lacked the strength to even carry their wounded to safety. But that didn't matter anyway because they were being slaughtered en masse by the Maccabean soldiers.

Judah saw an Amazon warrior dressed in bright Scythian color-painted leather with pointed Phrygian cap. She appeared to be a leader voicing commands and had stayed on her horse. Judah whistled, and his stallion came running down to him.

These girls think they know horses? I know horses. And my horse knows me.

Judah leapt onto his mighty white Arabian stallion without it breaking stride and steered right at the Amazon. She saw him and bolted. They galloped down the hillside past the dead elephant and onto the plain. She led Judah away from the phalanxes. He kept her on target like a lion on prey.

She was good.

But he was gaining.

Then she turned around in a surprise move and aimed her bow at him. Her horse kept going forward at full speed, but the prey was now facing her predator. It was the signature move of Scythian horse archers.

Judah had only a moment to duck. He could swear he felt the arrow pass through his hair flying in the wind.

But that was her last arrow. And his mount was faster.

Judah caught up beside the racing Amazon. She pulled out a dagger and swiped at him. He grabbed her wrist and held her tight. She jerked and squealed, but she couldn't pull loose from his iron grip.

As Judah slowed his horse down, his animal seemed to know the general's thoughts and acted to force the Amazon's mare into submission as well. They all came to a stop.

The Amazon would not stop squirming. Hatred seemed to fill her face. A face so beautiful it almost distracted Judah. Her war paint looked like Egyptian make-up, which accented her stunning facial features. She must have been in her thirties, but she was fit and lively.

Judah yanked her off her mount and over his saddle onto the ground beside him. She was so light. Like a child.

She landed with a grunt at the impact. Rolling over to face him, she tried to catch her wind. Judah got off his horse and stood over her.

She looked pathetic. He wanted to comfort her.

Throwing her dagger at her feet, he said, "Return to your people and family. Or your fellow women or whoever."

She had nothing to say.

He added, "You need some real men in your lives."

At those words, she screamed hysterically, grabbed the dagger, and got up to attack him like a panther.

He punched her once, and she fell unconscious at his feet. He still felt bad having to do it. But it *was* self-defense.

Such a waste of beauty. Judah turned to see his stallion snuggling and snorting with the Amazon's mare. "No time for romance, big fella."

He jumped up into his saddle and patted the stallion's neck. "Good boy."

And they were off back to the battlefield.

When Judah returned to the ravine, he found the hillside around them filled with the corpses of crushed, mangled Amazonian women, their horses wandering riderless phantoms. Not one Amazon was left alive.

John stood smiling with his war hammer in hand, bloodied and full of gore. The Seleucid army was on the run back to Beth-Zur without their supreme commander.

Their supreme commander. Judah had forgotten about Eleazar's sacrifice. He jumped off his mount and ran down to the head of the line where the giant war elephant lay dead, conquered by the hand of Eleazar Avaran, the Piercer.

When Judah arrived at the tangle of bodies lying around, he spotted the red-plumed commander but no king. Looking down into the face of the commander, he realized it was not Lysias at all but some other Seleucid leader in charge of the elephant squad.

Big John stepped up next to Judah, following his stare.

Judah muttered, "What a tragedy. What a waste of my brother's life."

"No," replied John. "Eleazar's life was not wasted. His act became the inspiration that led us to victory. It empowered our warriors as if he had indeed killed the supreme commander and king. And we routed the enemy just the same. That's not a tragedy, brother. That is God's help in God's way."

Judah nodded in agreement. "You're right, brother. I am humbled."

John said, "I think I know a little about such humbling as well."

Judah looked at him with a knowing smile. He had figured out the Nephilim incident with John.

Judah said, "I suppose each of us brothers in our own ways have sought our significance in achieving glory or fame. Thucydides wrote that the whole world is a graveyard of famous men."

John quoted from the prophet Isaiah, "All flesh is like grass, and all its glory like the flower of grass. The grass withers, and the flower falls, but the word of the Lord remains forever."

Looking down at the dead elephant, Judah spoke to his younger brother resting in peace somewhere beneath the beast. "Well, Eleazar, we'll see you in the Resurrection."

They held a funeral and mass burial for their dead that day. But the broken body of Eleazar was brought back to their base camp in the Gophna Hills to be buried next to their father, Mattathias ben Hasmon.

Judah had lost over a thousand men at the battle of Beth-Zur. But they all stood strong and proud knowing they had killed over five thousand of the enemy. Lysias had fled back to Antioch after receiving Judah's demand for Jewish freedom of worship in their temple.

As Judah stood with his three surviving brothers, Simon, John, and Jonathan, they said a prayer for Eleazar. Then Judah looked them each in the eye and stated resolutely, "Brothers, God has given us this victory. But we are not done."

CHAPTER 65

Jerusalem

Judah, and his brothers Simon, John, and Jonathan arrived at the gates of the holy city with their commanders of thousands and hundreds followed by a column of five thousand infantry and cavalry. They were received with much fanfare as the residents had heard of their victory at Beth-Zur. Hundreds had lined the road to the southern Dung Gate where Judah arrived. Waving ivy wreaths and palm fronds, they shouted to heaven, "Hosanna, Adonai," which meant "Save us, O Lord."

Judah led his procession all the way to the temple mount in a triumphal Pompe. In the front of his parade, he had wheeled in various artillery machines they had captured from the Seleucids over the previous year. They were prepared to besiege both the Akra fortress and the temple mount to face down Seleucid forces.

Several large wooden catapults were placed before the walls of the Akra, as well as Scorpions, huge crossbows the size of wagons that were operated by two soldiers and would fire bolts the size of small trees into the fort. The Seleucid forces watched them set up below their walls. Judah ordered a blockade of the gates to stop any sortie attacks.

Next, Judah turned his attention to the temple mount. Smoke rose from inside. It looked much more voluminous than animal sacrifices would make. He was surprised to find the gates wide open and Jewish priests beckoning them in. They were dressed in their Levitical garb. He could see no Greek priests of Zeus.

Simon rode beside Judah on his steed. He queried, "Is it a trap?"

John and Jonathan were now beside them as well. John said, "If it is, we'll be right by your side, brother general."

They walked their horses up with a battalion of a thousand soldiers and entered beneath the glorious arches thirty feet over their heads. The clip clop of their horse's hooves on the stone pavement sounded in Judah's ears like a rainfall before a storm.

They passed the colonnaded exterior and entered the outer court. Judah could now see where the smoke was coming from. The Beautiful Gate of the holy temple. Kicking his horse, he galloped all the way to the front stairs of the temple followed by his battle-ready forces.

No one was around. The Beautiful Gate had been left open as its huge wooden doors burned with flames. Judah ordered a regiment of his men to find the water cart and put the fire out before it spread.

He and his brothers got off their horses in awe before the burning gates as the smoke rose in billows. Judah dropped to his knees. Reaching up to his tunic, he ripped it. His brothers followed suit.

Glancing around at the unkept pavement, Judah brushed dirt together, which he tossed onto his head.

"Hosanna, Adonai!" he cried out in prayer.

A group of a dozen Jewish priests approached Judah and his brothers in dirty, tattered robes. The brothers stood to their feet to receive them. The leader was elderly with years of experience etched into his wrinkled face. Another priest looked so young and zealous he reminded Judah of his beloved Eleazar. Pangs of loss burned in his memory.

The general said, "I am Judah ben Mattathiah, general of the Maccabean resistance against the Greeks. Who are you?"

"Samuel," the old priest said. "Keeper of the temple grounds."

"Where is the temple guard?"

"They are outside the north gates in submission, happily awaiting your orders to enter. They will not fight. They have been waiting for this day."

"The Greek priests?"

"When they heard of your victory at Beth-Zur, they fled back to Antioch, burning the gates on their way out. And inside, they destroyed the priests' chambers."

Judah saw the golden image of Zeus through the flaming gate in the inner temple. The wavering heat and smoke made the image look eerily alive, trembling at its fate. "I see they didn't bother to take their Abomination of Desolation with them."

"No, they did not," said the priest smiling.

"And the high priest Menelaus?" Judah asked.

The old man pointed to the Akra peeking over the temple walls. "I do not think he is happy to see you."

Judah smiled. "He will not be too happy when he sees what I have in store for him."

He turned to his men. "Well, my brothers, it looks like it is finally time to clean this mess up."

He turned back to the priest. "Samuel, I am going to need your help in finding blameless priests devoted to the Law of God to help me purify the profane from this holy temple and return her to Adonai's service."

Samuel grinned wide and replied, "Sometimes God uses the voice of a prophet, and sometimes he uses a hammer."

•••••

Year 148 of the Kingdom of the Greeks, 25th day of Kislev (December), 165 B.C.

The shofar trumpet rang out from the corner of the temple. It was early morning daybreak and time for the Tamid, the morning sacrifice. This would be the first regular burnt offering in three and a half years since Antiochus Epiphanes had stopped the daily sacrifice—over six years since he had trampled the temple underfoot with his occupying forces. That had been 2,300 evening and morning sacrifices until the sanctuary was restored to its rightful state—as the prophet Daniel had predicted—and on the very day of the month it was originally profaned.

From his perch over the rebuilt Beautiful Gate, Judah looked out upon the thousands of Jewish citizens who now filled the outer courtyard of the temple in repentance and worship. His brothers Simon and John stood with him like throne guardians over their ward.

They had spent the last few weeks purifying the temple of its corruption. The first thing they had done was dismantle the Abomination of Desolation, the gilded image of Zeus Olympius that had sat before the altar. They had burned the sculpted wood, melted down the gold, and poured it into a crevice in the earth.

Priests now took two unblemished male lambs, each a year old, and slaughtered them, pouring their blood into a small bronze basin. They then used large simple brushes to sprinkle the blood on the sides and horns of a new altar. They had decided to replace the original altar that had been defiled by forbidden sacrifices. Not one stone had been left standing as they dismantled the unhewn sacred blocks and carried them away to a secret place. They would await a prophet to rise in Israel to tell them what to do with them.

They had rebuilt the altar with new unhewn stones anointed by the priests with oil and prayer for its holy function. No metal tools of man were allowed to touch Adonai's sacred altar, which had necessitated carefully chosen rocks to recreate the massive edifice forty-five feet square and fifteen feet high.

Judah watched the lambs slain and laying on the new structure. Grain offerings of flour were mixed with oil and frankincense. At the base of the altar, priests poured out drink offerings of wine.

Down below, a priest raised his hands to heaven and waited. This was an act of faith replicating King Solomon's prayer of supplication before God for the people of Israel before the original altar upon the completion and dedication of the first temple. The priest was calling upon Adonai to bring fire down from heaven and consume the burnt offerings as Adonai had done in response to Solomon's prayer. The same had occurred under Moses upon the dedication of the wilderness tabernacle and ordination of Aaron and his sons as priests. This divine fire had been the heavenly affirmation of the earthly system. That God was in their midst and he approved of both temple and altar.

Unfortunately, Judah had discovered that Menelaus the high priest had barricaded himself in the Akra but had fled in the night back to Antioch. That creature was no high priest. He was more like a harlot riding the beast of Greece. They would need to start a new line of high priests. Judah thought his brother Jonathan should be the first to take that role.

Judah noticed that the priest still stood before the altar with his hands held high. Nothing had happened for several minutes as he had stood there. The sacrifices on the altar remained untouched. No fire had come down from heaven. The priest looked agitated and confused about what to do next.

Finally, the priest motioned frantically to other priests, who lit the sacrifice with their torches. He made another gesture. Musicians quickly walked into the center and began singing a song accompanied by harp, lutes, and cymbals. It was a psalm of David calling for the arrival of Messiah to enter the temple.

> *Who shall ascend the hill of the Lord?*
> *And who shall stand in his holy place?*
> *He who has clean hands and a pure heart,*
> *Lift up your heads, O gates!*
> *And be lifted up, O ancient doors,*
> *that the King of glory may come in.*
> *Who is this King of glory?*
> *The Lord of hosts,*
> *he is the King of glory!*

It seemed to Judah like a distraction from the failed expectation of heavenly approval. They had believed that Adonai would provide the fire from heaven to legitimize the dedication of their cleansed temple and new altar. But it had not come. The hoi polloi of the masses hadn't even noticed. They continued to join in the song with joy and merriment.

But Judah was disturbed. How could they have been through so much by the hand of God, including miraculous victories and deliverances, and yet God had not shown up for the celebration and consecration? Was Adonai not returning to his temple? Why would he do all this and not return?

His musings were interrupted by Jonathan. "Judah, I have received word from the temple priests that there was not enough pure oil to keep the Menorah lit for eight days. They said they would pray for a miracle and light the lamps anyway."

That struck Judah as a lie. He had supervised the entire purification of the temple, including the recreation of the sacred instruments: the table of shewbread, the incense altar, the seven-branched lampstand, along with a new veil to cover the Holy of Holies. He had watched over the woodworkers who rebuilt the Beautiful Gate. He had made sure the replacement of the golden crown at the top of the temple was perfect. He had even personally inspected the pure olive oil set aside for the Menorah. He had seen that they had more than enough to last several weeks, let alone eight days. Why would the priests lie and say they didn't have enough?

And then it hit him. The priests needed to legitimize their consecration of the temple with a miracle. But God was not here. He had not spoken to Israel for over two hundred years. Ezekiel had seen the presence of Ha Shem leave the temple in the Babylonian exile, but he had never returned. The consecration of the temple had not brought forth the approval of fire from heaven. There was only one answer. Daniel's Seventy Weeks prophecy was not finished. The 490 years were not completed. Yahweh had not returned.

The priests were trying to create confidence in the people with an artificial "miracle" to justify a priesthood that did not have the approval of God.

What should he do? What should he say? Judah felt himself caught in a dilemma. On the one hand, God had providentially saved his people and restored his temple. Yet God had still not returned to his house. The transgression of Israel would not be finished until the Anointed One came to put an end to sin, atone for iniquity, and establish his kingdom of everlasting righteousness.

The music had stopped, and it was his moment.

Judah turned to the people and shouted as loud as he could to the crowd before the temple, "Children of Abraham, Isaac, and Jacob, listen to my words! These past several years, God has delivered us through many trials and tribulations to some defeats and many victories!"

The massive crowd cheered wildly. Judah waited until he could be heard again. "But most importantly, today marks the beginning of a new memorial in Israel to celebrate Adonai's victory and cleansing of the temple from the Abomination of Desolation! This festival shall be observed every year with joy and gladness for eight days, beginning with the twenty-fifth day of the month of Kislev! It shall be called Hanukkah, our feast of dedication of the altar and temple!"

The crowd cheered even more enthusiastically. The music started up again. For just a moment in time, the people of Israel celebrated their freedom to worship their God in peace and in their land.

Judah had never forgotten the old scribe Eleazar's mission of gathering the Scriptures together. The wicked Antiochus had been a satan to that goal by destroying any Scriptures he could find in the land. Well, now Judah would fulfill Eleazar's calling. He had sent out a command to find all those Scriptures hidden from the king and to bring them to Jerusalem where they could be stored in the sacred library of the temple.

"Someone has to do it," the old scribe had said.

Judah muttered aloud the rest of Eleazar's words. "God will provide."

How he missed that old friend now. The man who had patiently loved Judah even while he had rebelled against Adonai and his Law. The true example of a mentor. He would never forget Eleazar's zeal or devotion for the rest of his life.

Even more so, he would never forget his beloved Sophia. He pulled out the small silver amulet he had taken from her hands beneath the walls of Jerusalem. He felt it in his fingers, its engraved words now etched into his very soul.

> *May the Lord bless you and guard you; may the Lord make his face shine upon you.*
> *The Lord lift up his countenance upon you and give you peace.*

"Judah," came Simon's voice, interrupting his thoughts. "Judah, I don't mean to be the killjoy here again …"

Judah smiled and interrupted him, "Brother, you will always be both my wise brother and my most important killjoy."

Big John and little Jonathan laughed along with them.

Simon said, "I'm afraid our work is not yet done. The intelligence we have received is that Gentiles in Samaria, Idumea, and up in Galilee are starting to persecute our Jewish brethren in the cities and countryside."

With a sigh, Judah placed his arms around John and Jonathan. Simon followed suit from the opposite side. The four brothers embraced tightly in a holy huddle of Hasmonean kinship.

"It seems evil will never leave us alone," said Judah. "So I suggest, we never stop fighting."

"Until the Resurrection," corrected Simon.

"Until the Resurrection," affirmed Judah.

CHAPTER 66

Persia

Antiochus Epiphanes burned with a rage that could only be extinguished by the stabbing pains in his belly and the itching in his anus. The bumpy ride on this chariot was not helping his gut any. He had just had another episode of explosive diarrhea before he left, and he had seen worms in the stool. It made him sicker just thinking of those thin, white little squirming creatures living in his bowels. This damned Persian food was too exotic for him. He was going to swear off their spices, especially that floral-smelling saffron, if he ever came back.

But right now, he was trying to make it to the city of Ecbatana just within his sight a mile ahead. His phalanx forces were marching behind him, and they would meet up at the city. Antiochus would then regroup and make his way back to Syria, back to his Antioch.

"Faster!" he yelled to the chariot driver. Several guardsmen rode alongside him. As bumpy as the chariot was, it was better than the damage that would have been done to his intestines on a galloping horse.

Antiochus grabbed the bronze railing on the chariot. He tried not to focus on the four horses pulling the chariot since their motion made him dizzy and nauseas. He coughed from the dirt cloud created behind the animals. Once he arrived in Ecbatana and organized for the march home, he would sit in the leisure and comfort of a royal carriage, to which he so looked forward.

The king's rage was twofold. First, his failure in the Persian city of Persepolis to extract more money from the people. To be fair, he had tried to plunder their temple. The citizens had risen up and rioted against him, driving him from the city to where he was at this moment.

In the temple of Nanaia, the Persian equivalent of the Greek Artemis, Antiochus had seen a glorious display of golden shields, armor, and weapons from the infamous troops of Alexander the Great, the Macedonian conqueror of the world. The artifacts had been used as decoration by that glorious emperor as a historic reminder of the eastward expanse of his Hellenist kingdom. Antiochus had wanted to get his hands on them to bring them back to Antioch. But these ridiculous Persians were too selfish, uncivilized, and unruly.

And that was only the half of it. Antiochus had also recently received a message about the great losses of the Mysian commander Lysias, whom the king had put in command. What a moronic mistake.

How could I have been such a fool? And for that bald-headed, lurching vulture to be routed and put to flight by that Maccabee Jew and his motley bandits!

Enough was enough. The king was going to have to do it himself.

More stabbing pain made Antiochus almost keel over. He grabbed the rail tighter.

As acting proxy regent, Lysias was teaching Antiochus's son Eupator how to be a ruler—an incompetent one. Well, that was going to stop. The king was returning to Antioch. And he had already decided to appoint one of the King's Friends, Philip, to take over as co-regent with his son Eupator.

Then I am going to Jerusalem, and I am going to turn that city into a mass graveyard of Jews. A permanent necropolis.

Suddenly, Antiochus felt the wheel of his chariot hit something in the road. He found himself flying through the air. The sky spun around him.

Then he felt his body hit the dirt and tumble. He rolled like a log, his arms like snapped branches. When he came to a stop, it felt like all his bones had been broken. He lay on his back looking up at beautiful, puffy clouds in a blue sky.

He had never noticed the sky before. Bright azure blue. An ocean in the clouds.

Pain brought him back to earth as several of his guardsmen jumped from their horses to help him. Both of them cringed with horrified looks on their faces. They held their noses in repulsion.

Raising his neck, Antiochus looked down at his belly, where they were staring. His abdomen had been split open, and some of his intestines had spilled out onto his thighs and the ground.

In shock, he desperately tried to scoop his bowels and shove them back into him. A foul odor came from his innards. Raising his hands, he saw them smeared with feces and little white worms. The stench made him nauseas.

"Philip!" he cried out. "Where is Philip?"

"I am here, your majesty." The voice was accompanied by the tightly-bearded, dark-skinned, effeminate face of Philip, a courtier who had become close to the king over this Persian excursion. Very close.

Antiochus's shaking hands took off his signet ring. He gave it to Philip, coughing out, "Take the scroll of declaration I gave you and my signet and present it before my son Eupator. You shall be his co-regent over Lysias of Damascus."

"Yes, your majesty," came the soft, painful voice of the King's Friend—and lover.

Then Antiochus's vision went blurry. He felt himself falling, falling.

A new face came into his view. It wasn't Philip or his chariot driver. It didn't look like the guards he had seen riding with him.

It was a blonde male with long hair and a thin angular face with chiseled cheeks and jaw. His eyes were bright blue. Antiochus had never before seen anyone like this.

The blonde male looked like an angel.

No, he was an angel! Come to bring Antiochus home.

As all the sounds around Antiochus faded away, the angel leaned in to whisper, "Do you remember the king of Babylon? You tyrants are all the same." Then he recited ancient verse.

How you are fallen from heaven,
  O shining one, O Venus star!
How you are cut down to the ground,
  you who laid the nations low!
You said in your heart,
  "I will ascend to heaven;
above the stars of God
  I will set my throne on high;
I will sit on the mount of assembly
  in the far reaches of the north;
I will ascend above the heights of the clouds;
  I will make myself like the Most High."
But you are brought down to Sheol,
  to the far reaches of the pit.
Sheol beneath is stirred up
  to meet you when you come;
it rouses the Rephaim kings to greet you,
  all who were leaders of the earth;

it raises from their thrones
>*all who were kings of the nations.*
All of them will answer
>*and say to you:*
"You too have become as weak as we!
>*You have become like us!"'*
Your pomp is brought down to Sheol,
>*the sound of your harps;*
maggots are laid as a bed beneath you,
>*and worms are your covers ...*
Until the time of the end.

By the time the archangel Uriel finished reciting the poem of judgment inscribed by the prophet Isaiah, Antiochus IV Epiphanes—the willful king—was dead.

· · · · ·

Antioch

Lysias sat on the co-regent's chair beside the crown prince Eupator in the king's hall. The King's Friend Philip stood before them with several guards. He had brought them the body of King Antiochus as well as his signet, diadem, and robe, all of which the crown prince now held in his hands.

Lysias looked with contempt upon the effeminate man before them. He knew full well why this creature was one of Antiochus's latest "Friends." The foppish Ganymede was surely there to satisfy the late king's taste for perverse variety. Everything about the young man from his effete curls in his chestnut hair to the ornate brooch holding up his soft purple cloak screamed catamite companion to Lysias.

When the man handed Lysias the so-called "last testament" scroll of King Antiochus IV Epiphanes, Lysias suspected the worst. He unrolled it to read. It *was* the worst.

"The late king left me as co-regent, your majesty," Philip stated smugly. "Signed in his own hand."

Lysias looked down upon the crown prince, now almost ten years old, shortly to be king. Lysias had spent the past couple years grooming the little prick and controlling him. This dandy twat was not going to jeopardize all that.

Lysias leaned in and whispered to Eupator, "It is exactly as I predicted, your majesty. An attempted usurpation."

Eupator told the guards, "Incarcerate him."

"Your majesty," protested Philip. "The king's own words. He spoke them as he died."

"I'm sure he did," said Lysias as the guards dragged the catamite away.

Turning to one of the torches standing beside the throne, Lysias lit the document on fire. He made sure it was consumed into ashes. Then he leaned in judiciously to Eupator and whispered, "Now that you will be crowned king, there are some matters we have discussed that require your immediate attention."

Eupator listened hungrily. Lysias had the boy wrapped around his finger. He continued, "First you must end the hostilities with the Jews. They have been a drain on your forces and finances. A treaty would shut them up for now, stop their acts of sabotage against the crown, and allow you time to rebuild your war machine and fill the treasury with taxes."

"Are we done with the Maccabees?"

"Not yet, my student. But as I've said before, they are not the cause of our conflict. They are the symptom."

Eupator said, "I have a good idea of some of the cause."

"I will take care of it," said Lysias. "And the other matters. You need to prepare yourself for your coronation and enthronement."

"I am so glad you are here to help me, Lysias. I don't know what I would do without your loyal devotion to the crown."

That was exactly what Lysias wanted to hear.

He bowed and repeated with his own interpretation, "To the crown, your majesty."

• • • • •

Philip the King's Friend had been waiting for hours in this dark and dreary cell block with rusty iron bars, a smell of mold, and the sound of rats squealing. He wasn't sure how much longer he could endure it all.

The sound of guards arriving and the clinking of keys excited him. He rose to meet two guards leading his rescuer up to the cell door. "Lysias."

Ignoring him, Lysias signaled to the guards. "Let him out."

Philip brightened with hope as a guard pulled out his keys and jangled one in the lock. Opening the door he pulled Philip out to face Lysias.

"What is the crown prince's decision?" asked Philip.

Lysias looked down at him. "To clean up the mess."

Immediately, the guards grabbed Philip and pulled his arms behind his back. One of them drew a dagger and swiftly cut through Philip's windpipe. He dropped to the ground choking and gasping, eyes wide with shock.

Lysias walked away with a casual gesture to the guards. "Clean up the mess."

· · · · ·

Antiochis and her daughter Ophelia were visited by four of the king's court, who escorted them to meet Lysias in a secret location in the woods on Mount Silpius. It was one of their frequent trysting spots just up the hill from the new quarter being built. Antiochis had made such sweet love with Lysias there. It held precious memories for her.

Since her daughter was accompanying her, she knew this was not an amorous visit. Both women dressed in nice clothes: newly washed and pressed himations with shined golden brooches over modest but elegant peplos undergarments. Their hair had been pinned above their heads, and golden headbands matched their bracelets and earrings.

When they arrived at the spot, Antiochis was confused. No one was there.

"Where is Lysias?" she asked.

The guards said nothing.

"He must be on his way," she assured herself.

Then she saw two holes in the ground next to two piles of dirt with shovels sticking out of them.

Her mind raced as she tried to fill in the blanks of what she could not understand.

The two women were marched up to the holes, which were rectangular and matched their heights.

Her daughter said fearfully, "Mother?"

Lysias hadn't the heart to be there. He had grown fond of his royal whore and couldn't bring himself to watch her and her daughter get their throats slit. He had asked the guards to make it as quick and painless as possible. He did after all have a conscience.

• • • • •

Menelaus had traveled from Jerusalem to Antioch under much duress. Though he had a Seleucid escort, he had continuously glanced behind him on the roads and trails, expecting his traitorous Jewish comrades to chase him down and exact their fanatical vengeance. The horse party had moved quickly, making the three-hundred-mile trip in a mere fortnight.

With the oppressive Hasmoneans now in charge of the temple and priesthood, Menelaus knew his life was in danger. The future of Israel was in danger as far as he was concerned. The more fanatical the Maccabees became, the more likely they were to bring down the wrath of the new king Eupator and his co-regent Lysias, who did not appreciate the finer nuances of Jewish idiosyncrasies.

Menelaus was grateful to be back safe and sound in Antioch. He actually preferred the Greek Athenian city as a Hellenistic paradise of sorts. But with his status as high priest rejected by the Hasmoneans, his power was severely in jeopardy.

He stood now before King Eupator and his co-regent, the ambitious Lysias of Damascus. Lysias would understand his claim since the co-regent himself was deeply focused on maintaining his own power within the structure of the kingdom. He knew how important it was to be given recognition. And to have Menelaus as an ally.

Menelaus wore most of his high priest outfit in order to impress the king with the unique importance of his position. A large white turban on his head. His blue tunic with bells. His checkered apron of many colors. The only things he did not have was the ephod breastplate of gemstones or the golden forehead plate.

"Your majesty," said Menelaus, bowing low. "The purpose of my visit is to press for my rights as the chosen high priest of Israel. As you know, your father appointed me almost ten years ago as the representative for Seleucid interests in the Jewish priesthood. Royal appointment is the way to maintain peace and stability *and* your control over Judea. If I may humbly remind you, I also helped your father to implement his Edict of Unity in relation to Judea and the temple in Jerusalem. The reason why I am here is because when the hasidim took back the temple, they forced me out of the city and out of the office of high priest."

Menelaus paused to let it all sink in. Then he concluded. "Your majesty, I ask that you reinstate me as the only recognized high priest of Judea. If you do not, you may have another insurrection on your hands. I can help to avert that tragedy."

Lysias interrupted him. "Menelaus, as I recall, your original appointment to the position was achieved through a bribe of many talents of silver and gold from the temple treasury."

"And I will procure it again to assure you of my loyalty."

"What about your loyalty to your own rules?"

"What do you mean?"

"Well, as I understand it, you advised Antiochus and Apollonius on how to implement the Edict of Unity that in fact forced your own people to deny their rules and their god in order to live in peace."

"I sought the peace of the Seleucid kingdom," Menelaus protested. "I am not ashamed of that."

"But you did so by betraying your own people and religion, which plunged them into chaos. If you are willing to betray your own people and rob your own temple, why should the king not expect you to betray him and rob from him as well?"

Menelaus began sweating. He felt his face flush with angry heat. He said to Lysias, "I thought I was having an audience with the king, not with his advisor."

Eupator snapped at him, "Lysias is my co-regent! He represents my interests. So you *will* respect his position."

"Forgive me, your majesty," groveled Menelaus. "I was out of line."

Lysias had a smug look on his face. "You are more than out of line, Menelaus, I think you are to blame for all the trouble that has led to the Jewish revolt in the first place. And now you come begging for your installation into office instead of the welfare of your people."

Menelaus couldn't look at Lysias. He felt humiliated. The co-regent was right. The high priest couldn't deny it. Though he had lived in denial for ten years. He didn't know what else to say.

Lysias broke the silence. "Your majesty, I recommend the tower of ash."

Menelaus felt his whole body freeze in fear. He looked up in shock. "No, please, your majesty. Please. I will be loyal. I will be loyal!"

But it pleased his majesty to send Menelaus to the tower that stood at the edge of town, a seventy-foot-tall round edifice of stone that was filled with cold ash from old fires.

The high priest was brought to the top of the tower's ledge and cast down into the ashes, where he fell a great height and suffocated to death, leaving his body to rot inside the cremated debris without proper burial.

And so the man who had violated the daily burnt sacrifice was executed in the ashes of his own sacrifice.

• • • • •

Scroll

Antiochus V Eupator ruled the Seleucid kingdom for three years with his co-regent Lysias.

In 161 BC, Demetrius I was released as hostage from Rome and placed as king over Seleucia. Eupator and Lysias were executed.

The cleansing of the Jerusalem temple and return of the burnt sacrifice was only the beginning of the Maccabean wars for independence.

Five years later, Judah Maccabee was killed in the battle of Elasa by the Seleucid forces of General Bacchides. He was outnumbered 800 to 20,000.

The wars would continue under the brothers of Judah Maccabee for twenty-plus years as they regained territory for Israel.

The success of the Maccabean Revolt established the Hasmonean dynasty of both princes and priests in Judea until the time of Herod the Great.

Some Jewish zealots refused to accept the Hasmonean priesthood and left Jerusalem to establish a separate community called the Essenes, who lived in Qumran beside the Dead Sea. They would await the final War of the Sons of Light Against the Sons of Darkness.

In 37 BC, Herod the Great defeated the last Hasmonean ruler and made Judea a client king of Rome.

Supporters of the Maccabees split into two main parties, the Sadducees and Pharisees, whose sectarian differences became the heart of Israel's divided people …

… until the days of the fourth kingdom of iron and clay, when a voice of one came crying in the wilderness, "Prepare the way of the Lord. Make straight in the desert a highway for our God."

EPILOGUE

Mount Zaphon

Baal-Set climbed the rocky incline of his cosmic mountain in Syria, the far reaches of the North. As he did, he recalled his victory over the serpent Apophis, known as Leviathan in the Levant. Since he was returning to take back his temple, he would also be calling himself Baal again with its Semitic compounds, such as Baal-Shamem, lord of the sky, Baal-Hadad the storm god, and Elyon Baal, god most high.

He was the Prince of Canaan, and it would take more than a slimy seven-headed sea dragon to defeat him. When he had been thrown into the Nile from Ra's solar barque, Baal had found himself alone in the water, which was one of his weaknesses as a daemonic Watcher. As Leviathan drew him under, one of its heads swallowed Baal whole.

As a chaos monster, Leviathan was universally feared in the spiritual world. It was the strongest and most unruly of Yahweh's creatures. But it was not one of the smartest.

It had not taken care to realize that when it swallowed Baal, he still had his sword sheathed by his side.

So the storm god had waited until he ended up in the belly of the beast before taking out his blade and cutting his way out. Unfortunately, the blood of Leviathan was supernaturally poisonous, one of the only things that could permanently poison or cripple a Watcher. But the blood had dissolved into the saltwater that protected Baal's skin. The sea dragon's own wound would heal with preternatural speed, so Baal knew he had not seen the last of this troublemaker of the Abyss.

He remembered the lyrics to his own epic poem from the Baal Cycle.

> *What manner of enemy has arisen against Baal,*
> *or foe against the Charioteer of the Clouds?*
> *Surely I smote the Beloved of El, Sea?*
> *Surely I exterminated River, the mighty god?*
> *Surely I lifted up the dragon,*
> *I overpowered him!*
> *I smote the writhing serpent,*
> *Encircler-with-seven-heads!*

Once he swam to the surface, Baal had discovered that he was in the waters at the bottom of the crevice at the Gates of Hades, the infamous cave at Panias at the foot of Mount Hermon. Leviathan had access to many portals of the Abyss around the world. Baal was glad he had been taken here where he could hide out on Mount Hermon until he found out when and where the conflict would end between the Seleucids and Ptolemies. And more importantly, with Rome.

Baal had spied on the Olympians as they conspired on Mount Hermon. He had concluded that there was going to be massive upheaval in the pantheon that would not end well. So he had waited it out until he saw his chance of taking back his own house.

He now stood before his house on that cosmic mountain. Its sacred pillars and altar were overrun with weeds. The Olympians had been horrible occupiers. They had left everything in ruins. He would have to do some renovation on his house, but he had time. And he had patience.

Yes, Baal was back. And from everything he had heard from the Prince of Rome, he knew Messiah was almost here. So Baal had much preparation to do.

• • • • •

Rome

In the spiritual world, Sammael sat on the throne of the temple of Jupiter Optimus Maximus on the Capitoline Hill, the most sacred of the seven hills of Rome, a cosmic mountain range. The temple's massive stone walls and columns rose to the heavens overlooking a spread of sacred buildings below.

Sammael was the true "king of the gods." Jupiter and the other Roman deities genuflected before him on the marble floor. Neptune of the sea, Pluto of the underworld, Jupiter's wife Juno, Apollo, Mars, and all the others had been called to assembly in the grand hall. In time, he would have the gods of Greece, Egypt, Gaul, and Spain at his feet as well. He wanted all the world, and he was going to take it.

"I have called you here to announce the next phase of my plans," he announced to his minions. "The Little Horn Epiphanes is dead. The Abomination of Desolation is overtaken. The Greek beast is in its death throes. The kingdoms of the earth are ripe for the taking. Persia and Parthia in the far east remain an annoyance, but they too will ultimately bow. As for the Republic of Rome, I am done with it. I want an empire."

The gods shuddered at the thought. They knew what that meant.

"It will still take some time, maybe a few more generations, but I need an emperor to unify this world again."

And Sammael would be the god of this world.

"Regarding my plans for Judea and her Messianic Seed, I have in mind a new kind of king. One who shall do as he wills just like all the others. But this one will not be a Gentile. He will be an Edomite. A son of Abraham and Isaac but from the lineage of Jacob's hated brother. Yahweh hates this people, so I love them. For whom Yahweh loves, I hate. He chooses Jacob, so I choose Esau. I will make this Edomite king of the Jews, and I will use him to stop the Seed of the Woman."

The crowd of gods murmured with interest and agreement.

Sammael finished his proclamation. "Babylon could not crush the Jews. The Medes and the Persians could not crush the Jews. And now the Greeks have failed as well. But a Roman Empire shall not fail. I will use the iron teeth on my Beast of Rome to be my fatal bite on the heel of Messiah.

"Yahweh shall yet taste of my venom."

• • • • •

Alexandria

Joseph, a young Jewish apprentice scribe of twenty-two years old, walked down the long aisle of a huge study foyer in the Great Library of Alexandria. He had come from the far side of the huge complex, where he had been retrieving some obscure documents. He felt a bit winded from the walk and knew he should exercise more, but his devotion to books was all-consuming. The result was a pudginess in his belly that bothered him but not enough to take a minute away from his studies to exercise.

The young scribe carried a handful of scrolls carefully in his arms. He was draped in the linen of a scribe's tunic and well-worn sandals. He looked up at the ceiling fifty feet above his head carved with scenes of world mythology. Not merely Greek and Egyptian but exotic stories of the far East, Persia, India, and even the land called Tianxia or Ch'in.

Large Corinthian columns lined the foyer that contained dozens of large cedar tables used for studying books. Joseph could hear his footsteps echo on the marble floor. He loved the grandiosity of the Hellenistic fusion of Grecian architecture with Egyptian hieroglyphs and art on the walls. He could smell the mustiness of the hall of parchments, a blend of papyrus and glue that could carry you away into worlds of the imagination. He felt so blessed to be able to do this for a living, as meager as it was.

Arriving at the table of his master, Jason of Cyrene, Joseph laid the scrolls down. Jason was a middle-aged, dark-skinned Jewish scholar with thick black hair and an academic concentration that made him unsociable with normal people. He lived and breathed books. For the past year, he had been writing a history of the events that had been occurring during the Jewish Revolt of the Maccabees. He had already written three volumes. He was projecting five to finish.

Joseph had apprenticed with Jason for a year now and knew his every quirk. So he was surprised to see the older man with tears in his eyes as he took notes with his quill. Jason expressed very little emotion as a matter of course.

Joseph asked, "What is wrong, master?"

Jason put down his quill. "I am writing about a fellow scribe I met on my travels to Jerusalem. His name was Eleazar. He was executed by King Antiochus because he would not disobey Torah."

"I am sorry to hear it," said Joseph.

"He was faithful to the end," said Jason.

"So it was not in vain," Joseph concluded.

Jason sighed. "I do not know that. The Hasmoneans now reign in Judea, but there is still much civil unrest. We have not seen the end of this conflict."

"That is why my family and I will not return to Judea yet," Joseph commented. "We are waiting for some stability."

"You may be waiting a long while. What is your hometown?"

"Bethlehem."

Jason returned to his work. Joseph soon lost himself in the rows of wooden scroll cubicles, diamond-shaped cases filled with parchments and tablets of clay from all over the world.

By the time his attention returned to his surroundings, he realized the light had greatly diminished. Dusk was descending on the city. It was not wise to carry out scribal work under too much candlelight. Parchment and candle flames were not good bedfellows.

Putting away the scrolls he had been examining, Joseph returned to his master's table. Jason was packing up his own work, closing his jar of ink, rolling up his scrolls.

"We have stayed too late," the older scribe said. "I am done for the day. You may go home."

"Thank you, master. I will see you tomorrow."

Joseph left the library and walked quickly to his home several blocks away in the Jewish quarter. The sun was already disappearing beneath the Mediterranean, and most people were in their homes eating their evening meal. Joseph thought eagerly of seeing his wife and child as he hurried through half-empty streets of lined mudbrick homes.

Suddenly, he had a strange feeling that he was being followed. Looking behind him, he saw nothing but the shadows of buildings growing in length with the deepening twilight like ghostly phantoms.

Joseph had felt this ominous presence before, and he wondered if he was just worrying too much. He had been reading so much about the Maccabean revolt in his work that it was overwhelming him with sadness and fear for his Jewish brethren still in the Land. The war, the violence of it all, and the sufferings of his people were getting to him.

Then he remembered when he had first felt that same presence. He had been in Alexandria during the siege of Antiochus Epiphanes years ago. He had never forgotten the vision he had seen of heavenly armies in battle in the clouds. Many others had seen the vision as well, but they had never understood why. Why would Ha Shem bother to come all the way down here to Egypt to fight with such fury? Was there something he was protecting down here?

Such high and mighty concerns were distracting to Joseph. He just wanted to get home to his wife and child.

And then he saw it. The front door of his home with a faint light emanating from within. It stood amidst a neighborhood of other houses with their lamps lit, their families safe and warm behind mudbrick walls.

But how safe were they really?

Joseph opened the front door. He entered and barricaded it shut behind him with the heavy wooden security crossbar. Taking off his woolen outer cloak, he turned to see his wife holding their son, a two-year old with bright eyes that lit up joyously when he saw his abba.

Joseph kissed his wife. She handed him their son, who reached out to grab and hug his father in an ecstasy of delight after not seeing him all day.

"My little Jannai." Joseph snuggled and kissed his son as though he might never see him again.

His wife looked at him, wondering if there was anything wrong.

Seeing her worried eyes, Joseph reassured her, "I am just glad to be home with my family and that we serve the living God in a world of turmoil and danger. He watches over us."

Her frown turned into a smile, and they kissed again.

They did not see the shadow figure standing outside their window, peering in, watching, waiting.

Outside Joseph's home, the shadow figure turned and noted the arrival of two more cloaked and hooded figures. Anyone on the street that evening or looking out their windows would not see these creatures because they inhabited the unseen realm of the heavenlies. If humans were allowed to see these beings, they would most likely be frozen in fright or fall at their feet as dead men.

The one by the window pulled off his hood as the others met him. He was handsome with black flowing hair, dark complexion, and a muscular build the cloak could not completely hide. He was Michael the Archangel.

He greeted the others with a whisper. "Any sign of Watchers?"

"No," came the whispered answers. The other two pulled down their hoods. The tall black Gabriel and the small blonde Uriel, fellow archangels from the throne of the Most High.

"I'm telling you, they still have no clue," Uriel said. "That whole incident with Hephaestus snooping around a few years back was unintentional. I don't think he was lying to us. I think he suspected, but he didn't know."

They had interrogated the Greek god of volcanoes before they had cut him up and cast his pieces into a volcano in the heart of the sea. He had told them his journey to Egypt was a secret of his own and that the Olympians had no knowledge of his whereabouts.

"Still, we cannot be too careful." Michael turned to look in at the family. "Jannai ben Joseph is safe in his father's arms for now. The Adversary's attention is distracted. But we have a few more generations of the messianic seed line to protect."

Uriel sighed. "I'm so tired of this silence and absence thing. I want to stop hiding and start fighting."

Gabriel smiled and slapped Uriel on the back. "Don't worry, little brother. Messiah will be here before you know it, and he brings a winnowing fork in his hand with an unquenchable fire. You'll have your opportunity for plenty of battle."

Michael affirmed, "We will tread on the head of the serpent."

The angels gave each other a solemn murmur of approval. Taking their places around the house, they all dissolved into the night shadows to watch and to wait.

• • • • •

The Gospel According to Luke

Jesus, when he began his ministry, was about thirty years of age, being the son (as was supposed) of Joseph, the son of Heli, the son of Matthat, the son of Levi, the son of Melchi, the son of Jannai, the son of Joseph.

• • • • •

For the next book in this storied timeline get Jesus Triumphant **(Chronicles of the Nephilim, Book 8). Though it is in a different series than this one, it is the next book you want to get. This is because**

Chronicles of the Watchers is interwoven with Chronicles of the Nephilim to fill in the gaps of the storyline of the Nephilim series.

Sign up for Godawa Chronicles Updates at Godawa.com to be the first to hear about new releases, special deals and articles on strange things in the Bible.

APPENDIX:
THE ABOMINATION OF DESOLATION
PAST AND FUTURE

Introduction

The abomination of desolation is a biblical term that is a part of eschatology, which is the study of "last things" in the Bible. Since one of the most common eschatological views propagated in Christian circles is premillennial dispensationalism, let's call it the Left Behind view for short (and who doesn't know about the mega-selling hit novel series *Left Behind*?). It conjures up fantastical supernatural scenarios in one's mind of a "rapture" of Christians out of this world, followed by an "Antichrist" who rises up as a world leader and makes a covenant with Israel, which he eventually breaks and sets up some kind of image of himself called "the abomination of desolation" in the Jewish temple in Jerusalem. The Antichrist makes it "come alive" and even speak. But eventually he requires Jews to worship it, which is the catalyst that wakens many of them up spiritually and leads to their turning toward Jesus Christ as their true Messiah. Jesus then returns to fight that Antichrist, destroy his allied nations, and set up his kingdom on earth.

Okay, I know that's only one interpretation of many that are out there. But I use it as one of the more popular examples of what is called "futurism," which is a broader term than the Left Behind view when applied to Bible prophecy. A futurist interpretation simply speculates that a specific Bible prophecy is yet to be fulfilled in *our* future. The belief that a Bible prophecy has already been fulfilled in the past is called a "preterist" interpretation. "Preterist" comes from the Latin word that means "past."

For example, all Christians are preterist in their interpretation of the Old Testament Bible prophecies of a coming Messiah to be born in Bethlehem to a virgin and who would be crucified for our sins because those are fulfilled in our past (preterist). But if you believe a certain Bible prophecy is yet to be fulfilled in our future, such as a coming Antichrist, then you would have a futurist interpretation of that prophecy.

Sometimes the terms futurist and preterist are used in a summary way to refer to two dominant (though by no means monolithic) schools of thought about "last days" or "end times" prophecies. In general, futurists believe that there is an abomination of desolation (among many other things) to come in *our* future while preterists tend to believe that the abomination of desolation was fulfilled in our past *and only in our past*.

Like I said, there are so many views within each school of thought that I am sure some will quibble with various designations. But I am sure it will become clear that these are not the main issues to address on this subject.

To begin, let's take a look at all the places where the abomination of desolation shows up in Scripture. These are almost all in the book of Daniel and once in the Olivet discourse by Jesus, who is quoting Daniel. Notice that the exact phrase "abomination of desolation" is not always used. Sometimes it is described using the words or concepts of abomination and desolation together (bold underlines provided for focus).

> Daniel 8:11–14
> And the regular burnt offering was taken away from him,
> and the place of his sanctuary was overthrown.… "For how
> long is the vision concerning the regular burnt offering, the

transgression that makes desolate, and the giving over of the sanctuary and host to be trampled underfoot?" And he said to me, "For 2,300 evenings and mornings. Then the sanctuary shall be restored to its rightful state."

Daniel 11:31
Forces from him shall appear and profane the temple and fortress, and shall take away the regular burnt offering. And they shall set up the **abomination that makes desolate**.

Daniel 9:26–27
And the people of the prince who is to come shall destroy the city and the sanctuary. Its end shall come with a flood, and to the end there shall be war. **Desolations** are decreed. And he shall make a strong covenant with many for one week, and for half of the week he shall put an end to sacrifice and offering. And on the **wing of abominations shall come one who makes desolate**, until the decreed end is poured out on the **desolator**."

Daniel 12:11
And from the time that the regular burnt offering is taken away and the **abomination that makes desolate** is set up, there shall be 1,290 days.

Matthew 24:15 (Mark 13:14)
So when you see the **abomination of desolation** spoken of by the prophet Daniel, standing in the holy place (let the reader understand)…

A cursory examination of all these verses show a common pattern of elements or events that seem to overlap in creating a scenario. That scenario includes the *tamid*, or daily sacrifice, in the temple being "taken away" and the temple being "trampled underfoot," "profaned," or "destroyed." But what does this have to do with the abomination of desolation?

Let's take a look at the words and concepts "abomination" and "desolation" in their ancient context. The Hebrew word for "abomination" is *siqqus*, which the *Theological Wordbook of the Old Testament* describes as "always used in connection with idolatrous practices, either referring to the idols themselves as being abhorrent and detestable in God's sight or to something associated with the idolatrous ritual. Idols generally are referred to as an abomination (Jeremiah 16:18)."[1]

The god Chemosh is called "the abomination of Moab." Molech is "the abomination of the Ammonites." Ashtoreth is "the abomination of the Sidonians" (2 Kings 23:13). And so on.[2] The context of all the passages describing these abominations of the nations was physical idols (images) to which the pagan deities were linked.

The slight variation "transgression that makes desolate" (Daniel 8:14) is contextually about the same abomination. The Hebrew word for "transgression" means a crime that breaks relationship in some way.[3] So the idolatry that makes the temple desolate is a part of God's broken relationship with Israel.

The Hebrew word for "desolation" (*mesomem*) means to lay waste or make deserted.[4] This does not necessarily involve destruction. It carries the idea of desertion and is used of cities being deserted (Ezekiel 36:35) or the wasteland of the desert that represents a return to the

---

[1] See also Ezekiel 5:11; 7:20; 2 Chronicles 15:8, etc. Hermann J. Austel, "2459 שָׁקַץ," in *Theological Wordbook of the Old Testament*, ed. R. Laird Harris, Gleason L. Archer Jr., and Bruce K. Waltke (Chicago: Moody Press, 1999), 955.

[2] See also Deuteronomy 29:17; I Kings 11:5-7; 2 Kings 23:24; 2 Chronicles 15:8; Isaiah 66:3; Jeremiah 7:30, etc.

[3] G. Herbert Livingston, "1846 פָּשַׁע," in *Theological Wordbook of the Old Testament*, ed. R. Laird Harris, Gleason L. Archer Jr., and Bruce K. Waltke (Chicago: Moody Press, 1999), 741.

[4] Willem VanGemeren, ed., *New International Dictionary of Old Testament Theology & Exegesis* (Grand Rapids, MI: Zondervan Publishing House, 1997), 167.

precreation state of chaos (Ezekiel 33:28). So in the context of the temple, it most likely refers to being deserted of the presence of God or at least deserted of the rituals and practices of its purpose.

Put together and applied to the temple and/or city of Jerusalem, these words create the image of the presence of a pagan deity inside the temple of Yahweh that pollutes that temple and makes Yahweh leave its presence. Profanation is an intolerable violation of God's holiness, so he leaves that temple which has become host to a detestable abomination of idolatry.

THE PAST ABOMINATION OF DESOLATION

Now that we have looked at the basic meaning of the term abomination of desolation, let's find out exactly how it is fulfilled in history. For the sake of clarity, I will announce my conclusion up front. There are so many different opinions on this matter that I want the reader to follow my argument without confusion or inaccurate assumptions.

Some interpret all the passages about the abomination of desolation to be talking about one and only one instance in history. Others add to that interpretation by suggesting that there is one concept of abomination of desolation that is repeated through history in partial fulfillments or multiple fulfillments. I will argue a third option, which is that Daniel is predicting exactly two separate abominations of desolation. The first one is in Daniel's near future when Antiochus Epiphanes erects an altar to Zeus in the Jerusalem temple in 168 BC. The second one is a similar offense in Daniel's distant future that mirrors Epiphanes but with significant differences.

So what about Jesus? What did he mean when he said, "So when you see the abomination of desolation spoken of by the prophet Daniel" (Matthew 24:15)? Jesus is referring to the second abomination. The first one had already happened in his past during the days of Antiochus Epiphanes. But the second one had not yet happened in his day. It was in his future.

Just who this second abomination is and when it occurs will be discussed below. But first let's see how the Daniel passages apply to the first abomination of desolation. To do so, we must get to know Antiochus IV Epiphanes.

Antiochus IV Epiphanes

The coming king foretold in Daniel's prophecy (Daniel 11:21-35) as a "contemptible" (ESV), "despicable" (NASB95), or "vile" person (NKJV) who would eventually bring about the "abomination of desolation" (v. 31) is also symbolized as "a little horn" that would grow out of Alexander's broken reign (Daniel 8:8-9) and grow powerful enough to defy Yahweh and oppress his holy people (8:9-14). That king would be the model and reflection of a future "little horn" that would also oppress God's people at a different time, the "time of the end" (Daniel 11:35, 40).[1]

That is why this story of the Maccabees is so important to the unfolding of God's plan to bring forth the Seed of the Woman that would crush the head of the Serpent—the very storyline of all three of my Chronicles series of novels (Genesis 3:15). That despicable and vile little horn was none other than Antiochus IV Epiphanes, the Seleucid king in Syria.

As 1 Maccabees says, Antiochus IV Epiphanes began to reign in the 137th "year of the Greeks," or about 175 BC. He was the youngest son of Antiochus III the Great, so he was not heir to the throne. He usurped the crown through political manipulation just as Daniel had prophesied.

---

[1] The second "little horn" in Daniel 7:20-21, 24-25. The Beast of Revelation who matches that little horn of Daniel I found in Revelation 13:5-7; 17:9-10. For a full narrative depiction of this fulfillment, see my series, Chronicles of the Apocalypse.

Daniel 11:21 (NASB95)
A despicable person will arise, on whom the honor of
kingship has not been conferred, but he will come in a
time of tranquility and seize the kingdom by intrigue.

In order to understand the "intrigue" that Antiochus IV used to
"seize" or usurp the crown, we must understand the historical situation of
the time. The Republic of Rome would require the son of a king who was
under their control to be held hostage in Rome in order to ensure the client
king's compliance. As an Italian mobster might put it, "You get outta
line, we gotta you son." Antiochus IV had the unfortunate circumstance
to be one of those hostages when his father was king. But later, Antiochus
used that hostage experience to his benefit. Commentator Robert Doran
explains Antiochus IV's intriguing kingdom situation.

> After the Romans decisively defeated Antiochus III at the
> battle of Magnesia (190 BCE), this youngest son
> [Antiochus IV] was handed over to the Romans as a
> hostage. Antiochus III was succeeded in 187 BCE by his
> older son, Seleucus IV. Around 176, the Romans
> exchanged Antiochus [IV] for Seleucus IV's son
> Demetrius [because he was son of the new king]. On
> Seleucus IV's death in 175 BCE, Antiochus [IV] seized the
> opportunity to gain control of the kingdom in place of his
> brother's son.[2]

Some scholars believe Demetrius's death was too well-timed for
Antiochus's rise not to have been an assassination. But Antiochus's
previous stay in Rome was also fortuitous in educating him in the Roman
way of politics and war. He would know his ultimate opponent well.

---

[2] Robert Doran, "The First Book of Maccabees," in *New Interpreter's Bible*, ed. Leander E. Keck, vol. 4
(Nashville: Abingdon Press, 1994–2004), 31.

Daniel 11:23
And from the time that an alliance is made with him he shall act deceitfully, and he shall become strong with a small people.

As this prophecy indicates, Antiochus was in alliance with Rome because of their support for him when he came to power. But in 170 BC, Egypt demanded Coele-Syria back from Antiochus in a territorial dispute. Antiochus's capital city Antioch was in Coele-Syria, and he was not going to wait for such a personal attack to take place. So he consolidated his forces and invaded Egypt first in what would be called the Sixth Syrian War with King Ptolemy VI of Egypt in 169 BC.[3]

But Ptolemy could not stand against Antiochus. He was betrayed by his own advisors. Antiochus then swept in and took Ptolemy VI prisoner. But after he did so, the city of Alexandria installed Ptolemy's younger brother, Ptolemy VIII Euergetes II, to the throne. Angered by this affront, Antiochus plotted with his prisoner Ptolemy VI against the installed opponent by leaving and supporting Ptolemy VI as king in Memphis to counter Euergetes's claim. Eventually, the Ptolemy brother kings became allies and united over Egypt, which spoiled Antiochus's hopes of control.

Daniel foretold this all [my explanations in brackets].

Daniel 11:25–28
And he [Antiochus IV of Syria] shall stir up his power and his heart against the king of the south [Ptolemy VI of Egypt] with a great army. And the king of the south [Ptolemy] shall wage war with an exceedingly great and mighty army, but he shall not stand, for plots shall be devised against him. Even

---

[3] The rest of this section on Daniel's prophecies fulfilled in Antiochus Epiphanes is drawn from Bruce W. Gore, *Historical and Chronological Context of the Bible* (Trafford Publishing, 2006), 10.19-23.

those who eat his food shall break him. His [Ptolemy's] army shall be swept away, and many shall fall down slain. And as for the two kings [Antiochus and Ptolemy VI], their hearts shall be bent on doing evil [plotting against Ptolemy Euregetes]. They shall speak lies at the same table, but to no avail [the Egyptian Ptolemy brothers unite], for the end is yet to be at the time appointed.

On his way back home to Syria, Antiochus decided to stop off in Jerusalem and plunder the temple for its treasury, described as imposing or "working his will."

Daniel 11:28
And he [Antiochus IV] shall return to his land with great wealth, but his heart shall be set against the holy covenant [Israel]. And he shall work his will and return to his own land [Syria].

This first invasion of Egypt by Antiochus IV was a high cost for the Seleucid king, who often pillaged temples as repositories of wealth to pay for his enterprises. Antiochus took the golden altar from the holy temple as well as the famous Menorah lamp stand and table of the Presence in addition to all the gold and silver temple utensils and any other hidden treasures he could find (1 Maccabees 1:20-23).

The prophet Daniel explains what would happen next. A year later in 168 BC, Antiochus decided to return to Egypt to finish what he had started and take the city of Alexandria. However, Rome would not tolerate this and sent an emissary, Caius Popilius Laenas, to put a stop to the Seleucid advance. This was the infamous incident where Popilius drew the line in the sand and told Antiochus to give him an answer of submission to Rome before he crossed it. If Syria did not pull back from

Egypt, they would be at war with Rome. Not a cheerful prospect of victory. Here is how Daniel described it.

> Daniel 11:29
> At the time appointed he [Antiochus IV] shall return and come into the south [Egypt again], but it shall not be this time as it was before. For ships of Kittim [Rome] shall come against him, and he [Antiochus] shall be afraid and withdraw.

So Antiochus obeyed Rome and returned to Syria. But upon hearing of a possible uprising of Jews in Jerusalem, Antiochus became enraged and sent forces to the holy city to punish the Jewish insurgents and re-establish his authority over the region.

> Daniel 11:30
> And [Antiochus IV] shall turn back and be enraged and take action against the holy covenant [Israel/Jerusalem]. He [Antiochus] shall turn back and pay attention [favor] to those who forsake the holy covenant [Hellenist Jews].

See my chart at the end of this book about the fulfillment of Daniel 11 in the lead-up to and including the Syrian Wars of the second century BC.

Antiochus and the Abomination of Desolation

As Daniel describes above, Antiochus affirmed the Jews who had embraced Hellenism, but something inside him snapped against those Jews who did not. He decided to employ a violent strategy to end the religious freedom that the Jews had enjoyed since his predecessor, Antiochus III, had granted them autonomy.

On December 6, 167 BC, Antiochus IV stopped the daily Jewish sacrifices to Yahweh in the temple and set up an altar to the Greek god

Zeus to replace those sacrifices to his patron deity. This was called by Daniel the "abomination of desolation" that profaned the temple.

> Daniel 11:31
> Forces from him [Antiochus] shall appear and profane the temple and fortress, and shall take away the regular burnt offering. And they shall set up the **abomination that makes desolate**.

The book of 1 Maccabees details the abominable desolation foretold by Daniel.

> 1 Maccabees 1:44–54 (LES)
> And the king [Antiochus IV Epiphanes] sent letters in the hands of messengers to Jerusalem and the cities of Judah, going after the customs of foreigners of the land, and to withhold burnt offerings and sacrifice and drink offering from the sanctuary and to profane Sabbaths and festivals, and to defile the sanctuary and holy things…. And on the fifteenth day of Kislev, on the ⌊one hundred and forty-fifth⌋ year, **they built an abomination of desolation on the altar**.

More details on what the pagan worship of the abomination of desolation included are given later. But in short, the profaning involved not merely erecting a detestable idol but suppressing Jewish circumcision, dietary laws, and sabbaths while requiring sacrifices to Zeus with animals that the Jews considered unclean such as pigs.

The Hellenist Jews flattered the king by participating in the profane abomination of these demands, but others did not. Many would not stop circumcising their sons, worshipping on sabbaths, or refraining from eating pork and other unclean animals. And they would certainly not participate in sacrifices to Zeus. The result was the massive persecution and martyrdom of Jews by Antiochus described in the books of the Maccabees. Daniel prophesied the suffering and martyrdom as a refining fire of holiness.

> Daniel 11:32–35
>
> He [Antiochus] shall seduce with flattery those who violate the covenant [Hellenist Jews], but the people who know their God [holy Jews] shall stand firm and take action [disobey Antiochus's decrees]. And the wise among the people shall make many understand, though for some days they shall stumble by sword and flame, by captivity and plunder. When they stumble, they shall receive a little help [from the Maccabean uprising] … and some of the wise shall stumble, so that they may be refined, purified, and made white, until the time of the end.

The family of Mattathias led by Judas Maccabeus not only refused to obey but stood in violent resistance and built an army of defiance. Their war against the Seleucid king ended with temporary victory in 165 BC, and Judas cleansed the Jerusalem temple of its abomination with a reinstatement of biblical sacrifices.[4]

Amazingly, Daniel foretold the amount of time this entire series of events would take: 2,300 days ("evenings and mornings").

> Daniel 8:13–14
>
> "For how long is the vision concerning the regular burnt offering, the transgression that makes desolate, and the giving over of the sanctuary and host to be trampled underfoot?" And he said to me, **"For 2,300 evenings and mornings**. Then the sanctuary shall be restored to its rightful state."

---

[4] 1 Maccabees 4:36-61; 2 Maccabees 10:1-9.

2,300 days comes out to about six years and three months (the "evening and morning" phrase may refer to the fact that the daily sacrifice was actually performed in the evening and in the morning of each day). The description of the sanctuary and host being "trampled underfoot" does not refer to physical destruction but to the polluting presence of pagan forces of idolatry occupying that temple. Commentator Jay Rogers explains this fulfillment.

> This is the time period, exactly six-years and three-and-a-half-months, during which Antiochus occupied the city of Jerusalem. Although the Jews were oppressed for over six years under the tyranny of Antiochus, for the last three years of the occupation, the sacrifices ceased to be offered.[5]

In all his defiance, the "little horn," Antiochus IV Epiphanes, did not thwart the will of God. But he had tried. This incident marks Epiphanes as one of the most infamous of villains in Jewish history, indeed in Christian history since he would become a template for another future ruler who would set up a second abomination of desolation in the Jerusalem temple. A pattern of historical repetition.

The two places where Daniel describes this second abomination of desolation are Daniel 9 and 12.

> Daniel 9:26–27
> And the people of the prince who is to come shall destroy the city [Jerusalem] and the sanctuary. Its end shall come with a flood, and to the end there shall be war.
> **Desolations** are decreed. And he shall make a strong

---

[5] Jay Rogers, *In the Days of These Kings: The Book of Daniel in Preterist Perspective* (Clermont, FL: Media House International, 2017), 60. The 2,300 number could also represent a total of 1,150 days, each day of which included both morning and evening sacrifice. That would be approximately the three and a half years of the stopped burnt offerings. The result would be the same with a slight difference of perspective.

covenant with many for one week, and for half of the week he shall put an end to sacrifice and offering. And on the **wing of abominations shall come one who makes desolate**, until the decreed end is poured out on the **desolate**."

Daniel 12:7–11

When the shattering of the power of the holy people comes to an end all these things would be finished. I heard, but I did not understand. Then I said, "O my lord, what shall be the outcome of these things?" He said, "Go your way, Daniel, for the words are shut up and sealed **until the time of the end**.… And from the time that the regular burnt offering is taken away and the **abomination that makes desolate** is set up, there shall be 1,290 days.

Though we read in these passages similar terminology of "abomination of desolation" related to the holy people, temple, and city as we saw in Daniel 8 and 11, we know for several reasons that these prophesies are not about Antiochus Epiphanes but about a future abominator. First, Antiochus Epiphanes polluted the temple but did not destroy it or the city of Jerusalem. The second abominator would make the temple "desolate" (Daniel 9:27) *and* destroy both the city of Jerusalem and the temple (9:26).

Second, the new abomination would occur at "the time of the end" and "when the shattering of the power of the holy people comes to an end." The era of the Maccabees was not the end of anything in relation to God's timeline of history since the power of the Jews did not come to an end but kept on with the success of the Maccabees. That power would only be shattered for good when the Roman Beast destroyed the temple totally and permanently in the generation of Messiah Jesus.

Third, the return to the regular burnt offering in the days of Antiochus was 2,300 days (Daniel 8:14), not the 1,290 days spoken of here in Daniel 12:11.

So what we see then in Daniel are two different abominations of desolation that are called by the same epithet or nickname phrase because they share a pattern of behavior in relation to God's people and temple. They both invade God's holy temple, they both stop the daily sacrifice, and they both desolate the temple with idolatrous presence for a time. But the second one does worse in destroying both temple and city. At this point readers may want to engage in speculation as to who this new "prince" is and when he will arise in history. I have addressed that separate issue later in this book. For now, I want to continue with an exploration of the character of Antiochus IV Epiphanes as described by Scripture and history.

One aspect of that character is another repeating pattern of behavior in the kings of the "beastly" Gentile kingdoms: god-like pride. Arrogant ancient rulers always seem to want to overthrow God and take his place.

> Daniel 8:25
> And he [the little horn-Antiochus] shall even **rise up against the Prince of princes**, and he shall be broken— but by no human hand.

The phrase that Daniel uses to indicate the idolatrous arrogance of Gentile rulers involves derivations of "do as he wills." In Hebrew, do (*asah*) as he wills (*rason*). It carries the meaning of "doing what he pleases" as if the king was so great that like a god he could do whatever he wanted without resistance.

Daniel's first use of the phrase applies to King Cyrus the Great of Persia, who "*did as he willed* and became great. And there was no one who could rescue from his power" (Daniel 8:4). Daniel later describes Alexander the Great as "a mighty king who shall rule with great dominion and *do as he wills*" (11:3). After him comes Antiochus III the Great who would "*do as he wills* and none shall stand before him" (11:16).

The last king of which Daniel uses the phrase is one who would come "at the time of the end" of these kingdoms. This king would also "*do as he wills*" by "exalting himself and magnifying himself above every god and shall speak astonishing things against the God of gods" (Daniel 11:36). But this last willful king is not Antiochus IV Epiphanes because Antiochus was not the king *at the time of the end*. We will discuss who this king might be later. Let's stay with our focus on Epiphanes.

The willful king phrase takes an ironic twist when considered in its context of God, the king over all the earth, describing his sovereign predestination of their exact actions in history that would lead up to the finishing of the "transgression of Israel" against Yahweh (Daniel 11:36) through the coming of Messiah (Daniel 9:24). These kings all believed and behaved as if they were gods. But in the end, they were mere instruments in the true God's plans.

Antiochus Epiphanes is the only king in these chapters not referred to as "doing as he wills." Some English translations of Daniel 11:28 say that Antiochus "shall do as he will," but this is not in the Hebrew. It only says that he will act (asah) against the holy covenant. I.e., the first half of that phrase without the second willful component. Perhaps this is God's most demeaning and mocking gesture of all in avoiding even acknowledging the will of the "despicable" monster who profaned Yahweh's house with the abomination of desolation. He's just another axe in the hand of God chastising his people (Isaiah 10:5, 15).

That said, contextually Antiochus was certainly in the line of kings who acted with godlike pretensions. In another prophecy, Daniel details this blasphemous arrogance of Antiochus Epiphanes against Yahweh and his people and heavenly host.

> Daniel 8:9–11
> Out of one of them came a little horn [Antiochus Epiphanes], which grew exceedingly great toward the south, toward the east, and toward the glorious land [Israel]. It grew great, even to the host of heaven. And some of the host and some of the stars it threw down to the ground and trampled on them. It became great, even as great as the Prince of the host [Angel of Yahweh].

Could a mere human king actually be capable of casting angels of the heavenly host to the ground?[6] Could he really rival the greatness of the highest Prince of the heavenly host, the Angel of Yahweh himself?[7] In the context of the Scriptures, obviously not. Humans in the presence of real heavenly beings often tremble in deathly fright. These words are more likely a reflection of the little horn's blasphemous words of arrogance in the face of God. Something that history bears out and Daniel interprets just a few verses later as "in his own mind he shall become great…. He shall even rise up against the Prince of princes, and he shall be broken—but by no human hand" (8:25).

The epithet "Epiphanes" that Antiochus IV took meant "manifest god," a true affront to the only creator God Yahweh. This delusional surname expressed his tyrannical behavior and reflected a madness that

---

[6] Stars are often symbols or representatives of elohim/gods/angels in the Bible and other Ancient Near Eastern literature, including Intertestamental Jewish literature. See my explanation of this literary symbolism in Brian Godawa *When Watchers Ruled the Nations: Pagan Gods at War with Israel's God and the Spiritual World of the Bible* (Texas: Warrior Poet Publishing, 2021), 29-37.

[7] There are two strong possibilities for understanding "The Prince of the host." He is either Michael the archangel or Yahweh himself, Jesus in preincarnate form. For Michael the archangel, see Brian Godawa, *When Watchers Ruled the Nations: Pagan Gods at War with Israel's God and the Spiritual World of the Bible* (Texas: Warrior Poet Publishing, 2021), 314-317. For the Angel of Yahweh as the Prince of the host, see Michael S. Heiser, *Angels: What the Bible Really Says about God's Heavenly Host* (Bellingham, WA: Lexham Press, 2018), 71–72.

eventually inspired a satirical twist of the word Epiphanes into "Epimanes," which meant "utterly mad" or "madman."[8]

Roman historian Polybius wrote of Antiochus fancying himself a god come down to men by wandering around town in royal garb or plebian disguise to discuss technical matters of the arts and crafts with goldsmiths and jewelers. He would engage in drinking bouts in the taverns with a couple of his trusted advisors, Heraclides and Timarchus of Miletus. He would bestow godlike excessive gifts of ointments, food, or money upon unwitting strangers in the streets, sometimes out of the blue, sometimes in response to overheard desires.[9]

But his unpredictable acts of caprice could have their sinister side as well for as historian Edwyn Bevan warns, beware the caresses of a panther. "He felt no difficulty in pleasantries with the man at whom he designed to strike."[10]

Roman historian Livy writes that Antiochus would also adjudicate on the most trivial of legal matters as if divinely omniscient, then move on to petty common interactions with a rather short human patience. In Antioch, he spent extravagantly on religious and civic splendor. He began building the magnificent temple of Olympian Zeus, which was gilded with gold throughout, and splurged on Greek theaters and Roman gladiator arenas.[11]

Of all the Greek deities, Antiochus favored Zeus. Not only did the king build the Antioch temple dedicated to that Supreme Deity but had previously built a vast temple of "Zeus Olympius" in Athens. He also

---

[8] John Whitehorne, "Antiochus (Person)," in *The Anchor Yale Bible Dictionary*, ed. David Noel Freedman (New York: Doubleday, 1992), 270.

[9] Polybius, *Histories* XXVI https://penelope.uchicago.edu/Thayer/E/Roman/Texts/Polybius/26*.html

[10] Edwyn Robert Bevan, *The House of Seleucus* (London, Edward Arnold Publishing, 1902), 129-130.

[11] Livy, Books XL-XLII With An English Translation, ed. Evan T. Sage and Alfred C. Schlesinger, *Ab Urbe Condita (Foster-Moore-Sage) English Text* (Medford, MA: Cambridge, Mass., Harvard University Press; London, William Heinemann, Ltd., 1938), 249–251.

put the storm god's face on newly minted coins in his realm. There are some grounds to believe that Antiochus identified himself with Zeus as the king of the gods.[12]

Ironically, most scholars agree that Antiochus did not originally have a particular animosity toward the Jews. Despite this ostentatious display and public dedication to Zeus, Antiochus himself was quite without religion. As Barry explains:

> His devotion to the worship of Zeus was but part of his
> idea that there be, instead of divers local and tribal faiths,
> a formal state religion, to become a powerful unifying
> factor, as a means of giving securer basis of solidarity to
> his empire.[13]

The king's imposition of Hellenism was that attempt to unify the empire through the transcendence of deity and religion. In a sense, he was playing with fire, the fire of true believers that he could not understand.

The death of Antiochus Epiphanes has more than one narrative in the books of the Maccabees. In 1 Maccabees 6, the Seleucid king is in Persia unsuccessfully seeking to plunder the city of Elymais to increase his waning wealth. A messenger tells Antiochus of Lysias's defeat to Judas Maccabeus in the battle of Beth-Zur and the subsequent cleansing of the temple. Whereupon the king becomes physically sick with disappointment. A sickness that he thought would kill him. In his deathbed pondering, he painfully regrets his poor treatment of the Jews but doesn't repent so much as suffer spiritual punishment for his choices. He then appoints a regent over his young son until he is of age

---

[12] Bevan, *The House of Seleucus*, 150.

[13] Phillips Barry, "Antiochus IV, Epiphanes," *Journal of Biblical Literature*, Vol. 29, No. 2 (1910), pp. 126-138

to reign. Then Antiochus dies. The writer wants to console himself that the king experiences some kind of justice in this world before he dies.

In 2 Maccabees 9, a different and more interesting tale is told with no less a religious agenda and a far greater hunger for earthly judgment. Antiochus is in Persepolis, Persia, seeking to rob its temples and gain control. He fails and retreats to Ecbatana near Babylonia, where he receives a message of Seleucid defeats to the Maccabees but *before* the cleansing of the temple has occurred.

Antiochus becomes so angry he leaves for Jerusalem, shouting in arrogance, "When I get there, I will make Jerusalem a cemetery of Jews" (9:4). We are then told that God in his providential retribution strikes the king with "a pain in his bowels, for which there was no relief, and with sharp internal tortures—and that very justly, for he had tortured the bowels of others with many and strange inflictions" (9:5-6). This does not stop Antiochus from his journey of rage. In fact, he tells his chariot driver to go faster. Unfortunately, the king falls out of the vehicle, and "the fall was so hard as to torture every limb of his body" (9:7).

In a verbose display of literary poetic justice, the writer mocks the king's epithet of "god manifest" by saying that he who once thought he had the "power of God manifest to all" was now "swarmed with worms" with an "intolerable stench" from the "rotting of his flesh." The storyteller really wants Antiochus to suffer deeply in this life for the pain he has caused as otherwise the Jewish suffering would seem without just recompense.

But Antiochus is enlightened and expresses his regret, not unlike King Nebuchadnezzar's revelation in the wild: "It is right to be subject to God; mortals should not think that they are equal to God" (9:12). Still, the writer does not want Antiochus to have the full release of forgiveness so he reminds us that even though the king made a vow to God to free the Jews from persecution and return the wealth he had stolen from the temple, "the Lord would no longer have mercy on him" (9:13).

Antiochus then appoints his son to take the throne. The writer concludes, "So the murderer and blasphemer, having endured the more intense suffering, such as he had inflicted on others, came to the end of his life by a most pitiable fate, among the mountains in a strange land" (9:28).

Abominable. Miserable. His flesh rotting. His bowels swollen with worms. His suffering unabated. In summary, the reader of 2 Maccabees can safely say of Antiochus Epiphanes, "Good riddance."

So we have come to understand the man behind the first abomination of desolation. Now, let us look at the detestable thing itself to see what it is.

Zeus and the Abomination of Desolation

Though there are many different versions of Greek mythology, the poet Hesiod (circa 700 BC) and his book *Theogony* is one of the foremost references for the origins, identities, and stories of their gods.[14] In it, we see a succession narrative of early gods overthrown by later gods.

In Greek mythology, first there was Chaos and Gaia (earth) with Night and Day. Ouranos (sky) and Gaia (earth) birthed the first set of primordial gods called the Titans. One of those Titans, Kronos, ambushed Ouranos, castrated him, and separated him (sky) from Gaia (earth), their version of a common component in most creation stories, the separation of heaven and earth.[15]

---

[14] Other main sources of Greek mythology used by scholars that vary in some of their details are Homer, Orpheus, Apollodorus, Pausanius, and Greek historians such as Herodotus, Diodorus Siculus, and Plutarch.

[15] Hesiod, trans., Barry B. Powell, *The Poems of Hesiod: Theogony, Works and Days and the Shield of Herakles* (Oakland, CA: University of California Press, 2017), *Theogony* 95-145, pp 36-41.

Kronos then took over and mated with his sister goddess Rhea. They gave birth to three female deities, Hestia, Demeter, and Hera, and three male deities, Pluto, Poseidon, and Zeus. Because Kronos did not want to be overthrown by his offspring as he had overthrown his own father, he swallowed his children.

Rhea, however, tricked Kronos and got him to swallow a stone wrapped in swaddling clothes instead of the real Zeus. Zeus grew up and managed to get Kronos to vomit Zeus's siblings into the world. Along with these freed captives are several Cyclopes, one-eyed monsters, who then provided the powerful weapons of thunderbolts to Zeus, a magical helmet of invisibility to Pluto, and a mighty trident to Poseidon.[16] The mountain Olympus became their home.

Zeus and the twelve Olympians defeated Kronos and the other Titans in the Titanomachy and imprisoned them in Tartarus, after which Zeus took his place as king of the gods and was allotted the sky as his domain. He became known as a storm god with the epithet "Cloud-Gatherer."[17]

Though most people know about Zeus taking his sister goddess Hera as his wife, they may not be aware that Hera was his seventh and last wife. Nor was Zeus satisfied with only seven wives. He also took many mistresses, both goddess and human. Zeus was a randy, promiscuous adulterer. He became known for fathering many gods such as Apollo the sun god, Ares the god of war, and Athena goddess of war. He also mated with mortal women to birth human/god hybrids, the most famous of which was Heracles.

---

[16] Apollodorus, *Library of Greek Mythology* 1.1.5-2.1 pp 27-28.

[17] Homer, *Illiad* 1.511.

There is little doubt that Zeus's sexual interaction with humans was modeled on the ancient Near Eastern narrative of the divine Sons of God mating with human daughters of men. Though Heracles was not a giant like the human/angel hybrid Nephilim, he was certainly in the category of the Hebrew *gibborim*, the mighty men of old, the men of renown (Genesis 6:4). His character reflected the excess of a demigod as well. He had extraordinary strength and extraordinary passions, including many sexual conquests of both men and women.

Like father, like son.

When Antiochus Epiphanes set up the "abomination of desolation" in the Jerusalem temple, he renamed it the temple of Zeus Olympian (2 Maccabees 6:2). But what did the abomination look like and what rituals did the king demand from the Jews? To answer that, we begin with the text of the Maccabees. 1 Maccabees is the least detailed. It simply states:

> 1 Maccabees 1:54-55 (LES)
> Now [the Seleucid officials] built an **abomination of desolation** on the [Jerusalem] altar, and in the cities around Judah, they built altars. And at the windows of their houses and in the streets, they burned incense.

> 1 Maccabees 1: 44-47 (LES)
> And the king [Antiochus] sent letters by messengers to Jerusalem and the towns of Judah; he directed them … to build altars and sacred precincts and shrines for idols, to sacrifice swine and other unclean animals.

Ancient Jewish historian Josephus wrote, "And when the king had built an idol altar upon God's Altar, he slew swine upon it, and so offered a sacrifice."[18]

In Hebrew, the word "abomination" (*siqqus*) was a word used in the context of physical images of pagan gods (idols) that Yahweh considered detestable in his presence.[19] The Hebrew word for "desolate" (*mesomem*) reinforced that alienation. It meant to make uninhabitable, thus implying the withdrawal of God's presence due to the presence of the abominable idol. Yahweh simply did not tolerate any gods before him (Exodus 20:3).

So the Hebrew conception in the words "abomination of desolation" involved the presence of the image of a false god. Desolation did not require actual destruction of the temple but simply religious pollution of images/idols that resulted in God's presence being withdrawn.

Josephus wrote that "the king [Antiochus Epiphanes] built an idol altar upon God's altar,"[20] which echoes 1 Maccabees 1:59: "They were sacrificing on the altar [to Zeus] that was on [Yahweh's] altar for burnt sacrifices." We are told nowhere what the idol altar built upon Yahweh's altar may have looked like. Most assume the simple description of new stones placed upon the existing stones of the Jerusalem altar. But why would there be a need to add additional stones to an existing functioning altar? Unless they were adding something distinctly Greek to that altar.

The implication is that the stones may have been actual idol images of some kind as those indicated by the Hebrew terms defined above. Though

---

[18] Josephus, Antiquities 12.4 (253) Flavius Josephus and William Whiston, *The Works of Josephus: Complete and Unabridged* (Peabody: Hendrickson, 1987), 324.

[19] Deuteronomy 29:17; 2 Kings 23:24; 2 Chronicles 15:8; Jeremiah 13:27; 16:8; 32:34; Ezekiel 20:7; 32:23.

[20] Josephus, *Antiquities* 12.5.4 [12.253].

we know the Jerusalem temple was renamed for Zeus Olympian by Antiochus Epiphanes, we also know that altars to Zeus could include his image as well as those of other deities such as Athena.[21] A common ancient view of the abomination of desolation was that of Roman philosopher Porphyry (AD 234-305), who suggested that it was an actual statue of Zeus enthroned on the altar.[22] Such large statues of Zeus were known in other Greek conquered cities. Ancient historians wrote of a golden statue of Zeus 12 cubits (18 feet) high in the precinct of the Babylonian temple, a 40-foot-tall golden statue of Zeus at the temple of Belus, and a 72-foot-tall bronze statue of Zeus at Tarantum.[23]

While the possibility of a statue on the altar has been rejected by more recent interpretations, it would make sense to place such a statue of Zeus into the Holy of Holies because that inner sanctuary was supposed to be the throne of God, with the ark of the covenant as his footstool. Such an act would represent Zeus taking over Yahweh's throne.

The Anchor Bible Commentary suggests the "abomination of desolation" may have consisted of three meteorite cult-stones (*massebot*) that represented the God of the Jews [Yahweh/Zeus], his female divine consort the Queen of Heaven [Anat/Athena], and his divine son [Dionysus].[24] Though entirely speculative, this would synchronize well with the idol worship of cult standing stones (*massebot*), already long practiced by the Jews historically.

---

[21] This is the case with the famous altar of Zeus at Pergamum that includes Athena.

[22] John Collins and Peter W. Flint, Ed., *The Book of Daniel: Composition and Reception Volume 2* (Boston, MA: Brill, 2001), 677.

[23] James Alan Montgomery, *A Critical and Exegetical Commentary on the Book of Daniel* (Edinburgh, T&T Clark, 1959), 193-194.

[24] Jonathan A. Goldstein, *I Maccabees: A New Translation with Introduction and Commentary, vol. 41*, Anchor Yale Bible (New Haven; London: Yale University Press, 2008), 224.

Though the Jews would not have required cult-stones to be meteorites,[25] the Greek king would find commonality with massebot in the fact that the famous temple of Apollo at Delphi housed the Omphalos, a large meteorite conical stone that was believed to have been placed at that location by Zeus to mark it as the "navel" or center of the earth.[26]

Since it is likely the high priest Menelaus would have counseled Antiochus in this matter, Menelaus might have suggested a subversive way of syncretizing the gods of Canaan with the gods of Greece. Zeus had already been worshipped in Syrian cities as Ba'al-Shamem, and his consort was Anat (Athena). So massebot standing stones that represented gods interchangeable between Canaan and Greece might be one way of seeking the smoothest transition.

But a strong argument against this massebot view is that Antiochus was extremely hostile to the Jewish religion and sought to deny them their distinctives in Torah, so it would not be as likely that he would seek a syncretistic blending as opposed to an explicit and hostile replacement of deities.[27]

Though an attempt to decode this nefarious abomination of desolation leaves us with a plethora of questions and unproven possibilities, it remains a fascinating subject for fictional speculation in the novel Judah Maccabee.

---

[25] "Standing Stones," Brian Godawa, *The Spiritual World of Jezebel and Elijah* (Texas: Warrior Poet Publishing, 2021), 97-99.

[26] Robin Hard, *The Routledge Handbook of Greek Mythology, 8th edition* (Oxon, OX: Routledge, 1928, 2020), 136-137.

[27] Bible scholar Johan Lust concludes, "These passages seem to identify the 'abomination of desolation' with an 'idol altar,' a kind of superstructure built upon the altar of the Lord. No mention is made of a statue of a pagan deity, nor of meteorites." Johan Lust, "Cult Sacrifice in Daniel. The Tamil and the Abomination of Desolation," John J. Collins and Peter W. Flint, Eds., *The Book of Daniel: Composition and Reception Volume 2* (Boston, MA: Brill, 2001), 684.

Regarding the activities of idolatry imposed by Antiochus, 2 Maccabees describes in more detail the imposition of Greek gods upon the Jews (bold emphasis added).

2 Maccabees 6:1-6 (RSV)
Not long after this, the king sent an Athenian senator to compel the Jews to forsake the laws of their ancestors and no longer to live by the laws of God; **also to pollute the temple in Jerusalem and to call it the temple of Olympian Zeus, and to call the one in Gerizim the temple of Zeus-the-Friend-of-Strangers, as did the people who lived in that place.**

Harsh and utterly grievous was the onslaught of evil. For the temple was filled with debauchery and reveling by the **Gentiles, who dallied with prostitutes and had intercourse with women within the sacred precincts,** and besides brought in things for sacrifice that were unfit. The altar was **covered with abominable offerings that were forbidden by the laws.** People could neither keep the sabbath, nor observe the festivals of their ancestors, nor so much as confess themselves to be Jews.

After this, the writer of 2 Maccabees adds that at a festival for Dionysus, the Greek god of bacchanalia, the Jews were also forced to wear "wreaths of ivy and to walk in the procession in honor of Dionysus" (6:7). What the writer is too diplomatic to describe is that the procession of the festival, called the Dionysia, involved carrying large wooden or bronze "phalloi," images of phalluses on poles. A cart with a huge phallus image was pulled behind.

This is because the origin of the celebration was rooted in a mythical incident where the city of Athens rejected a gifted statue of

Dionysus, so the god had sent a plague on the genitals of the male citizens. Their epidemic malady was only healed by the acceptance of the cult of Dionysus.[28]

But back to Zeus.

According to 2 Maccabees, the pagan worship of Zeus involved temple prostitutes in the sacred precincts of the temple mount. But again, this behavior was already well-known in Israel's history of Canaanite idol worship, so it would be another familiar addition to the imposed apostasy.

But the focus of worship was an idol altar built upon the Jerusalem altar of burnt offerings upon which unclean animals such as pigs were sacrificed. This idolatrous altar was considered the "abomination of desolation" predicted by Daniel the prophet.

> Daniel 11:31
> Forces from him [Antiochus Epiphanes] shall appear and profane the temple and fortress [in Jerusalem], and shall take away the regular burnt offering. And they shall set up the **abomination that makes desolate**.

This same abomination of desolation is implicated in another prophecy of Daniel that foretells the Maccabean incidents. And this one brings in the spiritual powers involved in the incident.

---

[28] "Dionysia," Wikipedia: https://en.wikipedia.org/wiki/Dionysia

"The date of the desecration of the temple in the month just before the winter solstice (Kislev) may have coincided with a festival of Dionysus. Antiochus IV's Athenian expert may have suggested imposing on the Jews the "rustic Dionysia," which in Athens were celebrated in the month of Posideon=Kislev; indeed, the author at I 1:54–55 stresses that the rites were observed in the country towns." Jonathan A. Goldstein, *I Maccabees: A New Translation with Introduction and Commentary*, vol. 41, Anchor Yale Bible (New Haven; London: Yale University Press, 2008), 155.

Daniel 8:9–13

Out of one of them came a little horn [Antiochus Epiphanes], which grew exceedingly great toward the south, toward the east, and toward the glorious land. It grew great, even to the host of heaven. And some of the host and some of the stars it threw down to the ground and trampled on them. It became great, even as great as the Prince of the host. And the regular burnt offering was taken away from him, and the place of his sanctuary was overthrown. And a host will be given over to it together with the regular burnt offering because of transgression, and it will throw truth to the ground, and it will act and prosper. Then I heard a holy one speaking, and another holy one said to the one who spoke, "For how long is the vision concerning the regular burnt offering, the **transgression that makes desolate**, and the giving over of the sanctuary and host to be trampled underfoot?"

As explained earlier, this little horn is a descendant of the great single horn of the goat that represented Alexander the Great of Macedon. After the Greek conqueror's death, his kingdom was divided between four of his generals. Out of one of those generals, Seleucus, came this little horn, Antiochus IV Epiphanes.

Those who would seek to find a mere earthly historical narrative here see Antiochus growing so great and specifically with regard to the "glorious land" of Israel that he would overcome the "Prince of the host," interpreted as the high priest, from whom the regular burnt offering would be taken. A host of Jews would then be "given over to" Antiochus in both war and slavery. Antiochus then tramples the temple and God's people underfoot.

But this earthly naturalistic interpretation does not take into account the supernatural context that includes the spiritual powers at war in the heavenlies.

First, the context of this prophecy within the book of Daniel is quite supernatural. The chapter before it, Daniel 7, charted out the four Gentile kingdoms ending in Rome which culminate in the ascension of the Son of Man (Jesus) to his throne in heaven. We read of "ten thousand times ten thousand" who stood before that fiery throne as "the court sat in judgment" (Daniel 7:10). This phrase is always used of Yahweh's heavenly host of divine beings that surrounds him, often in judgment.[29]

So when Daniel 8:10-11 refers to the little horn Antiochus Epiphanes becoming "as great as the Prince of the host," this is not a mere reference to a human high priest but likely a supernatural reference to the godlike pretensions of Antiochus Epiphanes ("god manifest") in taking over Yahweh's house (the temple of his presence) and with it the spiritual authority over Israel.

In Daniel, the Aramaic word for "prince" (*sar*) is used of spiritual princes over nations (Daniel 10:13, 20-21). Daniel interprets for us later in the passage that Antiochus becoming "as great as the Prince of the host" was another way of saying that the little horn "shall rise up against the Prince of princes," that "in his own mind he shall become great" (8:25). In fact, he would not be a god but "he shall be broken—but not by human hands" (8:25). This was spiritual warfare with historic consequences. There is only one Prince of princes in both heaven and earth, and that is Yahweh.[30] And there is only one Prince of the host,

---

29 Jude 14:15; Psalm 68:17; Revelation 5:11; Deuteronomy 33:2-3 LXX.

30 "Prince of the host" in Hebrew was the same phrase used of the Angel of Yahweh, Yahweh himself (Joshua 5:14)

Yahweh, God of hosts.[31] This Prince of the host of heaven is the Angel of Yahweh (Joshua 5:14-15), who is ultimately Jesus pre-incarnate (Revelation 9:11-16), our high priest (Hebrews 4:14).

The "host" of this Prince is defined by Daniel as "host of heaven," including the stars (8:10). I have described in detail elsewhere that "host of heaven" in the Bible is not merely a reference to the physical sun, moon, and stars but also to angelic Sons of God (Job 38:7), other angels (Psalms 148:2-3), and gods of the nations (Deuteronomy 4:12-20).[32]

This leads to the most natural conclusion that this symbolic prophecy of stars "being thrown to the ground and trampled" is fulfilled in heavenly powers being overthrown along with their earthly counterparts. This is the conflict of gods over nations. When the pagan ruler Antiochus captured the temple and profaned it, some of Yahweh's heavenly host were "given over to it together with the regular burnt offering because of the transgression" (Daniel 8:12). The heavenly conflict was tied to the earthly conflict. Because Israel had transgressed against Yahweh in her unfaithfulness, this empowered the pagan earthly and heavenly rulers to maintain temporary power over the holy temple of Yahweh. On earth as it is in heaven (Matthew 6:10b).

When Daniel hears a "holy one" speaking to another "holy one," some think that "holy one" is a reference to Israelites, or "saints" as it is sometimes translated. But "holy one" is tricky because it is used of both human Israelites[33] and heavenly divine beings around God's throne as well as Yahweh himself.[34] So context would dictate the meaning. The

---

[31] Psalm 59:5; 89:8; Isaiah 10:24, 33; Jeremiah 5:14; 15:16; 38:17; Amos 4:13; 5:27.

[32] See also Deuteronomy 32:8-9, 17, 43. For detailed investigation of stars as divine see Brian Godawa *When Watchers Ruled the Nations: Pagan Gods at War with Israel's God and the Spiritual World of the Bible* (Texas: Warrior Poet Publishing, 2021), 27-37.

[33] Daniel 7:18, 21-22; 25, 27; 8:24; Psalm 34:9; 16:3; 30:4.

[34] Psalm 89:5, 7; Deuteronomy 33:2; Zechariah 14:5; Jude 14; Job 15:15.

context of Daniel contains both. But when it comes to visions in Daniel, the holy ones are described explicitly as heavenly beings.

For example in Daniel 4, the prophet sees a vision where he defines "a watcher, **a holy one**, came down from heaven" (4:13). Those Watchers make decrees, "decisions by the word of the **holy ones**" (4:17). And let us not forget that in Daniel 8, the original passage we are looking at, Daniel is also having a vision of these holy ones who are "host of heaven," not of earth.

So the context of Daniel 8 is very clearly a story of the earthly Antiochus trampling God's temple and people underfoot but with the simultaneous spiritual reality of the heavenly host over Israel being temporarily overcome.

The "transgression that makes desolate" is therefore a reference to the sin of Israel that brought on the abomination of desolation, i.e., the imposition of Zeus worship with its altars and pagan ritual behaviors coupled with the spiritual power that comes with such earthly victory.

But of course, Yahweh's will is never ultimately thwarted. Ultimately, both the power and defeat of Antiochus as well as the spiritual powers behind him are by the hand of Yahweh (Daniel 8:24-25). As king Nebuchadnezzar would ultimately learn:

Daniel 4:35
[Yahweh] does according to his will among the host of
     heaven
     and among the inhabitants of the earth;

and none can stay his hand
     or say to him, "What have you done?"

Partial or Dual Fulfillment?

At this point, some Bible prophecy speculators will concede that the little horn and abomination of desolation in Daniel 8 and 11 are fulfilled in Antiochus Epiphanes in 168-165 BC. But they argue that he is only a "partial fulfillment" of this prophecy. That there is still an abomination of desolation in our future which will also fulfill these prophecies in an ultimate sense. Put another way, they believe there is a short-term fulfillment in Antiochus and a long-term fulfillment in another ruler yet to come. Antiochus then becomes only a type of fulfillment but not the final one. He is either a "partial fulfillment" or one of dual or multiple fulfillments of the same prophecy. These speculators believe the prophecies are *really* pointing toward someone else in our future. Sometimes they will even argue that there are many "abominations of desolation" and "little horns" in history (Hitler, Mussolini, Stalin, etc.) that point toward this ultimate abomination of desolation.

This is a dangerous unbiblical hermeneutic.

Those who hold this view have not thought through what they are really arguing for. Their view ultimately reduces Bible prophecy to subjective arbitrary putty that can be pressed into any shape according to the personal subjective tastes of the interpreter. The result is that Bible prophecy can mean whatever any interpreter can make it fit. Let's look at how this plays out.

First, what does "partial fulfillment" even mean? Does that mean Antiochus only fulfilled some of the prophecies but not all of them? That would be empirically false. I have shown how that little horn Seleucid king and his abominable idol fulfilled *all the prophecies* related to the abomination of desolation in Daniel 8 and 11. To say that he only partially fulfilled those prophecies is to deny the biblical facts.

If by "partial" the interpreter means that it is only one of two or more fulfillments of the same prophecy, then they still have the problem of imposing their preconceived bias upon the text. Where in the Bible does it say these prophecies are about anything other than the singular historic events they predict? Nowhere. It either fulfills the prophecy or it does not. If it fulfills the prophecy, where does the prophet say there will be others? To see the historic fulfillment of these prophesies and declare two or more fulfillments of one prophecy is to claim a mystical or secret knowledge of the "real meaning" of the prophecy that is not apparent in the text. This would reduce prophecy to the arbitrary whim of every private interpretation.

Another problem with partial, dual, or multiple fulfillments is that Daniel's prophecies are specifically rooted in historical events that explicitly point to one time period of history that ended in Messiah in the first century. Consider the fact that Daniel's dream interpretation in Daniel 2 is all about the arrival of Messiah, who brings the Kingdom of God "in the days of these kings" (2:44). What kings? Daniel explains that Nebuchadnezzar's dream of the metallic statue symbolically represented four kingdoms in succession—the Babylonians, the Medo-Persians, the Greeks, and the Romans (2:36-43). These are exactly the kingdoms that we see in past history.

Daniel then says that the Messiah would bring his kingdom in the days of the last kingdom, that of Rome (2:34, 44-45). From that day forward, the Messiah's kingdom would grow to overcome all the other kingdoms (2:44-45). This all happened in history just as Daniel predicted. The Babylonians were conquered by the Medo-Persians, who were then conquered by the Macedonian Greek kingdom of Alexander the Great, whose kingdom was eventually overtaken by ancient Rome.

Some futurists try to deny the contiguous history in the prophecy, claiming that it is not about the first coming of Jesus but his second coming. They believe that the Roman kingdom of iron mixed with clay is not the ancient Roman kingdom into which Jesus came but that Daniel skips right over the coming of Messiah, jumping thousands of years later to his second coming. The Roman empire in the prophecy then becomes a "rebuilt Roman empire" in our future, not the ancient Roman empire that came right after the Greek empire in actual history.

This makes no sense and doesn't fit the prophecy. Why would Daniel, whose entire purpose is to predict the coming of Messiah after all these Gentile kingdoms, just ignore that first coming and jump thousands of years later to a second coming? It would turn the first coming into an inconsequential event.

There is nowhere in the text that says there is a gap of thousands of years before the last kingdom. On the contrary, they are successive kingdoms which happen to match history perfectly. Ancient Rome came after ancient Greece just as Nebuchadnezzar's dream predicted. Messiah came during that kingdom and brought it all down just a few centuries after his arrival—just as the "rock cut without hands" in the prophecy struck the statue at the Roman feet, demolishing it.

The futurist prejudice is so blinding it will eliminate or downplay the prophecy of the first coming of Messiah to maintain its presumed scenario for the future. Such interpretation denies the obvious fulfillment and inserts a two-plus-thousand-year gap that is not in the text to push the last kingdom into the future. The futurist engages in revising the Bible itself to keep their eschatological system from collapsing into absurdity.

To reinforce the interpretation that Daniel is speaking of the four kingdoms of our past history, the rest of his book chronicles that history in more detail through various other visions. Daniel has another vision under the Babylonian king Belshazzar that zooms in on the Medo-Persian kingdom and then the Greek kingdom to come (Daniel 8). He depicts Alexander the Great as a mighty goat that overcomes a ram symbolizing Medo-Persia. This actually happened in history. Then in 8:9-14, Daniel explains Antiochus Epiphanes and his abomination of desolation coming out of that Greek kingdom as a little horn that we have exegeted earlier.

In Daniel 10, we read about the spiritual principality of Persia who will soon be battling the principality of Greece just as the Greek kingdom of Alexander the Great eventually took over Persia in history. Then in Daniel 11, we get a dizzying series of wars between the "kings of the north" and the "kings of the south," which refer to the Syrian Wars between the Greek Seleucids and Ptolemies after Alexander (see my chart at the end of this book about fulfillment of Daniel 11 in the lead-up to and including the Syrian Wars of the second century BC). Antiochus Epiphanes appears in 11:20 as the final willful king of that series who brings his abomination of desolation.

After Antiochus comes the final king at the time of the end and the events of Daniel 12 that are during the days of ancient Rome. All this narrative requires more exegesis than this small booklet can offer.[35] But I think I have shown enough details to make it clear that the context of Daniel from beginning to end is all about the four Gentile kingdoms that would oppress Israel until Messiah came. And that's what biblical history is, a history of Israel, not the Gentile world.

---

[35] For more details on Daniel's prophecies of history see my podcast series, "Daniel and End Times Prophecy": https://www.youtube.com/playlist?list=PL5TyMLcYh4AOPA4WGoSAr9rSxUEMgv2hC

Over and over again, the book of Daniel spells out prophetic and symbolic references to the Babylonians, the Medo-Persians, the Greeks (especially the Seleucids and Ptolemies), and then the Romans. The context of Daniel is so clearly about Israel's past history until Messiah that to say it is also symbolic of a future fulfillment is to engage in interpretive violence against the text. It is wrenching prophecies out of their full context in the book and arbitrarily applying them to some speculative future that only the interpreter can know.

This brings me to another problem with this futurist catastrophe of interpretation. Some will argue that there is precedent for dual fulfillment claims in Daniel by pointing to Messianic prophecies that seem to have a short-term fulfillment in the Old Testament and a long-term fulfillment in the New Testament in Jesus. For instance, they will claim that prophecies like Isaiah 7 about the virgin birth of Messiah apply to a local referent. God is speaking to king Ahaz and telling him that a young maiden in his presence would have a child who would not be fully grown before King Rezin of Damascus and "the son of Remaliah" of Israel would find their land deserted.[36] New Testament writers then tell us that these prophecies also apply to Jesus as the Messiah (Matthew 1:22-23).

This kind of dual fulfillment in messianic prophecy is another subject too complex to address here. It is sometimes called typology. But for the sake of argument, I will assume it is true. That some Old Testament prophecies spoken of Jesus as Messiah may also have a local referent in Old Testament history. Here is the problem for the futurist. The ones who have made the claim of dual fulfillment of Messianic prophecies are New Testament apostles, who were the New Testament

---

[36] Gene M. Tucker, "The Book of Isaiah 1–39," in *New Interpreter's Bible*, ed. Leander E. Keck, vol. 6 (Nashville: Abingdon Press, 1994–2004), 111.

equivalent of the Old Testament prophets. They spoke for God, and their writings became Scripture. Jesus had actually invested them with his authority as his representatives (John 14:26), his ultimate authorities on earth (1 Corinthians 12:28).

For a Christian to look at the New Testament apostles and to conclude that we now have the same authority to claim dual fulfillments of prophecies *that the apostles did not claim* is to place ourselves and our subjective interpretations in the place of apostolic authority or prophets of God.[37] One would be saying, "I have new revelation from God that tells me that the prophecies of Daniel, though fulfilled in the past history of the four Gentile kingdoms, *also* have a future fulfillment to come." That claim by definition is "new revelation" because there is no dual fulfillment in the text according to Daniel. Such a claim is bringing a new interpretation that extends beyond what the prophecy actually predicts and fulfills. It is adding to the Word of God.

I don't know any Christian who would want to make such an explicit claim. But that is exactly what one is doing when one says, "I can do what the apostles did. I can declare dual fulfillments beyond the text." Only a bona fide prophet of God can claim to speak for God and therefore make such connections as that "out of Egypt I called my Son" is also about Jesus (Hosea 11:1; Matthew 2:15). We do not have the right to do what the apostles and prophets of God did in exegeting dual fulfillments, if that is in fact what they did.

But the implications are far worse. If one claims prophecies have dual or multiple fulfillments, then every prophecy can be so interpreted. That would mean there could be another Son of David born in Bethlehem of a virgin who would take the sins of the world upon

---

[37] The New Testament spiritual gift of prophecy is not the same as Old Testament prophets. The apostles are.

himself. Outrageous! Yes, but as soon as you say you cannot do that, you have put an arbitrary restriction that contradicts your original interpreting principle. You have said prophecies can have dual fulfillments, just not *those* prophecies. But where do you get that restriction? And where do you stop? It's arbitrary. If the standard is that prophecies can have dual fulfillments, that means messianic prophecies can too. And why not triple fulfillments? Or more?

Well, you may say, Jesus already came and died for our sins once and for all, so that can't happen again. Precisely. Once a prophecy is fulfilled, there is no "dual fulfillment," or you reduce it to subjective putty that is hostage to the whims of interpreters and makes us all New Testament apostles of God. If I can find any kind of similarity or connection between arbitrary words in the Old Testament and something in today's world, I have claimed a new revelation of God's Word.

This is not so absurd or unrealistic as it sounds. There are religious "Christian" writers and speakers right now who interpret the Bible this way, taking Scriptures out of context and finding mystical new fulfillments in our day. I have read one of them claim that historical events of the Old Testament such as the story of Jezebel and Elijah are prophecy "templates" for events being fulfilled in our day in America. With the wave of an interpretive wand, the historical Old Testament account has been turned into prophecies for today without any justification from Scripture whatsoever. This man does not claim analogies, he claims actual prophecies. And this man claims it is revelation from the Holy Spirit.

By that claim, his writing of these so-called prophecies should be considered Scripture. He probably wouldn't claim that, but it is the logical conclusion of his premises. If God is giving him new revelation that some historical story in the Old Testament is now a prophecy, then he should logically conclude that his "revelation" is the Word of God and should be written down as scripture. This is an obvious blasphemy in claiming new revelation after apostolic authority has passed away. This is not some obscure preacher in a small church somewhere. This is a mega-bestselling "teacher," and untold hundreds of thousands of Christians are following his delusion of false prophecies.

I hope you can see how this concept of multiple fulfillments of prophecy becomes an arbitrary rule of Bible interpretation that results in every person appointing themselves a prophet of their own interpretation of out-of-context Scripture. If prophecy has multiple fulfillments, why can't I claim that Abraham Lincoln's emancipation of the slaves is a "partial fulfillment" of "proclaiming liberty to the captives" in Isaiah 6:1? Or that the lion with eagle wings in Daniel's vision about Babylon is a dual prophecy about America because the eagle is our national bird and we are like a powerful lion in the world. All analogies become prophecies. The possible interpretations are literally endless, reducing Bible prophecies into putty that can be shaped by a million interpretations, making a million prophets of God. In the dual or multiple fulfillment view, prophecy becomes meaningless words that can be applied to anything to which the interpreter can make a connection.

THE FUTURE ABOMINATION OF DESOLATION

Daniel 9:26–27

And the people of the prince who is to come shall destroy the city and the sanctuary. Its end shall come with a flood, and to the end there shall be war. **Desolations** are decreed. And he shall make a strong covenant with many for one week, and for half of the week he shall put an end to sacrifice and offering. And on **the wing of abominations shall come one who makes desolate,** until the decreed end is poured out on the **desolate**."

Daniel 12:11

And from the time that the regular burnt offering is taken away and the **abomination that makes desolate** is set up, there shall be 1,290 days.

Spoken of by Daniel

As we saw earlier, Antiochus IV Epiphanes fulfilled the prophecies about the abomination of desolation in Daniel chapters 8 and 11. But there are two other passages in Daniel that talk about a second abomination of desolation to come long after Antiochus Epiphanes is gone. This abomination appears as indicated above in chapters 9 and 12. This is not partial or dual fulfillment but a biblically defined second abomination of desolation that is different from the first.

I do not have the space here to explore this topic exhaustively. It is one of those prophecies that has a dozen different interpretations. I recommend *The Seventy Weeks and the Great Tribulation* by Philip Mauro. Some Bible scholars suggest that the abomination of desolation spoken of in Daniel 9 and 12 is the same being as in Daniel 8 and 11. But they cannot be the same for three big reasons I have previously stated. One, the first abomination by Antiochus was described as only a desecration of the temple (religious pollution) while the second abomination includes both the desolation *and* the destruction of that temple, as well as the city (9:26). That is a very big difference. Two, the period of desolation for the first abomination was 2,300 days, or evenings and mornings (Daniel 8:14), while the period of desolation for the second abomination would be 1,290 days (Daniel 12:11). Three, the first abomination was to occur long *before* "the time of the end" (Daniel 11:27, 35) while the second abomination was explicitly stated to occur *during* "the time of the end" (Daniel 11:40; 12:4, 9), at "the end of days" (Daniel 12:13). No matter how one interprets "the end," it is a definite time period that was to occur long after that first abomination of desolation.

The informed reader will naturally ask if this is the abomination that Jesus predicted.

> Matthew 24:15–20
> [Jesus:] "So when you see the **abomination of desolation** spoken of by the prophet Daniel, standing in the holy place (let the reader understand)

I believe it is. And I will address Jesus later. For now, I want to see where Daniel himself is pointing. Then we will look at how Jesus confirms that future monster.

So, who is this second abominable desolator to come? Let's take a closer look at Daniel 9.

The Seventy Weeks

Probably the most famous messianic prophecy in the Old Testament is Daniel's vision of the 70 Weeks. This is because it predicts the coming Messiah within a specific number of years from a specific historical event—the decree to restore and rebuild Jerusalem, most likely fulfilled in the decree of Artaxerxes I around 457 BC (Nehemiah 2:1). From 457 BC to AD 30 (the death of Jesus the Anointed One) is 487 years, the middle of the 70th week of years (Daniel 9:27).[57]

The English phrase "70 weeks" is a translation of the Hebrew "70 sevens" of years, or 490 years. That chronology would place Messiah in the very lifetime of Jesus.[58] This is why messianic expectation was so high in the first century. But it also places the arrival of Messiah right before the arrival of one who would set up an "abomination of desolation," going on to defile and destroy both Jerusalem and her holy temple. Just exactly how are these two things, the Anointed One and Abomination, related in time and space? And what do they have to do with the abomination of desolation in the days of the Maccabees as discussed earlier in this book? Let's take a closer look at the 70 Weeks prophecy.

---

[57] It is important to note that our dates for these events are not set in stone. At best, we can only get close, but not exact, as much as some Christians would prefer. Jay Rogers, *The Prophecy of Daniel in Preterist Perspective: The Easy Parts and the Hard Parts* (Media House, 2021), 13.

[58] Another theory is that the decree to restore and rebuild Jerusalem was that of Cyrus the Great of Babylon in 538 BC, which would still place Messiah in the rough time period of Jesus. In this view, the prophecy does not claim scientific precision, but rather approximation, which is not unwarranted in prophetic interpretation.

Daniel 9:24–27

24 Seventy weeks are decreed about your people and your holy city, to finish the transgression, to put an end to sin, and to atone for iniquity, to bring in everlasting righteousness, to seal both vision and prophet, and to anoint the most holy.

25 Know therefore and understand that from the going out of the word to restore and build Jerusalem to the coming of an anointed one, a prince, there shall be seven weeks. Then for sixty-two weeks it shall be built again with squares and moat, but in a troubled time. 26 And after the sixty-two weeks, an anointed one shall be cut off and shall have nothing. And the people of the prince who is to come shall destroy the city and the sanctuary. Its end shall come with a flood, and to the end there shall be war. Desolations are decreed.

27 And he shall make a strong covenant with many for one week, and for half of the week he shall put an end to sacrifice and offering. And on the wing of abominations shall come one who makes desolate, until the decreed end is poured out on the desolate.

Let's take a closer look at the first part of this passage. Daniel's prophecy was given to Israel. Because Israel had been unfaithful to Yahweh, he had punished his people with exile in Babylon, the city from which Daniel was writing. When Daniel states that 70 weeks is decreed for God's holy people and city, he is referring to Jeremiah's prophecy that the exile would last for 70 years (Jeremiah 25:8-12). Daniel is now amplifying that the 70 years of judgment would be multiplied because of the multiplied wickedness of Israel (Daniel 9:2, 5-7). Though they would come back from exile in 70 years as promised (Ezra 1:1), their transgression would not be forgiven for 70 weeks of years. The Hebrew word for "weeks" is actually seven. So Daniel is saying that the prophecy will be fulfilled within 70 sevens of years, or 490 years. At the end of that time, the Anointed One, Messiah, would arrive to complete the punishment and bring in the New Covenant of forgiveness.

When Daniel wrote of "**finishing the transgression, to put an end to sin and atone for iniquity**" (9:24), he was writing about the sin of Israel. When Messiah came, he would put an end to sin and atone for Israel's transgression of continuing disobedience to Yahweh. This was fulfilled when the angel of the Lord told Mary to call her child Jesus, "for he will save his people from their sins" (Matthew 1:21). When Jesus cried out "It is finished" on the cross, he was putting an end to sin with his once-for-all sacrifice that atoned for iniquity and **brought in everlasting righteousness**, just as Daniel prophesied (Hebrews 9:12-14).

Jesus confirmed the promise, or "**sealed both vision and prophet**" (Daniel 9:24), in fulfilling the messianic promise to which all the prophets had looked forward (1 Peter 1:10-12). Jesus was the seal on the scroll of God's prophecies. And he was the "**anointed, most holy**." The English translation that there was to be an "anointing of a most holy *place*" is not in the original language. In the Hebrew, it only says "anoint a most holy." Contextually, that would be Jesus. Since Jesus was the Anointed One, he was the most holy for only he could stand in the Holy of Holies of Yahweh's temple as our perfect sinless high priest.

The prophecy then returns to proclaim when this prophecy clock would begin. But this is sometimes translated in a confusing way that throws off interpretations. Does Messiah the prince come after the first seven weeks as the ESV translates or after 69 weeks (7+62)? The NASB95 cuts through that confusion with some clarity.

Daniel 9:25 (NASB95)

"So you are to know and discern that from the issuing of a decree to restore and rebuild Jerusalem until Messiah the Prince there will be seven weeks and sixty-two weeks; it will be built again, with plaza and moat, even in times of distress.

Consider reading the passage this way. There are three events coming—the decree about Jerusalem, its actual rebuilding, and the coming of Messiah. Those are three events within two different time periods. The first event, the decree, launches the first time period of 7 sevens, or 49 years. The city of Jerusalem was rebuilt in Nehemiah's day within 49 years after the decree during the **"times of distress"** or **"troubled times"** of Nehemiah 4:18. Then after the next 62 sevens of years, or about 483 years after the decree, the prophecy predicted the coming of Messiah. Messiah comes after 7+62 weeks of years, or 483 years.

After Messiah comes (i.e., after that 62nd week), he would be "**cut off and shall have nothing**" (Daniel 9:26). We see this fulfilled in Jesus's words on the cross: "My God, my God, why have you forsaken me?" (Matthew 27:46, taken from Psalm 22:1). Sin cuts off spiritual relationship. "For our sake he made [Jesus] to be sin who knew no sin, so that in him we might become the righteousness of God" (2 Corinthians 5:21).

Messianic Context of Daniel 9:24-26	
Daniel Verse	**New Testament Fulfillment**
Finish the transgression.	Daniel 9:5-6, 10-11.
Put an end to sin.	Hebrews 9:26; 1:3.
Atone for iniquity.	Colossians 1:14; John 1:29; 1 John 2:2.
Bring in everlasting righteousness.	2 Corinthians 9:9; Daniel 7:14; Matthew 6:33; 1 Corinthians 1:30.
Seal both vision and prophet.	Luke 18:31; 24:44; 21:22; Matthew 5:17-18.
Anoint a most holy place.	Luke 4:17–21; Isaiah 61:1-2.
Temple rebuilt in troubled times.	Nehemiah 4:18.
Messiah cut off and have nothing.	Matthew 27:46 (Psalm 22:1); 2 Corinthians 5:21.

So, 69 of the 70 weeks are fulfilled up to the time of Messiah Jesus. But the text actually says that the Messiah is cut off "after" 69 weeks (7 + 62). So, his cutting off occurs sometime after his arrival at the start of the 70th week. Jesus started his ministry at age 30 around the years AD 27-29. That was the end of the 69th week and the beginning of the 70th week. And we know that about 3-1/2 years into his ministry, Jesus was crucified. Remember that 3-1/2 years because it is going to be important.

Next, we are told that a people of the **"prince to come"** shall destroy the city and sanctuary (Jerusalem and the temple). Some link this prince to the one who later "comes on the wing of abominations" (Daniel 9:27). I do not believe this to be the case because in the previous verse, the Messiah ("anointed one") is described as *the prince who is to come*. There are not two princes here. There is only one, and he is the Messiah prince.

Christians might react negatively to this by asking how it is possible that the Messiah would destroy Jerusalem and the temple. After all, it was the Romans who destroyed Jerusalem and the temple in AD 70. Therefore, they must be the people of the "prince to come" this passage is talking about. To many Bible readers, it may sound contradictory to call the invading Roman armies "the people of Messiah." But biblically speaking, this is exactly how God talks. Whenever God judges a city or a people, he sovereignly uses pagan armies to achieve his purposes, and he describes the event as God's own armies or servants bringing judgment. Indeed, the pagan armies are often described as God's own hand bringing judgment. They are in effect, God's people or instruments.[59]

When Israel first entered the Promised Land, Yahweh told them that if they would disobey him, he would "bring a [foreign] nation against you from far away, from the end of the earth, swooping down like the eagle" (Deuteronomy 28:49).

When God judged Israel in Isaiah's day, God stated that he was using the pagan nation of Assyria and her king as an axe in his own hand (Isaiah 10:5, 15-16), that it was God who sent the Assyrians against Israel (v 6).

When the first temple and Jerusalem were destroyed by the Babylonians in 586 BC, Yahweh described Nebuchadnezzar as "his servant" and the invading pagan armies as his tribes sent upon Israel (Jeremiah 25:8-9).

When Babylon was then overthrown by the Medes, Isaiah described it as Yahweh mustering and sending his own army host (the pagan Medes) to punish and make the land a desolation (Isaiah 13:1-5, 11).

---

[59] Interestingly, even if one interprets this "prince to come" as a king separate from Messiah whose people destroy the sanctuary and city, it still fits with my paradigm. For I will argue that the "prince" or king was Titus Vespasian, Roman Imperial ruler of the Roman armies.

So it is most consistent with Scripture to understand that Daniel is saying that the Messiah will be the one who destroys Jerusalem and her temple by sending a pagan army to do his work of judgment.

And that destruction of Jerusalem would happen *after* Messiah was cut off.

We know Jesus was cut off from the Father on the cross sometime around AD 29-32. So how long after the cross is the destruction of Jerusalem and the temple? Some Christian prophecy pundits impose a two-thousand-year gap here and say that the last seven years of the prophecy have been put on hold to be fulfilled in our future. This prince must be a future "Antichrist" who destroys a new temple that has been rebuilt after its destruction in AD 70.

This is problematic for a couple reasons. First, there is no reference in the text to a *second* rebuilt temple, only to the temple that was built after 49 years in the days of Nehemiah. The text says that this rebuilt temple will be destroyed *after* Messiah is cut off. Historically, this occurred a mere generation after Jesus Christ was cut off from the Father on the cross. There is only one destruction and one rebuilt temple in the text. So when futurists insert a belief in a *second* rebuilt temple and *second* destruction after the one that actually happened in history, they are adding to the Word of God, not exegeting it.

Do you see the pattern of adding gaps where there are none in the text and skipping over biblically significant events for imaginary ones? In Daniel 2, they skip over the prophecy of Christ's first coming and apply it to the second coming. Now, they skip over the actual prophesied destruction of the temple and apply it to a future destruction of a temple that the text never claims will be built.

There is also no indication in Daniel's prophecy of a time gap between any of the weeks of years as some futurists seek to impose.

These prophecy speculators believe that everything in the first 69 or 69-1/2 weeks of years was fulfilled by the time period of Messiah Jesus. But depending on their interpretation, they believe that either the last 7 years of the prophecy or the last 3-1/2 years of the prophecy have yet to be fulfilled in our current future. They place a gap of over two thousand years into the prophecy to maintain it is not yet entirely fulfilled, therefore we are still waiting for the last 7 or last 3-1/2 years to happen.

The big problem with this gap theory is that the seventy sevens of years are described as occurring continuously *without a gap*. There is not even the slightest hint of a gap of thousands of years between any of the continuous 70 weeks of years. Inserting a gap of two thousand years reveals a preconceived system that imposes an external artificial construct which does not exist in the actual biblical text.

So what did happen to that last 7-year part of the prophecy after Messiah? The answer can be found in the very next verse. In Daniel 9:27, we read that "***he* shall make a covenant with many for one week, and for half of the week, he shall put an end to sacrifice and offering.**" Many futurists interpret this "he" to be a so-called Antichrist and that the last week of years is a seven-year tribulation in the distant future. In their speculative paradigm, this Antichrist supposedly makes a treaty with Israel that he breaks after three-and-a-half years. Then he puts an end to sacrifices in a rebuilt temple in Jerusalem.

But the grammar of the Daniel text does not support this interpretation. In fact, the "he" referred to in verse 27 is grammatically a reference to the prior **Messiah prince**. "He," the prince in this passage who makes a covenant and puts an end to sacrifice, is the Christ, NOT the Antichrist. It is literally the opposite of what many prophecy speculators suggest. As scholar Kenneth Gentry has written:

The indefinite pronoun "he" … refers back to the last dominant individual mentioned: "Messiah" (v. 26a). The Messiah is the leading figure in the whole prophecy, so that even the destruction of the Temple is related to His death. In fact, the people who destroy the Temple are providentially "His armies" (Matthew 22:2-7).[60]

Let's reread the prophecy and that seventieth week with this clarity.

> Daniel 9:27
> And he [Messiah] shall make a strong [new] covenant with many [remnant believers] for one week [7 years], and for half of the week [3 1/2 years] he [Messiah] shall put an end to sacrifice and offering [the cross ends sacrifice and offering].

So we see that the initiation of the new covenant kingdom begins with Christ's ministry (Matthew 4:17). The "half-week" of years is not in the middle of some 7-year tribulation future to us. It represents the approximate 3-1/2 years of Christ's ministry. Jesus was crucified and therefore cut off from the Father 3-1/2 years into that 70th week of years. That is the creation of the new covenant.

In the Bible, Satan does not make covenants with God's people. God does. The "strong covenant" cannot therefore be of an Antichrist. It is the new covenant of the Christ. The earlier verse in Daniel 9 already stated it was Messiah who would **put an end to sin and atone for iniquity**" (9:24), not some future Antichrist. It was Jesus Christ's sacrifice that put an end to sacrifices and offerings once and for all (Hebrews 10:12).

---

[60] Dr. Kenneth L. Gentry, Jr., "Daniel's Seventy Weeks," (Covenant Media Foundation). http://www.cmfnow.com/articles/pt551.htm

It is also important to note that while the abomination of desolation in both the past and future versions in Daniel "takes away the daily burnt offering" (Daniel 11:31, 12:11), the text says that what Messiah the Prince does is different. With his once-for-all sacrifice on the cross, Messiah "puts an end to sin and atones for iniquity" (Daniel 9:24) and "puts an end to sacrifice and offering" (Daniel 9:27). The Abomination forcibly defies the covenant. The Anointed One fulfills and brings the covenant to an end.

So if Jesus put an end to sacrifice at the cross 3-1/2 years into the final 70th week of prophecy, what happens in the last 3-1/2 years of that last week of years? Nothing needs to happen. The break in the middle of the last week is a prophetic sign of the brokenness of Messiah at that point. That perfect last seven is broken in the middle by the cross. But because of that break in the 70th week, within the next three and a half years, the gospel was spreading all over the world to the Gentiles.

Now for the last verse of the passage. This is where the abomination is finally noted. And this is finally a different individual than the Messiah prince. This one is called "the one who makes desolate."

> Daniel 9:27
> And on the wing of **abominations** shall come **one who makes desolate**, until the decreed end is poured out on the **desolate**.

As we noted earlier, this is not the exact term "abomination of desolation," but it is a confluence of those exact terms in synonymous parallel. And this desolation is tied back to the previous verse 26 that describes the destruction of the city and sanctuary. "Its end shall come with a flood, and to the end there shall be war. Desolations are decreed."

Can you see how the two things are connected? Messiah ends old covenant sacrifice with the cross, then the city and temple of old covenant sacrifices are destroyed by an abominable one shortly afterward. In fact, within a generation.

So who is this abominable "one who makes desolate"?

Titus Vespasian

I will argue that the Roman general Titus Caesar Vespasianus is the bringer of the second abomination of desolation spoken of in Daniel 9 and 12. This occurred at the city of Jerusalem in the time period of AD 66-70. Let me set the historical stage for this fulfillment. In his Olivet discourse of Matthew 24, Jesus prophesied the destruction of the temple in Jerusalem of his day as God's judgment for their rejection of Messiah.

> Matthew 23:37-24:2
> "O Jerusalem, Jerusalem, the city that kills the prophets and stones those who are sent to it! How often would I have gathered your children together as a hen gathers her brood under her wings, and you were not willing! See, your house [holy temple] is left to you desolate...."

> Jesus left the temple and was going away, when his disciples came to point out to him the buildings of the temple. But he answered them, "You see all these, do you not? Truly, I say to you, there will not be left here one stone upon another that will not be thrown down."

Within 40 years of Jesus's prediction, the temple was destroyed just as he had predicted. This resulted from a Jewish revolt in Judea, then a province of Roman rule, around AD 66. The political, religious, and historical details of this series of events has fortunately been left to us in the writings of a Jewish historian named Flavius Josephus. His book *The Wars of the Jews* chronicles the narrative from before the revolt in AD 66 all the way up to the final destruction of the city of Jerusalem and its temple in AD 70.

At the time of the Jewish revolt, Nero was still Caesar of Rome, and he had been persecuting the Christians. This was the wicked king under whose reign the apostles like Peter and Paul were martyred. It was a major spiritual turning point in history for both Judaism and Christianity. In AD 67, Nero had sent his general Vespasian to quench the Jewish revolt. But when Nero died in 68, Vespasian came back to Rome to become the next Caesar. He sent his son Titus to finish the job in his stead.

Titus was a competent military general, but the revolt was widespread and took 3-1/2 years to put down (does that 3-1/2 number sound prophetically familiar?). He was described by Roman historian Suetonius as "the darling of the human race," a "highly educated Roman noble with diplomatic skill that served to conceal both his efficiency and his ruthlessness."[61] As a family representative of Vespasian, Titus was considered to carry the authority of Caesar. He was even called Caesar during the war.[62]

Titus first swept through Judea, subduing most of the Jewish cities before ending up in AD 69 at Jerusalem, where he besieged the city for 5 months before conquering it and entering the holy city and temple.

A story of Titus from the Talmud illustrates his blasphemous, abominable nature. It is written that Titus had entered the temple, now

---

[61] Brian W. Jones, "Titus (Emperor)," ed. David Noel Freedman, *The Anchor Yale Bible Dictionary* (New York: Doubleday, 1992), 581.

[62] Dio Cassius, *Histories* 65.1.1-4: "Vespasian was declared emperor by the senate also, and Titus and Domitian were given the title of Caesars. The consular office was assumed by Vespasian and Titus while the former was in Egypt and the latter in Palestine."

empty of its treasures, and demanded, "Where is their God, the rock in whom they trusted?" He then "blasphemed and raged against Heaven.… He took a whore by her hand, and went into the house of the Holy of Holies; he spread out a scroll of the Torah, and on it he f****d her."[63]

Josephus explains that the Romans brought their standards into the temple, "and there did they offer sacrifices to them and there did they make Titus imperator, with the greatest acclamations of joy."[64] Roman standards included an image of Caesar as god. They were a pagan abomination that signaled God's desolating absence from the temple.[65]

Josephus then claims that Titus plundered the temple of its treasures and ordered all the surviving priests to be put to death to perish along with the temple.[66] According to Josephus, the temple was burnt on the same exact day, the 10th day of the month Ab, "upon which [the first temple] was formerly burnt by the king of Babylon."

The historian concludes that in the Roman war with the Jews, 1,100,00 Jews perished and 97,000 were taken into slavery. He concludes with hyperbolic words that echo Jesus: "Accordingly the multitude of those that therein perished exceeded all the destructions that either men or God ever brought upon the world."[67]

Of this city and sanctuary destruction, Daniel 9:26 says, "Its end shall come with a flood, and to the end there shall be war." The use of "flood" here is not a literal tsunami of water but a metaphoric description of the overwhelming speed and unstoppable force of God's judgment, a common image in Old Testament prophecy (Isaiah 28:17;

---

[63] *Babylonian Talmud Gittin* 5:6, I.12.A–D. Jacob Neusner, *The Babylonian Talmud: A Translation and Commentary, vol. 11b* (Peabody, MA: Hendrickson Publishers, 2011), 243–244.

[64] Flavius Josephus, *The Wars of the Jews* 6.6.1, §316.

[65] Flavius Josephus, *The Wars of the Jews* 2.9.2 §169-170.

[66] Flavius Josephus, *The Wars of the Jews* 6.6.1, §316, 321

[67] Flavius Josephus, *The Wars of the Jews* 6.9.3-4, §420, 429.

Jeremiah 47:2). But there's even more to it than that. The use of flood language evokes Noah's flood, which was theologically communicated in Genesis as being a symbolic return to the chaos of pre-creation in order for God to start over with the creation of a new covenant with Noah. Biblically speaking, the destruction of the Jerusalem temple was symbolic of God reducing the old covenant system as embodied in that temple into chaos so he could establish his "new creation," the new covenant through Christ (2 Corinthians 5:17).[68]

So Titus would perfectly fit Daniel's prophetic portrayal of the "one who comes on the wing of abominations and makes desolate" by destroying both city and temple and bringing abomination and desolation to that sacred space. What's more, the desolation/destruction took place after Messiah made his new covenant just 40 years earlier— just as Daniel's prophecy stated. The Jerusalem temple was the incarnation of the old covenant. So once the new covenant was established, the old covenant symbol, the temple, was destroyed by God through the abominable pagan leader Titus (Hebrews 8:13; 9:8-9).

But we are not done with the abomination of desolation. There is one last passage in Daniel 12:11 that mentions it again. And again, the entire chapter has often been interpreted as yet-to-take-place in our future. And yet again, I would argue for a first century fulfillment of the second abomination of desolation under the actions of Titus Vespasian, the "one who makes desolate."

Let's run through the passage verse by verse.

---

[68] For more detail on the temple and the New Covenant, see, Brian Godawa, Israel in Bible Prophecy: The New Testament Fulfillment of the Promise to Abraham (Warrior Poet Publishing, 2021), 47-53. Interestingly, the first temple being destroyed by the Babylonians in 586 BC was also described by the prophets Isaiah and Jeremiah as a decreation return to chaos: Isaiah 24:1-23; Jeremiah 4:23-26.

Daniel 12

Daniel 12:11–13

[11] And from the time that the regular burnt offering is taken away and the **abomination that makes desolate** is set up, there shall be 1,290 days. [12] Blessed is he who waits and arrives at the 1,335 days. [13] But go your way till the end. And you shall rest and shall stand in your allotted place at the end of the days."

Daniel 12 is the final section of the prophecies of Daniel. This section actually begins at Daniel 11:36 with the final "willful king" at the time of the end. Remember, chapter separations are not in the original text. So when Daniel 12:1 begins by saying, "At that time shall arise Michael," he is referring to the "time of the end" that he was just addressing a few verses earlier in 11:35, 40. It is one continuous flow of history.

So when exactly is this "time of the end"? Many Bible prophecy speculators assume it is the end of history when Jesus returns. But they would be seriously wrong. I do not have the space here to exegete every detail of this section, so I will stick to a few major points that argue against the context of our future and for the context of our past in the first-century days of ancient Rome and Titus Vespasian (if the reader wants more detail, see my podcast series, Daniel and End Times Prophecy).[69] Please keep in mind I am not arguing here that there is no return of Christ in our future but simply arguing that Daniel is not talking about that event. He is talking about the first coming of Messiah at the end of the Gentile kingdoms.

---

[69] https://www.youtube.com/playlist?list=PL5TyMLcYh4AOPA4WGu3Ai9i3xUEMqv2hC

The final kingdom of Daniel's four kingdoms. First, remember the context of Daniel's prophecies that we established earlier on. Daniel's prophecies are all about the four kingdoms that would rule over Israel until Messiah came: Babylon, Medo-Persia, Greece, and Rome. The vision of the large statue of four metals (Daniel 2), then the vision of the four great hybrid beasts from the sea (Daniel 7), and then the vision of the charging ram and the one-horned goat (Daniel 8) all reiterate those four kingdoms with differing focus. We read about Babylon in Daniel 1-7, then Medo-Persia in Daniel 8-11, which occurred during the lifetime of Daniel. Daniel 11-12 follows with predictions about the final two kingdoms of Greece and Rome. Messiah would come "in the days of these kings," specifically Rome, to usher in Messiah's new covenant kingdom (Daniel 2:44-45; 9:24-27).

Remember we have already seen that Daniel 11 chronicles with amazing precision the third kingdom, Greece, with its Syrian Wars of the third century BC, ending with the abomination of desolation by King Antiochus IV Epiphanes (11:21-35). So when Daniel begins to address the final king that "shall do as he wills" at "the time of the end" in 11:36-45, we are in the fourth and final kingdom of Rome. After all, what kingdom comes immediately after Greece in Daniel's prophetic timeline? Not some future symbolic or speculative rebuilt Roman kingdom thousands of years later but the real-world Rome that arose after Greece in real-world history. The big picture context of Daniel demands that the time of the end is during the ancient Roman kingdom (empire).

But isn't the time of the end the end of all time?

Time of the end. In Daniel 12, the divine messenger explains that the second abomination of desolation comes at the time of the end or the end of the days.

Daniel 12:9, 13

He said, "Go your way, Daniel, for the words are shut up
and sealed until **the time of the end**.... But go your way
till the end. And you shall rest and shall stand in your
allotted place at **the end of the days**."

When they read those words, too many Christians impose their own
preconceived cultural assumptions upon the phrases "time of the end,"
"end of the days," or "till the end." They read them out of context. The
primary rule of understanding the Bible in its ancient context is to let
Scripture interpret Scripture. When we read the words "time of the
end," we must not *assume* it means what we want it to mean, the end of
all time or the end of the space-time universe. We must ask according
to biblical precedent and context, "The end of what?" Let's let Daniel
tell us exactly what he means by the end.

Daniel 8:19–23

[19] He said, "Behold, I will make known to you what shall
be at **the latter end of the indignation ["curse"],** for it
refers to the appointed **time of the end**. [20] As for the ram
that you saw with the two horns, these are the kings of
Media and Persia. [21] And the goat is the king of Greece.
And the great horn between his eyes is the first king. [22] As
for the horn that was broken, in place of which four others
arose, four kingdoms shall arise from his nation, but not
with his power. [23] And at **the latter end of their
kingdom, when the transgressors have reached their
limit,** a king of bold face, one who understands riddles,
shall arise.

The time of the end is the "latter end of the indignation" or curse
upon Israel when the transgressors have reached their limit. This occurs

at the latter end of the four Greek "horn" kingdoms that came out of the horn of Alexander. Antiochus Epiphanes was at that latter end of those Greek kingdoms. In fact, it was during his reign that the Roman republic asserted her power over the Greek kingdoms of Seleucia and Ptolemies of Egypt. After the death of Antiochus Epiphanes, those Greek kingdoms began to crumble under Rome's ascendancy. Shortly thereafter in 65 BC under Julius Caesar, Rome would evolve into the Roman empire, the last of Daniel's four kingdoms.

Daniel 9:24-27 states that Messiah would finish the transgression of Israel, put an end to sin, atone for iniquity, and bring in his everlasting kingdom of righteousness. Israel's curse would be ended with the coming of Messiah. In context, Daniel was writing about the Messiah *ending* the transgression of Israel and *ending* sin with his atonement for iniquity at the cross (Daniel 9:24). And that was linked to *the end* of the holy city and temple (9:26). Daniel reiterates this *end* of the temple again in 12:11 with the second abomination of desolation. So "the end" in Daniel's prophecy is not the end of history or the end of time. It is the end of Israel's sin of idolatry against Yahweh through Messiah that would occur in the days of Rome at the end of the four kingdoms.

11:36-45 – the final "king that shall do as he wills … at the time of the end" is a ruler who is a part of that fourth and final kingdom. There are several strong options for who this Roman king was: Julius Caesar and the line of Caesars, the Roman general Titus, or King Herod the Great. I am not certain as to which of these three positions I am most persuaded. I find them each compelling. I would recommend further study.[70] But I lean toward King Herod, the Edomite king over Judea and

---

[70] Jay Rogers argues that it is the line of Caesars beginning with Julius: Jay Rogers, *In the Days of These Kings: The Book of Daniel in Preterist Perspective* (Clermont, FL: Media House International, 2017).

client king of Rome. He certainly magnified himself above gods (Daniel 11:36). He was king when Messiah was born to end "the indignation" of Israel (11:36). As an Edomite, he paid no attention to the god of his fathers, Abraham, Isaac, and Jacob (11:37). He built mighty fortresses as he rejected Yahweh (11:38-39). He divided his land for favors (11:39). The final section of this king's interaction with the kings of the south and north (11:40-45) reflects Herod's experience with Caesar Augustus (king of the north) and Egyptian queen Cleopatra (king of the south). The major actor "he" in that section is the king of the north, Augustus. The passage describes his victory over Antony and Cleopatra in the battle of Actium in 31 BC.[71]

As Bible commentator James Jordan explains:

> Why is attention given to these events, out of the many in
> Herod's reign? I believe it is because these events (a) fully
> established Rome's domination over the near east once
> and for all; (b) ended the separate history of the South,
> thus bringing to an end the Alexandrian history that began
> in Daniel 11:3; and (c) established Octavian Caesar, soon
> to take the name Augustus, as ruler of the Roman empire,
> thus setting the stage for the events described when

Duncan McKenzie makes a good argument that Titus is the king of Daniel 11:36: McKenzie PhD, Duncan W., *The Antichrist and the Second Coming: A Preterist Examination Volume I* (Kindle Locations 2896-2903). Xulon Press.

Philip Mauro argues for Herod the Great: Philip Mauro, *The Seventy Weeks and the Great Tribulation: A Study of the Last Two Visions of Daniel, and of the Olivet Discourse of the Lord Jesus Christ* (Public Domain, 1921, 1944),

James Jordan also makes a persuasive case that the "Little Horn" of Daniel 8:9-26 is also Herod the Great, rather than Antiochus Epiphanes. This would not change the overall interpretation or the other passages that still refer to Antiochus. See James B. Jordan, *The Handwriting on the Wall: A Commentary on the Book of Daniel* (Powder Springs, GA: American Vision, 2007), 424-437.

[71] For a good narrative of this fulfillment see, Bruce Gore, *Historical and Chronological Context of the Bible* (Bruce Gore, 2006), Chapter 11, pages 15-16.

Daniel's sealed book is reopened in the book of
Revelation [in the first century].[72]

12:1-3 – "And many of those who sleep in the dust of the earth shall awake, some to everlasting life, and some to shame and everlasting contempt." This is a famous passage that many assume refers to the physical resurrection at the end of history and the return of Christ. But since it takes place in the days of ancient Rome, it is not in fact about the second coming. It is about the *first coming* of Christ. It wouldn't make sense for Daniel to completely skip over the most important hope of the Old Testament, the first coming of Messiah, to talk about a second coming out of context. This resurrection is simply Daniel's reiteration of his contemporary Ezekiel's obvious metaphorical resurrection of Israel when Messiah comes (Ezekiel 37). Many Jews would rise from their spiritual death to everlasting life in Christ (through faith) while some of those Jews would spiritually rise to shame in rejecting Jesus and end in everlasting contempt. Jesus would be the spiritual Promised Land of Israel unto which they would be regathered (Hebrews 9:15; 11:8-16; 12:22-24).[73]

12:7 – "[the length of time for these predictions to take place] would be for a time, times, and half a time…" A time, times, and half a time is another way of saying 3 1/2. "Titus's campaign of destruction against the Jews lasted exactly three-and-a-half years (March/April AD 67 to

---

[72] James B. Jordan, *The Handwriting on the Wall: A Commentary on the Book of Daniel* (Powder Springs, GA: American Vision, 2007), 606–607.

[73] For a detailed explanation of how Jesus Christ fulfills the Land Promise see my book, Brian Godawa, Israel in Bible Prophecy: The New Testament Fulfillment of the Promise to Abraham (Warrior Poet Publishing, 2021), 22-32.

August/September AD 70) and resulted in the destruction of the Jewish nation."[74]

12:7 – "...and that when the shattering of the power of the holy people comes to an end all these things would be finished." The "power of the holy people" in the Bible is the covenant. The shattering of that power or covenant was the end of the old covenant that was historically and publicly ended in AD 70 with the destruction of the incarnation of that old covenant system, the holy temple (Matthew 21:38-44, fulfilling Joshua 23:16; Galatians 4:24-31).

12:9 – "He said, "Go your way, Daniel, for the words are shut up and sealed until the time of the end."

12:13 – "But go your way till the end. And you shall rest and shall stand in your allotted place at the end of the days." The "time of the end" is not "the end of time." "End of the days" does not mean "end of all days" but merely the end of the days for these prophecies of the four Gentile kingdoms (12:12). Those days were ended with the AD 70 destruction of the temple in Jerusalem.

12:11-12 – "And from the time that the regular burnt offering is taken away and the abomination that makes desolate is set up, there shall be 1,290 days. Blessed is he who waits and arrives at the 1,335 days." The Hebrew grammar underlying this verse is unclear as to whether the taking away of the burnt offering is first, the arrival of the abomination of desolation is first, or whether the two incidents are to be considered together as the starting point for the days.

---

[74] McKenzie PhD, Duncan W., *The Antichrist and the Second Coming: A Preterist Examination Volume* I (Xulon Press. Kindle Edition).

The ancient Jewish historian Josephus indicates the exact date in AD 70 when the daily sacrifices had stopped during the war with Rome.

> Josephus *Wars of the Jews*, 6.2.1 (93)
> And now Titus gave orders to his soldiers that were with him to dig up the foundations of the tower of Antonia, and make him a ready passage for his army to come [into the Jerusalem temple] … on that very day, which was the seventeenth day of Panemus [Tamuz], the sacrifice called "the Daily Sacrifice" had failed, and had not been offered to God.[75]

Based on this interpretation of the ending of the sacrifice in AD 70, Bible scholar Philip Mauro concluded:

> The first approach of the Roman armies under Cestius is described by Josephus in his book of Wars, II 17, 10. This was in the month corresponding to our November, A.D. 66. The taking away of the daily sacrifice was in the month Panemus, corresponding to the Hebrew Tammuz, and our July, A.D. 70. Thus the measure of time between the two events was three years, and part of a fourth [or 1,290 days].[76]

Those Roman armies that were previously under Cestius would return 3 1/2 years later led personally by the co-emperor Titus. When Titus captured the holy city and temple, it was the end of the siege but not the end of the war atrocities that would commence upon victory. The additional 45 days that resulted in Daniel's blessing to those

---

[75] Flavius Josephus and William Whiston, *The Works of Josephus: Complete and Unabridged* (Peabody: Hendrickson, 1987), 731.

[76] Mauro, Philip. *The Seventy Weeks and the Great Tribulation* (K-Locations 2288-2319). K-Edition.

surviving 1,335 days is a reference to those few Jews who had been able to hide or escape the pillage and plunder of the Roman forces in the city.

To conclude, let's look at the whole of the Daniel prophecy again with my notations to see how it all flows.

Daniel 9:24–27 (NASB95)

[24] Seventy weeks [of years or 490 years] have been decreed for your people [Israel] and your holy city [Jerusalem], to finish the transgression [of Israel's spiritual idolatry], to make an end of sin, to make atonement for iniquity [through the cross], to bring in everlasting righteousness [with the gospel], to seal up vision and prophecy [that have all been pointing to Jesus] and to anoint the most holy [Jesus].

[25] "So you are to know and discern that from the issuing of a decree to restore and rebuild Jerusalem [by Artaxerxes in 457-8 BC] until Messiah the Prince [Jesus] there will be seven weeks [49 years] and sixty-two weeks [+434 years = 483 years]; it will be built again, with plaza and moat, even in times of distress [in the days of Nehemiah].

[26] Then after the sixty-two weeks [after 483 years around AD 30-32] the Messiah will be cut off [from the Father on the cross for us by taking on our sin] and have nothing, and the people [Roman soldiers] of the prince who is to come [Jesus as sovereign God using them] will destroy the city [Jerusalem] and the sanctuary [the temple]. And its end will come with a flood [in AD 70]; even to the end there will be war; desolations are determined [as Jesus predicted and Josephus described in *The Wars of the Jews*].

> ^{27} And he [Messiah Jesus] will make a firm [new] covenant with the many [remnant believers] for one week [the beginning of the 70th week of years in AD 30], but in the middle of the week [3 1/2 years later in AD 33] he [Jesus] will put a stop to sacrifice and grain offering [by his once for all sacrifice on the cross]; and [within that generation, or 40 years] on the wing of abominations will come one [Titus the Roman general] who makes desolate [the temple], even until a complete destruction [in AD 70], one that is decreed, is poured out on the desolate.

Because of their preconceived eschatology, most futurists separate the abomination of desolation from the coming of Messiah. They think that the Seventy Weeks prophecy is talking about the first coming of Jesus, then jumps ahead thousands of years into the future to talk about an Antichrist who is the abomination of desolation. They have to impose an imagined third rebuilt temple and destruction and ignore the second rebuilt temple and destruction spoken of in the text. They have to stick a 2,000-year gap into the prophecy, which simply isn't there. It's not even hinted at. They must add to the Word of God to keep their system working. In reality, the context consistently fits the first century where all those things occurred.

And if you don't believe me, let's ask Jesus.

Jesus and the Abomination of Desolation

It is well known that Jesus spoke of the coming "abomination of desolation spoken of by the prophet Daniel" (Matthew 24:15). When futurist prophecy speculators read his statement that took place on the Mount of Olives, they see it as the Antichrist, the Beast, some demonic person in our own future who has yet to appear and set foot in the temple in Jerusalem (which is supposedly yet to be rebuilt). This is alleged to happen in the midst of a "great tribulation" in our future and heralds a betrayal of a treaty made between the Antichrist and Israel. Unfortunately, none of this imagined futuristic science fiction is in the passage, let alone in the entire Bible. Let's take a look at Jesus's words in biblical context.

> Matthew 24:15–20
>
> [Jesus:] "So when you see the **abomination of desolation** spoken of by the prophet Daniel, standing in the holy place (let the reader understand), [16] then let those who are in Judea flee to the mountains. [17] Let the one who is on the housetop not go down to take what is in his house, [18] and let the one who is in the field not turn back to take his cloak. [19] And alas for women who are pregnant and for those who are nursing infants in those days! [20] Pray that your flight may not be in winter or on a Sabbath.

This Generation

So many Christians come to this passage with a preconceived assumption that it is in our future when the actual context of the prophecy through Jesus's own words says it already happened in our past to his generation.

Jesus himself tells us the interpretive key to the abomination of desolation in several ways. First and most important is that the entire prophecy of events to happen in Matthew 24, including the abomination of desolation," is bookended by a repeated phrase: *this generation*.

Matthew 23:36

Truly, I say to you, all these things will come upon **this generation.**

Matthew 24:34

Truly, I say to you, **this generation** will not pass away until all these things take place.

So Jesus tells us that all these things he was predicting—the destruction of the temple, wars and rumors of wars, persecution, apostasy, the abomination of desolation—were to come upon his generation that was rejecting him. In fact, most of them would not pass away until it occurred (Matthew 16:28).

Like the 40-year wilderness generation that was judged for their unbelief, so Jesus's generation would be judged for their unbelief. Their rejection of Messiah is exactly what Jesus was explaining in Matthew 23.

Matthew 23:36–24:2

"Truly, I say to you, all these things will come upon **this generation**. O Jerusalem, Jerusalem, the city that kills the prophets and stones those who are sent to it! … See, **your house [the temple] is left to you desolate**." … Jesus left the temple and was going away, when his disciples came to point out to him the buildings of the temple. But he answered them, "You see all these, do you not? Truly, I say to you, **there will not be left here one stone upon another that will not be thrown down**."

A generation was about 40 years, another symbolic number. And it just so happens that the second temple was destroyed about 40 years later in AD 70 before Jesus's generation had passed away.

There have been attempts to try to spin away the plain meaning of the phrase "this generation" to mean anything other than the generation to whom Jesus was speaking. All of them fall flat in the face of the explicit definition given by Matthew and all the New Testament. Everywhere Matthew uses the phrase "this generation," it is a reference *to the contemporary generation of Jesus*, the ones to whom he was speaking. Not only that, but it was also most often used as a derogatory term of judgment upon those who were rejecting Jesus as Messiah.[77]

> Matthew 12:41
>
> The men of Nineveh will rise up at the judgment with **this generation** and condemn it, for they repented at the preaching of Jonah, and behold, something greater than Jonah is here.

> Luke 17:25
>
> But first he must suffer many things and be rejected by **this generation**.

> Luke 11:50–51
>
> So that the blood of all the prophets, shed from the foundation of the world, may be **charged against this generation**…. Yes, I tell you, it will be required of **this generation**.

So when Jesus predicts the destruction of the temple in Matthew 23:37-24:2 as judgment upon the first-century Jews for rejecting Messiah and states that everything included with that judgment would occur to "this generation," he is referencing his generation to whom he was speaking. When Jesus uses the personal second person accusative "you" over 35 times—"when *you* see," "when such and such happens to *you*"—directly to his audience, it is safe to say that he meant the

---

[77] See also: Matthew 12:39–42 (Luk e11:29-32); 12:41, 45; 11:16-19; 17:17; Mark 8:38; 9:19; Luke 9:41; 17:25; Philippians 2:15; Acts 2:40; 1 Thessalonians 2:14-16.

generation to whom he was speaking, not some future generation of people.

Imagine being a person listening to Jesus telling you that when you see these things and when these things happen to you, then you should know that destruction is near. Then you discover that he wasn't talking to you at all but was speaking to and about a future generation of people thousands of years from your generation. You could fairly accuse Jesus of misleading his entire audience. Of course, I do not believe Jesus would ever mislead or lie. My point is that the claim that Jesus was not speaking to his audience but to an imaginary future one is tantamount to such misinformation.

In my novel series Chronicles of the Apocalypse, I tell the story of the destruction of Jerusalem and the temple in AD 70 by the Roman forces of Titus. I based it on the only existing full manuscript detailing the infamous event by one of its own participants, Jewish historian Flavius Josephus. His narrative reads like a virtual point-by-point fulfillment of Jesus's prophecy in Matthew 24.

Here are a couple paragraphs from Josephus's account of the AD 70 destruction of Jerusalem and its temple where he claims fulfillment of Daniel's two abominations of desolation as referencing successively Antiochus Epiphanes and Rome under Titus. Josephus also considered the Romans as God's means of judgment. If Josephus wasn't a Jew who most definitely didn't accept Jesus as Messiah, you would think he was a Christian quoting Jesus.

> Flavius Josephus, *Antiquities* 10.276
> And indeed it so came to pass, that our nation suffered these things under Antiochus Epiphanes, according to Daniel's vision, and what he wrote many years before they came to pass. In the very same manner **Daniel also wrote**

concerning the Roman government, and that our country should be made desolate by them.

Flavius Josephus, *The Wars of the Jews* 6.2.1 §110
And are not both the city and the entire temple now full of the dead bodies of your countrymen? It is God therefore, **it is God himself who is bringing on this fire, to purge that city and temple by means of the Roman**s, and is going to pluck up this city, which is full of your **pollutions**.

Flee to the Mountains

Another element of context to the abomination of desolation passage that reinforces a first-century fulfillment is the advice Jesus gives to his audience to flee Judea when they see the abomination of desolation at the gates.

Matthew 24:17-20
Then let those who are in Judea flee to the mountains. Let the one who is on the housetop not go down to take what is in his house, and let the one who is in the field not turn back to take his cloak. And alas for women who are pregnant and for those who are nursing infants in those days! Pray that your flight may not be in winter or on a Sabbath.

None of this could apply to the present-day thousands of years after Christ. Fleeing to the mountains today would be meaningless in the face of modern travel and war technology. Winter, Sabbath, and pregnancy would not be problematic for modern travelers. Back in the first century, the mountains surrounding Israel were actual places of refuge from the war that had spread throughout the land. But it would be difficult to flee there carrying small children, ferrying household goods in carts or wagons, or even just for the elderly, incapacitated, or heavily pregnant.

Jesus was telling his followers how to escape the judgment that was coming upon Jerusalem and Israel for rejecting Messiah. And escape they did. Early church historian Eusebius recorded how the Christians followed Jesus' warnings.

> Eusebius, *Ecclesiastical History* 3:5
> But the people of the church in Jerusalem had been commanded by a revelation, vouchsafed to approved men there before the war, to leave the city and to dwell in a certain town of Perea called Pella. And when those that believed in Christ had come thither from Jerusalem, then, as if the royal city of the Jews and the whole land of Judea were entirely destitute of holy men, the judgment of God at length overtook those who had committed such outrages against Christ and his apostles, and totally destroyed that generation of impious men.[78]

My second book in the *Chronicles of the Apocalypse* series, Remnant: Rescue of the Elect tells this story in dramatic fiction. The Christians were spared from God's judgment because they were no longer part of the old system, the old age of the old covenant. They had both figuratively and literally fled all of it. God was destroying the temple as the incarnation of that old covenant.

---

[78] Eusebius of Caesaria, "The Church History of Eusebius," in *Eusebius: Church History, Life of Constantine the Great, and Oration in Praise of Constantine*, ed. Philip Schaff and Henry Wace, trans. Arthur Cushman McGiffert, vol. 1, *A Select Library of the Nicene and Post-Nicene Fathers of the Christian Church, Second Series* (New York: Christian Literature Company, 1890), 138.

Since most Jews did not embrace the new covenant, they were in a dead religion. The Roman army was like vultures gathering around the carcass of that dead religion to finish it off just as Jesus stated in this same Olivet discourse.

Matthew 24:28
Wherever the corpse is, there the vultures will gather.

But there is even more hermeneutical help that Jesus gives us in interpreting his words. More precisely, Luke gives us a literal explanation of what the "abomination of desolation" actually was in his generation.

Surrounded by Pagan Armies

Let's take a step back for more context. Matthew uses the Hebrew term abomination of desolation. This is important because the book of Matthew was written to Jews. It has many Hebraisms and Old Testament references and concepts that most Jews would know when reading them.

The gospel of Luke was written more for a Gentile audience, so he tended to explain things or translate them for the non-Hebrew. The abomination of desolation is one of those things Luke translated for us.

Luke 21 and Mark 13 both contain the same sermon also found in Matthew 24. But there are some variations in the text. Let me put them side by side so you can see the obvious correlation.

Matthew 24:15–16	Luke 21:20–22	Mark 13:14 (NASB95)
"So **when you see the abomination of desolation** spoken of by the prophet Daniel, standing in the holy place (let the reader understand), then let those who are in Judea flee to the mountains."	"But **when you see Jerusalem surrounded by armies**, then know that its desolation has come near … Then let those who are in Judea flee to the mountains."	"But **when you see the abomination of desolation standing where it should not be** (let the reader understand), then those who are in Judea must flee to the mountains."

The Hebrew image of "abomination of desolation" in Matthew and Mark is translated by Luke to be "Jerusalem surrounded by armies." So Luke makes clear that the correct interpretation intended by Jesus of "abomination of desolation" is *Jerusalem being surrounded by armies.* Specifically, pagan idolatrous armies.

Did this happen in the first century as we have been arguing? Why, yes, it did. In A.D. 66, the abominable Roman armies did in fact surround Jerusalem just as Jesus had foretold. In this sense, they were "standing in a holy place" around the holy city "where it [the pagan army] should not be." Like Antiochus Epiphanes and his Greek armies setting up their idol of Zeus, so a general of Titus named Cestius with his Roman legions surrounded Jerusalem with their idolatrous standards of Caesar, the abomination of desolation (images of desolation). Providentially, Josephus tells us that for some unknown reason, Cestius stopped short of attacking the temple and just left with all his army. This allowed the Christians of the city the opportunity to flee to the mountains.

A couple years later, Titus returned with that army and finished what was started by conquering the city of Jerusalem and capturing the temple. While there, he set up Rome's idolatrous standards of Caesar in the temple as an abomination of desolation. Jewish historian Josephus described the event.

> And now the Romans … upon burning of the holy house itself, and of all the buildings round about it, brought their ensigns to the temple … and there did they offer sacrifices to them, and there did they make Titus imperator, with the greatest acclamations of joy.[79]

It could not be more clear. Pagan rulers and their armies are abominable defilers of sacred space.

The destruction of the city and temple were a main focus of the prophetic near-future for Jesus and the apostles. In fact, Jesus referred on another occasion to the destruction of the city of Jerusalem as punishment for the Jews not recognizing the time of the visitation of God in Messiah.

> Luke 19:41–44
> And when he drew near and saw the city [Jerusalem], he wept over it, saying, "Would that you, even you, had known on this day the things that make for peace! But now they are hidden from your eyes. For the days will come upon you, when your enemies will set up a barricade around you and surround you and hem you in on every side and tear you down to the ground, you and your children within you. And they will not leave one stone upon another in you, because you did not know the time of your visitation."

---

[79] Flavius Josephus, *The Wars of the Jews* 6.6.1, §316. Josephus also describes the standards as considered idolatrous by the Jews in *The Wars of the Jews* 2.9.2 §169-170 "Now Pilate, who was sent as procurator into Judea by Tiberius, sent by night those images of Caesar that are called Ensigns, into Jerusalem. (170) This excited a very great tumult among the Jews when it was day; for those that were near them were astonished at the sight of them, as indications that their laws were trodden underfoot: for these laws do not permit any sort of image to be brought into the city." Flavius Josephus and William Whiston, *The Works of Josephus: Complete and Unabridged* (Peabody: Hendrickson, 1987), 608.

Remember the language that Jesus used in Matthew 24 about God not leaving one stone of the temple upon another? Well, he used it here again, linking those two prophecies about the destruction that was coming in AD 70. At that time, Titus had his army set up a barricade all around Jerusalem, just as Jesus said they would. And just as Jesus had prophesied, they subsequently tore down both city and temple to the ground, not leaving one stone of that temple upon another.

Once again, Jesus makes clear that the reason for this judgment of destruction upon the city and temple was because its Jewish residents "did not know the time of your visitation" (v 44). That visitation was the visitation of God himself incarnate in the Messiah (Luke 1:68; 7:16). This first-century judgment for rejecting Messiah turns out to be a major motif of Jesus's own ministry (Matthew 11:16-18; 12:39-42; 21:33-45; 23:29-39; Mark 8:38-9:1).

The abomination that brought desolation to Jerusalem and the temple is not a prophecy of our future but a fulfillment in our past. It was the Roman ruler Titus Vespasian and his pagan armies who would defile the holy place and destroy both temple and holy city in AD 70, thereby fulfilling Daniel's prophecy.

> Daniel 9:26–27
> And the people of the prince who is to come shall destroy
> the city and the sanctuary. Its end shall come with a flood,
> and to the end there shall be war. Desolations are
> decreed.… And on the wing of abominations shall come
> one who makes desolate, until the decreed end is poured
> out on the desolate.

I am very aware that applying the abomination of desolation in Daniel 12 to Titus in AD 70 will offend some futuristic prophecy schemes and scenarios. As I have already indicated, there are many questions to be answered about the rest of Daniel's prophecies, but this booklet is a vanguard for addressing those issues by starting with the immediate context around the abomination of desolation before working outward to the rest of the story. The reader can pursue a fuller treatment in my teaching videos called <u>Daniel and End Times Prophecy</u>.

What About the Image of the Beast?

Another question may arise in the mind of the Christian who has a futurist orientation in their prophecy system. What about Revelation 13? That passage talks about the Land Beast creating an image of the Sea Beast for the people to worship. Isn't that the abomination of desolation that Jesus was talking about?

> Revelation 13:14–15
> [The land beast told the people] to make an image for the [sea] beast that was wounded by the sword and yet lived. And it was allowed to give breath to the image of the beast, so that the image of the beast might even speak and might cause those who would not worship the image of the beast to be slain.

Though this passage is certainly about idolatrous worship of an image, there is no connection to the abomination in Daniel or Jesus. First, the words abomination and desolation are nowhere mentioned or even hinted at. This is a minimum requirement if one is to make a connection to such a particular prophecy.

Second, this beastly image is not said to have any relation to the Jerusalem temple whatsoever, which is a key part of the definition of the biblical abomination of desolation. Some believe this image is placed in the temple, but that is an assumption simply not in the text. This is commonly called eisegesis when a person imposes their own extrabiblical system upon the text in order to keep their system from falling apart.

Third, the existence of an idolatrous image in a text does not automatically connect it to the abomination of desolation predicted by Daniel or Jesus. There are multiple places in the Old Testament where abominable images of Asherah and other Canaanite deities are spoken of being in the temple (2 Kings 21:4-7; 23:6). Any time an idol is brought into God's house, it could be accused of being an abomination. Though one could fairly call them abominations of desolation *by way of analogy*, one could never call them *the* abomination of desolation spoken of by Daniel and Jesus.

Of course, addressing Revelation further takes us far afield of the purpose of this examination. Many believe Revelation to be a prophecy about our future. But see my podcast series Revelation & End Times Bible Prophecy[80] for a detailed exegesis of Revelation as a prophecy about the first-century judgment of Jesus Christ upon Jerusalem and the temple with the coming of the new covenant kingdom of God. Or read my novel series Chronicles of the Apocalypse for the narrative telling of that story in the first century: the origin of the book of Revelation. Shocking to those who have been taught a futurist paradigm as if it were the only orthodox option. Shocking but more biblical.

---

[80] https://www.youtube.com/playlist?list=PL5TyMLcYh4AOz1_nbyeMQCQWW7pk097sG

Chart of the Syrian Wars in Daniel 11

Here is a chart of the possible fulfillment of the Syrian Wars of the Greek third kingdom in the prophecies of Daniel.[81]

Daniel Citation	Text or Symbols	Fulfillment
8:5-8, 21-22	Male goat and great horn	Alexander the Great
8:8, 22	Four horns from the broken great horn	The four kings that split up the empire after Alexander's death: Ptolemy (Egypt), Seleucus (Persia), Antigonis (Asia Minor), and Cassander (Macedon)
8:9, 23-26	Little horn grows exceedingly great toward the glorious land	Antiochus IV Epiphanes (Seleucid) turns his attention to Jerusalem
8:11-12	Burnt offering and sanctuary overthrown	Antiochus IV defiling the temple with a statue of Zeus and pig offering
11:3-4	A mighty king to arise	Alexander the Great
11:4	Kingdom divided to the four winds of heaven	The four kings that split up the empire after Alexander's death
Chapter 11	King of the South	Ptolemaic kings of Egypt
Chapter 11	King of the North	Seleucid kings of Syria/Babylon
11:5-6	North-South alliance	First Syrian War: Ptolemy II of Egypt vs. Antiochus I of Seleucia; Antiochus II marries Ptolemy's daughter Berenice in alliance
11:7-9	A branch arises in the South and attacks the fortress of the North	Ptolemy III arises when his sister Berenice is murdered and makes war on Seleucus II of Syria; Ptolemy occupies Antioch in Syria

---

[81] I have drawn much of the information in this chart from: Jay Rogers, *In the Days of These Kings: The Book of Daniel in Preterist Perspective* (Clermont, FL: Media House International, 2017), and Philip Mauro, *The Seventy Weeks and the Great Tribulation. A Study of the Last Two Visions of Daniel, and of the Olivet Discourse of the Lord Jesus Christ* (Public Domain, 1921, 1944), and Bruce Gore's teaching "Antiochus Epiphanes and the Maccabees," https://www.youtube.com/watch?v=6hwkThHYBXs

11:10-12	Sons of the King of the North wage war on the King of the South	Fourth Syrian War: Sons of Seleucus, Seleucus III Soter and Antiochus III the Great, attack Ptolemy IV Philopater of Egypt
11:13-18	The King of the North raises a multitude	Fifth Syrian War: Ptolemy IV dies and Antiochus III attacks Syria to regain; includes either the battle of Panium or battle of Sidon
11:17-19	"shall give him the daughter"	Antiochus III gives his daughter Cleopatra I to Ptolemy V in a peace treaty
11:21	"And in his place a despicable person will arise on whom they have not conferred the majesty of the kingdom, and he will come in without warning and he will seize the kingdom by deceit."	175 BC; Antiochus IV is the despicable one who was not next in line for kingship; he claims to rule on behalf of Demetrius, the heir, while Demetrius is in Rome as hostage
11:23	"After an alliance is made with him he will practice deception, and he will go up and gain power with a small force of people."	After Antiochus IV gets his small military force in place, he disavows Demetrius as heir and takes the throne for himself
11:22	"The overflowing forces will be flooded away before him and shattered, and also the prince of the covenant."	Sixth Syrian War: Antiochus IV comes to power and attacks both the Jews and Ptolemy VI of Egypt; the prince of the covenant may be the righteous high priest Onias III
11:24	"In a time of tranquility he will enter the richest parts of the realm, and he will accomplish what his fathers never did, nor his ancestors; he will distribute plunder, booty and possessions among them, and he will devise his schemes against strongholds, but only for a time."	Antiochus IV uses his wealth to buy loyalty in the Syrian provinces; he plunders temples, including the temple in Jerusalem, and plans a campaign against Egypt in the South; through the new high priest Jason, Antiochus Hellenizes Jerusalem, leading to the Maccabean Revolt
11:25-26	"He will stir up his strength and courage against the king of the South with a large army; so the king of the South will mobilize an extremely large and mighty army for war; but he will not stand, for schemes will be devised against him. Those who eat his choice food will destroy him, and his army will overflow, but many will fall down slain."	170 BC; Antiochus IV angers the King of the South, Ptolemy VI, and sends his army toward Syria, but Antiochus ambushes the Egyptian forces at Pelusium and takes much of Egypt, except for Alexandria; Ptolemy becomes his puppet king
11:27	"As for both kings, their hearts will be intent on evil, and they will speak lies to	Two Ptolemys now rule Egypt together: Ptolemy VIII governs

	each other at the same table; but it will not succeed, for the end is still to come at the appointed time."	Alexandria while Ptolemy VI governs the rest of Egypt
11:28	"Then he will return to his land with much plunder; but his heart will be set against the holy covenant, and he will take action and then return to his own land."	169 BC; Antiochus IV leaves Egypt and returns to Syria with his Egyptian plunder; he stops at Jerusalem and sacks it for gold and silver
11:29-30	"At the appointed time he will return and come into the South, but this last time it will not turn out the way it did before. For ships of Kittim will come against him; therefore he will be disheartened and will return and become enraged at the holy covenant and take action; so he will come back and show regard for those who forsake the holy covenant."	168 BC; Antiochus IV returns to invade Egypt a second time and take Alexandria but Rome stops him ("Kittim") Antiochus returns to Syria but again becomes enraged at a civil war that has begun in Jerusalem, prompting him to attack Jerusalem
11:31	"Forces from him will arise, desecrate the sanctuary fortress, and do away with the regular sacrifice. And they will set up the abomination of desolation."	167 BC; Antiochus IV halts the daily sacrifices and sacrifices a pig to Zeus on the altar; forces the Jews to forsake their covenant obedience by eating swine and not observing circumcision, dietary laws, or the Sabbath
11:32-35	"By smooth words he will turn to godlessness those who act wickedly toward the covenant, but the people who know their God will display strength and take action…Some of those who have insight will fall, in order to refine, purge and make them pure until the end time; because it is still to come at the appointed time."	Hellenist Jews are seduced to give up their obedience to the Mosaic covenant. But… 165 BC; the Maccabean Revolt against Antiochus IV results in many martyrs; the Maccabees successfully force the Seleucids out of Jerusalem, cleanse the temple, and resumes the Mosaic sacrifices
11:36-45	The Willful King who exalts himself against God and also enters glorious land rules at the time of the end	1st century BC; probably Herod the Great, but some argue for Julius Caesar and the line of Caesars, Titus, or (least likely) Antiochus IV

If you liked this book, then please help me out by writing a positive review of it on Amazon. That is one of the best ways to say thank you to me as an author. It really does help my sales and status. Thanks!—*Brian Godawa*

More Books by Brian Godawa

See www.godawa.com for more information on other books by Brian Godawa. Check out his other series below:

Chronicles of the Nephilim

Chronicles of the Nephilim is a saga that charts the rise and fall of the Nephilim giants of Genesis 6 and their place in the evil plans of the fallen angelic Sons of God called "The Watchers." The story starts in the days of Enoch and continues on through the Bible until the arrival of the Messiah, Jesus. The prelude to Chronicles of the Apocalypse. ChroniclesOfTheNephilim.com. (affiliate link)

Chronicles of the Apocalypse

Chronicles of the Apocalypse is an origin story of the most controversial book of the Bible: Revelation. A historical conspiracy thriller quadrilogy in first century Rome set against the backdrop of explosive spiritual warfare of Satan and his demonic Watchers. ChroniclesOfTheApocalypse.com. (affiliate link)

Chronicles of the Watchers

Chronicles of the Watchers is a series that charts the influence of spiritual principalities and powers over the course of human history. The kingdoms of man in service to the gods of the nations at war. Interwoven with Chronicles of the Nephilim. ChroniclesOfTheWatchers.com. (affiliate link)

Theological Thriller Novels

The *Theological Thriller Novels* series by Brian James Godawa is a series of standalone novels that explore good and evil, human nature and God. Some are modern, some are fictional, some are a blend of fiction and history. Sins of humanity are depicted in the novels with honesty and accuracy. Therefore they are for mature readers because the power of redemption in a story is only as great as the accuracy of depiction of the evil from which characters can be redeemed. TheologicalThrillers.com (affiliate link)

Get the Book of the Biblical & Historical Research Behind This Novel.

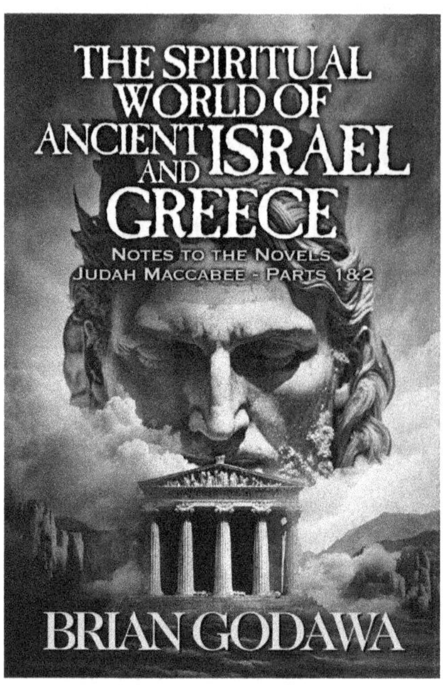

Learn the Story Behind the Historical Fulfillment of Daniel's Abomination of Desolation.

If you like the novel set *Judah Maccabee: Parts 1&2,* you'll love discovering the biblical and historical basis for the fascinating, mind-bending story of what happened between the Old And New Testaments.

Available for purchase in paperback, eBook, audio and large print.

https://godawa.com/get-spirit-world-greece/

(affiliate link)

GREAT OFFERS BY BRIAN GODAWA

Get More Biblical Imagination

Sign up Online For The Godawa Chronicles

www.Godawa.com

Updates and Freebies
of the Books of Brian Godawa
Special Discounts,
Fascinating Bible Facts!

ABOUT THE AUTHOR

Brian Godawa is a respected Christian writer and best-selling author of novels and biblical theology. His supernatural Bible epic novels combine creative imagination with orthodox Christian theology in a way that transcends both entertainment and preachiness.

His love for Jesus and storytelling was forged in the crucible of worldview apologetics and Hollywood screenwriting, as he began a career in movies and eventually expanded into the world of novels.

His first novel series, *Chronicles of the Nephilim,* has been in the Top 10 of Biblical Fiction on Amazon for more than a decade, selling over 400,000 books. His popular book *Hollywood Worldviews: Watching Films with Wisdom and Discernment* is used as a textbook in Christian film schools around the country. His movies *To End All Wars* and *Alleged* have won multiple movie awards such as Cannes Film Festival and the Heartland International Film Festival.

He lives in Texas with the most amazing wife a man could ever pray for and is accountable to a local church. He reads too many books and watches too many movies. He knows, he knows, he should get out more.

Find out more about his blog and his other books, lectures, and online courses for sale at his website, www.godawa.com.

NOTES

NOTES

NOTES

315

NOTES

NOTES

NOTES

NOTES

NOTES

NOTES

NOTES

www.ingramcontent.com/pod-product-compliance
Lightning Source LLC
Chambersburg PA
CBHW070408310726
48977CB00003B/606